An Artisan
Lovestyle

Kiltie Jackson

Jeff Rowland appears with the permission of

Jeff Rowland – Artist.

ISBN: 1999866614
ISBN-13: 978 - 1999866617

FOR MY MUM.

With love.
xxx

The Lovestyle Series

A Rock 'n' Roll Lovestyle (Book 1)
An Artisan Lovestyle (Book 2)

Acknowledgements

It is difficult to believe I've written a second novel and there are many people to thank for ensuring I stuck with it.

First up is Kym Wood – the best friend anyone could have. She has to suffer the early manuscripts, before they have been cleaned by my editor, and her feedback is vital. She provides constant encouragement and always makes me believe that I can do this.

My sister Rosie – the inspirational posts which you send each day always inspire me to keep believing in myself.

My dad – who read my debut novel at least four times and tells me, every time we speak, that he is proud of me.

My mother-in-law, Margaret, who still tells me I am brilliant. You keep me focused.

John Hudspith is the poor chap who, once again, had the pleasure of turning my error-riddled manuscript into something that people could read and make sense of. Thank you again for the new lessons taught. I hope they will have sunk in by the time you have to work on number three.

Henry Hyde came up with my beautiful cover design. I know it was a bit of a slog this time around but the effort was more than worth it.

Ian Peterson created the gorgeous 'Rock 'n' Roll Lovestyle' illustration and I love it to bits. The original has been framed and sits proudly in my study.

Jeff Rowland patiently answered all my arty questions and gave me the low-down on how it all works behind the scenes within the art world. Thank you for your constant support.

Neats Wilson – I thank you daily for the constant support that you give. Your honesty is highly valued and your friendship is too. Thank you for reading and proof-reading. I'll be sure to tell everyone that any leftover typos are your fault! ☺

Martine Fender and Percy Meadows – Thank you once again for being my guinea pigs and having to endure the barrage of questions thrown at you as you worked your way through the chapters. Your feedback is valued greatly.

No thanks would be complete without a mention of the fabulous Rachel Gilbey. This lady is responsible for my book tours and cover reveals. She works very hard to ensure these events run smoothly and I am deeply grateful to her for all she has done to help me.

I also extend my deep felt thanks to all the great bloggers and reviewers who read and promote my scribblings on their blogs, Goodreads and Amazon. The work you do is invaluable to us indie authors and this one thanks you all from the bottom of her heart.

It would be very wrong not to include the best book group on Facebook – The Fiction Café Book Club and Writers Group. The members are the most amazingly supportive people. For those who read my book and left the reviews on Amazon, Goodreads and on their blogs – I thank you all.

For the authors who are always astonishingly generous with their support and assistance – you guys are my writing family and you were always there to pick me up on the days when I was convinced I couldn't do it and you told me that I could. You're awesome.

I have to give a special mention to Natali Drake and Samantha Curtis – two ladies who have become dearest friends and who never hesitate to share their extensive knowledge and experience with me. Thank you for being my back-up buddies.

To my Facebook followers who continue to comment, like and share my news. This goes a long way in helping to spread the word and it is more appreciated than I can express. You guys rock!

The Moggy Posse – my funny, lovely, mischievous, little fur-balls. Mummy loves you very much.

My lovely husband Ian who still keeps telling me I can do it, and understands that Tuesday and Thursday nights will never be the same again.

Finally, for my mum, to whom this book is dedicated – good times, bad times and tough times; we've seen them all but, despite everything, we always find our way back to each other. Thank you for all of it.

The Middle Men

Death looked at the playing cards he was holding. As a hand in poker went, it was not one of the best. He absentmindedly ate some of his Twingle chips while he contemplated what to do next.

"You do realise you're eating your chips again!" said William McAllister, sitting across the table. "You're going to run out of funds!"

"Well, it won't be the first time," retorted Harry Clairmont, who was sitting between them.

Death grunted and poured himself another glass of Dementalated Zpirits.

"Don't you think you've had quite enough to drink?"

Death swung his head round to glare at the owner of the imperious voice sitting on his other side.

"Look, Vicky," he growled, "you may have been the Queen Bee back in your day but here, in this realm, you're just another non-mover with ideas above her station. So, button your lip and don't tell me what to do."

He looked at his cards again and then, picking up the remainder of the Twingle chips he hadn't yet eaten, threw them onto the pile in the middle of the table. "I see your bet and I'll raise you another twenty chips."

Queen Victoria closed her cards and laid them on the table in front of her. "I fold," she said. She gave her husband Albert a sharp nudge in the side. "Oh ja, I vold too," he mumbled, following his wife's lead.

She stood and caught William's eye as she turned away from the table. Smiling, she gave him a discreet wink before taking Albert's arm and walking away, leaving Death, William, and Harry to carry on.

A few minutes passed by in which the stakes continued to rise. When it was Death's turn once more, he looked down at his now non-existent pile of chips and asked in astonishment, "Where are my chips? I had a full tube of Twingles…"

"You ate them! Just like you always do!" Harry sighed in exasperation.

"It looks like you'll have to fold, dude," said William.

"No! I will not fold! Death never gives up. Fetch me some writing implements!" he snapped at a man passing by.

Two minutes later, he wrote on a piece of parchment:

I, Death, hereby promise to fulfil any favour to the bearer of this note – no questions asked.

Signing it with a flourish, he threw it onto the pile of chips on the table.

William looked at Harry before laying down his cards, revealing his uninspiring hand.

Death sniggered as he said, "I think maybe I do better than you," while putting his cards on the table and showing he held a straight flush.

William and Death looked at Harry who slowly placed his cards in front of him. William smiled but Death let out a loud groan as he took in the royal flush **Harry** had just trumped him with.

Harry leant forward, plucked the note off the top of the chips and, holding it between his fingers, he looked Death in the eye. "Right then, old chap, about this note…"

Chapter One

New Year's Eve

"OUCH! OW! OW! OW!"

Danny Delaney couldn't help but exclaim loudly. The back of his ankles felt as though they'd just been thumped with a cricket bat. He dropped the various cold and flu remedies he'd been holding and watched one bottle disappear underneath a shelving unit as he bent down to rub his sore and throbbing tendons.

He looked round and came face to face with a sleeping baby cosied up in its buggy. Clearly this was the ankle-level battering ram and peering from behind it was a pair of great, big, cornflower-blue eyes which were accompanied by a tiny little button nose, a poppet-sized, rose-bud mouth and were framed by an explosion of wild, blonde, goldilocks curls.

Suddenly, somewhere above his head, he heard an exasperated voice.

"Felicity! I TOLD you not to touch the pram. You are a very naughty little girl."

Immediately the cornflower eyes filled with tears and the rose-bud mouth stretched open to its full capacity, in preparation for emitting the air-splitting, ear-piercing wail that most three-year-old toddlers have honed to perfection.

"It's okay, it's okay! I'm okay." Danny rushed to console the little girl before she could let loose her screams. His head was already pounding in agony and the thought of trying to cope with any additional noise was more than he could bear.

"I am *so* sorry." Felicity's harassed mother bent down to help him pick up the packages he'd dropped. "She hates shopping so I normally let her push the pram to keep her quiet, but it's so crowded in here today I couldn't let her do it. Clearly she had other ideas."

Danny noticed the baby formula, bottle of Calpol, a very large tub of nappy rash cream and packets of nappies, in the mother's basket, and couldn't bring himself to add to her already stressful state. He remembered conversations he'd overheard in the office and took a guess that the baby was teething. The young mother didn't need more hassle on top of that.

"Hey, it's fine. These things happen. No harm done."

He ignored the stabbing pains still hanging around his ankles – they'd ease off eventually.

Felicity's mother straightened up, and handing over his medication, thanked him for being so understanding.

"You are very kind. Thank you again. Happy New Year." She looked down at her young daughter. "Say thank you to the very nice man, Felicity."

Felicity tipped her head right back to look up at the figure in front of her.

"Fankoo. Happy Noo Ear, very nice man."

"And a very Happy New Year to you, Felicity," Danny replied, forcing a smile on his face to ensure he

5

didn't grimace at her words. If there was one word in the English language he had come to detest it was the word 'nice'. So many times he'd heard himself described as 'nice' and he was sick of it. He wanted to be witty, funny, handsome, adventurous or zany. They were exciting words and described the kind of people you longed to hang out with. Nice, on the other hand, was just a little bit boring. A little bit safe. The fun people in life were never described as being 'nice'!

He waved goodbye to Felicity and her mother – the baby had slept through all the commotion – and, picking up another bottle of cough syrup, he walked over to the check-out area. He couldn't believe he'd been struck down with the lurgy on today of all days. His firm was hosting a New Year's Eve ball and his girlfriend Sandra hadn't stopped talking about it since it had been announced at the beginning of November. If it wasn't for her, he'd give it a miss and go straight to his bed. New Year held no excitement for him and, given the opportunity, he'd happily ignore it altogether. Sandra, however, had her heart set on going and he couldn't bear the thought of letting her down. Mostly because he wouldn't hear the end of it for weeks if he did!

He shuffled along the queue, waiting for the next till to become available. Soon he was scanning his items and putting them in his bag. He was sure that, once he got home and took some of these remedies, he'd feel much better.

The wind was howling when Danny walked out of the pharmacy so he put on his woollen hat, pulling it down over his unruly hair, tightened his scarf around his neck and, turning up the collar on his coat to keep the chilly December air at bay, he set off towards the tube station.

Five minutes later, he was walking onto the platform just as a train arrived. He checked it was going all the way to Morden, jumped on and couldn't believe his luck when he managed to get a seat. The way his head was pounding, he didn't think he could bear to stand right now. The swaying motion of the train would be too much for him. He took off his hat, shoved it in his pocket and sat with his eyes closed, gritting his teeth at the pain. He snapped them open, however, when a carrier bag swung forward and hit him on the head. He looked up to see a heavily pregnant woman standing in front of him, holding onto the rail above her for dear life. He knew she was pregnant as she was helpfully wearing a London Underground badge which declared 'Baby on Board'. He'd once gotten an earful from a lady whom he'd assumed was 'with child' only to get a flea in his ear when she loudly informed him she did not have a bun in the oven and was simply large-boned.

He looked around the carriage and, seeing that no one else was preparing to give up their seat, he let out a sigh, hauled himself up and said, "Please, have my seat."

The woman smiled at him gratefully and sank down into it. "Thank you so much. It was really nice of you to do that."

Danny simply smiled and replied, "No problem. You're welcome," as he drew in a sharp breath to try and counter the pain bouncing behind his eyes.

He stood swaying in time with the rocking sensation of the train as it hurtled along. He closed his eyes again – the bright overhead lights of the carriage were exacerbating his pain. When he opened them a few stops later, to see where he was and how much longer he would have to suffer, he caught the woman looking up at him with a smile on her face. He wondered if his nose was dripping and tried to wipe it discreetly with a tissue. At no point did it cross his mind that the mother-to-be was admiring his open, friendly face, his milk-chocolate brown eyes that were, ever so slightly, too close together, giving him a helpless, vulnerable appearance and the long dark lashes that framed them. The nose he was so conscious about was straight, slim and elegant, and his full, generous mouth was always quick to smile. Danny looked away but could still feel her eyes upon him. He ran his fingers nervously through his thick, dark brown hair – a habit which contributed to it being so unkempt and one he was unable to break.

Just then, the train gave an unexpected lurch which caused him to bump against the passenger standing next to him. He looked up to apologise and found himself facing a large, solid man who was easily a head taller than him. At almost six feet, Danny wasn't small although he was slim built which made him look a little on the lanky side. He hurriedly mouthed a 'Sorry' to his fellow passenger before moving his feet in an attempt to maintain his balance and gripped the handle even tighter as he wondered how much longer it would be till he was home.

Danny let out a sigh of relief when the tube train finally pulled into Colliers Wood station. He alighted, walked up the stairs – the darn escalator was broken again – and made his way outside. He saw the traffic lights were on red so sprinted across the road although he quickly wished he hadn't when his head began thumping again. He turned right to walk up the High Street and almost bowled over his friend Rob who was the manager of his local pub.

"Hey, careful there, Danny, you nearly had me on the deck!"

Danny peered at him through narrowed eyes. The bright sunlight wasn't helping his headache. "Oh, sorry Rob, didn't see you there."

Rob looked at him more closely.

"Bloody hell, Danny, you look like shit, mate." Being the true Aussie that he was, Rob didn't mince his words.

"Cheers, Rob, I needed that!"

"Well, you do. I hope you're going home to your bed. You're in no fit state to be out."

"That is exactly where I'm headed. I'll see you later."

"Sure thing, mate. And make sure you're better for football on Sunday. We're playing that bunch from up Tooting way and I need you on the side."

Danny gave him a wave as he walked off.

Ten minutes later he was home. He shed his coat and scarf, which fell in a heap on the hallway floor, walked into the kitchen and poured the contents of his carrier bag onto the work-top. He read the blurb on a few boxes and selected three that promised he'd be back to normal in no time. As he opened the packets, he looked at the cocktail of tablets in his hand before pouring a glass of water and throwing them down his throat. He knew he shouldn't mix the medication, and normally he wouldn't do such a thing, but needs must. He gave a small shrug. This was the one time he couldn't afford to be sensible – he had to get better ASAP.

He looked at the clock and saw it was only twelve thirty meaning he had plenty of time to get some much-needed shut-eye. He made his way to the bedroom, undressed and got into bed before quickly sending a text to Sandra to let her know that he'd still be picking her up tonight. Within minutes of lying down, he was fast asleep.

Sandra Harrison looked at her reflection in the mirror and huffed with annoyance.

"No! Not like that! I want it completely smooth with only a few tendrils around my face. Fix it!"

Sandra had recently seen a photograph in a magazine of Kate Middleton sporting a sleek and stylish chignon and wanted the same look for herself tonight. She hadn't considered that her tight, thick, curly hair made this task rather difficult for her hairdresser. The long-suffering stylist bit her tongue, turned up the heat on her straighteners and took out the pins she had just spent fifteen minutes putting in, doing her best to ignore the growing queue of women waiting for their own special, festive makeover. She couldn't help but think that sometimes her clients forgot where they were when they were demanding West End quality for East End prices. She'd happily take the verbal abuse if she was being paid Mayfair money but here, in the Elephant and Castle, it wasn't always so easy to buy into the old 'the customer is always right' philosophy when you were paid a pittance and relied heavily on your tips to get you through the week.

Sandra fitted perfectly into the stylist's vision of someone wanting everything for nothing. Despite going out with Danny for over three years now, she still believed she was destined for something, or someone, better. It was this belief which was behind her desire to look sophisticated tonight at the ball. There would be more-advanced-up-the-career-ladder–and-therefore-better -paid chaps there, and, if she played her cards right, she might be able to trade Danny in for an upgraded model. It wasn't that she disliked Danny; it was simply that she wanted more than he was able to provide.

In the three years she'd known him, he'd only had one small promotion and it didn't look as though there was going to be another anytime soon. Well that wasn't going to get her the detached house in the suburbs she'd always hankered for, so she needed to keep her options open and ensure she grasped every possible opportunity that came her way. And you didn't get many better opportunities than a massive party with a free bar and wall-to-wall City solicitors. Why on earth should she settle for a mere marketing supervisor when there was a whole company of corporate lawyers to choose from?

Hearing her phone beeping in her handbag, Sandra pulled it out and looked at the text message she'd received. It was from Danny, letting her know he felt really ill but was now at home and planning to have a few hours' sleep before he picked her up at 8 p.m. as planned.

Yeah, she thought to herself, you'd better pick me up after I've gone to all this effort. When she looked back at her reflection, she saw the stylist still struggling to control her crazy curls and let out another sigh of exasperation.

"Oh, for goodness' sake, get a move on will you! I want to celebrate New Year's Eve, not bloody Easter."

When Danny woke up, his eyelids felt really heavy, and he struggled to open them. He wondered how long he'd been asleep. He leaned over and, with half-opened, bleary eyes, looked at his watch on the bedside table. It was quarter to five. Oh good, he thought, he could catch another couple of hours sleep before he had to get ready to go out. The pain in his head was still bad – it felt as if it was being squeezed in a vice – and his throat was no better either. He was convinced a thousand invisible cheese graters were being rubbed up and down it. He decided to take some more of the various remedies he'd purchased. He'd had his first dose just over four hours ago, which meant enough time had passed for it to be safe to take a second one. He blundered through to the kitchen where he rummaged among the hotchpotch array in front of him and, deciding that none of the earlier potions had made any dent in how awful he felt, he opened three alternative packets. He balked again at the thought of mixing the medication, but he was desperate. Sandra could, and would, make his life a living hell if he didn't show up for this damned ball tonight. He opened a bottle of cough syrup and took a mouthful of it to wash down the tablets. He staggered back to bed, and pulling the quilt up to his ears, he burrowed beneath it.

He was already in a deep sleep by the time the clock in the lounge called out its hourly chimes.

Ding!

Ding!

Ding!

Chapter Two

Elsa Clairmont looked up from her book when she heard a tapping noise on the patio doors. On the other side was a little robin.

"Hey there, Robbie, have you come for your dinner?"

She glanced at her watch and saw it was 3.30 p.m. "You're early, little man. Did you see the light on and decide to try your luck?"

She went over to the kitchen, got out the tub of bird seed and put some water in a little plastic dish. The temperature was still several degrees below freezing today and she knew the bird bath in the garden was frozen over.

The country had been suffering a blast of icy Siberian winds for almost a week now and it was expected to last a few more days. She put the food and water outside and quickly closed the door before the cosy warmth of the flat escaped. She stood watching Robbie eat his fill and, when he flew off, she closed the curtains. Elsa stood for a moment, with her hands clinging tightly to the thick, velvet material, as she worked on quelling the agitation inside her. This was the sixth New Year's Eve she'd been through as a widow and it was still every bit as difficult as the first.

She looked at the photograph of Harry sitting on the shelf. Part of the deal she'd made with herself, when she'd sold their marital home and moved into the flat, was that she'd keep just one photograph of him on display. The rest were packed away. It was the only way she'd ever be able to move on.

Except... she hadn't moved on. Not really.

She'd gotten to a halfway point and had languished there ever since, unable to make that final break. Moving into the flat had helped as there'd been no ghosts to torment her, but it was the nearest she'd managed to a new start.

When her best friend Sukie had gotten married, and moved to Austria with her husband Pete, she hadn't wanted to sell her flat but hadn't been keen on letting it out to strangers either. Elsa moving in was the perfect solution and one which had benefitted them both.

She felt a cold, wet, nose bumping against her hand and looked down to see Puddle, her Golden Labrador, standing with his leash in his mouth.

"Yes, Puddle, I've seen the time. Give me a few minutes to get wrapped up and we'll go over to the park. Okay?"

Upon hearing the word 'park', Puddle let out a muffled woof of happiness.

A few minutes later, she was walking down the driveway when she saw her elderly neighbour Sadie coming towards her, carrying what looked like a heavy shopping bag. Elsa rushed over to help her. The last thing she wanted was for Sadie to fall on some black ice and harm herself.

"Oh, but it's a bitter one today," said Sadie, as she let

Elsa relieve her of the carrier bag and took Puddle's leash from her. "I can't wait to get home and put my feet up in front of the fire."

Elsa smiled as she walked back towards the house, Puddle walking calmly by her side. In the summer months, when the evenings were balmy, Sadie would often join Elsa and Puddle for a stroll around the park. She loved to hold Puddle's leash and pretend he was her dog. Elsa had asked why she didn't get one for herself, but Sadie had replied that, despite always wanting one, she'd never had the opportunity. Now she felt she too was old and it wouldn't be fair as she could 'pop her clogs any day' and then what would happen to the poor thing? No, she was quite happy to share Puddle with Elsa. She checked on him during the day when Elsa was at work, let him out into the garden to do his business and then sneaked him into her flat for a few hours before Elsa came home. Elsa knew of Puddle's little afternoon visits to Sadie but didn't let on. She'd guessed, correctly, that Sadie got a little thrill from being 'naughty' and she wasn't going to spoil it for her. Besides, where was the harm – both Sadie and Puddle got to enjoy some company and she didn't need to worry about either of them being lonely.

Elsa arrived at the park a short while later, once she'd seen Sadie into the warm safety of her flat. She let Puddle off his leash so he could enjoy a good run. When the weather was this cold, he didn't get so many long walks and his pent-up energy turned into boisterous tugging which could pull her off her feet. That's what came with being petite. Elsa was five-foot-two and everything about her was tiny – her hands, her feet, her dress size. With her shining blonde hair, big deep-blue eyes, perfect English-rose complexion and dark red lips, she really was the picture of perfection. As Harry used to joke, though, her looks were deceiving. Baked beans had been banned in their house as she would fart like a trooper for hours afterwards. Her singing was atrocious – she couldn't carry a song in a bucket – and, when she'd had one too many bottles of wine, her snoring could equal any ship's fog-horn you cared to compare her to. Harry had always told her that he loved her imperfections much more because it made her real – too much 'perfect' was boring.

She took a look around and saw there were a handful of dog walkers about, but she didn't recognise anyone, although, with it being so cold, everyone was fully wrapped up in hats, thick coats and with scarves across their faces.

She walked along, keeping her head down against the wind, and thought of Sukie and the invitation she'd turned down to spend Christmas with her in Austria. She'd visited last year and it had been a very difficult week. On the surface, she'd managed to appear as though she was having a great time but, inside, she'd been close to screaming.

She'd really struggled with seeing her best friend living a life which she had been denied. No one knew they'd been trying for their first child when Harry's brain tumour had been diagnosed, three years after they were married. The next twenty-two months, three weeks and four days had mostly been spent in hospitals, watching treatment after treatment fail and seeing the man she'd loved since they were both teenagers slowly fade away to a shell in front of her. In the end, death had been a blessed release for him. For her, it was the day the stabbing, churning sensation arrived in the pit of her stomach. Every morning when she woke, she had a few seconds of respite until the memory of Harry invaded her mind once again and the churning kicked back in. She'd become so conditioned to its presence that she would most likely miss it if it were to go away. Not that she wanted it to go away because that would mean she was forgetting about Harry and she could never do that.

Suddenly, there was a high-pitched yelp and she was startled out of her reverie. Looking around in the dark, she became aware that Puddle was no longer nearby.

She reached into her pocket, pulled out the little torch she carried with her and switched it on.

"Puddle… Puddle… Where are you, boy?" she called out loudly. "Puddle… Here boy…"

The high-pitched yelp came again.

She rushed towards it and realised it was coming from the lake in the middle of the park. When she reached it, her worst fear was realised. Puddle had run onto the frozen ice and had fallen through.

There was a reason her daft, lovable, dog was called Puddle and it was because of his obsession with water. Harry had bought the puppy as a gift for his parents. The puppy had stayed with them for the first four months while he was being trained and this was when they'd found out about his love of the wet stuff. It didn't take long for puppy Frank to become puppy Puddle and the name had stuck.

Not stopping to think, Elsa tore off her coat and boots. There was no way she was going to stand by and watch her precious dog drown. He was her last link to Harry now that both his parents had died. She couldn't lose Puddle too. She *wasn't* going to lose Puddle too.

She stepped slowly and gently onto the ice, testing it to see if it would take her weight, and then edged out onto the frozen lake. She could see Puddle trying to get out of the watery hole he'd fallen through, but she knew he'd be cold and may not have much time left. She eased down onto her belly, trying to distribute her weight more evenly

– just as she had seen people do on television programmes and in films. There hadn't been many times in her life when Elsa had been grateful to be only five-foot-two and small built, but this was definitely one of them.

She inched along as fast as she could, all the while calling out to Puddle, letting him know she was coming for him.

"It's okay, boy… Mummy's here. Hang on, baby! I'm coming to get you. That's a good boy. I see you. I'm coming."

Puddle let out another yelp and Elsa slithered along the ice faster, taking less care in her hurry to reach him. When she got to the hole, which had grown in size thanks to Puddle's escape efforts, she reached down and, grabbing a hold of his harness, tried to pull him out of the water, but he was a big dog and she couldn't quite manage. He slipped back in and disappeared under the water.

"PUDDLE!" she screamed, at the top of her voice.

His head came back up and she reached down to grab his harness again. Desperation leant strength to her arms and this time she managed to haul him out and onto the ice next to her. She gave him a gentle push towards the bank of the lake and he ran off towards it, clearly happy to be out of the freezing water. He may like water but not *that* much!

"I hope you've learnt your lesson now, you stupid mutt," she muttered, as she worked on swivelling herself around so that, she too, could get off the ice and back home to the warmth of the flat. Her teeth were beginning to chatter now that the relief of saving Puddle was leaving her and the effects of her fright, along with the cold, were beginning to set in.

She was about to begin her cold, belly-slithering

manoeuvre back to solid ground, when her bootless foot slipped into the watery hole behind her. The surprise of the icy wetness on her toes made her jump. The action caused the ice beneath her to let out an almighty creak and, before she could do anything, it broke into several pieces and she fell through into the lake.

The sudden shock of being fully immersed in the freezing-cold water dragged the breath right out of her body. She came back up from the murky depths, gasping for air but her muscles seemed to have stopped working. She was struggling to get her lungs to work. They sprang into action just as she sank down once more and the feeling of the ice-cold water flowing into her body made her panic further. She tried to get back to the surface again but could no longer see or feel the hole she had fallen through.

She felt her long, woollen scarf begin to weigh heavily around her neck, making her attempts to move even more of an effort. She tried dragging it off but one of the ends had gotten caught on something and she couldn't undo it. She tugged at the heavy, water-logged wool but only succeeded in making it even tighter around her neck.

She banged her fist against the ice above her, but the lack of air was quickly making her dizzy and light-headed. She hit the ice again but this time with less vigour. She was growing weaker. Little silvery stars began to swim in front of her eyes and the inside of her lungs felt like red hot pokers were being stabbed into them.

Who's going to look after Puddle? was her last thought as the blackness came over her.

Chapter Three

Joe Harrison let out a sigh as he picked up the remote control and turned up the volume on the television. Although, to successfully drown out the sound of Sandra's screeching from the kitchen, he'd need some heavy-duty ear-plugs and industrial ear-muffs. Boy, when that girl got started, she could scream for England.

She was now ripping-off because her boyfriend Danny hadn't turned up to take her to his company ball. To be fair, she *had* gone to some considerable effort to look good and so had every reason to be angry, but did she *have* to make such a racket about it? Joe figured there wasn't anyone in the whole street who didn't know she'd been stood up.

She was now on the phone to her best friend Kylie, calling Danny all the names under the sun. Personally, he thought Danny deserved a saint-hood for putting up with his spoilt brat of a child for this long. If only he would hurry up and marry the lass, then she'd be out of the house and they'd all have some peace. He'd lived with her dramas for thirty-two years and that was more than enough.

Joe loved his daughter, but he'd be the first one to admit she topped the charts when it came to being high-maintenance. He laid the blame for this firmly on his wife. Anita had always believed herself to be too good for the life she was living and had passed this belief onto Sandra. All through her childhood, Anita had told Sandra she was destined for great things and Sandra had lapped it up. Funny, Anita hadn't bothered to instil this same train of thought into their other daughter, Alison. Joe reckoned it was because Sandra was Anita's double in looks whereas Alison took after his side of the family – tall, slim, mousy brown hair and sharp, angular features. Sandra had the blonde hair, blue eyes and curvy, voluptuous, figure of her mother. There was no doubt that Sandra was the head-turner in the family. It was just a shame her inside wasn't as pretty as her outside. She was a lazy, demanding, stuck-up little cow and Joe found himself disliking her intensely most of the time.

He often wished she'd been like her older sister. Alison had put her head down, worked hard and was now a doctor at Guy's Hospital. Sandra on the other-hand, believing that one day some rich bloke would come along and sweep her off her feet, had done precious little in life and now worked in a boutique near Oxford Street. Every night she came home and all she did was bitch and moan about the customers and her colleagues. Although, when one stopped to think about it, Sandra never had a good word to say about anyone. Even her best mate Kylie would cop a mouthful if she didn't bow down to Sandra's whims.

Joe looked at the clock on the mantelpiece – it was after 9.30 p.m. Sandra still hadn't gotten a hold of Danny and he could hear her making arrangements to meet up with Kylie once she'd gotten changed. Thank goodness, he thought, at least it would all calm down after she went out. Mind you, it was unusual for Danny to let her down. He was always reliable and would usually arrive at least ten minutes early for their dates. Joe gave a small shrug as he picked up the remote to change the channel – he'd probably hooked up with some mates and decided he'd rather get pissed up with them. Joe couldn't say he blamed him. In his boots, he'd have done the same.

Joe heard Sandra stomping off up the stairs to her bedroom and he decided it was now safe to go into the kitchen for another beer. He'd finished his last one forty minutes ago, but he'd rather have died of thirst than face his youngest daughter when she was going off on one. Some things just weren't worth the hassle.

Chapter Four

Danny squinted his eyes against the soft, bright light shining around him.

What on earth... he thought as he turned to look about.

He was standing in a room, in the middle of a small queue of people. A woman with long, blonde hair was at the front, talking to a man standing behind a shimmering silver lectern. The man wore a plain, silvery-grey suit with a pale blue sash across his chest. From what Danny could see, the lettering on the sash said 'Host'. The man spoke with the woman, wrote something in the large book lying open in front of him and then pointed her towards a seat. She walked away to sit down and the man in front of him stepped up to the lectern.

He glanced down as he moved forward and saw a line painted on the floor with some wording politely requesting he stay behind it to allow privacy for those in front. He looked around again as he waited. The room was large and bright. Along one wall was a full-length window, although the glass was frosted. It appeared as though the sun was shining behind it, but the frosting muted the light coming through. Directly opposite the window was a full wall of clear glass and through this he could see crowds of people milling around. They were all wearing the same clothing – flowing tunics and long, loose trousers. The outfits appeared to be of a silvery, silky material, very similar to the suit worn by the host. It was then that he saw he was sporting the same apparel. He tried not to chuckle when he imagined himself looking like some hippy throwback.

The other walls, in both rooms, were painted white, although they also appeared to be shimmering. The room he was standing in had a large black 'A' painted on the wall. The room through the glass displayed a 'B'. Everything around him was soft around the edges – as though being viewed through a veil or a filter.

"Next!"

Danny started when he realised the man at the lectern was beckoning him forward.

"Name please," he asked politely.

"Err… Danny… Danny Delaney," he replied. "Where am I?"

Ignoring the question, the man said, "And your date of birth please?"

He gave him the details while asking again, "Where am I?"

The man just smiled and said, "Please take a seat," while directing him to a vacant chair next to the blonde woman.

Danny sat down and resumed his surveying. The room he was sitting in was considerably smaller than the one through the glass and was far less busy. That room was full to the brim with people although there appeared to be plenty of hosts in suits looking after them.

While he was watching, he saw a woman in his room

– also wearing a grey suit with a blue sash – walk over to a man seated against the opposite wall. She spoke quietly to him before guiding him towards a door in the corner. This happened on three more occasions over the next few minutes. It didn't take long for him to notice the anomaly within the room.

There was only one door.

People walked out through it every few minutes, yet no one ever entered by it. New people, however, were continuing to arrive in the room.

Suddenly, the woman next to him gave a loud sigh. He looked at her as she fidgeted in her seat.

"I hate waiting too," he said.

She looked up at him and Danny struggled not to let out a gasp when he saw how beautiful she was. She had the largest eyes, and their deep sapphire blue colouring was mesmerising. Long lashes swept up around them, enhancing their feline shape. Her cheekbones were as high as they came, and her chin was a pretty, delicate oval. Her lips were full with a perfect bow along the top. He really couldn't recall ever seeing someone this stunning in real life. On the cover of a magazine maybe, but never in the flesh and *never* sitting in a chair next to him. Women this beautiful just didn't come into his life. Ever!

"I'm sorry if I disturbed you," she said. "I've never been very good at sitting still for long. My mother was always telling me off for it when I was a child." She smiled as the memory of numerous scoldings crossed her mind.

"It's okay, no problem," he replied. "You'd think, if they're not going to provide us with some magazines to read, they'd at least put up a television we could watch. The walls are a lovely colour but there aren't even any posters to distract us."

The woman smiled at him then – a smile that revealed small, even white teeth and which totally blew him out of the water. For a brief second, the deep sadness he'd seen in her eyes disappeared.

"Where do you think we are?" he asked. There was nothing around them to give any kind of clue.

"I have got absolutely no idea," she replied. "I think we're dreaming. You know... those dreams you have where everything feels real and then you wake up and think you're in the wrong place, even though you're actually in the right place."

"Well, in that case, are you in my dream? Or am I in yours?" he asked.

"Hmmm, that is a good question," she replied. "What do you think would be here if this was your dream?"

Danny thought for a moment before replying. "Let me see, there would posters of big, shiny, motorbikes, Premier League footballers and high-action movies on the wall. The floor would be covered with a large, circular brown and orange rug, and we'd be sitting on a battered, cheap leatherette, sofa."

The woman looked at him with mild amusement. "Well... That's precise. Are those all your favourite things then?"

"Nope," he replied. "They're all the things I detest the most but, with the kind of luck I have – of always being in the wrong place, or doing the wrong thing, at the wrong time – it's exactly what I'd expect to find in my dreams. You know..., that sod's law thingy?"

The woman laughed at this – a light, tinkling laugh that sent a warm and mushy sensation flowing through his body. He'd made this beautiful creature laugh. If nothing else good happened in his life, he'd always have this moment to look back on. He knew he'd never forget it.

"Okay, then, what would you have if this was your dream?"

The woman stopped laughing and the pained sadness moved back into her eyes. She went quiet and didn't answer, choosing instead to look down at her hands which were clenched tightly together in her lap. He immediately sensed her dismay and began to apologise.

"I'm sorry, I shouldn't have said that, I've upset you now..."

She laid a small hand on his arm and her blue eyes looked up at him as she said, "No, this is not your fault. You said nothing wrong. Please don't feel bad. You should feel good, you made me laugh. I don't do that much anymore. It felt nice."

Looking around her, the woman let out a tiny giggle. She removed her hand from his arm and pointed to the furthest corner. "Over there, would be a rail full of beautiful, designer label clothes." She pointed to the other corner, "Over there would be a counter full of top quality make-up and hair products. In that corner, there would be floor-to-ceiling shelves full of Jimmy Choo and Louboutin shoes and finally, in that corner, more shelving groaning under the weight of Chanel, Radley, and Kipling handbags." She smiled back at Danny. "As you can tell, I'm the ultimate girlie. My best friend gives me earache over it but, what can I say? I am what I am."

Danny laughed as she shrugged her shoulders and assumed a resigned look on her face. He could tell she was making fun of herself and he found himself warming to her.

"Well, you're not quite *that* 'girlie'," he replied. "You missed out the fluffy kittens and cute puppies gambolling around."

"I wasn't finished. They would be in a giant pink, fluffy playpen in the middle of the floor."

At this comment, they both burst out laughing. It hadn't really been that funny, but it had been humorous enough to break the ice. It was a nice feeling to be able to indulge in silly, nonsensical chatter. Danny felt as though he'd made himself a friend. He didn't know exactly where he was but, with this lovely lady sitting next to him, he wasn't in any hurry to move on.

They carried on laughing and talking nonsense for a short while longer until one of the hosts came over to Danny.

"Excuse me, sir, may I ask you to come with me?"

Danny turned to the woman and put out his hand. "It's been lovely talking with you. I hope we meet again."

When she put her hand in his, he felt a jolt rush through him. It was as though her hand had reached right inside his being, wrapped itself around his heart and had given it a soft, gentle squeeze.

"It has indeed been a pleasure. I hope we meet again too. The question is… Will it be your dream or mine?"

Danny reluctantly let her hand go and replied, "I really don't mind. I'm rather partial to puppies and kittens." And, with those words, he smiled before following the host as she guided him towards the door.

Elsa watched Danny go and felt a small wave of sadness come over her. She'd liked him. His lovely, chocolate-brown eyes had pulled her in; he had a sweet kind smile and his habit of continually running his fingers through his thick, brown hair was really quite endearing. When he'd shaken her hand, a sensation akin to an electric shock had swept through her and had left all her nerve endings feeling fizzy and fuzzy. She hadn't felt those sensations since Harry had died. How bloody typical was that, she thought – she finally meets a man who could possibly reawaken her soul and he only existed in her dreams!

That was definitely *her* sod's law thingy!

Chapter Five

Danny walked through the door and it closed silently behind him. He was alone in a long bright corridor with doors set at regular intervals along each side. The floor beneath his feet was the same silvery hue as the walls. The ceiling above him was the same bright, frosted glass as the waiting room. Everything seemed to shimmer around him. He thought he could hear music playing but it was so faint, he wondered if his ears might be compensating for the silence. Not quite sure where he should be going, he walked slowly along the corridor, looking at each door as he passed by. They were all solid brown wood and no sound could be heard from behind them. He'd been walking for about a minute when he came upon a door that was different from the others. Its top half was glazed, and the lower half was solid wood. It reminded him of the door from his school art class as it had smudges of paint and charcoal fingerprints on it. He was smiling at the memory when he noticed a small card pinned to it and his name written upon it.

He knocked twice and waited for a response. When

there was none, he tried the handle and the door quietly swung open. Danny slowly walked in and found himself standing *in* his old art classroom. The door closed silently behind him.

He looked around and was astonished to see all the paintings and drawings he'd created when he was a teenager pinned up on the walls – back when his talent had still been fresh and blossoming. He'd forgotten most of them and seeing them again brought a lump to his throat as he remembered he'd always been happy when he'd been in the art room, messing about with the paints and pastels. He had just turned full circle when he became aware of a man sitting at a desk in the corner. He hadn't been there when he'd walked in. Danny recognised him immediately.

"Mr McAlister?"

"Hello, Danny, long time no see. Please, take a seat."

Danny crossed the room and slowly lowered himself down onto the vacant chair in front of the desk.

"So, how are you, Danny?"

"Urmm… I'm well, thank you. Confused, if I'm being honest and thinking that this is up there as one of the weirdest dreams I think I've ever had."

"Hmmm…" William McAlister looked at his young, ex-pupil and decided to jump right in. No point in beating about the bush. "This isn't a dream, Danny. This is the real deal."

"Err, Mr McAlister, I don't mean to be rude, but it can't possibly be real because… you see… you're dead. I read about it on the school website."

"That's correct, Danny, I am dead. And right now, so are you."

Danny jumped to his feet, knocking over his seat as he did so. "WHOA! Just back up your truck a minute there… I'm WHAT?"

He stood in front of the desk, feeling shock tremors rushing up and down his spine and stared at his old teacher who looked calmly back at him.

"You're dead, Danny. That's why you're here."

"But… how? How am I dead? And where am I? What is… where is this place?" Danny turned this way and that, looking for the door but it had disappeared. They were now surrounded entirely by walls adorned with his schoolboy pictures.

"Danny, please sit down and let me explain. It's not quite as bad as you think. We need to talk."

"Not as bad as I think?" he squeaked, as he struggled to breathe. "You've just told me I'm dead. I think that's as bad as it can possibly get!"

"Please, Danny, sit down."

Danny was breathing heavily as he picked up the fallen chair and sat down hard upon it, trying to make sense of this news. He couldn't be dead. How could he be dead? What on earth had happened? Why couldn't he remember it? And, come to think about it, he really didn't want to be dead. He wasn't yet ready for that…

He gazed at his old Art teacher and waited for him to speak. He'd always admired and respected Mr McAlister, so he was prepared to listen to what he had to say.

"Danny, first of all, you are here because you took an overdose of cold and flu remedies. You died at ten minutes past four this afternoon." At Danny's look of surprise, the older man stopped talking. "You seem surprised by this news," he said.

"I am," replied Danny, "very surprised indeed. I remember checking the time, it was nearly five o'clock. There had been over four hours between my medication doses. I made sure of that."

William gave him a soft smile. "I'm sorry, Danny, you got the time wrong. It was three o'clock when you took the second dose – barely two hours after the first. You took a cocktail of brands and… well… the combination caused a chemical reaction which brought on a massive heart attack. Your death was instant. I'm afraid taking that much medication in such a short space of time was only ever going to have one outcome. *That* is how you died."

Danny blinked hard, trying to prevent the tears which had suddenly gathered in his eyes from falling. He swallowed several times before he was able to speak.

"So, where am I? Is this Heaven? Or am I in Hell?"

William gave a small chuckle. "You're in neither. You're in Death's waiting room. Waiting Room **A** to be precise."

"Waiting Room **A**?" he asked faintly, unable to see why that would make any difference.

"Yes, didn't you notice the two waiting rooms were marked **A** and **B**?"

"Err… Well, yes I did, but I didn't really give the reason why much thought. Does it really matter?"

William leaned back in his chair and touched the tips of his fingers together, just like he'd done when Danny was his student all those years ago.

"It's really very simple," he explained. "Waiting Room **A** is for 'accidental' deaths and Waiting Room **B** is for 'booked in' deaths. In other words, the folks we're expecting go to room **B**."

"Ookaayyy…" said Danny, slowly dragging out the word as he tried to get his head around what he was hearing. "So, what happens now?"

"Well, this is where it gets interesting," said William, leaning forward in his chair and placing his elbows on the desk in front of him. His eyes shone with anticipation. "*This* is where it gets interesting…?" Danny didn't think he could cope with anything more, his head was all a-jumble with what he'd heard so far.

"Oh yes! This is when you get to choose what happens next."

"I get to choose? Choose what?"

"Yes, Danny, you get to choose. You get to choose whether to stay dead or whether to go back."

"Well, back of course! It's a no-brainer. Who would choose to be dead?" Danny gave a high-pitched laugh as relief washed over him. All was not lost after all.

"Hear me out, lad, it's not as straightforward as you might think." William looked at him gravely. "There's more to it. The deal comes with conditions and you need to hear them before you make your decision."

"Ok, I'm listening, tell me more."

"In a moment, first, tell me more about where you are in your life right now. Are you married? Got children?"

"No, I'm afraid not. I haven't met anyone that I felt I really clicked with and I wasn't going to marry someone just for the sake of it. After growing up with my mother, I've seen exactly how *that* turns out."

"Do you still paint and draw?" William looked genuinely interested in hearing more about him.

"Well... Err... Not as often as I should." If he was being very honest however, Danny knew he hadn't picked up a paintbrush or a pencil since he'd left school. Not in the way Mr McAlister was suggesting anyway. He did sketches for work but that wasn't the same. He always had the intention to get back to it one day, but it just never happened. It also didn't help that he often worked late and was too tired to draw by the time he got home. The realisation saddened him as he'd always enjoyed dabbing away on the canvas – it was the only time he'd ever felt a sense of peace.

"That's a great pity, Danny because your talent is exceptional. You know how much I wanted you to take up the place you won at The Royal Academy of Art. Such a magnificent achievement for one so young. It was sacrilege to turn it down."

"I couldn't accept it, sir, I needed to stay at home and begin earning a wage. My little brother…" Danny stopped when he thought about Patrick. Three years younger than him and never out of trouble. He didn't realise he'd reverted to calling his teacher 'sir' – it came automatically.

"Ah yes! Your brother! The one you gave everything up for. The one you *had* to look after and protect from your drug-addled, alcoholic mother. How are they both these days? Do they ever thank you for the sacrifice you made on their behalf? Hmmm? How is Patrick?" William's tone grew sharp as he spoke.

"Patrick's in prison, sir. Despite my best efforts, he got in with the wrong crowd, turned to drugs himself and began committing crimes – house-breaking, muggings, etc. – to pay for his habit. Eventually he stabbed a man and killed him. He was caught and is now doing a thirty-year stretch in Wormwood Scrubs."

"I see. What about your mother? Do you still see her? Did Patrick's downfall bring her to her senses? Did she waken up to the fact that the example she'd set her younger son had resulted in a man's death?"

"No, sir, she's still the same. She blames me, of course. If I hadn't left home, and had carried on giving her my money, then Patrick wouldn't have had to go out stealing. I try not to see her if I can possibly help it. She phones me every now and then when she's really desperate for money – usually when whatever bloke she's been fleecing gets wise to her and moves on."

"And you give her this money? This money which you know she will spend on drugs and alcohol?"

Danny sighed. "It's easier to give it to her to get rid of

her. If I don't, she phones constantly, at all hours of the night, waking me up. Once, when I was adamant I was not giving in, she turned up at my workplace. She walked in and began offering sexual services to my colleagues because, and I quote, 'my awful bloody son would rather see me starve than give me money to feed myself'. I nearly lost my job that day as we had important clients visiting and they witnessed the whole scene. I can't take that risk anymore, so I give her the money to keep her out of my life."

"So, even now, she continues to ruin your life, lad. Were you aware that she came to the school to see me after you won that scholarship?"

"No, I wasn't." Danny was shocked to hear this.

"Oh yes, she came in for a little visit. Said she would allow you to attend the Academy on the condition that the school gave her money. Otherwise, you could forget it. She would persuade you that you had to work because your wages were needed at home. Of course, the school *wouldn't* give her any money."

Speechless with shock, Danny just shook his head, mortified at how his mother had manipulated him. For the last twenty-plus years he'd been working in an office, having turned his back on the talent he loved dearly, and all because his mother had, yet again, thought of no one but herself. He could still recall clearly the guilt trip she'd laid on him. By the time she'd finished, he'd felt ashamed at even having thought about going to art school. Of course, it was his place to go out to work and start bringing home a wage.

"I wanted to tell you what she'd done but the headmaster forbade me. I had to keep quiet. It's been the biggest regret of my life, that I was partly involved in you throwing away your life's dream and wasting such a tremendous gift. That's why I'm here now, stuck in this middle realm – the regret over my actions is so intense. My soul is not at peace. I can't move on because of the guilt I feel at having ruined your life. I stopped you following the path you were meant to take. You had SO much talent and it is simply too bad that it has been wasted. Such a terrible waste…"

Danny looked at the old man in front of him. The spark of anger which had flared up when he'd told him of his mother's deceit quickly faded as he saw the intense pain on his face. Instead, he felt sorry for him – yet another person who had fallen victim to his mother's selfish, conniving and manipulative ways.

"Please, Mr McAlister, don't feel bad. You're not the only person my mother has done this to over the years and you won't be the last. She is what she is, and you can't blame yourself for the decision I made. I could have been equally as selfish and taken up that scholarship, *I* made the choice not to. What's done is done and it can't be changed." Feeling it would be better to change the subject, he said, "So, now we've gotten all that out of the way, can we discuss those conditions that come with me *not* being dead?"

"Ah yes, I think we're ready for those. Please keep any questions you may have until I am finished and please don't interrupt."

William cleared his throat as he sat up straighter in his chair.

"Right, there are three conditions which come with not being dead. Number one," he stuck up his thumb of his left hand, "You need to change another person's life." Holding up his left index finger, he said, "Number two, you need to change your own life. And finally, number three," he raised his left middle finger, "you need to find true love." He paused for a moment before continuing. "To help you along, you will have three small freckles on the inside of your left wrist. As you achieve or complete each condition, a freckle will fade. You get one year to clear all three freckles. If any freckles still remain by the last chime of midnight on the 31st of December, you will become properly dead."

William leaned back in his chair and waited for Danny to absorb what he'd said.

Danny sat quietly, turning his old teacher's words around in his head.

Finally, he spoke. "So, let's make sure I've got this straight. I need to make a difference to someone else's life, make a difference to my own life, *and* find true love. All in one year. Correct?"

"That's correct."

"Do I have to do them in that order?"

William shook his head. "No, you can achieve them in any order. Although, I should clarify that the changes you make must be good ones. Shooting someone would make a difference to their life but it's not really what we're looking for."

Danny smiled at the old man's humour. "I think we both know that is not really my style." He paused again, trying to see the catch in the terms but there didn't seem to be any. "And you're quite sure that's it? No catch? No 'selling my soul to the devil' or anything like that?"

This time it was William who smiled. "I can assure you there is no catch, no pitfalls to watch out for, no 'small print'." He made quotation marks in the air with his fingers at the last bit. "It is simply the three conditions and nothing else."

Danny felt himself relax at these words. If he failed, he would be no worse off than he was right now. It seemed as though he had nothing to lose and everything to gain.

"Ok, I'll do it. I accept the terms."

William smiled. "Are you quite sure now?"

"Yes, I'm absolutely sure!"

"Final answer?"

"Final answer!"

William stood up and held a hand out across the desk. Danny got to his feet and, when he put his hand in William's, the old man gripped it tightly with both of his. Danny heard the depths of his emotions in his voice when he said, "Good luck, son. Good luck!"

Chapter Six

Not long after Danny had left, one of the hosts came over to Elsa and directed her through the door. On the other side, she found herself in the same long, silvery-shimmering corridor Danny had walked down a short time before. Slowly walking along, she passed the solid wooden doors on each side until eventually she came to the one which was different. She stopped in her tracks when she saw it. It was identical to the kitchen door in the first flat she and Harry had moved into when they'd returned from university. It was a plain, white painted door with a huge orange stain a third of the way up. She remembered that stain very clearly – she'd been carrying a new bottle of nail varnish when she'd tripped on the rug in the hallway. The bottle had flown out of her hand and smashed against the door, the nail varnish splattering all over it. The more she and Harry had tried to wipe it off, the worse the stain had become. In the end they'd decided it improved the appearance of the dull hallway and agreed to leave it be. They'd given the door a fresh coat of paint just before they'd moved out and handed the keys back to the landlord. She smiled at the memory, she'd forgotten about that.

She stepped closer to the door, her hand outstretched to touch the memory, and saw a small card pinned to it with her name on. She laid her hand upon the painted wood for a few seconds before knocking and waiting for an answer. When none was forthcoming, she gently turned the handle and opened it slowly. She peered round cautiously and let out a gasp. Her hand flew up to her mouth and she let go of the door, allowing it to swing wide open. She was standing in the very kitchen from that same flat. Right down to the battered old dining table with the four, mismatched, chairs around it. She walked in and the door closed behind her.

Elsa stood looking around her. There, above the sink, was the squinty roller blind which had never quite rolled down properly. On the worktop stood the kettle – the one that didn't switch off automatically and which had resulted in several kitchen saunas when it was put on and forgotten about. Next to it were the old seventies-style ceramic tea and coffee canisters her mother had dug out of the loft when she and Harry had been too skint to buy new things for the flat. Everything they'd possessed had been donated by both of their mothers – from the pots and pans in the kitchen to the towels in the bathroom. Their only new items had been the bedding and some cheap cushions which Sukie had bought for them as a housewarming present.

She turned around slowly, feeling herself being swamped as memory after memory assaulted her. She could almost feel the throbbing under her feet from the parties they'd had when the stereo had been turned up to its limits and she could practically smell the scent of the fresh pizzas they'd had delivered far more often than they should have done. She looked over at the fridge freezer in the corner and saw it was covered in concert tickets – held there by the fridge magnets they'd picked up on their various travels. A happy reminder of the wonderful days and nights they'd shared with Sukie and whichever young man she'd had in tow at the time.

With a radiant smile on her face from the wonderful memories, she turned back to the dining table... and screamed.

For there, sitting where he had always sat, on the wobbly, blue chair, was Harry!

She stared at him, her mouth moving but she couldn't speak; trying to move but finding herself rooted to the spot. So many times over the years she had wished and prayed for this moment. A chance to see his face one more time, hear his voice, feel his touch. To hold him and tell him again how much she loved him. And yet, now the moment was here, all she could do was stare at him. She knew she wasn't dreaming. She'd had many dreams where she and Harry were together again but this...? This was something else. She couldn't say how she knew – she just... did!

"Sit down, Elsa," Harry pointed to the chair opposite him. It was the one with the padded seat that she'd always preferred.

She stood for a moment longer before, with a deep breath, she managed to step forward, pull the chair out with a shaking hand and sit down. For a few minutes neither of them spoke as they drank in the sight of each other. Harry's hands were clasped together on the table in front of him. She reached tentatively across to touch him, but he pulled back sharply.

"No! Not yet."

Elsa finally found her voice. "What do you mean 'not yet'? I haven't seen you for over six years and you're telling me I can't touch you?"

"I need to explain some stuff to you first."

"Such as...?"

"Well, Elsa, where exactly do you think we are?"

"Well, I initially thought I was dreaming but I can sense now that I'm not. If I didn't know better, I'd say I'd died and gone to heaven." She gave a small laugh at this.

"Not bad. You're fifty percent right." Harry's tone was gravely quiet.

She looked at him as his words sunk in and she grasped their meaning. "I'm dead?" Her eyes widened and her voice was barely more than a whisper.

"Right now, yes, you are."

"What do you mean 'right now'? Harry, stop talking in riddles. What's going on? What has happened? And if this isn't heaven, where exactly is it?"

Harry had a look of sadness on his face. "What's the last thing you remember?"

Elsa scrunched her face up as she tried to think back to before she'd arrived in wherever the heck she was now. "Cold... wet... couldn't breathe..." She suddenly sat upright as it all came flooding back to her. "I fell in the lake in the park while trying to rescue Puddle. I went under the ice. I couldn't find my way out and I couldn't breathe..." She stopped as the realisation hit her. She looked at Harry, her blue eyes filling with tears.

"I'm dead..." she said quietly.

"I really am dead."

Chapter Seven

There was silence for a few minutes as Elsa absorbed this news. Eventually, Harry broke it.

"Well, I don't know what you're so upset about," he said harshly, a look of total disdain on his face.

Elsa stared at him in complete shock. Harry had never used such a tone with her, not in all the years she'd known him. "What do you mean?" she asked him. "Of course I'm upset! Being dead is quite a big thing."

"Aw, Elsa, don't give me that. You've been dead as long as I have. Now it's just become a reality. I thought you'd be glad to be here."

"I have not been dead, Harry Clairmont! What are you going on about?"

"Elsa, with the greatest of respect, you've been dead in every way it is possible to be dead while still having a pulse and breathing. You stopped living when I died and have merely existed since then. Look at you, all skin and bone. You might think you're being healthy with all your organic foods and obsessive gym work-outs but it doesn't look like that from where I'm sitting. To me you're just a bloody mess! You haven't even taken off your rings! At least that would have been a start."

She looked at Harry, trying to blink away the tears of anger in her eyes. How dare he speak to her like that.

"Who the HELL do you think you are, judging me like that? What did you expect, Harry? Hmmm? We lived in each other's pockets for the best part of twenty years. I grew up with you always by my side. You walked with me to and from school. We sat next to each other in all our shared classes. We went away to university together. We came back home and moved into our first flat, this place!" She waved a hand around before thrusting it angrily in Harry's face. "When we got married, I told you that day that *you* had put this ring on my finger and only *you* could ever take it off again. You know that. But then you went and left me!"

By now she was furious. Every nerve ending was pulsing in anger as her blood raced through her veins. She stood up, her chair scraping the floor as it was pushed back and, raising her voice to hear herself over the pounding in her head, she said, "I didn't know what to do or what to think. It felt as though everything inside me had been viciously ripped out and all that was left was an empty shell. Yes, I admit that when we buried you, it felt like I'd buried myself with you. You think I've gone too far with my eating habits and gym trips – well, let me tell you something – focusing on those things is what stopped me from doing something much, much, worse." She put her clenched fists on the table and, leaning forward, she screamed at him, "YOU HAVE GOT NO IDEA HOW BAD I FELT!"

"I HAVE EVERY IDEA BECAUSE I FELT IT TOO!" Harry jumped up, shouting back. "While you mourned me and clung onto my memory so bloody tightly, *I* couldn't move on. I've been stuck in this halfway, middle realm all these years because YOU couldn't bloody let go and get on with your life without me. Instead of burying me, you'd have been better off burning me on a funeral pyre – at least then you could have thrown yourself upon it and saved us both years of misery!"

They stood glaring at each other, breathing heavily. They'd never fought or had arguments. There had been silly disagreements but never a full-on shouting match like this.

"Sati was made illegal in the 1800's!" replied Elsa, sitting back down in her chair. She felt quite weary now her anger was fading.

"I'm sorry, what?" Harry, following Elsa's lead, sat down too.

"Sati – it's the old Hindu custom where wives would kill themselves to honour their dead husbands."

"Yeah, I knew that!" Harry grinned at Elsa.

Elsa grinned back. They were now on familiar territory. She would impart little bits of trivia and Harry would pretend he already knew it. Sometimes he had, more often though, he hadn't.

"Didn't!"

"Did!"

"Did not!"

"Did too!"

"I miss you, Harry."

"I know, Elsa, I know, but you should have let me go. You had so much living to do, so much to see and enjoy. It was unfair of you to waste it. When I think of how hard you worked to get your Art History degree, followed by the day you got your perfect job at The Ashmolean Museum, only to throw it all away and become what? A P.A. in some faceless, corporate business... Well, I become very angry and frustrated. You had so much to live for and you chose not to. You promised me, before I died, that you would live your life for both of us. That you would do so much to make up for what I could not. You broke your promise, Elsa, and that saddens me more than you will ever know."

"I had to leave my job, Harry. I couldn't bear to walk through those rooms every day, remembering all the times we'd shared there together. Every corner held a memory, every painting mocked my loneliness. It was my perfect job because I could share so much of it with you. Without you, it simply became a place that was too painful to endure."

"Ok, I get that, but look at you. What are you doing? You've done nothing. You work, you eat, you sleep – just about. You make very little effort to see Sukie and you've lost touch with all your other friends. You don't go out anymore. What's going on, Elsa?"

She thought for a moment, trying to find the best words to explain.

"I'm terrified." Seeing Harry about to speak, she held up a hand. "Hear me out... I. Am. Terrified. In the pit of my stomach is a churning sensation which has been there since the day you died. And the cause of it is fear. Fear at being alone. Fear of doing things wrong. Fear of making mistakes and not knowing how to fix them."

"But you were always so confident, Elsa, why are you scared?"

"I was only confident because you were by my side. Every decision I made I ran by you first. I didn't realise it until you'd gone. I never 'asked' for your opinion but we'd talk and discuss things, so I always knew what I had to do, safe in the knowledge that you'd backed me up. I haven't made a decision completely on my own since I was about eight years old. And then suddenly, you were no longer there, and I lost my belief in myself. I didn't trust myself to do anything right. It felt so wrong not having you by my side that every decision I made also felt wrong. As time's gone by, it's gotten worse. It's crippling me. I feel like I'm in a twisting, whirling spiral of fear and despair and I'm sinking more and more beneath it."

"But Elsa, it was always you who made the decisions. I merely followed along behind, happily agreeing to all that you wanted because it made you happy."

She gave him a little watery smile. "It was knowing you were behind me that gave me the confidence, Harry. If I stumbled or fell, you were there to catch me and pick me up. Now I'm flying on the trapeze on my own, my safety net has gone, and I'm terrified about letting go."

"Well, you need to let go, Elsa, because this can't continue. You need to be brave. You need to make a decision now and you have to do it on your own. I can't help with this one."

"What is it?"

"You can stay dead or you can go back and put things right?"

She looked at Harry, an expression of scepticism on her face. "Oh yeah," she said. "You wanna tell me how *that* one works?"

So he did. Just as William had done with Danny, Harry went through it all with Elsa.

"…And to help you along, you will have three small freckles on the inside of your right wrist. As you achieve or complete each condition, a freckle will fade. You get one year to clear all three freckles. If any of your freckles still remain by the last chime of midnight on the 31st of December, you will become properly dead."

Elsa didn't say anything as she worked on taking in what Harry had told her.

"So, just to clarify, I can choose whether to stay here

48

or go back?"

"That's correct."

"If I stay here, or rather, stay dead, we would be together again, wouldn't we? Okay, it might be a different kind of life but, if we're together, we'd be able to deal with it." Elsa couldn't help but become excited as she began to imagine them both being together in some cosy little cottage with roses around the door.

The joyful expression on her face let Harry know exactly where her thoughts were headed.

"I'm sorry, Elsa but it won't be like that. We won't be together and won't even see each other. You will have a different path to follow from myself and I don't know if they will ever cross or even run parallel."

Elsa slumped in her chair. She hadn't wanted to hear this but, somehow, she had expected it. It had been one last, desperate, grasp to keep hold of the life they'd once shared but her soul already knew she wouldn't be staying. Despite everything, she wasn't ready to be here. She wasn't ready to be dead.

She raised her head and looked at Harry again, her eyes drinking in every last part of him, because she knew this really would be goodbye. Wherever he needed to go, it had to be without her and she had to live without him. It was time to finally let go. Over six years of grieving was more than enough.

"I've got one question – Do you *really* want me to find someone else? Do I need to accept that condition? I mean… That's rather a big deal. It would feel like I was betraying you, being unfaithful…"

"Elsa, I love you and I will always love you. And that means I need to let you go and find happiness with someone else. If you choose to remain single for the rest of your life, then that is fine, but let it be because you *choose* to, not because it would be a betrayal to me and our memories."

She looked at him, the silence wrapping itself around them as she made her decision.

Finally, sitting up straight, she fluffed her hair, straightened her shoulders and said, "I'm going back. I'll take the deal."

Harry smiled at her actions – whenever she needed a confidence boost, the first thing she always did was fluff her hair.

"Just wait till I tell Sukie about this, she's never going to believe me."

Harry started at her words. "Elsa, you won't be able to tell anyone about this. If you try, you'll find it impossible to do so. It's a safety thing because people who've never been here won't understand. You would find yourself seriously compromised."

"But Sukie—"

"No one, Elsa!"

"Ok, fair enough. No one... I accept *all* the terms."

Harry smiled. "Are you quite sure now?"

"Yes, I'm absolutely sure!"

"Final answer?"

"Final answer!"

She had barely finished uttering her reply when a sense of lightness settled upon her and she knew she had made the right decision.

Harry got up and walked around the table. He'd pulled it off. He didn't know how he'd managed to speak so sternly to Elsa but he had and it had worked. He'd made her realise – or at least he hoped he had – that she had to move on. Only time would tell though.

He turned her to face him and, putting his hands on her shoulders, he placed a soft, tender, kiss on top of her head before bending down to lean his forehead against hers. He looked into her eyes while whispering, "Be strong, my darling. Keep the promise you made to me. Never forget you are living for two – go and do all the things I never got to do, see all I never got to see, be everything I never got to be. Live for me as well as for yourself. Will you do that for me?"

"Oh yes, Harry, I'll do that for you. I promise to keep my promise."

"I love you, Elsa. I always will."

"I love you, Harry."

He wrapped his arms tightly around his beloved wife, holding her against him, feeling her heart beating against his chest for the last time while she clung to him, finally crying the last tears she would ever shed for him.

The Middle Men

"WHAT? Say that again!"

Death roared before putting his delicate head in his hands, trying not to shake it. His hangover had kicked in and boy, was he feeling rough.

"You heard us the first time," said William, showing absolutely no sympathy for his friend's tender state.

"But HOW did that happen? They don't get to go back…"

Harry and William looked at each other. Now was the time to remind Death of the favour he'd granted the night before.

As they spoke, Death placed his head on the table and groaned loudly.

"Stop!"

He raised a bony hand. "Before we go any further, could someone please find me some Eye-Be-Ruffin for my headache, it feels like it's been replaced by Big Ben. And a bucket of Kevin's-Funky-Chicken would be good too. The munchies are beginning to kick in."

He peered up at Harry and William through slitted

eyes – opening them fully wasn't yet an option.

"So, let me see if I have got this right. You both felt your incumbents die and saw them arrive in the waiting room. You took advantage of the time-delay differential to engineer a poker game with me. A game you *knew* I would most likely lose, in order to extract a favour which would be to send them back."

"That pretty much sums it up," replied William, "although, in fairness, we'd already arranged the poker game three days ago, if you recall. It was merely a bit of lucky timing for us."

"I don't suppose it crossed your tiny minds that I have a yearly quota to meet and now you have created a problem because my numbers will be out."

William burst out laughing at this. "Oh puh-lease... Who are you kidding? You fudge the numbers every year because you're always getting pissed and half the time, you don't know who's coming or going anyway."

Death had the decency to look sheepish at William's keen observation. "Okay, okay, it's too late to change it now. Please fill me in on how you achieved this. Did you tell them where they were?"

William and Harry took it in turns to explain to Death how the meetings with their incumbents had gone and what had been said.

"So, you let them believe that all accidental deaths have the choice to stay or go? I'm impressed with your inventiveness given that Accidentals have their own room because they take longer to process. At least give me some peace of mind by telling me you applied conditions or forfeits?"

Harry and William let out sighs of relief – their plan had worked. "Of course we did," they replied in unison and filled him in on all the details.

"And this 'find true love' thing – are you hoping these

two get it on together? Is their 'true love' each other?"

"That's kind of what we're hoping for."

"Hahahahahahahahahahaha! Ow!"

"Hahahahahahahahahahaha! Ow!"

Death couldn't stop himself laughing, a great big belly laugh that really wasn't helping his sore head. Tears began to run down his face.

"Oh, this I have GOT to see. You two... Playing matchmaker... this is going to be priceless! Bring it on, guys! Bring it on!"

Chapter Eight

January

BANG! BANG! BANG!

"Argh...! What the fu...?"

Danny sat bolt upright in his bed. Daylight streamed through the gap in his curtains, stabbing his half-opened eyes.

BANG! BANG! BANG!

"Huh? Wha...?"

He shook his head, trying to clear the thick muggy sensation from his brain. He pushed back the quilt and stumbled out into the hallway where he heard a key being inserted into his front door. He quickly made his way to it, yanked it open wide and was almost flattened by the body that came flying in. Thankfully the hallway wasn't that big and the wall behind Danny was close enough to stop them both landing on the floor.

"Guy? What the *hell* are you doing, banging on my door like that?"

Guy Stevenson straightened himself up, smoothed down his shirt and looked at his best friend. "I'm here to check you're okay. No one has been able to get a hold of you for almost twenty-four hours."

"I'm fine! I've been here sleeping."

"Well, maybe if you'd bothered to waken up and turn up for the date you'd arranged with that dumb bint Sandra, she wouldn't have been on the phone to me half the night telling me what a complete bastard you are. Or, better still, you could have answered her phone calls which would have kept *me* out of the loop altogether. That would have been much better. Why didn't you answer *my* calls? I get why you'd ignore that mad cow but you never ignore me. I'm here early because I was worried about you – you never avoid a phone call. Is this a New Year's resolution – to finally stop being so damned nice?"

Guy eventually stopped talking, his relief beginning to calm him down. He walked through into the lounge and dropped onto the sofa. Danny followed behind him, still not fully with it.

"Do you want a coffee?" he asked because *he* definitely needed one. Probably even two if he had any hope of clearing his head and making some sense of Guy's words.

Guy looked up and replied, "I sure do, but I think I'll make it. You look as rough as old boots, mate." He stood up and walked into the kitchen but stopped in his tracks when he saw all the bottles and boxes of flu potions littering the worktop.

"Danny, what the fuck has been going on here? What's all this shit on your kitchen counter?" He picked up various boxes, reading them as Danny walked in.

"I was really ill yesterday. I bought a load of stuff to try and make me feel better. Sandra knew I was feeling bad because I sent her a text. Clearly, she didn't stop to think that might be the reason I didn't turn up for her. I must have slightly overdone it and slept right through."

"*Slightly* overdone it? Danny, with this amount of remedies, it's a miracle you're not standing here dead!"

Guy's words triggered something in Danny's head. He'd begun to tidy the boxes away but stopped as a sliver of a memory came to him – something about being dead and sitting in a room with his old Art teacher.

"Hey, Dan, you okay? You've gone as white as a sheet."

"Hmmm what? Oh, yes, yes, I'm fine. I dunno about killing me but they certainly gave me one hell of a dream, that's for sure."

"Oh yes, what was it about?" Guy finished making the coffee and, handing a mug to Danny, they walked back into the lounge.

Danny thought for a moment. "I… I… I don't know. I can't recall it really. It's all fuzzy. I just know it was very weird."

"Hmph, you're no fun! You know you're supposed to remember the crazy ones – they make life much more interesting. So, how are you feeling now?"

Danny paused before replying. His head was still a bit sore but not as bad as it had been, and his throat seemed to have calmed down too – drinking his coffee didn't feel like he'd stirred razor blades into it. His nose was no longer bunged up which meant his breathing was back to normal. "Not too bad actually. Now the thick head is easing off, I feel almost normal again."

"Well, tell you what, why don't you go and have your shower and stuff while I cook the traditional New Year's fry-up. We can watch the early game on the telly rather than the later one."

Danny's stomach gave out an almighty rumble. He hadn't eaten for almost forty-eight hours. "Mmm, that sounds like a plan, Guy." He went to walk out of the room but stopped and turned back. "I'm really sorry if I worried you. I didn't mean to. I didn't expect to fall into such a deep sleep."

"It's okay, Dan, I know you'd never do anything like that intentionally. That's why I was so worried. But hey, that's what best mates are for – to keep an eye on each other!"

"I hope Nigel isn't too annoyed that you're here earlier than planned?"

"Of course he's not. He was more than happy to see his bed. I think he imbibed a bit more than usual last night, so a few extra hours of sleep won't do him any harm. Now go and get showered and dressed, I'm starving too."

They both left the room and headed in opposite directions. Something was niggling at Danny as he walked into the bathroom, but he couldn't put a finger on what it was. Maybe it was the remnants of the strange dream he'd had – the one that was much clearer in his head than he'd let on to Guy. He couldn't bring himself to describe it to Guy though as it was just too fantastical. I mean, seriously? If you told someone that you'd died, then struck a deal to come back but you had to fulfil three conditions or you would end up dead again... Well, they'd have the men with the straitjackets round at your door before you could say 'Grim Reaper'! Even Guy, who was pretty open-minded on most things, would struggle to get his head around this one. Nah, it was better he kept it to himself.

He closed the bathroom door behind him and turned on the shower. While waiting for the water to warm up, he grabbed his toothbrush with one hand and the toothpaste with the other. He was squeezing out the toothpaste when something caught his eye.

He looked closer...

With a loud gasp, the brush and toothpaste were dropped into the sink and he was staggering over to the toilet where he dropped the lid down and sat on it.

Slowly turning over his left wrist, he looked down at it trembling in front of him.

There was no mistake.

His previously flawless skin was now sporting three small, brown, freckles.

Chapter Nine

Elsa let out a quiet groan. Her mouth was dry and her eyelids felt like lead weights. She gradually prised them open, but closed them quickly when the bright light in the room hit her eyes. She took a moment to think before trying to open them again. She was lying in a bed, but it was not her own. She could also sense someone else was nearby. It was quiet, but she could hear muffled sounds in the distance. There was a strong smell invading her nostrils. A smell she recognised immediately. She was in hospital!

Elsa had spent so many hours in clinical, sterile units with Harry, as his health had deteriorated, and it was a smell she now associated with illness and death. She hated it with a passion.

The knowledge of her whereabouts had her snapping her eyes wide open. The light was less painful this time and it receded quickly. She carefully moved her head to look around. Her mother was sitting in a chair by the side of the bed. She'd dozed off and had a little bit of dribble hanging off her bottom lip. She was wearing her black party dress and her best pearls although her face was devoid of any make-up. Her up-do was now a half-up-

and-half-down-do with several strands of hair hanging over her face

Elsa was both confused and disorientated. What could possibly have happened that had resulted in her being here?

She tried to sit up, realising she needed a drink to ease the dryness in her mouth. The movement woke her mum who was instantly alert.

"Elsa, you're awake. At last! You had us so worried." Her mum stood up and leaned over her, smoothing her hair back off her face, a small gesture of comfort she had performed so many times in her life.

Elsa struggled to work her parched lips. "Drink," she finally managed to whisper.

"Oh honey, of course. Here, let me help you sit up a little and I'll pour you a glass of water. I also need to call for the doctor." Jean Benton pushed the button at the side of the bed before helping her daughter to sit up and giving her some small sips of water. A moment or two later, a young nurse popped her head round the door.

"Is everything ok?"

Jean replied, "Elsa has woken up, please could you let the doctor know."

"Of course," the nurse said. "I'll see that he is paged straight away."

She turned back to Elsa, and straightened the bedsheet as she said, "You gave us a terrible fright, darling, thank goodness you're okay."

"Mum, what happened?" Elsa's head felt foggy and her memory was hazy. Her throat was sore and felt bruised.

"Oh sweetie, don't you remember? Puddle fell through the ice on the lake in the park and then you fell in when you rescued him."

"Puddle! Is he okay?" Elsa croaked as concern flooded

through her.

"He's fine and is at home with your dad. Luckily for you, another dog walker saw what happened and came to your rescue. Unfortunately, he was on the opposite side of the lake when you fell through and by the time he'd run around to where you were, you'd disappeared underneath the ice. Fate was definitely on your side though as your scarf had caught on a jagged edge and he was able to use it to pull you out. Your throat might be sore for a few days but, given the alternative..." She stopped as a sob escaped through her words.

"Oh Mum, I'm so sorry to have caused you all this worry," Elsa whispered as she patted her mum's hand. Memories of the incident were slowly beginning to come back. Before she could think any further however, the door opened and a blond man wearing the most hideous Hawaiian shirt walked in.

"Ah good, nice of you to join us, Mrs Clairmont, how are you feeling?"

Not giving her a chance to answer, he whipped the stethoscope from around his neck, put it on and began to listen to her chest and back. With a grunt of satisfaction, he went through the rest of his checks, making sure everything was as it should be.

Once he'd finished, he looked down and asked again, "How are you feeling?"

Elsa replied in a whisper. "Quite groggy, to be honest, and my throat is sore, although Mum has just explained why that might be."

"Can you remember what happened?"

"I didn't, but Mum started to explain. It's beginning to come back to me now, although it's still quite hazy."

"Good, good." The doctor nodded. "That doesn't sound too worrying. You may remember more, you may not. I expect dying is quite a traumatic experience, even though we did manage to bring you back."

"Dying?" The shock was evident on her face as she tried to sit upright.

The doctor sat on the side of her bed and, easing her gently back onto the pillows, he carried on with the part of the explanation her mother hadn't gotten to yet. "Yes, Elsa, you were technically dead. You'd swallowed a lot of water and had stopped breathing by the time you were pulled out. Your rescuer performed initial first aid on you while waiting for the paramedics to arrive. They then had to shock you because your heart had stopped."

"How long have I been here?"

"Just over twenty-four hours. It's nearly six p.m. on New Year's Day."

Elsa didn't speak, as something had begun to niggle at the back of her mind.

"We're going to keep you in for a few days, for observation. There are many bugs and bacteria in lake water, so we want to be sure you don't succumb to anything nasty, okay?" He looked at Jean and continued, "Mrs Benton, now Elsa is safely back with us, I think you should go home and have a good night's sleep. You need it. Elsa is going to be fine now."

"Oh, I couldn't possibly—"

"Mum, go home." Elsa put her hand over her mum's. "You heard the doctor. I'm going to be okay. Please, go home."

"Well, if you're sure…" Jean began.

"Mum, I'm sure. I'm very tired and I'll be asleep again shortly. You go home and do the same. I'll see you tomorrow. Give Dad and Puddle a big cuddle from me, okay?"

"Okay, I'll see you tomorrow." She gave Elsa a hug and a kiss before gathering up her things and walking out of the room with the doctor.

Elsa began thinking when the door had swung closed behind them. The accident was now completely fresh in her mind – she could recall it all clearly.

But it wasn't the only thing she'd recalled. When the doctor had said the word 'dying' something else had come back too. She lay there, going over it all in her mind and began to realise how fanciful it was. Clearly, she'd had some kind of weird dream, no doubt brought on by the trauma of falling in the lake. The mind did funny things to help it cope with shock.

Although… The persistent churning in her stomach had stopped. Now there was nothing. She looked down at her tummy lying flat beneath the bed-clothes, as though by doing so, the churning would begin again, but it didn't. There continued to be nothing. She thought about Harry and speaking with him in the dream… Nope! Still nothing! In fact… This was the first time she'd thought about Harry and it didn't feel like she was being kicked in the chest by a horse. Now there was no pain at all, just a warm feeling of love.

The more she thought about it, the more she convinced herself it had all been some strange hallucination, most likely the result of oxygen deprivation. There was one way to prove it was all nonsense.

She raised her right hand up in front of her and, closing her eyes, she turned it so the inside of her wrist was facing her. She took a deep breath and opening her eyes, looked at her arm.

Her eyes opened even wider.

As she began to shake, she dropped her hand back on the bed and, squeezing her eyes closed, she took several deep breaths, trying to calm the heart now thumping hard in her chest.

Minutes ticked by as she worked on trying to pluck up the nerve to look a second time.

When she could no longer hear the blood rushing through her head, and the shallow breathing had eased, she finally felt ready to look again.

Nothing had changed.

Her pale wrist now had three small brown freckles.

Freckles which, most definitely, had not been there before.

Chapter Ten

Guy was walking down the road, chewing his lip and deep in thought. He was heading home earlier than expected as Danny had said he still wasn't feeling right and wanted to go back to bed. He'd looked really pale when he came out of the bathroom after his shower, and had barely touched his fry-up. Guy had agreed it was the best thing for him. He hadn't let on just *how* worried he'd been when none of his calls had been answered last night. It was so out of character that Guy had known something wasn't right. At any other time, he would have marched straight round to Danny's flat to see for himself what the problem was, but he and his husband Nigel had been at a party in Maida Vale and he hadn't been able to travel home until late this morning. He'd gone straight to Danny's from the tube station, leaving Nigel to go home and feed their spoilt, indulged cats, before going to bed for some shut-eye. Nigel had been just as concerned and had no problem with Guy heading straight off to check that Danny was okay.

Guy thought about his best friend of twenty years as

he walked, remembering how they'd met. Danny had walked into the gent's loos in a West End pub just as two thugs had been about to give Guy a battering for being 'a poncey little shirt lifter'. Danny had stepped in and, upon seeing the martial art stance he'd taken up, the two cowards had legged it. Danny had sagged against the wall, breathing a sigh of relief at their departure. It transpired that the 'stance' was the only bit of martial arts he knew, and had been gleaned from watching a few too many Jackie Chan movies. He'd have been stuffed if Guy's attackers had chosen to stand their ground.

When they'd returned to the bar, Guy had bought Danny a pint as a thank you. At the same time, he'd introduced himself as 'Guy the Gay' – using his schoolboy nickname for a laugh. Danny, however, hadn't been amused. He'd proceeded to give Guy an ear-bashing on undermining himself. He said that Guy was just Guy and the fact he was gay was no one else's business. By introducing himself this way, however, he was making it folks' business and thus opening himself up to abuse. Guy had been gobsmacked to hear a clearly heterosexual bloke speaking to him like this. People were less tolerant back then and he'd used the nickname to deflect trouble. He'd accepted Danny's wisdom however and had never used the expression since. Finding out that Danny was a life-long Liverpool FC supporter, like himself, had sealed their friendship.

Seven years later, Danny had introduced him to his work colleague Nigel and it had been love at first sight for them both. Thirteen years down the line and they were still crazy about each other. As soon as they could be married, they'd tied the knot. Danny had been best man to both of them.

Absentmindedly pushing the button on the traffic lights by the main road, Guy was still lost in his thoughts while waiting for them to change, mulling over the fact that Danny hadn't yet met a wonderful woman, who loved him as much as he loved her, and settled down. That Sandra one he was seeing was a money-grabbing little baggage and Guy loathed her. Sandra detested him as much as he detested her. He was sure this was down to the fact he could see right through her and the 'helpless little woman' act she always pulled with Danny didn't cut it with him. In truth, she was a conniving, manipulative, she-devil who would twist anything to suit her own agenda or make her look good. The woman wouldn't know the truth if it slapped her around the face with a wet kipper. Guy would never describe himself as a bitch but, when it came to Sandra Harrison, he could give Alexis Carrington a run for her money.

When she'd phoned him last night, telling him of Danny's failure to pick her up, she hadn't been at all concerned for his welfare. She hadn't even mentioned that Danny had been ill. Oh no, she'd been too busy thinking only of herself and the inconvenience he'd caused after all the effort she'd put in to getting ready for her big night out. Guy knew what had really pissed her off though – it was the missed opportunity to get her false talons into a well-off lawyer and move up her social climbing ladder. The stupid tart had confirmed this when she'd phoned him for the third time in a drunken rage, screaming the odds over Danny's continued absence. He had switched his phone to silent after that, ignoring all further calls.

Guy had been witness to the way she spoke to Danny, on many occasions, and the grief she gave him over his apparent lack of ambition. It annoyed him no end. Danny had a good job and had worked bloody hard for the position he now held. He was employed by a good company who'd put him through night-school and various courses which had given him a career. He'd gone from office junior to marketing supervisor and Guy was proud of his friend's achievements. He knew about the dream Danny had abandoned long ago and how hard his life had been, being raised by an abusive, druggy mother. Sandra knew nothing of that, however, and there was no way Guy would ever tell her. He knew the cheap little harpy wouldn't ever understand.

Guy turned the corner into his own street and saw the welcoming twinkle of the Christmas tree fairy lights in the window of their flat. He quickened his step, anxious to be home with his own little family. He considered phoning Sandra to let her know Danny was alright but, as she'd shown zero concern for him the night before, he decided against it. She wasn't worth the effort.

He closed the front door behind him and heard the sound of eight paws thundering down the stairs as he removed his jacket and scarf. He turned around, scooping the small furry bundles up into his arms.

"My babies!" he exclaimed. While continuing to whisper and croon in their little furry ears, he walked up the stairs, Sandra now completely forgotten.

At that same moment, Sandra Harrison was letting out a groan as she slowly began to waken up. She was lying in bed, her face buried in the pillow. Her head was thumping and her mouth was drier than the Gobi Desert. With her eyes closed, she turned over onto her back. The movement made her feel as though everything was spinning.

She was lying still, in an effort to quell the effects of her hangover, when she felt a hand move over her breast and begin to massage it. She pushed it away, muttering,

"Not now, Danny, leave me alone."

"The name's Robbie, love, but you're close enough."

"WHAT THE FUCK?"

Sandra shot upright, the shock moving her headache into second place. She looked around and saw she was in a room she didn't recognise, lying naked in bed with a man she'd never seen before.

"Who are you?" she squealed, trying to wriggle away from him. "What am I doing here? Where am I?"

Robbie grabbed her wrist and pulled her back towards him. "Aw c'mon darlin', no use playing hard to get now, not when you were all over me like a rash last night. To be sure, you couldn't keep yer hands off me so there's no use trying to be coy now." The soft Irish accent, and the cheeky smile on his face, took the edge off his words.

Sandra squinted against the light of the streetlamp coming in the window. She stared at Robbie as snippets from the night before began finding their way into her head. A vision of her and Kylie staggering along the Old Kent Road, trying to flag down a taxi to take them home... Meeting some old friends who'd invited them to a party nearby... Where she'd bumped into a gorgeous, sandy-haired Irishman in the hallway, just as the New Year countdown began... Screaming 'Happy New Year' at the top of her lungs before grabbing him and tonguing the gums off him... Robbie, she now recalled, had been quite happy to join her in some hot and heavy snogging. He'd eventually asked her back to his flat and she'd accepted without question, thinking as she did so 'fuck you, Danny Delaney. If you don't want me, there are plenty of men who do'.

She looked at him for a few minutes more until, eventually, she lay back down, pulling the quilt up to her neck, belatedly thinking of her decency.

"So, how about it, my sweet mavourneen, you fancy

another go? You were begging me not to stop earlier so why don't we continue where we left off?"

Sandra became aware of the throbbing between her legs and guessed that they must have really been going at it hard last night. When she realised that Robbie was playing with her breast again, giving the nipple little hard nips, she felt herself becoming aroused. Hot dirty sex with a total stranger? Oh, why not, you only live once!

She moved towards him and pushed him onto his back as she straddled herself across him. Leaning forward, she let her breasts dangle above his mouth and said, "Okay then, show me what you've got!"

As she succumbed to the pleasures of Robbie's mouth, not one single thought of Danny crossed her mind.

<u>*Chapter Eleven*</u>

<u>*February*</u>

Beth McClaren ran her hand over the bedcover, smoothing out invisible wrinkles. Her daughter Sukie was arriving tomorrow, along with her husband Pete and their toddler twins, and she wanted everything to be perfect for them in their new home.

She looked around once more and, satisfied the master bedroom was ready for them, she walked out, closing the door behind her. Two minutes later, she was walking down the grand staircase, her keen eyes taking in everything around her, making sure nothing was out of place. She was so excited. Tomorrow her family were finally moving into the manor. The renovations had been completed six weeks ago and Beth, along with her partner Jordie Ray, had come home in early January from Austria – where Sukie and Pete currently lived – to assist with the deliveries of the new furniture.

When she reached the foot of the sweeping staircase,

she glanced over the polished marble floor to ensure there were no scuff marks. Pleased to see that it had a perfect mirror finish, she looked up at the antique roof lantern high above her. It was very beautiful now, a far cry from how dilapidated it had been when Sukie and Pete had first found their new home...

Eighteen months earlier

"Mum, how do you and Jordie fancy doing a spot of babysitting?" Sukie and Pete were visiting Beth and Jordie for the first time since their twin babies had been born barely five months earlier. They walked into Beth's living room, having finally gotten the twins off to sleep upstairs. "I want to take Pete out to see some of the gorgeous Oxfordshire countryside."

"Oh, I think we could manage that, don't you Jordie? You two go out and have some alone time together."

"Thanks, Mum." Sukie gave her a hug before pulling on her cardigan and grabbing the car keys. "C'mon, Pete – August is totally the best time of year to see all the pretty villages in the Cotswolds."

They'd been meandering through the beautiful country lanes for a couple of hours when Sukie drove into a picturesque village called Lower Ditchley. The sight of a pretty little pub near the village green and duck pond prompted them to park up and have a look round.

"Oh, this is glorious!" Sukie was standing by the pond, watching the feathered occupants swimming around in the sunshine. The village was quiet, and she could hear the crickets chattering in the long reeds around the edge of the water.

Pete peered over the top of his sunglasses and agreed. "It is quite something. Look at that building over there. I'd put good money on that being the real deal." He pointed towards a shop with black and white frontage which looked as if it dated back at least two hundred years, possibly even more.

They strolled around the small village, stretching their legs, and as they walked up the lane towards the church, Sukie said, "I do love little country churches." She put her arm through her husband's and squeezing it tightly, she continued "Those little kissing gates are always so cute to see, I hope there's one here." When they arrived at the church, Sukie was not disappointed, and she quickly took a few pictures on her phone to share with her mum when they got back. She was snapping away when she spotted a broken wooden gate hanging off its hinges and surrounded by bramble bushes. Beyond it, an overgrown pathway ran along the side of the church wall. Sukie might now be a mother to twins but that hadn't curbed her sense of adventure and, grabbing Pete's hand, she pulled him along to see where it led.

It led them, a few minutes later, to a house which was not far off being an empty, derelict shell. As they walked towards it, they began to fall in *like* with the old building. It was built (they discovered later) from local Cotswold stone, which gave it a lovely, warm welcoming appearance. Half of the roof was missing, although the tall chimneys appeared to be intact, and all the lower windows were boarded up. Several of the windows on the first and second floors, were missing their glass panes.

They were walking around the perimeter when they turned a corner and found themselves at the front of the house. Sukie knew then that she was done for! The porte cochere was her undoing. The beautiful flat-roofed, pillared structure was something she'd always had a fondness for. After all, who didn't desire a covered area where you could pull the car up to the front door, unpack the kids – and the shopping – without getting soaking wet in the rain? She stepped back, and looking up, saw French windows which opened out onto the top of the porte cochere and some black, rusting, iron fencing, albeit with gaps, around the perimeter. With a turn to gaze at the land behind her, Sukie could see it would be the perfect spot for keeping an eye on the long, sweeping driveway. Any unexpected visitors would quickly be spotted, giving the ladies of the house time to make themselves suitable to greet to them.

The driveway was full of holes and covered in weeds but Sukie didn't need much imagination to see how glorious it once had been. It was the same with the landscaped gardens which were also overgrown and full of weeds. The small box hedging – despite having grown phenomenally itself – was struggling to maintain the vegetation within its borders.

Sukie and Pete looked at each other and knew, without exchanging a word, that they'd found the perfect family home. For as much as they both loved living in Pete's ancestral schloss in Austria, Sukie was finding it a bit lonely and she missed her friends and family back in the UK. She and Pete had been discussing the option of splitting their time between Oxfordshire and Austria for the last few months. So, to now find themselves standing right in front of the perfect house, when they hadn't been looking for it, was, Sukie decided, a good omen. Yes, it was a rather decrepit house, it had to be said, but it was still the perfect house all the same. They were no longer 'in like' with it, they were in love.

"What do you think?" she asked.

"I think it would give us a lot more privacy than the Notting Hill house, there's plenty of space for visitors and we can be closer to our friends again." Pete put an arm around Sukie's shoulders. "I know you've been lonely without Elsa."

They continued to explore and Sukie was trying to peer through some broken bits of the wood-covered windows when a voice called out behind them.

"Excuse me, this is private property. What do you think you're doing?"

They both quickly turned and saw a tall, slim-built man walking towards them. He drew closer and they saw he had a kind and inviting face which looked as though it was forcing itself not to smile. He was wearing a white dog-collar at his neck which suggested he may be the vicar of the church they had passed by.

Pete stepped forward, stuck his hand out and introduced himself. "Good afternoon, I'm Pete and this is my wife Sukie, very pleased to meet you."

With a return of the handshake, the vicar replied, "Very nice to meet you too. I'm Jeremy Taylor, the local vicar." He shook Sukie's hand when she walked over to join them. "You haven't answered my question, however, what are you doing?"

Pete looked up at the house as he spoke. "We were having a walk around the village when we came across a path at the side of the church. We followed it and found ourselves here. We've been considering buying a family home in the UK and I believe we may have just found it. Do you know anything about the property, Mr Taylor, and if it's for sale?"

"Please, call me Jeremy," the vicar replied, "and you're in luck, the house *is* for sale and has been for a very long time."

Sukie grabbed Pete's hand in excitement and smiled at him with joy before turning back to Jeremy.

"Do you know its history, Jeremy? It's clearly been

empty for some time."

"I know some of it," he replied. "The house was built in the mid-1700's. I don't know the name of the family at that time. It comes with about six thousand acres of land which encompasses two villages, some woodland, a river and the remains of an old windmill. All the properties in the villages have one thousand year leases on a peppercorn rent. The last resident was Sir Anthony Featheringstone and he died, aged eighty-nine, back in the late eighties. He lived here alone most of his life. He was an only child who never married. Upon his death, and in accordance with his will, all of his possessions were sold and the proceeds donated to charity. No one, however, would touch the house. Even then, it was in a poor state of repair – like most of these historical stately homes, the money is eaten up in death duties, which means each generation inherits fewer funds to maintain the property. The land itself brings in very little revenue as farming is becoming less of a viable occupation."

"With that much land, I'd have expected developers to have been beating a trail to the estate agent's door," said Sukie.

"Oh, they tried," replied Jeremy, "but the property has a long-standing covenant on it that decrees the land may not be split up and sold off in lots, nor may it be built or developed upon in any commercial manner. In other words, it has to stay like this." He swept his hand around him.

By the time he'd finished his explanation, Sukie's excitement was overflowing. "Do you happen to know who the estate agents are?"

Jeremy shook his head. "Not off the top of my head I don't, however, if you drive out of the village along the Charlbury road, you'll pass the gates at the bottom of the drive. I believe there used to be an estate agent board with details on it. I don't use that route very often, but I would expect there will still be something there."

Sukie and Pete, after thanking the vicar for his time and the information, rushed back to the car and drove off to find the information they needed.

Within four days, the property had been viewed – twice – and a price agreed upon.

There was some trouble with a local resident, George Walton, who took umbrage that a world-famous rock star would be moving into the neighbourhood. He started up a petition against the purchase, citing wild parties, drunken hooligans and hordes of groupies taking over the village and causing mayhem. He only got three signatures however, as most of the villagers were excited that a world-renowned celebrity was coming to live among them. The proprietors of the village shops – of which there were quite a few – were thrilled at the prospect of more money being spent in their establishments and the owners of the two small village inns had visions of seeing their sales treble as fans and media gathered to try and catch a glimpse of the Wallace family. Any opportunity to see an increase in sales was welcomed by all.

George, a solicitor in London, tried every legal approach possible to prevent the sale of the manor but to no avail. The day arrived for the renovations to commence and in a fit of desperate rage, he drove to the manor, parking his car – a newly purchased Jaguar – across the gates to prevent access to the grounds. He didn't bargain on the ingenuity of the forklift driver, however, who, having driven his little vehicle off the large transporter, proceeded to carefully lift the Jaguar, with George still inside, and move it to the opposite side of the road. Unfortunately, not being a local man, he wasn't aware of the hidden ditch there which the Jaguar, unexpectedly, fell into.

George Walton was enraged, but the gathered villagers simply laughed. He'd always been too big for his boots. Up till now, his house had been the biggest in the village and he often looked down his nose at his neighbours. Many thought he fancied *himself* as the lord of the manor. Well not anymore. The big fish in the pond had just been relegated and there was a much bigger name on his way in.

From start to finish, it took just over a year for the manor to be restored to its former glory. There were a few tussles with English Heritage due to some restrictions they wanted to put in place but, overall, the house was rebuilt how Sukie and Pete wanted it. Now it was ready for them to move in.

Beth, realising the time, made a small harrumphing sound – she had so much more to look over, including what groceries needed to be ordered. She scurried off towards the large family kitchen, checking the surfaces for dust as she rushed past.

Chapter Twelve

Danny was sitting on his sofa watching the television. It was Saturday night and he should have been out with Sandra but she'd cancelled late this afternoon, saying Kylie had boyfriend troubles and she wanted to be with her to cheer her up. Danny wasn't too bothered – the odd Saturday night in by himself was quite nice. Sandra was hard work, high maintenance they called it, and sometimes he'd rather be on his own than have to deal her. Although... This was the third weekend she'd cancelled at the last minute in the past six weeks. First she'd had a headache, and then her mum hadn't felt too good and now Kylie – she was certainly having a run of it lately.

He picked up the remote control and flicked through the channels to see what was on. He'd been struggling to focus on anything over the last few weeks. He just couldn't seem to concentrate for any length of time. He channel-surfed for a few minutes after which he let out a sigh, switched the TV off and threw the remote onto the coffee table, his eye catching sight of the freckles on his wrist as he did so. He could now remember talking to Mr McAlister as clearly as anything. After Guy had left on New Year's Day, everything had swept back into his head with total clarity.

The first week he'd been a nervous wreck, unable to eat or sleep as the events of that night had sunk in. He'd found himself staring at people – complete strangers – wondering if they'd had the same experience. He would have sworn it had all been a dream if it wasn't for the freckles on his wrist reminding him it really *had* happened.

Towards the end of the second week, he began to calm down, realising he wasn't going mad after all, and, by the end of January, he'd finally accepted it for what it was. Worrying about dying wasn't going to change anything so he might as well get on with the job of living. After all, he had three challenges to deal with, although he had no idea what he was supposed to do that would change *his* life never mind how he was going to change someone else's. And as for the 'find true love' part… Well, he was nearly forty – if it hadn't happened in the last twenty years, then it wasn't looking good for that particular challenge either.

He let out another sigh, picked Priscilla off his lap and stood up. With a small meow, she stretched out and began to groom herself. Danny rubbed her head before closing the curtains and switching on the lamps. He turned back to face Prissy and smiled, watching her antics as she gave herself a good going over. His thoughts went back to the day he'd received a panicked phone call from Guy, screaming at him to come to his place as quickly as possible and to bring the car. When he'd pulled up outside Guy's flat, the front door was flung open and Guy ran to get in. Guy *never* ran so Danny knew something was very wrong. He'd thrust a large box into Danny's hands, saying "Hold that carefully" while buckling himself in before taking the box back. He'd carefully opened it to reveal three small, fluffy kittens inside who were clearly very ill. Two were white with ginger patches, the third was completely white. He'd given Danny directions to a vet's in Tooting and explained that Florrie, his down-stairs neighbour, had found the box lying on the path which ran alongside the railway line. She'd been about to walk past it when she'd heard a mewling noise from inside. Upon opening it, she'd found the kittens, and picking it up, had walked home as fast as she could. She would have run but she didn't want to jolt the little ones inside. She'd asked Guy and Nigel to help as her Jack Russell terrier would not have been happy with the kittens being in her flat.

They'd arrived at the vet's, and were ushered straight to a consulting room. The vet had estimated the kittens were six weeks old, informed them that they were riddled with fleas – which had almost caused Guy to faint – and they all had a bad case of cat flu. He'd doused them with flea-spray, had given them some worming medication and an antibiotic shot each. He'd then advised they would need to be given further medication each day, plus some special kitten milk as they were too young to be away from their mum. He also supplied several tins of calorie-packed food to help them put on some much-needed weight. When he'd finished with all his instructions, he'd presented them with the bill. The sight of *that* had almost caused Danny to faint!

In the end though, they had been worth every penny. Guy and Nigel had kept the two ginger and white kittens and he'd taken the white one. He adored Prissy just as much as Guy and Nigel adored Anthony and Abigail. He placed a kiss on her furry head before heading into the kitchen to make himself a coffee, spitting cat hairs out of his mouth as he walked. Long-haired cats were beautiful to look at, but their fur did get everywhere. Not that he cared – he knew Prissy could make whatever mess she wanted and he'd always be her willing slave, cleaning up behind her.

While he stood waiting for the kettle to boil, he felt waves of restlessness moving around his stomach. As the days since New Year had passed, the unsettled feelings had slowly grown more intense. He sloshed the now-boiled water into a mug and, giving it a quick stir, he threw the teaspoon into the sink and walked into the hallway with the mug in his hand.

He stood sipping his drink while staring at the closed door at the far end. Finally, making a decision, he put his mug down, marched towards it and, before he could change his mind, pulled it open and switched on the light. The wooden flight of stairs rising up steeply in front of him, mocked him from beneath the cobwebs. He could almost see the spiders rushing out to buy sunglasses to protect their little eyes from the unexpected glare. It had been over eight years since he'd ventured up these stairs and that had been only the once – the day he'd moved in.

Danny had bought this flat because it came with a great loft area which had been properly floor-boarded and boasted two large skylights in the roof. He'd hoped having such a light and airy space to work in would encourage him back to his painting.

But it hadn't.

The truth was, he hadn't picked up a paintbrush since turning down the scholarship offer from the Royal Academy. The pain of what he'd thrown away had been too much for him and it had been easier to turn his back on his talent altogether. His marketing job gave his creativity some degree of an outlet, but everything was designed using computer graphics – no chance of getting his hands dirty with some oil paint or linseed oil.

Now, however, he had an overwhelming urge to put paint onto canvas once more. It was a sensation that had been gradually growing inside him. It had started when he'd found the freckles on his wrist. He'd tried ignoring it, but it had simply grown stronger and stronger.

So here he was, standing in front of the stairs which led up to the attic. Given the way his stomach was tumbling around, he might as well have been looking at the north face of the Eiger.

He took a deep breath and placed a foot on the first step.

Then on the second.

And then on the third.

It took another seven steps before he was standing in the loft. The only light came from the two naked lightbulbs – one at either end of the empty space.

Well… almost empty.

Over in the corner, against the far wall, was his easel, various drawing pads and a large box which contained his other materials such as chalks, pencils, pastels and paints. Wherever he'd lived, his painting materials had always gone with him. He'd never been able to dispose of them no matter how many times the idea had crossed his mind.

He walked slowly across the floorboards, his socked feet making no sound, until he stopped in front of the pile. For several moments he stood there, his head spinning as it flashed back to his schooldays when he'd spent every spare moment in Mr McAlister's classroom, drawing and painting. Not for him the thrill of kicking a football around the playground – no, he'd found the peace and quiet of painting helped to soothe his inner turmoil. His home life was so crazy, with his mother's drunken, drugged-up abusive behaviour, that painting was the only thing which gave him some respite, if only for a short period of time.

He opened the flaps on the cardboard box and the first thing he saw was the box of pencils Mr McAlister had given him on his last day at school. They were brand new, and even back then, Danny had known they were an expensive gift. A tin of sixty, top quality, Faber-Castell pencils did not come cheap. Not then and not now.

He reached in and pulled the tin out. From behind the box, he retrieved one of the smaller drawing pads he had stashed there. He checked the paper inside and was pleased to find it dry and useable. He walked back down the stairs, carrying his booty, and sat on the chair opposite the sofa where Prissy was still engrossed in her ablutions. He opened the tin of pencils and, taking one out, he turned over the pages of the drawing pad, preparing to sketch. He held the pencil in his hand for a time, growing used to the feel of it and remembering how to channel his thoughts down into it so it became an extension of his hand rather than a tool within it.

Prissy now had her leg stuck up in the air as she worked on cleaning her under-carriage. Very tentatively, Danny put the pencil against the blank page and began to draw.

Five minutes later, the page was ripped off and dropped to the floor at the side of the chair. He tried again. A few minutes later, that page was also ripped off, scrunched up and thrown across the room. He tried again, this time making a huff of annoyance. His strokes were too heavy and Prissy looked more like a bad caricature than a delicate feline. Her beautiful fine fur resembled clumps of tarmac. It wasn't long before that page also joined the others. Half-an-hour later, dumping the pad on the floor and storming back up to the attic, he rummaged deep inside the box. He found the pencil sharpener he required, returned to the lounge, sharpened his pencil and tried again. By now Prissy, having finished her grooming, had curled up and gone to sleep. Danny picked up the pad and began drawing again. This time, the page was discarded after fifteen minutes, the next after twenty and the next after thirty. He, eventually, began to feel the flow returning. His lines were becoming smoother, his strokes were softer and his curves less stilted.

It was after midnight when he was finally satisfied that he'd produced a passable likeness of his sleeping cat. He stood up and, stretching to ease the knots out of his back, put the pencils back in their tin and tidied up the paper from the floor before getting himself ready for bed. It was as he switched off the bedside lamp he became aware that something was different.

The turmoil in his stomach had ceased.

Chapter Thirteen

March

Elsa had been out of sorts since finding the freckles on her wrist. She'd been discharged from the hospital three days after the accident and her parents had wanted her to stay with them, but she'd convinced them she was well enough to go home.

That first night on her own, she'd sat down and gone through all she could remember. Without the distraction of nurses, and the nauseating smell of disinfectant, she was finally able to concentrate. The time she'd spent with Harry came back to her, right down to the very last detail.

She'd been surprised by how calm she felt – most people would have been losing the plot, knowing, firstly, that they had died and then, secondly, panicking over how little time they had left. A year is either a little or a lot, depending on how you looked at it.

Elsa chose to look upon it as a gift.

Harry had been right. Since his death, she *had* barely

existed and *had* wasted all those years. Now, however, she had the chance to make up for lost time. Even if she failed the challenges, she'd still been 'gifted' one more year.

What she was going to do, however, was another matter entirely. She'd been racking her brains on how to move forward but inspiration was simply not striking.

She no longer had the feeling of fear which had crippled her progress. Since waking up in the hospital, she'd waited for it to return but it never had. She was now experiencing something else instead but couldn't say exactly what that was. If she had to give it a name, she'd say restlessness, maybe dissatisfied, perhaps even unsettled. Whatever it was, it was turning out to be a lot worse than fear. At least with the fear, she hadn't been losing her temper at every turn or snapping at people when they made small mistakes. From being a sweet, kind-natured person, she'd turned into a grumpy old woman who lost her rag at almost every opportunity.

She let out a sigh, and picking up a file, headed to the print room to do the board report photocopies she required. Another secretary, Marjorie from Customer Services, came out of the room with an armful of paper and smiled at her as she passed by.

Elsa walked over to the copier, put her file on the machine and went to enter the number of copies she needed only to find an error message sitting on the screen.

"Oh, what now?" she exclaimed, looking at the details in front of her. It appeared there was a paper jam in three different sections of the copier.

With a "Grrrrr" of disgust, she set about clearing the jams, her temper rising as each piece of scrunched-up paper was rescued from its depths. The last straw, however, was when she burnt her hand on the hot roller while trying to get the last torn-off piece out.

"Oh, bloody hell!"

She shook her hand in an attempt to ease the pain and, looking at the paper she'd retrieved, it didn't take her two seconds to see it related to the Customer Services department. That damned Marjorie, she thought. She'd purposely left the machine all jammed up. She was a right lazy cow that one. No wonder she'd smiled at Elsa – she knew she was the mug who'd be sorting out her crap.

"Well, I am no one's mug and certainly not hers!" she muttered as she strode down the corridor to the Customer Services department.

She flung the door open with such force it slammed off the wall and yelled, "Oy, Marjorie, you lazy bitch, the next time you jam up the copier, at least have the decency to clear it and not just leave it for the next person to sort out."

Marjorie jumped at Elsa's shouting. "I don't know what you're talking about," she mumbled, although the guilt was clearly written all over her face.

"Like hell you don't, you lying cow!"

"Who are you accusing of lying?" Marjorie was now on the defensive and glaring at Elsa.

"Don't give me your slapped-arse, bitch-face, girlfriend. D'you want me to come over there and punch it off?"

"ELSA!"

Elsa looked at Marjorie's manager who was now bearing down on her. "You can't go around calling people names and threatening violence."

"I'm only telling the truth. Everyone knows that she's a lazy bint. I've just burnt my bloody hand sorting out her damned mess."

"You can't prove it was me..."

Elsa turned on her heel. "Oh, can't I? We'll soon see, shall we?" She walked over to Marjorie's desk and picked up the pile of photocopying sitting on it. Quickly looking at the original file sitting on the top and then grabbing the copy on the bottom, she saw it was missing the last three pages.

"See, Marjorie, as I said. You're a lying, lazy cow. You need a bloody good slapping!"

"ELSA! That is quite enough. Leave this office now. I'll be reporting you to the HR department for this." The Customer Services manager loomed behind her.

Silence descended across the office as Elsa slowly turned to look at the manager now in front of her – an officious little man who took the expression 'jobsworth' to an entirely new level. She looked him up and down for a few seconds before leaning in and saying in a chillingly calm voice, "Fuck. You."

With these words she turned back, picked up the pile of paperwork from Marjorie's desk and threw it in the air while yelling, "Fuck the whole bloody lot of you! I don't need this shit. I'm out of here!"

Elsa stormed back out of the office, slamming the door hard behind her. She marched up the corridor to her office, went straight to her desk where she picked up her coat and handbag and walked out.

She changed out of her work suit, when she got home, and took Puddle for a long walk, which helped to calm her down. It was growing dark by the time she returned to the flat where she found a voicemail from her boss, telling her to take the rest of the week off and return refreshed on Monday. He added that he understood she'd been under a lot of stress recently and he hoped this small break would be helpful.

Later that evening, as she was getting ready for bed, she stared at her reflection in the bathroom mirror, trying to work out what to do now. She knew she was finally ready to move on, but the problem was how? Where did she want to go? What did she want to do? Her reflection, however, refused to supply an answer, so she turned off the bathroom light, walked into her bedroom, and quickly got under the quilt. It might be early March but the weather outside was still cold and blustery. She turned on the television and flicked through the channels until she came to the news which she watched while absentmindedly stroking Puddle's ears.

Suddenly she sat upright.

She grabbed the remote control and rewound the image on the screen. She definitely wasn't interested in the news item being reported – some film star leaving London's Annabel's nightclub in a very drunken state – but rather something else which had caught her eye. She replayed the news article, watching carefully until she saw it and then, pausing the television screen, she leant forward to peer at it closely. In the background behind the reporter, she'd spotted a discreet brass plate with the word 'ROWLANDS' engraved on it. It was situated to the side of a glossy black door on one of the elegant Mayfair buildings.

Rowlands?

Rowlands, Rowlands, Rowlands? Why was the name familiar? Why was it jumping out at her?

Elsa stared at the television for several minutes, waiting for her brain to work it out. When the lightbulb moment finally arrived, she jumped out of bed and ran through to the spare bedroom where, yanking open the wardrobe door, she rummaged among her old handbags until she found what she wanted – the handbag she'd taken to Sukie and Pete's wedding.

She walked back to the bedroom, returning to the warmth under the covers again before opening it.

And there it was, hiding away in the little zippy pocket, the business card Jeff Rowland had passed to her when he'd asked her to come and work for him.

As she held the little piece of embossed cardboard in her hand, she remembered the day and the conversation. It transpired Jeff had been very helpful and kind to Sukie in Italy on the night Pete had been shot by a security guard at the gig he was playing. Sukie's inability to speak Italian had made it difficult for her to convey to the hotel receptionist why she needed to know which hospital Pete had been taken to. Jeff had stepped in and sorted everything out, right down to covering the cost of the taxi fare. Sukie and Pete had gone on to become good friends with him and he'd been at their wedding. Jeff, when he'd found out Elsa had a degree in Art History, had immediately offered her a job as his PA / Girl Friday / Office Manager – whichever title she preferred – covering his two London establishments. She'd laughed at the time and said that, although she was very flattered, she didn't think it was for her. Jeff had placed his card in her hand and told her that, should she ever reconsider, she mustn't hesitate to get in touch. She'd placed the card in her handbag and had promptly forgotten about it.

Until now…

Her mind whirling, she stared at the business card for a while longer. Could she do this? Was this what she needed to do? Eventually deciding there was only one way to find out, she picked up her phone and booked a train ticket to London for the following day.

Elsa looked at her watch and sighed. It was 11.40 a.m. and she'd been sitting on the tube for twenty minutes. Normally she loved coming into London but sitting in a tunnel of darkness for ten minutes, due to some points issue, was not helping her jangling nerves in the slightest.

A sudden jolt signalled the tube train was on the move again and soon they were approaching Bond Street. With a quick glance at the map above the head of the passengers opposite, she saw it was only one more stop for Green Park where she needed to alight for Mayfair and Berkeley Square where Jeff's flagship gallery was based.

She looked down at her wrist again and, turning it round, saw the three brown freckles staring back up at her, taunting her almost. What *had* she been thinking? She was mad to be doing this! It was nearly three years since she'd seen Jeff – he was never going to remember who she was, never mind that he'd offered her a job.

She was an idiot!

A grade-A fool!

In the cold light of day, this all seemed like a really stupid thing to be doing.

But no!

No more fear!

She was going through with this. So what if he didn't remember her, she would simply remind him. And if he no longer wanted her to work for him? Well, so what? She would have had a nice day out and he might be able to recommend some other galleries she could contact. She was NOT backing down from this now. She was going to see it through. She took a few deep breaths and, pulling her small travel mirror out of her handbag, checked her hair and make-up looked okay and fluffed her hair before smoothing it down into place. The train began to slow down as it came into the station and she stood up, moving towards the doors.

Five minutes later, Elsa was outside, standing on Piccadilly as she got her bearings. She turned left, then left again into Berkeley Street and walked quickly along the pavement. Within a few minutes she was standing in

Berkeley Square. She stopped to look around her, working out where Jeff's gallery would be while remembering the news report from the previous night. She veered left and walked over to the opposite side of the square from where she was standing. Slowly walking along the pavement, she stopped when she found what she was looking for and, turning to face the beautiful old building in front of her, she immediately noticed the stunning painting displayed in the window. It was a Canaletto and she'd bet her last penny on it being an original.

Elsa stood for a time, looking at the door in front of her. Suddenly turning around, she crossed the road, making her way into the quiet garden the square was named after and found a bench which faced the gallery. She sat down, staring at the building across from her. Her heart was beating furiously while her breathing was rapid and shallow. The fear was back in her stomach, shouting at her to go home. Go back to the safety of the flat. Go back to the surety of her quiet, solitary, life where the cocoon she'd wrapped around herself ensured no one could ever hurt her again.

Every part of her being was screaming noooooooooo!

Except...

Except for her heart...

Still beating furiously, but now with anticipation, her heart was drowning out the noise in her head. A warm liquid-like sensation was flowing through her, telling her it was ready to take this step. *She* was ready. It was time

She stood up, and with trembling hands, brushed down her black gabardine trousers, making sure no stray Puddle hairs were stuck to them. She straightened her favourite cornflower-blue jumper, tweaked her blue paisley silk scarf and buttoned her coat. Satisfied her outfit was neat and tidy, she picked up her handbag, pulled her shoulders back, lifted her head high and walked out of the shadow of her fear.

Today she was going to embrace the sunlight.

Today was the start of a new life.

Jeff Rowland sat in his office, trying to make some kind of sense of the piles of paperwork in front of him. He loathed paperwork. This was why he employed a PA to deal with it. Although, watching his PA on the CCTV, she was far more concerned with faffing around on her phone than actually doing any work. He'd had about six PA's in the last three years. The problem was few proper PA's had the artistic knowledge required for the role and the people with proper art qualifications didn't want to be PA's in a gallery. They were either trying to get into the museums or become artists in their own right.

He let out a sigh – having to deal with the admin took time he didn't have. He needed to be out and about, finding new artists and purchasing the old works his clientele expected him to find on their behalf. He most certainly did not have the time to be doing filing.

"Tamara!" he called out. "Could you come in here please?"

A few minutes passed by and he could see Tamara was either ignoring him or hadn't heard him calling as she was still sitting engrossed with her phone. He called again, louder this time.

"TAMARA! PLEASE COULD YOU COME IN HERE?"

Still she didn't move. When he looked closer at the screen, he noticed her head bobbing ever so slightly from side to side. She had those damn earbuds in again.

He got up, stormed out of the office through to the

front of the shop, walked over and slammed his hand down hard upon the desk in front of her. Tamara quickly pulled the buds out, just in time to hear Jeff telling her to gather her belongings together and leave.

"What?" she questioned. "Why? Are you sacking me?"

"Yes, Tamara, I'm sacking you," Jeff replied. "I have asked you, and then I have *told* you, not to listen to music on the showroom floor but still you continue to do so. I have explained, numerous times, that I have important clients who like to be served the second they walk through the door. If you are otherwise engaged on your phone, face-twitting or whatever it is, or listening to music, then you are not providing that service."

"But it's so booooring here," Tamara whined. Her dad was going to cut off her allowance again if she lost this job.

"It would be less boring if you attended to the paperwork and did the filing which is part of your job remit. When was the last time you did it? That pile in the office is almost falling off the desk."

"Am I supposed to do filing?" Tamara's eyes widened as she asked this question. Clearly she'd missed that part of the job description.

"Yes, Tamara, you are supposed to do filing!" Jeff's voice was filled with pained resignation as he realised he was going to have to go through the whole interviewing rigmarole again.

"Oh well, I could try to do it now…" Tamara tried to sound as though she really did want to do the filing, but she failed dismally. She'd only taken this job because her father believed she shouldn't be sitting around the house all day and out partying all night.

"Well, you need to pay me my money." Tamara stuck her hand out, palm upwards.

Jeff tried really hard not to sigh. "Tamara, you've only worked a few days this month. Today is the fifth of March. Any money due to you will be paid at the end of the month in the usual manner."

"Tough! I want it now!"

"Well, you're not getting it now. It will be in your bank at the end of the month, so I suggest you get your coat, pick up your bag, put your phone away for five minutes and leave."

"You can't just sack me without paying me my money."

"Oh, I think I can!"

"You haven't heard the last of this!"

"Oh, I think I have! Here, let me get the door for you."

When Tamara was on the other side of the threshold, Jeff closed the door and made his way towards the office. He had a phone call to make.

Tamara stormed out of the gallery, down the steps to the pavement and, turning around when she reached the bottom, she shouted back at the closing door, "You're a fucking wanker, that's what you are!"

As she spun on her heel, she bumped into a small blonde woman standing just behind her. "You don't want to go in there, he's an arsehole!" she said, walking away while taking her phone out of her bag to update her twit-face status.

Chapter Fouteen

Jeff picked up the phone and began dialling the employment agency. He knew the number by heart.

"Good morning, Arlington Employment. How may I help you?"

"Good morning, may I speak with Amanda please?"

"Hold the line one moment please."

Jeff was waiting for his call to be put through when he heard the security buzzer. Glancing down at the small CCTV screen, he saw a woman walking through the door. Oh bugger, he thought, just what I need right now.

"Good morning, Amanda speaking."

"Hi Amanda, it's Jeff Rowland. I'm sorry but I'm afraid I'm going to have to call you back, a customer has just walked in."

"No problem, Jeff, I'll speak with you soon."

He hung up the phone and picked his jacket off the back of his chair. Quickly shrugging it on, he hurried out to the showroom. The woman was standing in front of the other Canaletto painting he currently had on show.

"Good morning, may I help you?"

The woman turned around at the sound of his voice. Smiling, she held her hand out. "Hello, Jeff, how are you today?"

Jeff looked at her for a moment, trying to place why she looked familiar. Then he smiled broadly, stepping forward to shake the outstretched hand. "Sukie's friend? Is that correct? We met at her wedding. Yes... you were her maid of honour. Lisa?"

"Nearly, it's Elsa," she replied.

"Ah yes, of course. I'm very well, thank you, Elsa, how are you? It's lovely to see you again."

"I'm well too, thank you. Your showroom is stunning," she replied, as she slowly gazed around, taking in the pale cream walls, the high ceiling with the gorgeous crystal chandelier hanging down from the ornate, ceiling rose, the pristine white woodwork and highly polished oak floor. The walls were adorned with a cacophony of art, covering all genres – from Turner and Hogarth, to modern day Warhol and Francis Bacon.

Jeff watched her with interest, noting that she loved the eclectic mix and was struggling to take it all in. It thrilled him to see her face changing right in front of his eyes. When she'd walked in, he'd noticed the stress behind her smile. Her greeting to him, while completely genuine, had still been forced. It hadn't reached her eyes but instead hovered somewhere below. Now, however, those same eyes were crinkled up at the corners and the smile was wide across her face. Her back straightened a little more and her steps became more confident as she walked from piece to piece. She put him in mind of a parched rose unfurling as it soaked up the rain. She was soaking up the beauty of the masterpieces in front of her and was blooming from the experience.

With a view to enhancing her obvious joy, he said quietly, "There's another two floors above with even

99

more to see."

Elsa turned to him in delight. "May I look?"

"Of course! Here, let me take your coat, I'll pop it in the office. You go on up. Would you like a cup of tea or coffee?"

"Oh, thank you. I'd love a black coffee please, if it's not too much trouble."

"No trouble at all, Elsa. I'll sort that out, you head on up the stairs. There's a good mix which I'm sure you'll enjoy." He relieved her of her coat and led her to the bottom of the grand marble staircase behind the main showroom.

Elsa couldn't help but gawp at the artwork around her as she walked slowly upwards. She was convinced that Jeff's collection could give the National Gallery a good run for its money. Was that a Stubbs over there? She peered across at the wall opposite the staircase and stared hard at a breath-taking painting of a horse. The sleek lines, the muscle structure and the sheen from the coat were all suggestive of a Stubbs. She would have to ask Jeff when he joined her.

On the first landing, she saw the room structure of the old house had been maintained and each room appeared to contain differing genres of art and artists. She walked into the first room and her eyes were treated to the sight of a Basquiat, a Jackson Pollock and another Warhol. Clearly this room was the contemporary art. The next three rooms she walked into were filled with old masters. Her breath caught in her throat when she saw the Rubens collection – one of which was large enough to cover the entire wall. There were Rembrandts, Titians, a Caravaggio and even a Da Vinci. All of the works were carefully placed to catch the natural light coming in through the specialist sheer-covered windows. Jeff was making sure his priceless pieces were not harmed by the UV rays which can cause so much damage.

She walked round twice, taking in her fill of the well-known artists. This was the first time she'd been surrounded by such glorious works of art since she'd left her job at the museum, barely three months after burying Harry. Already, the empty void inside was beginning to fill up as she drank in the sights in front of her.

She had just stepped back out into the hallway, about to go up to the second floor, when she met Jeff. They climbed the stairs together while he said, "Up here you'll find the modern and impressionist artists. Everyone wants to see a Van Gogh or a Picasso or a Gauguin, so I keep them on the top floor. That way, the buyers have to walk past all my other stock to reach them. That is VERY good for business." Jeff gave her a little side-long wink, clearly letting her in on one of his sales secrets. "I also place my newly discovered artists up here. The ones I like to try and help make their breakthrough. The popularity of the old guys helps to sell the work of the new guys because all art collectors want to be 'the one' who discovers the next Pollock, Van Gogh or Warhol."

They stepped into a vast, simple open space adorned with stunning splashes of colour around it. There were no picture rails, dado rails or ornate cornices here. It was just a straightforward, simply decorated room with a pale wooden floor and magnolia walls. Jeff explained to her that he'd had the flooring removed from the front rooms on the third floor to allow as much light in as possible. It had certainly worked as there were three large windows at floor level and then a further three smaller ones directly above, allowing plenty of natural light to stream in. The plain décor only served to enhance the beauty of the paintings around them.

Elsa couldn't help but be stunned by the works she

was seeing as she strolled round, and, turning back to Jeff, she said, "I don't want to appear rude, but you must be exceptionally successful to have this much art to sell. I don't even want to think what your Knightsbridge gallery must be like."

"Knightsbridge is very different. The focus there is predominately on modern European art, especially modern Russian art. The latter is a burgeoning market and, by placing the gallery near Harrods, I am guaranteed very good passing trade. The customers might pass by the first time, stopping only to look in the window, but, by the time they pass a second or third time, they've usually become clients. Have you seen the works of Lupanov, Annenkov or Shulzhenko?"

She shook her head. "I can't say that I have."

"Well, you must look them up. Their work is spectacular. And as for Stanislav Plutenko – well, he could give Dali a run for his money in the surrealism stakes."

"If you wouldn't mind writing those names down for me, I'll have a look this evening when I get home."

Jeff looked at his watch and suddenly exclaimed, "Oh bugger!"

"What's up?"

"I've just remembered I have an appointment with a client at one o'clock."

Elsa immediately turned towards the stairs. "I'm so sorry. I'm standing here keeping you talking when you have a business to run. How very thoughtless of me. If you could just get me my coat, I'll be on my way." She rushed down the stairs so quickly Jeff struggled to keep up with her and was a touch breathless when he met her at the bottom.

"That's not what I was inferring Elsa. I'm annoyed because I had to sack that stupid girl and now I'll need to close the showroom when I go out."

"Oh, I see." Elsa paused for a moment as a thought entered her head and she pondered on what to do next. She felt the familiar churning of fear begin to twist in her gut again.

This was it.

This was the threshold moment.

She could step back and walk away.

Or she could step across into a new chapter and begin the change.

Could she do it?

Was she brave enough?

Her heart decided for her as she suddenly heard herself speaking. "If it's any help, I don't mind staying and holding the fort for a bit, as they say."

"I couldn't possibly ask you to do that. You're having a day out, what about your other plans?"

"You didn't ask, I offered, and I don't really have any other plans. So, if it helps you out, I'm happy to stay."

"Elsa, it would be an *immense* help. Thank you."

Jeff quickly showed her the pass-code for the inner showroom door – the one between the front showroom and the stairs – which, he said, remained locked when there was only one staff member on the premises, as did the front door. She helped him put on his jacket, straightening his collar at the back, and picked up the portfolio folder sitting on the desk by her side. "Do you need this?" she asked.

"Yes I do! Thank you." He called out his mobile number, which she quickly scribbled down, as he rushed out the door and down the steps. "I'll be back in about two hours, thank you so much!" he yelled before scurrying off along the pavement.

Jeff trundled through the leafy green square two and a half hours later, thinking about the outcome of his meeting. It had been a great success and the Arabian sheikh had made not one, but two purchases. He waited for traffic to pass while looking across the road at his showroom and wondering how Elsa had gotten on. He couldn't believe he'd run out like that and left her in charge, but he'd been desperate, and she *was* Sukie's best friend so surely she could be trusted. Well, he'd soon find out.

Quickly crossing the road to avoid being knocked down by a maniac in a white Transit van, he walked up the steps and into the gallery.

He immediately noticed the smell of polish when he opened the door and looking about him, he saw all the surfaces were gleaming, and the brass door plates and handles were shining. He was closing the door behind him when Elsa walked out from the office carrying a stack of paperwork in her hands.

"Oh, hi there, how did it go? Did your client make the purchase?"

"Err... yes, he did. Two actually..." He tried not to be too obvious, as he glanced around the showroom and was impressed by how tidy it now was. The various brochures he had dotted about had been neatened up, the old dog-eared one removed and a fresh clean one put in its place. The special window blinds looked cleaner. Had they been hoovered? He also saw three piles of paperwork on the desk. "What are you doing there?" he asked, inclining his head towards the items in her hands.

Elsa walked across to the desk. "I got bored and, as there wasn't much happening, I decided to do a spot of tidying. Once that was done, I cracked on with sorting out this paperwork. I'm guessing you DON'T want it lying in the tray all higgledy-piggledy?"

"No, no, not at all. I mean, no, I'm quite happy for you to do it but you were only helping out, you didn't need to do that. I am, however, very grateful. Thank you."

"It was no trouble at all. It helped to pass the time. I also rather enjoyed being surrounded by these beauties," she replied, sweeping her hand around her. "And, one more thing, there was a phone call from a Mr Western, asking you to go ahead with the reserve on the painting you discussed. He said you'd know which one it was, although he left a number should you need to call back to confirm."

Jeff thought back to the inefficient assistants he'd had over the years and said, with a laugh, "Are you *sure* I can't interest you in a job, Elsa, you're amazing!?"

While walking to his appointment, he'd recalled making such an offer to her when they'd met at the wedding, and she had turned him down, so he wasn't expecting her reply to be any different this time.

Therefore, when he heard her say, "Well, actually, yes you can as it happens…" he spun around in shock.

"Seriously? You would take the job?"

"Yes, I would. I would love to come and work for you."

He let out a whoop of joy, walked across and, grabbing both of her hands, began shaking them profusely. "This day just keeps getting better and better."

Chapter Fifteen

"You're doing WHAT? I can't believe I'm hearing this. I haven't seen you for almost six months and now, here you are, telling me you're moving to London!" Sukie sat down heavily on the nearby sofa.

It was the day after her trip to London and Elsa was sitting across from her best friend in the manor's newly decorated family room. Despite the high ornate ceiling and vast windows, Sukie had managed to make it feel cosy and snug. Well, it had been managed after the two of them had spent three hours moving all the furniture around trying to get it right.

Once Sukie had decided everything was where it should be, she'd brought through a tray of coffee and cakes and that was when Elsa dropped her bombshell.

"You heard me! I've got a new job and I'm moving to London next month."

She hid her face behind Poppy, Sukie's two-year old daughter, who was currently enjoying being jiggled up and down on Auntie Elsa's knees. Her twin brother Drew was playing with some toys on the floor in front of them.

"But why? What's brought this on? I've really been looking forward to spending loads of quality time with you. It was one of the main reasons for buying the manor – to be closer to our friends and family!"

"I know you did, Sukie but I'm finally moving on. It's been a long time coming," said Elsa. "That's the funny thing about dying – it kind of gives you a good kick in the pants to sort your life out."

"Dying? Excuse me? What the hell do you mean by that?"

"Oh crap, I'm sorry, I forgot I hadn't told you everything." Elsa hesitated for a moment, trying to choose the right words to explain what had happened that fateful night. "When I had the accident, I actually 'died' for a short time. I suffered a cardiac arrest from the shock of the cold water. They had to do CPR, including the use of a defibrillator, to get me going again."

"Why didn't you tell me? You used to tell me everything."

Elsa saw the shock and upset on Sukie's face. "Oh Sukes, I didn't mean to upset you. It's not really the sort of thing I wanted to talk about over Skype or in a text message. But hey, I'm fine, as you can see." She raised her hands up in a small shrug and winked at Sukie.

Sukie said nothing and took a drink of coffee. Elsa saw her hands shaking and, placing Poppy on the floor with her brother, she moved over to sit on the sofa. She put an arm around Sukie's shoulders, placed her other hand on top of the clenched fist in Sukie's lap and said, "Sukes, I am *really* sorry I've upset you by not telling you this sooner but, the absolute truth is, I've been getting my head around it myself. It's left me feeling quite out of sorts."

She explained to Sukie about all she'd been dealing with since Harry had died. Everything she'd told Harry that night, she now told Sukie

"But you were never alone, Elsa, I was always here for you. I thought you knew that. I thought I'd made that clear."

"Oh, Sukie, you did and you were. But this was something very different. When we were kids in primary school we were always together. It was either 'Elsa and Sukie' or 'Sukie and Elsa' – we came as a pair. Then Harry came along, and we were the Musketeers. When we split up to go to university and college, I became part of 'Harry and Elsa'. Because you went off on your own, you found 'you'! You became just 'Sukie'. You learnt who YOU were, what you liked and disliked, how to make decisions – and sometimes mistakes – and you learnt how to cope with them on your own. You learnt how to be alone. The first time I was 'alone' was when Harry died. Up till then, I could've told you what *we* liked, who *we* were, what *we* did but I had no idea who *I* was. I knew who Harry and Elsa were, but I didn't know who Elsa was. And it scared the absolute crap out of me. It sounds so silly and stupid – a thirty-something woman who can barely think for herself, who didn't know herself. Who didn't know how to make a life on her own. I know that, in the early days, my grief was the major factor in everything but then this really heavy fear of everything began to grow. And it *really* grew. It took over. It stopped me socialising. It stopped me moving on with my life. It stopped me being alive. I didn't know how to deal with it and I was too scared to talk about it. How's that for irony?" Elsa gave a wry grin as she squeezed Sukie's hand.

Sukie squeezed back. "And now? Do you still feel this way?"

"No. After the accident, I realised how lucky I was to be alive, but another feeling has replaced it."

She described her recent restlessness and of the anger which had been building up, telling Sukie how she'd been so bad-tempered with everyone and everything.

"You had a screaming match in the office with Marjorie in Customer Services?" Sukie looked at Elsa in amazement. "Well done you! Did you get a round of applause afterwards because I know several folks who'd like to tell that lazy bitch a thing or two?"

"I told her she had a slapped-arse bitch face!"

Sukie threw back her head and roared with laughter. When she was finally able to speak she said, "Oh, Elsa, you are wonderful!" Doing her very best Yoda impression, she continued, "Taught you well, I have, my little padawan."

Elsa laughed. "Oh, Sukie, I know it's funny now but that's not me. I'm not that kind of person. I hated it. The anger kept taking over and I didn't know what to do. Then, when I saw Jeff's gallery on the news, I was overcome with this absolute certainty that I had to go and see him. It's weird but... In the blink of an eye, it suddenly feels as though everything is slotting into place for me. I mean... Seriously? Jeff sacking his assistant five minutes before I walk through the door? Leaving me in charge while he visits a client? And then offering me a job when he returns... Honestly, Sukie... What are the chances? It has to be right. It *feels* so right. In here." Elsa placed her hand over her heart.

In truth, she was totally shocked herself at how her life had changed within forty-eight hours. Two days ago, she was having a screaming match with Marjorie in the office, now she was getting ready to pack up her old life and begin a new one in the big city. She couldn't help the feelings of excitement that were skipping through her.

Sukie turned to face Elsa and looked into big blue eyes which were sparkling in a way they hadn't done for a very long time. She leaned in and gave her the biggest and tightest of hugs.

Eventually, she let go and asked, "What about Puddle? Will you leave him with your mum?"

"I'm hoping to rent a flat that'll allow me to have pets. Jeff has said he's more than happy for me to take him to work. He likes dogs and wouldn't mind him being around. When I mentioned some of his clients may not take to a dog being on the premises, he informed me he actually lives in the basement flat underneath the showroom, so we can pop Puddle down there if anyone has an objection. I'm beginning to think he would've agreed to anything to ensure I took the job."

Before Sukie could reply, Pete walked into the room. "Elsa, how wonderful to see you, how are you? Nice…erm… haircut…" Going across to her, he gave her a kiss on the cheek before turning to Sukie and kissing her too.

"Oh, don't!" Elsa put her hand up to the short, geometric-bobbed haircut she was currently sporting. "I wanted a change and told the stylist to give me something different. This was the end result. And I know it's awful because your wife hasn't made a single comment on it."

"Well, mum's always said, 'If you can't say anything nice, don't say anything at all', so I'm saying nothing."

"Sukie, when did you join the diplomatic corp?" Elsa laughed.

"When I realised my best friend needs positivity in her life, not negative shit!"

Elsa looked at Sukie and squeezed her hand again. "I need to apologise for all the pain I've caused you since Harry died," she said quietly.

"You do NOT need to apologise for anything, Elsa Clairmont!"

"Yes, I do Sukie. You don't walk on eggshells for

anyone, but I can tell you've been doing exactly that, with me, for some time now. I've been in a very dark place and I've treated my friends badly. I need to make amends to many people but you more than anyone. I really am *very* sorry and thank you *so* much for sticking around. It means a lot to me, it really does."

She gave Sukie the tightest of hugs, trying not to cry as she did so, but failing dismally.

Sukie held her tightly before sitting back and saying, "Well, honey, the good news is your hair will grow. That can only be a blessing!"

They both burst out laughing again while wiping their eyes.

In an attempt to lighten the mood, Pete picked up his daughter and swung her around above his head. "Hey, Poppy-poppet, have you got a kiss for Daddy."

Poppy squealed with delight before placing a big, wet, slobber on Pete's cheek. "Doo-Doo," she said. "Kiss Doo-Doo."

Pete put her back on the floor and picked up Drew. He was named Andrew in honour of Pete's father, but it had been shortened to Drew because Poppy always called him Doo-Doo. Poppy had originally been called Elizabeth, after Sukie's mum, but Beth had put her foot down on that one. She'd never liked the name. It was why she changed it to Beth. They'd compromised by naming Poppy after Beth's favourite flower instead. Sukie now agreed it was the perfect choice, for her daughter suited it perfectly.

"Elsa's moving to London." Pete sat down on the chair Elsa had been sitting in earlier, Drew still in his arms. They both filled him in on Elsa's news.

"Wow! That's a big step. Good for you. Jeff's a great bloke. I'm sure you'll really enjoy working with him."

"When do you go?"

"Hopefully in about six or seven weeks. The first week in May is when I'm due to begin work," Elsa replied. "It depends how quickly I can find a flat to rent. Which also means Sukie," she looked at her friend, "that I'm giving you notice on your flat in town. I'm sorry."

"Hey silly, don't you worry about that. This is your time now. You focus on yourself.

"Oops, phone call… Excuse me ladies." Pete stood up and patted his jeans pocket, pulling out his mobile phone as he left the room.

"I *am* glad for you, Elsa, honestly I am. And London is not quite as far as Austria, so we'll still see each other often."

"Of course we will, Sukes. I'll be up to visit Mum and Dad all the time and I'll see you too."

"Well, you'll always have a bedroom here, it's not like we don't have enough of them!" Sukie jerked her head upwards and Elsa grinned knowing that, even though Sukie had lived in an Austrian schloss for over three years now, she still hadn't fully adapted to having so much space around her. There had been many times when Sukie had told her how much she missed her snug little flat in Oxford – usually when she couldn't locate her cats, Tony and Adam, who'd found yet another little cosy, hidden nook to curl up in.

Pete walked back into the room, pushing his phone into his pocket. "Well, Elsa, the good news just keeps on coming!"

Elsa gave him a puzzled look. "What do you mean?"

"I've been on the phone to my property management company. They received notice from one of our rentals, *only this morning,* advising he'll be vacating at the end of the month. The property is a two-bedroom basement flat only a few minutes' walk from Jeff's gallery. It's right up your street, you could say, and it's yours, Elsa, if you want it."

Elsa looked at Pete, her mouth open in an 'O' of surprise. Quickly composing herself, she immediately protested. "Oh, Pete, that's very kind of you but I can't afford Mayfair rental prices. Jeff's not paying me that much. Thank you so much, though, for the offer, it's really kind of you."

"Hey, who said anything about rent? You're our friend, I'm not going to charge you rent."

"Pete, I couldn't live there without paying, it wouldn't be right. No, I couldn't do it. I really appreciate the offer, but I can't accept."

"How much rent were you thinking of paying?" Pete asked.

Elsa named the price she'd earmarked as being affordable.

"Okay, pay me half of that and let's be done with it. Use the other half to go out, make friends and enjoy all London has to offer. It's not a cheap place to live in so you'll need the extra cash if you're to build a new life for yourself. You don't want to be eating into your savings."

Tears pooling in her eyes, Elsa swallowed hard to clear the lump which had suddenly appeared in her throat, overwhelmed by the generosity of her friends and the support they were giving her. No matter how right this change felt, it was still a massive step she was taking.

"What about Puddle? Do you mind me having him there?" She wasn't sure if a Mayfair flat was the right place for her lump of a mutt.

"Of course I don't mind." Pete's reply came without any hesitation. "The flat has a small garden for him to play in and there's a large square nearby where he can have a good run about."

Elsa looked at Sukie. "I can't believe I'm doing this! I don't know anyone in London, apart from Jeff. I hope I manage to make friends okay." She bit her lip as it suddenly hit her just how big a move this was.

"I'll have a word with Kara. She's living in the Notting Hill house now – it's sort of become our HQ so it makes sense for her to base herself there. She and Gareth are now engaged, and I know they'd be more than happy to take you under their wing while you find your feet. I'll have a word with her later."

"I don't want to be putting anyone out, Pete." Elsa immediately worried she might be a burden and that was the last thing she wanted, although it would be nice to know someone other than her boss when she got there, and Kara, Pete's PA, was lovely. They'd met a few times and got along well."

Just then, Pete's phone gave off a loud buzz. He pulled it from his pocket to look at the text he'd received. "Ah, here we go. I asked the office to mail over the photographs we had on file for the property, so you can see if you like it first." He passed the phone over and Elsa held it so Sukie could look too.

She slowly scrolled through the photos and felt her heart begin to beat a little bit faster. The flat was lovely, bright and very modern and the layout was quite straightforward. The large master bedroom was located at the front of the building. It had a bay window dressed with white wooden shutters inside to let in the light but providing privacy from people walking past on the pavement above. Across the hallway was a smaller, second bedroom and a stunning wet-room. Both of these had smaller half-arched windows at the top of the walls, close to the ceiling. Pete explained that they ran under the hallway of the flat above and the light came from the small pedestrian alleyway which ran along the side of the house. The kitchen and lounge were open plan with a breakfast bar breaking up the space. Large bi-fold doors led out onto a pale decking area and a garden that would be just right for Puddle.

"It also has under-floor heating for the winter and under-floor cooling for the summer," Pete advised.

Elsa passed the phone back to Pete, with the broadest of smiles, and stuck out her hand. "Okay then, mate. I like what I've seen and I'd love to live there. We have a deal. Thank you."

"Oh, away with that!" Pete swiped at her hand and, bending down, he pulled her to her feet into a big hug. "That's what friends are for, Elsa. If there's *anything* we can do to help, you let us know, okay?"

Elsa returned his bear hug. "Okay!"

Pete let her go and said, "Right then, I think this calls for a glass of something cold and bubbly to celebrate. Are you ladies up for that?"

"Oh yes," they replied in unison.

When he'd left the room, Elsa turned to Sukie and said, "He really is a decent bloke. You got a good one there."

Sukie grinned widely and replied, "I know, that's why I married him. But, if you ever tell him I said that, I will have to break your legs!"

Chapter Sixteen

Danny, very gradually, became aware of banging below him. He'd been so engrossed in his painting everything around him had totally faded out. It was the last Saturday in March and he'd been painting all day. He tried not to sigh at the interruption as he put down his palette, wiped his hands on the rag at the side of the easel and walked down the stairs to his front door. He opened it to a very harassed Guy standing on the other side and stepped back to let him in, closing the door behind him.

"Danny, is this going to be regular thing?"

"What?" he asked, looking perplexed.

"Me getting worried because you're not answering your phone and then having to come round to ensure you're okay? This is the second time in three months!"

"Well that's hardly 'regular' is it? My phone's in the lounge, I didn't hear it." He walked through to the other end of his flat and picked the phone up from the coffee table. Sure enough, he had seven missed calls from Guy and two from Sandra.

"So, what were you doing that you didn't hear the

phone?" Guy peered at Danny. "Hang on... Have you been painting?"

"Eh?" Danny looked as shocked as he felt. He hadn't yet told anyone he was painting again. "Are you doing your body language thing again? I've told you not to do that to me!"

A few years ago, Guy and Nigel had discovered a new crime author whose main character was a woman on the autistic scale. She'd studied the art of reading body language to help her interact with the people around her. Guy had been fascinated by this and had enrolled on a few courses. He'd picked the basics up very quickly and now claimed it was the best thing he'd done. It had proved invaluable in his work as an interior designer – he used the skills to assess if clients were genuine or time wasters, or which colour schemes they really liked over which ones they thought they *should* like. He maintained that, of all the courses he'd done for his design business, this one had paid for itself several times over in both money and time saved.

Guy sniggered. "Danny, while I am impressed you think my skills are *that* good, I'm afraid that, on this occasion, it's the big dollop of paint in your hair that's the giveaway!"

Danny put his hand to his head and felt the wet, slimy lump of oil paint sticking there – he must have run his fingers through it while he'd been lost in his painting. Guy stared at him hard, impatient with getting no answer. "Well? Are you?"

With a large sigh, Danny turned around. "Follow me."

Guy trailed behind him along the hallway and up the stairs to the attic. Just like Danny, the last time Guy had seen this room was when Danny had moved in. He'd helped to carry a box up all those years ago but hadn't been back since.

When his head came up into the attic, his jaw practically hit the floorboards.

Floorboards that were buried beneath paintings and drawings!

There were paintings leaning against walls and sitting up on boxes. Charcoal and pastel drawings were stuck to the walls and two easels were both perfectly positioned under each skylight to catch the best of the daylight.

"Oh wow!" Guy walked around slowly, giving his full attention to each piece. There were several of Prissy – curled up, stretched out and mid-wash, a few of famous landmarks – the Eiffel Tower, the leaning tower of Pisa, and St Mark's Square in Venice and some depicting the profile of a woman, although her features were extremely vague. One thing was for sure – it wasn't Sandra.

"Who's the woman?"

"Don't know… no one. She's just some vision I've got in my head. I can't see her face, that's why she's always in profile. It's probably someone I saw on the tube or walked past in the street and she's stuck in my mind."

Guy walked around the attic again. Finally, he turned back to Danny.

"Dan, these are fantastic. Seriously mate! They're exceptional. What made you start again? After all, how long has it been since you picked up a paintbrush?"

"Twenty years, or thereabouts. I hadn't held one since the day I left school."

"So why now?"

He shrugged before replying, "Dunno really. I was feeling restless and dissatisfied with life and stuff. One night I came up here, picked up a pad and some pencils and simply began sketching. The next thing I knew, several hours had passed, I'd used up nearly all the pad and the restless sensation had gone. Since then, I've been unable to stop and I'm up here nearly every night after work and all day at the weekends."

"What does the slapper have to say about it?"

"Don't call her that!" He glared at Guy, who glared back.

"She doesn't know. I've barely seen her since New Year so there hasn't really been an opportunity to tell her."

"She probably wouldn't get them anyway. She's not the brightest pound coin this side of the Elephant, is she?"

"Guy...!" Danny shot him another look, letting him know he didn't approve of him being rude about Sandra. Although, if he was being fair, she never had anything nice to say about Guy, so he was wasting his time trying to be the good dude in the middle. Besides, Guy did have a point – Sandra wasn't one of the most intelligent women he'd been out with.

"So, what do you intend to do with them? It won't be long before you're stuck for space."

Danny looked around him. "I don't know. I haven't found my style yet. I've got some ideas in my head but I'm not ready to try them. I'm not yet back to where I used to be. I need another two or three weeks."

"Well, mate, all I can say is this – if this is you on your B-game, I cannot *wait* to see what you produce when on you're on your A-game!"

Danny said nothing and simply smiled. He cleared away his brushes and paints, while Guy walked around once more, studying each of the pieces again. He really was impressed.

"C'mon then, let's go down and have a beer. I think there's footie on the TV tonight..."

"Well, Danny... it is why I'm here!" Guy replied, scathingly. He'd clearly forgotten their arrangement.

Danny was walking towards the stairs when he stopped and looked back. One of the profile paintings had caught his eye. Was something finally going to come to him…? Nope! It was gone again. Whoever she was, she'd made an impression. He just wished he could remember who, how or why.

Sandra Harrison was annoyed. She'd cancelled her date with Danny tonight as Robbie had said he'd take her to the cinema to see the new Tom Cruise movie. Robbie, however, had just cancelled on her as he wanted to go the pub with his mates to watch the football match on the big screen. She'd tried calling Danny to say she could now see him, but he hadn't answered.

Sandra knew she was walking a very fine line with Danny. In the last three months she'd cancelled several of their dates and had barely seen him. They'd gone out to dinner together last week and she'd really had to make an effort to be nice. She was so close to ending their relationship, but she was stopping herself from doing so. She didn't want to finish with him just yet because she still saw him as her ticket to finding someone better. When he'd asked her if she was coming back to his, she'd nearly choked on swallowing down her initial refusal. Making love with Danny wasn't unpleasant, he was a very considerate lover, but he lacked the wild abandon she'd become used to with Robbie.

She was drawn to Robbie like he was a drug. He gave her absolutely no respect, did his own thing when he felt like doing it – regardless of any previous arrangements he might have made – and seemingly only called her when he was at a loose end himself. Every time she vowed she would refuse to see him and every time she found herself giving in without any resistance. She'd always been the one to call the shots in her relationships and yet he only had to say jump and she asked how high. She seriously disliked the pathetic woman she turned into whenever he was around but, at the same time, she couldn't seem to stop herself. She was addicted to him and, she knew, this was a dangerous thing to be.

With a deep sigh, she picked up her mobile to call Kylie. It was Saturday night and there was no way she was staying in.

Chapter Seventeen

April

Elsa stood in the middle of the lounge and looked around her new London flat. Puddle was exploring the walled garden and she'd just finished emptying some of the boxes and bin bags she'd brought down this morning. Sukie and Pete, along with her mum and dad, had driven down in a large van which Pete had borrowed. Jeff had met them when they'd arrived and had helped to carry in the heavier pieces of furniture such as her bed and sofa. Sukie and Jean had washed down the kitchen and she'd done the bathroom. Despite Pete informing her a cleaning company had already been in to do a deep clean that week, Elsa knew she wouldn't feel at home until she'd done it herself. Now, everyone had left, and she was finally alone.

She made a cup of coffee and, picking up her laptop, went to sit at the small table in the garden. She sipped her drink and watched Puddle having a good sniff round, still unable to believe she'd really done it. She had left her job, given up her home and moved to the biggest city in the country. All by herself! She only knew two people and one was her boss.

Jeff had very kindly offered to take her out to dinner tonight, but she'd declined. She wanted to spend the weekend by herself, adjusting to the new sights and sounds around her. Sukie would be back in London with Pete on Monday and they were going out sightseeing together while Pete went to his meetings. In the meantime, Elsa wanted to discover her new neighbourhood. She'd looked around the area on the internet maps and now she longed to discover everything for herself. She wasn't due to start work for another week, but she'd agreed with Jeff that she'd pop in over the next few days to discuss how he'd like her to manage the shop, the expenses and all the billing. It would be an induction of sorts, but it would make her first proper day on the job a bit less stressful.

She opened her laptop and was typing in her password when she was distracted by her engagement ring twinkling in the sunlight. She stopped to look at her rings – the wedding ring which had never left her finger since her wedding day and her very unique engagement ring. When Harry had proposed, they'd been poor students and the only thing to hand at the time was a ring-pull from a lager can. One of their arty friends had said he would make them a ring as practise for his course. Somehow, he'd managed to twist the ring-pull around a small silver band and had placed two small amethysts on the top. He'd polished the ring for several hours until it was smooth and comfortable to wear.

As she looked at her hand, she felt a small shift inside her. This was a new life and she had to commit to it fully. No blatant reminders of her past could be allowed. With that thought, she swiftly pulled off both rings, placing them gently on the table in front of her while looking at the marks they'd left behind on her finger. There were two clear indents where they'd been, and her hand felt light and bare. She picked the rings up, holding them in the palm of her hand while her head and heart argued over what to do next. Her chest began thumping as she contemplated the prospect of keeping them off. Her head was saying it was time to do just that. She picked up her engagement ring and looked at the little purple stones. She loved this ring – apart from what it had stood for, she'd always thought it was very pretty and unusual. She slipped it onto the ring finger of her right hand and, deciding it looked quite good there, kept it on. It seemed a shame to hide it away. She looked again at her wedding ring – their initials were engraved inside, along with their wedding date. Her finger was so small the ring had actually been able to fit inside Harry's wedding ring. He'd smiled when she'd shown him – "Proving again, my darling Elsa, that I will always surround you with my love."

She pushed back her chair, stood up and hurried through to the bedroom. Her suitcases stood in the corner, waiting to be unpacked. She picked up the larger one, dropped it on the bed and opened it. She rummaged inside until she found her jewellery box. The suitcase was pushed out of the way and she sat on the bed before slowly opening the box up. The small velvet jeweller's bag the rings had come in was lying on the bottom. Elsa picked it up and opened it. She tilted it upwards and Harry's wedding ring slid out onto her palm. She took her own ring and placed it inside. The two were together once more. While she was looking at them, she felt a soft sense of peace wash over her. She was ready to close another door on her past and face her new future. She slipped both rings carefully into the little velvet bag which was then placed back inside the jewellery box. She stood up and put it on the shelf inside the fitted wardrobe. Well, there was no point in putting it back in a suitcase that would shortly be unpacked, was there?

Elsa decided she'd earned herself a glass of wine and some nice chocolate. She went back to the garden and opened up the maps on her laptop to refresh her memory on the location of the nearby late-night supermarket. She called Puddle in from the garden, pulled on a jacket and, picking up her purse, went out to explore her immediate surroundings. Oh sod it, she thought, let's really push the boat out and get some prosecco. This was a new chapter in her life which needed to be celebrated. For the first time since Harry's death, she didn't feel lost. She was finally in charge. She was getting on with her life and, damn, it felt good! She was putting the key in the front door to lock it when she caught a glimpse of her wrist.

Something was different.

She looked closer.

A large smile crossed her face and she ran up the stairs to the pavement with a spring in her step.

She now had only two freckles.

Chapter Eighteen

It was Sunday night and Danny was sitting in front of the television. He had the next week off work and he was planning to really knuckle down to his painting. He wanted to begin trying out the ideas he'd had. He needed to find a style – he was close, but it was floating around, just out of conscious reach. A blank sketch pad lay on his lap and the pencil in his hand hovered above it. If only that wayward thought would settle on him, he'd be able to start on some basic sketches. The time was fast approaching when he'd need to decide where he was going with this – doing a few hours after work and over the weekend wasn't enough anymore. Apart from anything, he was tired in the evenings and it was detrimental to the quality of his painting. He was also finding work harder to cope with. It wasn't that he disliked his job or the people he worked with – no, the problem was the urge to paint was now so strong that suppressing it during working hours was making him irritable and bad-tempered.

Guy, bless his cotton socks – okay, silk and cotton mix to be precise – had said he'd be able to use his paintings in his interior designing as many of his clients liked to have original work by new artists. Danny sighed. He knew Guy would need to sell to half of London for him to be able to pay his mortgage. He was in a difficult place right now and he needed time to think. He glanced down at the pad on his lap and was surprised to see he'd drawn a small village scene. Where on earth had that come from? He looked up and, seeing a well-known murder mystery programme was on the television, realised he'd inadvertently drawn the village from that. Suddenly an idea jumped into his head. He grabbed a fresh pencil and began adding to his sketch. A few minutes later, he held it up for scrutiny. Oh yes, he liked that. He *really* liked that. In front of the village shop, he'd drawn in two figures. One was a boy dressed like a 1950's rocker, complete with quiff, leather jacket and drainpipe trousers. He was standing facing a blonde, pony-tailed girl. She was perched on the seat of a BSA motorcycle with her back to the viewer.

Danny looked at the sketch, realising he may just have found the elusive signature style he'd been searching for. A small frisson of excitement skipped through him. He continued to gaze at the drawing, letting his mind wander and allowing it to come up with ideas.

To begin with, just to get started, he could locate some picturesque villages to visit and sketch. He put the pad on the coffee table, picked up his laptop and did an internet search. With the use of different key words, he jotted down names of places that looked promising and then expanded his search to the online maps to get a better look. He added Brighton to his list as that had been a hot spot for the rockers in the early sixties. It wouldn't hurt to do a few sketches there and, as he rather liked the town, it gave him a good excuse to visit.

He'd put together a list of about a dozen locations, and was about to close the laptop, when a small picture jumped out at him. He enlarged it for a better look and was thrilled to see another truly traditional English country village. It had the village green and duck pond just across from a row of quaint, lead-glass, bay window-fronted shops. There were window boxes filled with colour and hanging baskets outside every doorway. The accompanying blurb informed him the village had barely changed since the late 1500's and nearly all the buildings were made from the local Cotswold stone which made it look both bright and fresh. Danny looked on the website to find out what this little bit of heaven was called and its location. If it wasn't too far, he would drive there tomorrow. He found the information he wanted and looked at the map to see if the whole village matched the online photographs. He was delighted to find it did and, furthermore, it was fairly easy to get to. The village was called Lower Ditchley and wasn't too far from Oxford. He jotted down the directions, closed the laptop and headed for bed. He wanted to set off early tomorrow.

He had a really good feeling about this place.

Chapter Nineteen

Sukie sat in the passenger seat of the Range Rover, staring at the cars passing by on the motorway. It was Monday morning and they were on their way to London for a couple of days. Pete had meetings with Kara, his PA, and his record company. She was looking forward to spending the day with Elsa and playing tourist by visiting some of the sights.

She wriggled in her seat and let out a sigh.

Pete glanced across from the driver's side. "You're looking bothered. What's up?" The little frown line between her eyebrows was the giveaway sign.

"Oh, I don't know. There's something niggling at the back of my mind, and I just can't put my finger on it. It's annoying me."

"Did you switch off your hair straighteners?"

"Yes, they're in my bag."

"Did you pack your toothbrush?"

"Don't need one, we've got spares at the house."

"Did you remember to put on your underwear?"

"That's it! Thank you, darling, you're always so helpful.

"Well dear, now you've turned forty, your mind is"

beginning to go…"

"Oh yeah? Well, you'll be going through that window if you carry on with your cheek… *Darling*!"

Pete laughed. "Try not to dwell on it too hard, love, it'll come to you in its own sweet time." He quickly took his hand off the steering wheel to give Sukie's hand a little squeeze.

The next fifteen minutes passed in silence when suddenly she let rip with some colourful expletives.

"I'm guessing 'the niggle' has stopped niggling huh?" Pete gave her a wry smile.

"Oh damn, damn, damn!" Sukie exclaimed a bit more.

"Are we playing a guessing game here or are you going to fill me in on the details?"

Sukie half-turned towards Pete. "I forgot to tell Mum that Poppy can now open the buckles on her old pushchair. The little madam can perform an escape act faster than Houdini! I meant to tell her to pick up the new buggy from the house if she plans on taking the twins out."

"Why didn't you get her a new one at the same time? Wouldn't that have been the most sensible idea?"

"I needed to check if Poppy could undo them first. If she couldn't – which she can't, by the way – *then* I was going to get a second one for Mum to use."

"Well phone her and tell her."

"I'm already on it, babes." Sukie smiled as she sat back up from digging her mobile out of her handbag.

A minute later she muttered, "Shit!"

Pete raised his eyebrows. "Now what?"

"Hmmm…" Sukie looked up from her phone. "There's no reply. The land-line went to the answer-machine and both the mobiles are going straight to voicemail. There's probably no signal again."

After they'd bought the manor and explored the

grounds more thoroughly, Pete and Sukie had been thrilled to discover several old workers' cottages, some not too far from the main house. Like the manor, they'd also been in need of serious repair. Two had been adjoining so they'd knocked them into one, making a larger single cottage which Beth and Jordie now occupied.

Jordie hadn't been too sure about the arrangement initially – he'd wanted to be the one to provide a home for him and Beth. He felt it was his place to look after her. Beth had told him to get over himself and stop being so old-fashioned. She'd been delighted with the offer as it meant she'd be close enough to see the twins regularly but she'd still have her own space. Jordie couldn't refuse Beth anything and so they'd moved in a few months before Sukie and Pete moved into the manor.

"Did Beth say anything about going out?" Pete asked.

"No, she didn't."

"Well, they'll probably just keep the twins at home until we return. After all, we're only away for two days. We'll be home tomorrow night."

Sukie let out a sigh. "You're right. I'll call again and leave messages on the land-line and both of their mobiles. They're bound to find one of them. I'm over-reacting. I'm sorry." She gave Pete a big smile and rubbed his shoulder affectionately.

"Hey, it's fine. You *are* allowed to fret over our children you know. I can assure you it is quite normal." He picked her hand off her lap and, raising it to his lips, he quickly kissed the back of it. He looked over at her again and said, "I *do* love you, Mrs Wallace."

Her insides flipped over at his words. "And I *do* love you, Mr Wallace."

She picked her phone up and, dialling again, she proceeded to leave a message on all three phones.

Beth looked up from the plants she was placing in the flower bed when she heard Drew let out a scream. She gave a small sigh. Poppy had hit him with a stick because he wasn't playing their game correctly. Her granddaughter was feisty, strong-minded, knew no fear and wouldn't do anything she didn't want to. She was so much like Sukie that Beth often felt she'd time-travelled back thirty-odd years. Drew, according to Jordie, had a lot of his grandfather, and namesake, about him. He was quieter and more thoughtful. You could almost see his mind working as he calculated his next move. It was this slower thought process which often frustrated Poppy as, being the leader of the two, she expected Drew to follow her regardless. When he didn't, she wasn't slow in letting him know of her annoyance.

She decided it would be better for the twins to be apart for a couple of hours so got up to wash her hands and change into something more presentable than her gardening clothes. She needed to tackle a job which she'd been putting off – buying her wedding outfit.

Jordie had been asking her to marry him for almost three years and, when he'd asked again at Christmas, she'd said yes. When he'd asked why she'd finally changed her mind, she'd simply replied, "The time is right, my love."

What she hadn't told him was that she'd been deeply affected by his words a few nights earlier when he'd mentioned that while he loved Pete, Sukie, and the twins with all his heart, when all was said and done, he wasn't actually family and it really saddened him. Pete's father and mother had been his best friends and he'd known Pete, and his twin sister Claire, from the minute they were born. Now the twins had started talking, they were calling him 'Pappy' but he felt like a fraud because he wasn't really their 'Pappy' at all.

As she'd listened, Beth realised she had the power to change this and make Jordie a 'real' pappy – all she had to do was say 'yes' the next time he asked her to marry him. Which she did!

Beth had no problem with being 'married'– it was the wedding part she couldn't really be bothered with. She'd discussed it with Jordie, hoping he'd be enthused by her suggestion to run away to Gretna Green and do it quietly, but he'd said he'd really like his new family to be a part of the day when it became official. And, as she'd also feared, Sukie had become her unofficial wedding planner. Her ideas had gradually become more and more grandiose until, eventually, Beth had told her to stop. It was all too much. If there was going to be a wedding, it had to be small, quiet and tasteful.

The wedding itself was taking place in the village church on the first Saturday in July. Being a divorcee, she'd been concerned she may not be allowed a church wedding but, having talked it all through with Jeremy the vicar, he was satisfied that she'd been the injured party within her previous marriage and he would be more than happy to perform the ceremony.

She walked back into the garden and went over to Jordie. "I'm going down to the village to have a look in the new dress shop that opened last month. I want to see if they have anything which might be suitable as a wedding outfit. I'll take Poppy and you can keep Drew here with you. Are you okay with that? Some time apart might stop them being so fractious."

Jordie stood up and leant in to place a kiss on her cheek, taking care not to get any dirt on her clean clothes. "That sounds grand, pet. I'll tell Drew we need to find some worms and he can help me to turn the soil over."

"Try not to get him get dirty please. I don't want to have to bathe them twice and you know what he's like about having a bath without Poppy."

"I'll pop him into the little overalls you bought for him – they should keep the worst off."

"Okay, my love, I'll see you in a couple of hours."

Going over to the children, Beth scooped Poppy up into her arms. "Shall we take a walk to see the quack-quacks?" she asked her.

"Yis, yis, yis…" exclaimed Poppy, bouncing with excitement. "Doo-doo come too." She twisted round, looking at her brother still sitting on the grass.

"No, darling, just you and Nanny. Drew is staying with Pappy to help him look for wormies."

"Me find wormies too!" Poppy wriggled to be let down.

"You can't find wormies AND feed quack-quacks, Poppy. You can only do one."

Poppy gazed into Beth's eyes. She had a way of looking at you with her bright, emerald eyes that made you feel as though she could see right inside your head. "No wormies, just quack-quacks?"

"That's correct, just quack-quacks."

Poppy looked at her for another few seconds. "Okay, Nanny, quack-quacks. Bye-bye Doo-doo. Bye-bye Pappy." She waved her little hand at Drew and Jordie as Beth carried her around to the front of the cottage and placed her in the buggy.

Beth held the floaty confection in front of her and looked at her reflection in the full-length mirror. The colour was perfect against her pale skin and fair blonde-white hair. It was a pale coffee shade and the dress fell to just above her ankles. It had a matching frock-coat and the two items together looked very elegant. She wasn't sure about the dropped neckline though – it seemed a little too risqué for a woman of her age.

She turned the dress around to look at it more closely and, peering at the neckline, noted there was a reasonable amount of spare material inside it. Maybe she could put in a false panel – something lacy would be nice and it would make the dress a bit more 'wedding' like. She would have a look in Hilda's Haberdashery next door to see what she had in stock before committing herself to buying it.

Beth held it up in front of her again and turned back to the mirror. Hmmm… If she did add some cream lace to the neck, and maybe also along the hemline, she'd be able to accessorise with cream shoes and handbag. A hat might be overkill but a fascinator would definitely work. For a few minutes she imagined herself walking up the aisle, wearing the dress and envisioning how she would look…

Suddenly, a loud scream, the sound of screeching tyres, and the sickening thud of something, or someone, being hit by a vehicle shocked her out of her reverie. Beth thrust the dress back on the rail and grabbed the buggy to go outside but, when she looked down, she found the buggy empty and Poppy was nowhere to be seen.

Chapter Twenty

Danny drove slowly through Lower Ditchley. It was bigger than he'd expected. To his left was the row of shops which had piqued his interest the night before and the village green with the duck pond was on his right. It was a no parking zone in front of the shops, so he continued driving until he found a small car park at the end of the road. He parked up and decided to take a walk around before getting his sketching gear out. It was now a warm, sunny day, far removed from the rain which had been lashing down as he'd driven out of London. There was a pedestrian gate at the far side of the car park and, when he walked through it, he found himself at the bottom end of the triangular-shaped green. A road ran down either side of it while, at the far end, was a woodland area with what, he guessed, was a cricket hut or village hall in front of it. To the right of the hut was a quaint pub with seating outside while hanging baskets and window boxes adorned the front. He could see two people pushing lawn mowers or rollers over the grass near the hut and he suspected they were getting the pitch ready for the cricket season which was only a week or so away.

What was really making him smile, however, was the pleasing sight of the traditional red phone box in front of him, just where the green tapered to a point. He stepped across the road and opened the door to find a fully operational phone inside along with a small folding stool. A gel air-freshener, and a small vase containing fresh flowers, sat on the little ledge where the directories were usually kept. Closing the door, he turned around and smiled at a man walking past with a small white dog at his heels.

"Good morning," he said. "I'm impressed to find one of these here and still in full working order."

The man returned his greeting before saying, "The mobile phone signal around here is a bit hit and miss. We had a right battle with the phone company to keep it – they were all set to do away with it, saying the upkeep was costing them money. It was agreed the village would maintain the box and they'd maintain the phone and the line. The local WI take turns to clean it, and every year it gets sanded down, repaired where needed and repainted. The villagers are very proud of their phone box."

"They should be," Danny replied. "It's a fine-looking specimen."

He bade the man farewell and took a walk along the road on the other side of the green to the one he'd driven in on. An old-fashioned black and white signpost told him he was heading in the direction of Upper Ditchley, which was three miles away. Well, I won't be walking that far, he thought to himself.

He stopped by the bus shelter to look at the shops across from him. There was a newsagent, a butcher, a bakery with a quirky little name that made him chuckle – *Sam C's Cakes* – and a large, double-fronted shop that was an ironmongers. There was also a card and gift shop, a florist and, at the end of the row, a convenience store.

He crossed the road and walked into the ironmongers. He couldn't remember the last time he'd been in one of these. There used to be one on the Old Kent Road when he was a kid and the sight of the men in their brown overall coats had fascinated his younger self. He could remember his grandpa taking him there. Afterwards, he'd be allowed to visit the sweet shop next door where he always came away with a huge gobstopper and a small white bag full with fifty pence worth of chewy sweeties. He opened the door and couldn't help but smile as the little bell above it tinkled. While closing it behind him, an elderly man came through from a back room and Danny's smile grew wider when he saw him wearing a brown overall coat.

"May I help you, sir?" the old man asked.

"No, thank you. I don't need anything, but I had to come in for a look around. I haven't seen a shop like this since I was about eight or nine."

"Aye, we're a dying breed that's for sure. Feel free to look and don't hesitate to give me a shout if you need anything."

"Thank you," Danny replied.

He noted a wall of wooden drawers behind the counter and they were just as he remembered from the shop of his youth. He walked through the shop, looking at the various electrical appliances, and was impressed to see some of the more expensive models being stocked. Mind you, he supposed, there were probably a lot of high-flying London commuters living in the area as Oxford was only about an hour away on the train from the capital.

He continued to stroll round and entered a bright room with a conservatory area which housed a pretty display of garden tables and chairs. There was a large paved patio space beyond it and the patio doors were open to let the warm sunlight in. He could see flowerpots, watering cans and wheelbarrows out there. He stepped through another doorway and found himself back in the front of the shop again where the shopkeeper was still standing.

"What a fabulous shop you have."

"Thank you. It's been in my family for four generations although I'm the last in the line. Neither of my daughters are interested in taking it on when I go."

"I'm very sorry to hear that," replied Danny, picking up the sadness in the man's voice as he spoke.

"Oh, it is what it is."

"Well, thank you for your time, sir, and allowing me to be a bit nosy while reminiscing of my childhood."

"You're welcome. It's been a pleasure chatting with you."

Danny left the shop, and carried on along the pavement a bit further where he came across a tarmacked path running through the green to the duck pond on the other side. He walked along it and, as he drew closer to the pond, he chuckled at the antics of a little dark-haired girl trying to throw some seed out to the ducks on the water. The lady with her, he presumed it was her grandmother, was trying to explain that she was opening her hand too soon and this was why all the bird seed was now lying on the grass behind her. He smiled a hello as he passed by and stopped when he came to the pavement. The shops on the other side looked exactly as they had done on the internet. Standing back, he gazed at them, his view unhindered thanks to the no-parking zone. There were six shops along the row and all were bathed in sunlight. Most of them had full bay windows complete with old-fashioned crown glass.

He noted there was a restaurant, although it was currently closed, a hairdresser and beauty salon, a dress shop, a haberdashery, a post office and finally a fish and chip shop. He spotted a small lane running down the side of the chippy so crossed over the road to explore a bit further. He walked along it, passing a doctor's surgery with an adjoining chemist, until he came to a church complete with a lovely kissing gate a bit further on. This discovery caused a little surge of joy to run through him. He'd definitely be back to draw that later. It was perfect.

He walked back towards the green where he looked once again at the shops. His artist's eye noted the slight slope on the old roofs, the solid wooden lintels above the doors and the pretty hanging baskets filled with spring floral arrangements. He couldn't wait to begin drawing and almost sprinted back to his car to collect his equipment. He decided he would sketch for a few hours, taking in different aspects of the little village, before heading home.

He returned to the pond to find the little girl and her grandmother had gone and, barring some curious ducks, he was on his own. He set up his small portable easel, unfolded his little stool, sorted out his pencils and began to draw.

He'd been sketching for about twenty minutes when the little girl he'd seen earlier came clambering out of the door of the dress shop. She stopped for a moment to look around and then, seeing the ducks on the other side of the road, began toddling towards them. There was no sign of her grandmother.

Just then he noticed a large, black, four by four, vehicle driving down the road. It was moving quickly and showing no signs of slowing down as it approached the shops. The child was still making her way towards the road.

Before the realisation of her imminent danger had even hit his brain, Danny had thrown down his pencil and was pushing the easel out of the way. Leaping to his feet, he ran towards the road. The blood rushed like a torrent to his head and his heart was thumping in his chest. He wouldn't be able to save her. He wasn't moving fast enough. Instinct took over and he threw himself headlong across the road, managing to brush her forehead with his fingertips, pushing her backwards and away from danger as the vehicle slammed into his side. He bounced onto the bonnet, seeing a mouth opening in a scream as his head sped towards the windscreen, hitting it with enough force to create a spider's web of cracks before rolling off when the car screeched to a halt.

Darkness had engulfed him by the time he hit the road.

The Middle Men

Death was sitting at his desk in his office. He was holding a large mug of Koughee, a discarded newspaper lying on the desk in front of him as he stared out of the rain-battered window. He sighed deeply. He could reside anywhere he wished and yet his preference was London where the weather was usually shocking. Despite having lived in various locations around the world, he always ended up coming back here. He loved the buzz of this city. This was his home. It was that simple.

He glanced down at the newspaper and his eyes were drawn once more to the news of the continuing war in the Middle East. His deputy in that area was very busy and his overtime costs were becoming ridiculous. It looked like he was going to have to make some adjustments and appoint more deputies. He sighed again. This job used to be so easy, but, in recent centuries, the earthly population had exploded and he'd had to appoint deputies and delegate the workload. Most of the dead, thankfully, did move on. In the grand scheme of things, the Middle Realmers, as they liked to be called, were a minuscule percentage, but every expired life, regardless of species, still had to be processed.

There was a bang on the office door before it was flung open and William McAlister stormed in, a thunderous look on his face.

He banged his fist on the desk while yelling, "What the HELL do you think you're playing at?"

Looking behind him, Death saw Harry sidle into the room. He returned his gaze to William, and said, "I'm taking an educated guess here and assuming you're referring to the accident your incumbent has just been involved in."

"You know damn well I am! You'd better not be trying to renege on our deal by killing him off early."

"Is he dead?"

"No—"

"Then shut your face, old man and stop jumping to conclusions."

William clamped his lips together. After fifteen years of hanging out with Death, he knew when to do as he was told.

Death glared at him. "As it happens, you cantankerous old git, I'm giving you a helping hand. It hasn't gone unnoticed that the other party in this arrangement appears to be having a much easier time of it. Isn't that so, Harry? The new job and the London flat, happening as they did, was rather serendipitous, was it not?"

Harry stepped forward, looking a bit sheepish. "Erm, well... I suppose..."

"In the meantime, William, your incumbent is sitting drawing pretty pictures and not doing much else. Clearly he needed the same push from the 'hand of fate' that Harry's incumbent has been receiving."

"There's a big difference between a 'push from the hand of fate' and pushing him over the bonnet of a bloody car!"

"Look, you need to trust me on this. It will all be okay."

"Well… I'm still not happy about it."

"William, you're a miserable sod, you're never happy about anything. Now bugger off and close the door *quietly* behind you."

He caught Harry's eye as they left the office, and gave him a wink. Harry grinned back while closing the office door, leaving Death on his own once more.

Chapter Twenty-One

Elsa was flicking through her CD collection. She was in the mood for something loud and heavy but had nothing of that ilk on her shelf. She stared at her options while wondering when her musical tastes had become so safe and boring. She called over to Sukie in the kitchen making coffee.

"Sukie, when exactly did my musical preferences become so dull? This stuff here is pants."

Sukie walked over to the breakfast bar and asked, "Do you have any champagne in?"

Elsa looked up, puzzled by the question. "Err... No. Why?"

"Because I want to celebrate the day you finally came to your musical senses." She laughed when Elsa stuck her tongue out at her. "To answer your question," she continued, "you became 'dull' when you got engaged – deciding it was time you began *behaving* like a grown-up. YOUR words, not mine, before you start arguing. That's what you said when I suggested getting tickets for a Green Day gig."

Elsa closed the mouth she'd opened to protest at Sukie's words before smiling widely.

"Green Day! That's what I'm in the mood for."

"Well, you might just be in luck there," answered Sukie, passing over the coffee mugs. "I think I've got one of their CDs at the bottom of my bag. Hang on…" She walked over to the table where she'd placed her bag earlier, sighing as she glanced out of the patio windows, seeing the rain lashing down in the garden. They had both been looking forward to going up in the London Eye but, in this weather, it would have been a waste of time. Instead, they'd stayed in and were sorting out the remaining boxes Elsa hadn't yet unpacked.

"Here you go." She passed the disc to Elsa.

A moment later, the first chords of American Idiot filled the air and Elsa sat down in the chair opposite Sukie. Barely a few seconds had passed when she jumped up onto her feet, yelling, "Air guitar challenge!" and whacked the volume up louder on the player,

Elsa laughed at Sukie watching her in surprise. They hadn't messed about like this since their early twenties. She had been giving it her all for a couple of seconds when Sukie abandoned her coffee to join in. For the next ten minutes, the two of them sang badly, played air guitar and head-banged for all they were worth, oblivious to the sound of Sukie's mobile ringing frantically in her handbag.

"Here you go, pet, get this down you." Jordie handed Beth the plastic cup from the vending machine. Beth took a sip of the coffee and shuddered.

"Urgh! That's awful. And you've put sugar in it."

"Sugar is good for shock, and you've certainly had

one of those. Has the doctor been to see you?"

"No, not yet." She looked at Poppy lying on the hospital bed, so small and helpless. She was still trying to get her head around what had happened. She'd found the phone message from Sukie, warning her Poppy could get out of her buggy, so she knew that she hadn't done anything wrong, but she couldn't stop feeling guilty that she hadn't been paying close enough attention.

"Are you sure Drew was okay with going to Sarah's?"

When Beth had tried to phone Jordie to let him know what had happened, he'd still been in the garden with Drew and hadn't heard the phone ringing. Eventually, in desperation, she'd called Jeremy the vicar and he'd offered to go up to the manor. Sarah, his wife, had said not to worry about Drew, they would look after him – he knew her from his playgroup visits and he'd be happy to play with her two boys.

By the time Jordie had arrived at the hospital, Poppy had been examined and the doctor was telling her she was a very lucky little girl. She'd sprained her wrist when she'd fallen, after being pushed away from the car, and she had a few cuts and scrapes on her hands and legs. Once they'd plastered her wrist, the doctor had advised they would be keeping her in overnight. There was no evidence she'd hit her head – they couldn't find any bruising – but they'd prefer to observe her for twenty-four hours just in case.

"Did you manage to get hold of Pete or Sukie? I tried Sukie about four times on the way here but got no answer. Pete's phone kept going to voicemail."

Jordie hugged her before replying. He could see she was trying hard not to cry. "I called Kara. She got in touch with the record company and they've informed Pete. He'll text me when he's picked up Sukie and they're on their way back."

"What about the young man who saved Poppy? Do you know anything more about him?"

"Sam from the bakery saw it all through her window. It was she who called for an ambulance before going across to help. She gathered up his belongings – looks like he's an artist – and handed them over to the police. They found his wallet. Apparently, his name's Danny Delaney and he lives in London. They got an emergency contact name too so they're going to get in touch. When they know more, they'll come to see you for a statement. Assuming you're up for giving one, of course."

"Yes, yes…" Beth flapped her hand at all the details Jordie was giving her. She only wanted to know how the young man, Danny, was faring. "But how *is* he? Was he badly injured?"

"I don't know. He's currently in theatre. He must have hit the windscreen pretty hard though as I overheard the ambulance driver telling the surgeon it was cracked."

"I do hope he'll be okay. He saved Poppy's life. He's a hero…" Her voice broke as once again the horror of what could have been came over her.

Jordie placed his hand on her shoulder and squeezed it gently. "There, there, pet. Everything's going to be okay."

A young nurse came over to them. "Miss McClaren, would you mind coming with me please. We need to give you a quick check-up since you've had such a shock. We won't be too long."

"Oh, but Poppy…" Beth got flustered at the thought of leaving her little granddaughter's side.

"I'll be here with her," said Jordie. "You go and get yourself seen to."

She leant over to place a soft kiss on Poppy's head and smoothed her hair. She noticed the little flush of colour coming back into her cheeks and, feeling slightly better, she followed the nurse from the ward.

Sukie was sitting by herself, holding Poppy's hand, when she returned. Seeing her mum walking towards her, she stood up, wrapping her arms around Beth in a tight hug. "Oh, Mum, are you okay? What a terrible shock you've had. Come, sit down."

Sukie sat her down in the comfortable armchair by the side of the bed while she sat on the hard, plastic thing that was supposed to pass for a chair but felt more like an instrument of torture.

The tears welled up again and this time Beth was powerless to stop them. She couldn't let go of the feeling she'd let her daughter down and kept repeating, "I'm sorry, I'm so, so sorry."

"Mum, it was *my* fault. I forgot to warn you about the buggy. You weren't to know Poppy could open it. You were right to think she was safe because she was strapped in. She *should* have been safe, and it's completely my fault she wasn't."

"Hey! Less of that! It wasn't anyone's 'fault' – it's just one of those horrible accidents that can happen. No one is taking any blame here for this." Pete put a hand on Sukie's shoulder and rubbed it gently. She looked up and gave him a small smile. She hadn't seen him and Jordie come back onto the ward.

"Have you got any more news on Danny?" Beth looked up at them both.

"Yes," replied Jordie. "He's out of theatre. His left shoulder was badly dislocated – it required surgery – and he's severely concussed. His arm is currently strapped up and he'll need to keep it in a sling for a couple of weeks for it to heal. He got the concussion when he hit the windscreen, so they've stitched up his forehead and he's being kept under sedation, and observation, until the morning. There's also extensive bruising down his left side where the car hit him."

"We've spoken to his emergency contact, a chap called Guy," Pete picked up where Jordie had left off. "I explained about Danny being kept in for a few days, and the extent of his injuries. He told me Danny lives alone and, with his arm out of action, he'll be rather incapacitated, so I said he can be our guest for the next week or so until he's out of the sling. I hope that's okay."

Sukie took Pete's hand. "Of course it's okay. He must stay with us, it's the least we can do. We owe him so much."

A small moan from the bed had them all turning towards Poppy who was beginning to waken up. As she lay on the bed beside her and gathered her gently into her arms, Sukie knew she would spend a lifetime indebted to the man who had saved her daughter's life.

Chapter Twenty-Two

Slowly opening his eyes, Danny wondered where he was. It was very bright. His head was throbbing and his left arm felt odd. He tried to move but it was too painful, and a groan escaped from his lips. Someone moved at the side of the bed and a gentle voice spoke to him. "Hi, Danny, try not to move. You're in hospital. I've called for the doctor to come in now that you're awake. My name's Beth. You saved my granddaughter's life."

He closed his eyes as the memory swept over him – pushing the toddler out of the way, the horrific pain when the car hit him, the look of terror on the face of the passenger in the car and his head hitting the windscreen. He couldn't remember anything else.

"The little girl... Is she okay?" he whispered, his words a little slurred.

"She's absolutely fine, thanks to you. She'd never have survived being hit by that car. You're quite the hero."

"No, I'm not. Just did what anyone would have done." He fell silent. It was taking a great deal of effort to talk.

Beth didn't reply. She just placed her hand softly on his and held it gently.

A few minutes later a young blond-haired doctor walked in. Beth had stayed by Danny's side through the night – it didn't seem right that he should be alone – and she'd gotten to know the doctor from his hourly visits to check on his patient. She wasn't sure about his taste in shirts though. The Hawaiian number he was wearing today was particularly lurid. She didn't fancy having to look at that after sustaining a brain injury. He was, however, a very capable doctor and that was what mattered most.

"Mr Delaney, you're back with us. Excellent! Ah-ah, try not to move. Your head will be throbbing like billy-o, I imagine, and any movement will feel like a wrecking ball is bouncing around in there. I'm afraid that's concussion for you. Now, I'm just going to do a few checks on you so please bear with me."

The doctor took Danny's pulse, checked his temperature, shone a light in his eyes and prodded him gently in various places.

"Okay, Danny, everything's looking good. Now that I'm satisfied you're on the right road, I'll get your pain relief increased. Once that kicks in, we'll sit you up and you can greet your visitors."

"Visitors?" Danny mumbled.

"Oh yes, everyone wants to meet the hero of the day."

"I'm not a hero."

The doctor ignored his reply as he fiddled with the drip at the side of the bed. "There we go. You should begin to feel more comfortable in a few minutes. I'll tell the nurse to check with you before anyone is allowed in. See you later."

The doctor rushed out of the room and Danny felt the peace descending around him again. The medication was already working its magic and the throbbing in his head was beginning to recede.

"Wow! He's a bit of a whirlwind," he said to Beth.

"Be grateful you didn't see his shirt!" Beth replied with a smile.

Danny opened his eyes again and was pleased to find it didn't hurt so much now when he moved his head. His gaze fell upon a petite, blonde lady whom he instantly recognised as the woman who'd been feeding the ducks by the pond. The grandmother of the little girl he'd saved.

"Thank you," he said quietly.

"For what?" she asked, unable to keep the shock off her face

"For staying with me, you didn't have to do that. You don't know me."

"I most certainly did have to. My family owe you a massive debt of gratitude for what you've done. The very least I could do was ensure someone was by your side while you slept."

"How is the little girl? I think I pushed her quite hard. It wasn't intentional. The car was moving too quickly. I didn't have time to be gentle. I'm sorry."

"Hush now, don't you be apologising. You've got nothing to be sorry for. Poppy is doing very well. She sprained her wrist when she fell and has a nice selection of cuts and bruises on her hands and legs, but she'll get over those in no time. She has a plaster cast on her wrist and she's thrilled with it. Well, she is now. The original cast they put on when she was sedated was pink. She *really* dislikes pink – takes after her mother in that respect." Beth smiled as she recalled the look of horror on Poppy's face when she awoke and saw her pink-clad arm.

"Did they change it for her?" Danny asked.

"Yes. She now has a blue one and is showing it off to everyone."

"I hope I get to see it." Danny smiled at the thought of meeting the little girl who was so strong minded.

"Oh, you will, there's no question about that."

The door opened and a nurse came in. "How's your head feeling now, Mr Delaney? Do you think you can sit up?"

Danny confirmed the pain had receded and said he'd really like to sit up. It felt weird having a conversation while lying on his back.

The nurse sat him up and forward with a gentle touch and, taking care not to bump his shoulder, she sorted the bed behind him and laid him back on the pillows.

"I'm sorry, but could someone please tell me exactly what my injuries are?" Danny realised that while the doctor had checked him over, he hadn't offered any information other than he had a concussion.

The nurse looked at his notes. "Your left shoulder was badly dislocated and required surgery to fix the torn tendons. If they'd been left, they may not have healed properly and there was a good chance your shoulder could have popped out again in the future. You need to keep your arm in the sling for roughly two weeks to give everything time to heal. After that you can begin using it, but it will be minimal movement and no lifting for a few more days. Strenuous sports or weight-lifting is not recommended for about six months. You may also need some physio, but you can arrange that through your GP. You have dissolving stitches, so you won't need to worry about having them removed. There is extensive bruising on your left side from the impact with the car. This will slowly fade but you're probably going to feel very stiff and tender for at least a week. Finally, the head injury, and concussion, will heal in its own time. Again, however, you can't indulge in rough or strenuous sports for about six months. You must let the brain heal fully.

So, no rugby I'm afraid." She smiled as she said this.

Danny pointed at his slim physique. "Does this seriously look like a body that does weight-lifting or plays rugby? The nearest I get is watching the Six Nations on the TV. I can assure you there is no risk of me doing myself any further injury from participating in either of those past-times." He grinned at the nurse, his sense of humour coming back now the pain had ceased. All in all, he figured he'd gotten off quite lightly. It could have been so much worse.

Shortly after the nurse left the room, there was a gentle tap on the door. It opened a second later and in walked a woman with wavy chestnut hair and a big smile on her face. Behind her was a taller man with blond hair and brilliant green eyes. Danny immediately knew who *he* was.

"Hi, Danny, I'm Sukie Wallace, this is my husband Pete. I... *We* don't know how to begin thanking you for saving our daughter. You're a hero. Thank you so much." Walking over to stand beside Beth, she leaned down and kissed Danny on the cheek.

Pete followed her and, clasping Danny's good hand, he shook it firmly. "Saying thank you feels very inadequate."

Danny felt himself blushing under their gaze – accepting thanks or compliments was something he'd never been good at. He repeated again the words he'd uttered to Beth and the doctor.

"Honestly, I'm *not* a hero. I just did what anyone would've done. I didn't do anything special."

Sukie put her hand on his arm. "Oh yes you did and that makes you *our* hero."

Pete took her other hand and said, "Sukie's right, you *are* our hero and we'll be forever in your debt. We'll never be able to fully repay you, but we'd like to try."

"Look, you don't owe me anything, please… I'm just glad I was there and that Poppy is going to be okay. Please… Let's just leave it at that." He was horrified that these lovely people felt they owed him anything.

"Sorry, mate but no can do on that one. I've been talking to your friend Guy—"

"Oh, really? And how did that go?" Guy had more than a small crush on Pete. Danny wished he'd been a fly on the wall when that conversation had taken place.

"Well, he was okay to begin with. He'd gotten over the shock of the phone call from the police, which helped. Naturally, he was concerned when I explained about your injuries. We discussed a few details – such as he's collected your cat and taken her back to his place. He then explained you live on your own in a top floor flat. We both agreed that wasn't practical right now, so I suggested you stay with us until you're more capable again. Well, at that point, he began asking questions and demanding to know who I was. When I told him, there was a strange, choking, strangling sound. I said I would text him my phone number and, if he had any questions or wanted to call to check on you, to please use it. He coughed a few times and then squeaked a goodbye of sorts before hanging up."

Danny was unable to contain his laughter. He just *knew* Guy would've been running around the flat, squealing like a seven-year-old child, when he'd learnt who'd called him.

"Guy's been a massive fan of yours for quite a few years. I think I'm very safe in saying he was probably rather surprised, and very excited, when you told him who you were."

"Ahhh… I see!" Now it was Pete's turn to blush while Sukie and Beth laughed at his embarrassment. "Anyway, as I was saying, we'd like you to be our houseguest until your sling comes off and you're able to use your arm again."

"Oh, I couldn't possibly do that. I can go home, I'll be fine. I'll manage." He wasn't sure *how* he would manage but he didn't want to cause a fuss or put anyone out.

"I'm afraid it's not up for discussion, Danny," Beth chimed in from her chair at the side of the bed. "It's all been agreed, and your room is being prepared as we speak. We'll be in touch with Guy once we know when you're being released and ask him to pack some stuff for you. If he's a Pete Wallace fan, I'm sure he'll be more than amenable to bringing you a case of clothes."

"Amenable? You just try keeping him away," was all Danny could say. He knew any chance of Guy taking him back home to London had just been scuppered. He sensed he'd be seeing more of Guy over the next two weeks than he'd seen of him in the last two months.

Danny's speech started to slur and Beth saw he was beginning to tire. "Right you two, time to get out of here, Danny needs to rest. Let's go and locate the doctor to find out when he'll be released. We can then make arrangements for Guy to bring some clothing and things."

"Of course, Mum, you're right." Sukie picked up his hand again and squeezed it softly. "Danny, I understand you're probably feeling quite overwhelmed right now and you don't want to be thanked but I really need to say this. You saved our little girl. If it hadn't been for you, our world would have been shattered. Your actions have changed our lives in ways none of us can possibly imagine. Thank you." She leant down and kissed him on the cheek a second time before taking Pete's hand and following her mum out of the room.

When they'd left, and the door had closed behind them, Danny closed his eyes and lay for a few minutes enjoying the peace and quiet.

Suddenly, he sat bolt upright.

What had Sukie said? Something about 'changing their lives…'?

He closed his eyes and heard Mr McAllister's voice in his head. "You need to change another persons' life."

He gently eased back the sling his arm was resting within and, with slow, careful, movements, he turned his wrist.

Unable to stop himself, he held his breath, scared he might find nothing had changed, and glanced down really quickly.

He looked back up and stared out of the window. Had anything changed? His glance had been *so* quick, he hadn't been able to see.

He looked more slowly the second time and let out a whoop of joy, while doing a small fist-pump with his good arm.

He was down to two freckles.

Chapter Twenty-Three

May

"…in here we have the first of four viewing rooms. Each room contains a coffee machine, and a fridge which is always stocked with fresh milk, a selection of fresh juices and wine. The lights are all remote controlled using this touch-pad – they can be dimmed, switched on or off, or just random spotlights. Whichever configuration displays the art at its best."

Elsa followed Jeff out of the room, as she scribbled the details in her pad and made a mental note to come back later with the intention of working out the lighting system to ensure she learnt it fully.

She was paying very close attention to everything Jeff was showing and telling her. The intended induction days of the previous week had been cancelled due to a client unexpectedly requesting Jeff's services, so she now had to learn everything at once. And there was a *lot* to learn!

Jeff climbed the stairs to the next floor and went

through the security details for each room, informing her of the system he had in place to remember the code for each one. "We use the year of death, of whichever artist is the first on the left of the door frame, as the code. If that painting is sold, another artist is placed in that position and the code is adjusted accordingly. We never leave that space empty. The artist's name is written on the page which relates to that room number, in a book which is kept in the safe at all times."

As they walked up to the top level, Jeff continued, "I believe I mentioned before this is where we exhibit the unknown artists – the new kids on the block so to speak. We also hold exhibitions up here as we can line the walls along the stairs with the artist's work, which allows the clients to view as wide a range as possible."

Elsa gazed around the space she was standing in and decided this was her favourite area within the gallery. The high ceiling, large windows and pale décor gave it a wonderful sense of being open and airy. Behind her, the ceiling to the room above was still intact and, with only two small windows, the area was considerably darker. "What about back here? I'm guessing it's a bit dark for displaying."

Jeff replied with a smile, "Nope, not at all. We still have this..." He picked up one of the lighting touch-pads and threw the room into brightness.

"Oh! Duh!" She rolled her eyes. "I had totally forgotten about those.

"Don't worry about it. We've gone through a lot this morning. I don't expect you to remember everything. When we hold launches we usually place the bar and buffet in this area, it works better."

"And that corner there, is that a storage cupboard?" Elsa pointed towards a door.

"Oh no, that is something else. Here, let me show

you." Jeff walked over to the door, took a set of keys from his pocket and unlocked it. He opened it and she saw a flight of stairs. He stood back to allow her to walk up first and, when she reached the top, Elsa found herself in a small, roof-top conservatory. To her left, was a set of French windows which led out onto a decent sized roof terrace. Jeff unlocked the doors and they stepped outside.

"Wow! It's so peaceful." She could still hear the noise from the traffic below, but it didn't travel upwards and so was easy to ignore. The view, however, was fairly limited due to the other high buildings surrounding them.

When she'd walked around the perimeter, she stopped and leaned over the stone edging to look down below. "Jeff, this is amazing. I love it. Do you allow the clients up here when you have exhibitions?"

Jeff came over to stand beside her. "It depends who is exhibiting on the night and the size of the crowd. Most of the time, however, it's out of bounds."

"I really like it." She swung round to eye up the rooftops around her. "It's a pity these buildings are so high, I bet you could see for miles if they weren't there."

"I guess you probably could. What I can tell you is that on a clear night, and if the wind is blowing in the right direction, we can hear Big Ben chiming, so that almost compensates for the lack of a view."

"Fair enough, I'll take all I can get." She laughed, as she observed once again the Lego-sized traffic below her. "Right, come on then, Mr Rowland, let's go back down and I'll test my knowledge on the way. I want to be sure I have everything as clear as possible in my head."

Elsa made a sharp turn on her heel and marched back inside, leaving Jeff to wander in behind her. He burst out laughing, causing Elsa to stop in her tracks and look at him. "What?" she asked.

"Elsa, I usually have to chivvy my assistants along and

force them back to work. It's very rarely the other way round. I have a feeling that you're going to be keeping me on *my* toes."

With a smile, she replied, "You had better believe it!" before running off down the stairs.

She arrived back at her desk and heard her phone ringing in her handbag. "Jeff, I'm so sorry. I thought I'd switched it off." She fumbled around, trying to get a hold of the mobile, which was getting louder by the second.

"It's okay, take the call. It's not a problem," he said with a smile. "Unlike some of my previous employees, I can't see you spending all day on the phone, chatting to friends."

Elsa located her mobile and yanked it out of her bag to find 'Unknown Number' displayed on the screen. She hesitated before she answered as she really disliked taking unidentified calls. "Hello?"

"Good morning, am I speaking with Elsa Clairmont?" asked a woman's voice at the other end.

"Err… Yes, you are. Who's calling please?"

"Hi, Elsa, my name's Anna Kilpatrick. I'm the manager of the management company responsible for looking after Mr Wallace's properties. How are you settling in?"

"Oh, hi!" Further to Anna's introduction, she felt herself relax. Pete had told her to expect a call. "It already feels like home, thank you. It's a great flat."

"It certainly is and I'm glad to hear you like it. Elsa, I need to see you to go through some paperwork which needs to be completed and signed for insurance purposes. Usually this would all have been taken care of before you moved in, but the circumstances were a bit out of the ordinary on this occasion."

"Of course there would be paperwork! I'm sorry, I didn't even think about that. It's all been a bit of a whirlwind." Elsa felt herself growing flustered – it hadn't even crossed her mind she'd have to complete forms to register her tenancy. She'd been so thrilled and excited with moving and her new job, everything else had gone right out of her head.

"Don't worry about it, it's not a problem. Are you available either tonight or tomorrow? I can bring everything round after work."

"Anna, I couldn't put you out like that. I'm more than happy to come to the office. I don't want to trouble you." Embarrassed she'd given no thought to the official side of her move, she didn't want to inconvenience Anna out any more than she had done already.

"It's no trouble," Anna replied. "Part of the process is a walk through the flat together, taking an inventory of furnishings and so forth along with details of any damage incurred by previous occupants. I don't want you being held responsible for someone else's mishaps."

"I see, of course. That makes sense." It had been so long since she'd rented a property, she'd forgotten all the little hoops you have to jump through. Sukie hadn't bothered with any of that when Elsa had moved into her flat in Oxford. "Well, tonight is as good a night as any. I'll be home by five-thirty latest if that's suitable."

"Five-thirty is perfect, Elsa, I'll see you then. Goodbye."

"Goodbye, Anna."

Elsa switched her phone to silent, put it back in her bag, then went to find Jeff who'd disappeared into the office. She'd make them both a drink before carrying on with learning more of her new ropes.

Elsa had just let Puddle out into the garden when the doorbell rang. She rushed to open the door and found herself looking at a woman who was only an inch or so taller than herself, with a full-on curvy figure, short, dark, bouncing curly hair, lively grey eyes and a scarlet-encased smile so wide, it really did run from ear to ear.

"Hi, Elsa, pleased to meet you, I'm Anna." She stuck her hand out and, when Elsa placed hers within it, she was rewarded with a firm hearty handshake. She was already warming to Anna as she stepped back to welcome her into the flat. Anna waited while she locked the front door then walked with her down the hallway to the lounge at the far end.

Anna had just enough time, as she entered the lounge, to put down the bags and briefcase she was carrying before a big, golden lump came running in from the garden and hurled himself towards her.

"Puddle! No! Bad dog! Come here..." Elsa managed to grab his collar just before his muddy paws landed on Anna's smart, and clearly expensive, suit.

"I'm so sorry, Anna. He loves meeting new people." Elsa held the straining Labrador away from her guest, trying to direct him back towards the garden but Puddle was having none of it. He had a new human to meet. That meant lots of fussing and petting. He was going nowhere!

With a loud chuckle, Anna shrugged off her jacket, placed it carefully on the back of a chair and dropped to her knees in front of him.

"Well hello there, you gorgeous boy. Aren't you just a big handsome treat? Eh? Eh? Yes, you're adorable, yes you are!" Anna rubbed her hands vigorously along Puddle's back and scratched behind his ears.

Elsa noticed a slight Liverpudlian twang in her accent as she spoke. Ah, she thought, that explains the outgoing, bubbly nature. Elsa had yet to meet someone from Liverpool that she didn't like. There had been a couple of Liverpool lads with her at university and they'd been a right laugh – full of cheeky banter and high spirits. The only thing that had ever fazed them had been their beloved football team losing to either Manchester United or Everton. These results invariably had the outcome of sorrows being drowned for several hours in the Uni bar before they were carried home, via a kebab shop, and poured onto their beds as they lamented the woes which had befallen Liverpool F.C.

Elsa bent down and also gave Puddle a few big pets before shooing him back out into the garden. She pulled the patio door closed to stop him from barging back in again.

"Can I get you a drink? Tea or coffee?" she asked Anna.

"A cup of tea would be great, thank you."

"How do you like it?"

"Very strong, a splash of milk and no sugar please." Anna leant over and picked up a patterned gift bag which she'd brought with her and handed it to Elsa. "This is for you. It's a small house-warming gift from the company. Chocolates so your days may always be sweet, and wine so your nights may always be perfect."

Elsa laughed at the greeting. "Thank you very much, you are very generous." She accepted the gift and took it with her as she went to prepare the drinks. She had just placed the wine in the fridge when she noticed the label – more prosecco! This could become a habit she thought, with a small giggle to herself, as she closed the fridge door.

An hour later, the two women were sitting opposite each other in the lounge, the bottle of prosecco in a wine bucket on the coffee table in front of them. The inventory had been done, all the paperwork had been signed and completed and now they were just kicking back and relaxing. So far, Elsa had learnt that she and Anna were almost the same age and she lived in Hampstead. She was the owner of the property management company and had dumped her boyfriend just over a month ago "because he was a useless twat!" In some ways, Anna reminded her of Sukie – up-front, straight-talking, took no prisoners if you pissed her off. No wonder she found herself liking her more and more.

Feeling a bit shy, but not wanting the evening to end, she tentatively asked Anna if she fancied staying a bit longer. "I found a Chinese takeaway menu in the kitchen and there's another bottle of wine in the fridge."

Anna looked at Elsa for a moment then, with one of her wide, happy smiles replied, "Hmmm… If you add a Colin Firth movie into the mix, we have ourselves a deal!"

"Only the one? Are you a woman or a mouse?"

Anna laughed, picked up her wine glass and chinked it against Elsa's. "Elsa, you are my kinda woman! I think this is going to be the start of a great friendship. Cheers!" Elsa felt the smile split her face as she watched Anna drain her glass and lean over to do refills for them both. She felt the happiness bubble up inside her and took a moment to savour the emotion – it had been a long time since she'd experienced it. She lifted her own glass, drained it and stood up saying, "Right, let's see what this Chinese menu has to offer!"

Chapter Twenty-Four

Danny had just pushed back the quilt on his bed when there was a tap at the door. Every morning, Pete helped him to wash and dress although the latter was currently an interesting challenge as it appeared Guy had had his mind on other things when he'd packed Danny's clothes. Everyone agreed the jogging bottoms were a good move as the elasticated waist made them easy to pull up and down with only one hand. The T-shirts, jumpers and sweatshirts, however, didn't work for he couldn't raise his arm to put them on. When Pete and Guy had helped him to unpack his suitcase the night he'd arrived at the manor, Danny saw that Pete had realised the problem – his shoulders had shook as he'd tried not to laugh at the contents.

"Well, Guy, I should be grateful for small mercies, you did at least manage to put in my socks and underwear. I'm thankful for that…"

When he heard this, Pete had burst out laughing while Guy looked at him in confusion. Danny didn't want to hurt his best friend so quickly explained the dilemma of why the T-shirts and jumpers were not practical on this occasion. Pete, however, hollered and laughed until the tears ran down his face. Danny and Guy looked at him in bemusement. They didn't think the comment had been *that* funny but then the penny dropped – it was a release of all the tension from the last few days. Since the accident, Danny surmised, Pete must have been wound up tighter than an old clock as all the other possible outcomes of the accident went through his head. None of them, including Danny, was in any doubt as to what would have happened had he not taken action.

He got out of bed and called out to Pete to come in as he stood up and walked across to the window to open the curtains.

"Here mate, let me do that." Pete rushed over when he saw what Danny was about to do.

"Pete, I can open curtains. I've only got one arm out of action. You don't need to fuss so much." He smiled to take any sting out of his words.

"I know, I know. Sorry," Pete replied. "I'm not very good with seeing people struggle. I have a tendency to jump straight in to help. Please let me know if I'm being annoying, okay?" He stepped back to let Danny finish what he'd started.

"Well, I'll try but I'm not very good at speaking up like that. I'm a 'grin and bear it' sort of chap."

Pete smiled. "Looks like we're both rubbish then, eh?"

Danny returned his smile. He'd been living under Pete and Sukie's roof for a few days and was beginning to get to know them. So far, he'd found the couple to be very down to earth and Pete especially intrigued him as he was the least pop-star'ish person it was possible to be.

Pete held up a shirt. "I think this one should fit you," he said. He'd gone through his wardrobe to find some shirts to lend to Danny although, with Danny being smaller than him, they weren't a perfect fit.

Danny looked at the checked, lumberjack-style shirt Pete was holding up. With those blue and black checks, he was never going to win any fashion awards but hey, beggars' can't be choosers'! Fortunately, Guy was visiting again today and he'd promised to bring some more suitable attire.

"Thanks, Pete, I really do appreciate this."

"Danny, please stop thanking me. I'd happily give you every item of clothing in my wardrobe although, I confess, this is a monstrosity of a shirt. If, however, you don't want sleeves down to your knees, you are stuck with seeing some of the worst of what I have to offer. I think this was last worn ten years ago, maybe even longer. To be honest, I don't even know why I still have it."

Danny couldn't help but laugh at Pete's words – at least they both agreed it wasn't the most tasteful item of clothing in the world.

"I'm just gonna go and well… you know… before we begin washing and dressing," he said, walking into the bathroom and closing the door behind him.

While Danny was using the bathroom, Pete walked over to place the shirt on the bed. As he passed the old antique desk in front of the window, he accidentally brushed against the drawing pad lying on top and it fell to the floor. Several of the loose pages inside slithered out and scattered across the polished wooden floor. Pete bent down to pick them up and drew in a sharp breath when he saw what Danny had drawn since he'd arrived. There were pictures of the twins as they'd played in the garden, another where Jordie was holding Drew up above his head and the two of them were laughing at each other. There was one where Poppy had picked some small flowers and was presenting them to Beth. Pete picked up more sheets and saw portraits of Sukie, the cats, himself, the gardens – in fact, there wasn't much Danny hadn't drawn and each one was stunning. Every picture looked almost lifelike. He picked up a particularly gorgeous piece of Sukie, where Poppy had fallen asleep in her arms, and Sukie was gazing at her with such love and tenderness that Pete felt his heart tighten in his chest. When there was a cough behind him, he sprung up from the floor, quickly explaining to Danny what had happened.

"I wasn't snooping, Danny, honest. I brushed against the desk and the pad fell off. These slipped out when it landed on the floor." Pete hoped he sounded convincing.

"It's okay, Pete," said Danny, taking the picture of Sukie from his hand.

Pete noted the strange expression on Danny's face as he stared at the picture in his hand. He didn't speak and his silence made Pete uncomfortable, so he blundered on. "It's amazing. You've caught her so well – both of them, in fact." Pete nodded at the picture Danny was still holding. "It really took my breath away when I saw it. And these…, they're also fantastic. This one of Jordie is spectacular. I really love it. Actually…, I love them all." He placed the drawings back on the desk and said to Danny, "I've seen you sketching a few times since you came to stay, but I didn't realise you were so talented. Whenever someone approaches you, you close your pad. I assumed – quite wrongly as it happens – that you weren't very good and just liked to scribble for fun. These, however," he swept his hand over the drawings, "are much more than fun. These deserve to be exhibited."

Danny blushed at Pete's words. "Thank you. You're very kind. I hope you don't mind that there are quite a few of the twins," he said, as he shuffled his feet with embarrassment. "At that age, everything is a new discovery and they're too young to know how to hide their emotions. This makes them perfect little models. I've had to put some effort into getting each one exactly right. They've given me plenty of practise which I sorely need."

"I don't mind at all. And, if I'm allowed to show them to Sukie, I think she'll be buying a few from you."

"What? No!" Danny exclaimed. "I won't accept money for them. You can have any that you like with my compliments. It's the least I can do after all the help and care you're giving me right now."

Pete looked at him. "Are you for real?"

Danny's look of confusion told Pete he was.

"Danny, you have to stop thanking us for looking after you. We're the ones in *your* debt, not you in ours. And you will not 'give us' your work. We will buy it from you because it is worthy of being paid for. If you want to take your talent further, and something tells me you do, then the first thing you need to learn is to stop underselling yourself and know that quality comes at a price. And trust me, mate, these sketches are pure quality."

Danny swallowed down the lump in his throat before replying. "Thank you, Pete. I really appreciate your praise. It means a lot. However, right now, do you mind if we go about getting me washed and dressed because I'm beginning to get a bit chilly?"

"Goodness, of course not! Come on, into that bathroom with you," said Pete. He glanced once more at the pictures on the desk. This subject was not closed. Not by a long chalk.

Chapter Twenty-Five

Guy arrived in the doorway just as Danny had finished telling Sukie and Pete about his childhood ambitions to be an artist. They'd been so engrossed in Danny's story, and dumbfounded he'd passed over the chance to study at the Royal Academy of Art to look after his family, that no one had heard Guy arrive.

"Howdy there, folks, how y'all doin'?" He put on a mock American drawl in an attempt to hide his nervousness at being in the company of Pete Wallace again. He couldn't help it, he was totally star-struck. He'd fancied Pete something chronic for years and now, here he was, standing in his home for the second time in a few days. And, to find out he was one of the nicest, kindest human beings he'd ever met… Well! That was just the icing on the cake.

"I've brought you some more tops, Danny." He held up the rucksack in his hand. "Hopefully, these will be better."

To make sure he didn't look stupid in front of Pete again, Guy had tried on every shirt and loose top first, pretending he couldn't move his arm, to make sure they could all be put on with relative ease. Not that he intended to share *that* piece of information with them all.

"That's wonderful, Guy. Thank you so much." Danny walked over, took the rucksack from him, and placed it by the side of the door before hugging him with his good arm. "You've been so kind to help out like this, I really appreciate it."

Guy carefully hugged him back. "Oh, don't be so daft. That's what mates are for. And since you're my best one, it's no trouble at all. But we do have one small issue."

"What?"

"Your fortieth birthday bash is three days away. What are you going to do about that?"

"Shhh…" Danny quickly looked round to see if Guy's comment had been overheard. "Don't say anything. I don't want Pete or Sukie to know."

"Eh? Why not?"

"Because they might feel obliged to do something to celebrate it and they're doing so much already, I don't want to put them out further."

"Put them out?" Guy hissed in indignation. "Danny, you saved their daughter's life. They'd probably relish the opportunity to have a bit of a shindig to celebrate that."

"Well, I wouldn't feel comfortable about it, so say nothing. It's just some friends from work and the lads from the footie team. We can re-arrange it for when I'm back in London. Okay?"

"But—"

"I said 'okay'?" Danny cut in over his intention to object.

"Okay, okay. If you insist!" Guy threw his hands up.

"I insist! Now, let's change the subject. How is my girl doing?"

"I'm guessing you mean Prissy and not Sandra?"

173

"Of course!"

"The kits love having Prissy around. The three of them are tearing the flat up something chronic. They're driving Nigel mad. But in a good way, of course!"

"I do miss her."

Guy noticed the softening of Danny's face as he thought of Prissy. "I'm sure she's missing you too, mate but she's absolutely fine. The kits are doing their bit by keeping her entertained in your absence."

"Give her big snugs from me and tell her Daddy says she's to behave and not be a little drama queen for you."

"Will do! And err... Talking about drama queens... Does Sandra know where you are?"

Guy noticed Danny's look of guilt as he replied, "No, she doesn't. And I want it to stay that way. She'd only be up here, trying to muscle in and social climb if she was to find out. I wouldn't want to wish that on Pete and Sukie. They're far too nice to have to put up with that."

Guy's eyebrows almost disappeared into his hairline when he heard this. Danny never said anything against Sandra despite being fully aware of her faults. "Would I be correct in thinking you've had a change of heart over the-not-so-delightful Miss Harrison?" he asked.

"Yeah! It's run its course. It's over."

It took a lot of effort for Guy to stop himself dancing on the spot and hide his delight as he asked, "What brought this on?"

Danny let out a sigh. "I called Sandra from the hospital, letting her know I'd been in an accident, although I purposely kept the details vague. I knew she'd be a right pain if she found out I'd become acquainted with Pete Wallace. She'd arrive on the doorstep, in full glamour mode, if she knew where I was. As it was, she showed very little interest and only asked a few cursory questions. I don't think she even bothered listening to the answers before she began moaning she'd need to find someone else to go to some comedy gig we had tickets for. When she hung up, she didn't even bother to say 'Get well soon'. That's when I decided it was time to call it a day. I'll do it when I get back to London. Until then, however, I don't want you stirring it and letting on. She'll hear the news from me, not you. Have you got that?" Guy felt himself on the receiving end of a hard stare.

"You don't need to worry on that score, mate. She won't hear anything from me." He made a zipping motion over his lips with his hand. "What on earth makes you think I'd even want to speak to the evil little harpy anyway? I'm not that hard up for conversation!"

With a wink, and a throw of his head in a mock flounce, Guy wandered over to the table to see what Pete and Sukie had been 'oohing' and 'aahing' over. He was surprised to see a number of Danny's drawings lying in front of them. He knew he'd been, until now, the only person to have seen Danny's work. He was also aware Danny had been in quite the turmoil as he came to terms with knowing he had to let people see what he was capable of, if there was to be any hope of him progressing. To see his sketches laid across the table made Guy happy. This was progress.

"Ah, so you've discovered Danny's little secret. What do you think?"

"I think these are absolutely amazing. I've already said as much but he won't accept the praise," replied Pete.

Guy snorted in amusement. "Pete, that's the story of his life! Can't take a compliment, can't take anyone saying anything nice about him and can't accept he has awesome talent with a pencil or a paintbrush."

"He paints too?"

"Like a demon! If you think these drawings are good,

his paintings would blow your socks off. And I'm not just saying that because he's my best friend. It's my business to know quality from crud and that boy produces quality!"

"We want to buy some of these drawings from him, but he refuses to accept payment."

"Why am I not surprised?" Guy turned to look at Danny as he knelt down to speak with Poppy, a big smile on his face as the little girl showed him one of her drawings. He watched his friend humour the child, by making the appropriate noises of encouragement at her efforts and he saw once again what a lovely man he was.

He cleared his throat and said to Pete in an undertone, "I may have a solution for you."

Pete looked at him with interest. "I'm all ears. What do you suggest?"

Guy returned his attention to the drawings laid out in front of him. "Which pictures do you like the most?"

Without hesitation, Pete picked up the pictures of Jordie with Drew, and Sukie with the sleeping Poppy. "These two, I'd pay any sum of money for them."

"Good. Because what I'm about to suggest is going to cost you a few bob."

Pete said, "That's not a problem. What's your suggestion?"

Guy smiled. "Commission him to do you two paintings. Ask him to put those," he pointed at the drawings, "onto canvas. Then you can genuinely pay him a worthy price."

Pete thought for a moment and then a big smile crossed his face as he threw his arm across Guy's shoulder and gave him a hug. "Guy, that's a genius idea! Nice one, mate!"

Completely unaware he'd just turned Guy into a jelly

shake, Pete walked over to join Sukie and Danny. Poppy thrust a picture into his hand and Pete bent down to admire it. When he had looked at the multi-coloured scribbles for a few seconds he said, "Oh, baby girl, you are so clever. This is wonderful."

Danny smiled. "Actually it is, Pete. Her use of colour is very good. They all complement each other, none of them clash. For a two-year-old, that's quite exceptional."

Sukie caught Pete's eye. "Pete, I was just thinking, maybe we could have a word with Jeff—" She stopped when Pete give a very subtle shake of his head and quickly changed the end of her sentence "...about when would be a good time to go down for a visit. It's been a while."

Pete suddenly let out an "Urgh!" of disgust and looked down at his hands, "I think a certain little lady has been eating sticky sweeties and needs to wash her hands." He looked at Sukie who picked up his cue and got to her feet.

"Guy, I've been so rude. Would you like a tea or coffee? You've driven all the way here and I haven't even sorted out some refreshments for you. Danny, can I get you something too?"

Pete walked towards the kitchen with Sukie and waited until they were well out of earshot before saying, "You were going to suggest we talk to Jeff, weren't you? Ask him to have a look at Danny's work?"

"That's right. Why did you say no?"

"Because I'd rather talk to Jeff first and check with him if he'd be prepared to look at what Danny can do before saying anything. I'm not sure how Jeff operates with new artists and I'd hate to get Danny's hopes up only to dash them if Jeff's not interested or can't help."

Sukie smiled at Pete. "Oh husband of mine, I think my common sense is finally beginning to rub off on you. That's a much better idea." She grabbed a handful of his sweatshirt, pulling him in close for a kiss. Pete wrapped his arms around her, holding her tightly. There were times when he still couldn't believe how much his life had changed since this feisty, funny and caring woman had come into it. He'd been so lonely, living in his Austrian castle, hidden way from the prying eyes of the press who had caused so much damage in his life. Sukie had taught him to laugh again and, more importantly, to trust again. She'd picked up the pieces of his shattered life and had made him whole once more. His mother-in-law, Beth, treated him as if he was her own son and he loved her just as much for that.

He mentioned Guy's idea of how they could pay Danny for his work.

"What a clever suggestion! That'll work, surely. And, now that I think about it, those pieces painted up and properly framed would look spectacular. Let's ask him right now." She walked towards the kitchen door.

"Err... Sukie, we're supposed to be making drinks. I think it would look better if we did actually take them back in with us."

Pete burst out laughing when she turned round and replied, "Good point, well made! You do the kettle, I'll sort out the cups." She walked back to place another kiss on his lips, lingering for a moment before moving towards the cupboard to sort out the crockery and set the tray.

Chapter Twenty-Six

Elsa lay looking at the clock beside her bed. It was only seven a.m. She still had at least fifteen hours to deal with before she could go back to bed and forget about it.

Today was her fortieth birthday.

The last three weeks, since moving to London, had flown by. This day had crept up on her and she hadn't been prepared for it.

Recent birthdays had turned into non-events as she'd become more and more reclusive and she suspected this was the reason why Sukie and her parents hadn't made any suggestions to get together today. And therein lay the rub, for now that her life had changed so much, she would have been quite up for a little celebration or two. She tried to stifle a sniffle of self-pity and burrowed down into the middle of the bed, pulling the quilt cover over her head.

She was just dozing off when, suddenly, there was an almighty racket from outside her bedroom window.

"HAPPY BIRTHDAY TO YOU,
HAPPY BIRTHDAY TO YOU,

HAPPY BIRTHDAY DEAR ELSAAAAAAAAAAA, HAPPY BIRTHDAY TO YOUUUUUU!"

"C'mon you old reprobate, let us in! Time to party girlfriend!" Sukie banged loudly on the door as she yelled through it.

Elsa rushed to open it and found Sukie and Anna standing on the doormat with birthday hats on their heads, streamers around their necks and the makings of a Bucks Fizz in their hands.

"What on earth… What are you doing here?"

"Well, if you let us in, we'll tell you!" Anna pushed past, Sukie on her heel. She closed the door and followed them into the kitchen where they were already pulling glasses from the cupboard and uncorking the champagne.

"Did you honestly think we were going to let your fortieth birthday pass without celebration?" Sukie gave her a big hug before handing her a glass.

"Err… Well…" She was speechless.

Anna explained when she saw Elsa's bewilderment, "When you completed the tenancy forms for the flat, I saw your date of birth and noticed your birthday was soon. Then, when I realised how old you would be, I phoned Sukie to ask what was planned and could I please invite myself along. That's when I found out there were no plans for celebration. So we made some! This is part one."

"Part one?"

"Yup!" Sukie smiled at her. "A light cocktail breakfast, complete with fresh croissants," she held up a bag, "and then, once you're dressed we'll be heading out for the day."

"Can I ask where we're going?"

"Nope! That's a surprise, so get that drink down your neck while we warm up these lovely pastries."

Anna put the croissants in the microwave before

raising her glass and saying, "Happy fortieth birthday, Elsa. Here's to your happiness and good health."

"To Elsa. My almost sister, and my best friend forever."

Elsa felt herself filling up at Sukie's words, so took a large sip of her drink and blamed the bubbles going up her nose for the tears in her eyes.

"You have got to be kidding me! No bloody way! Forget it, it's not happening!"

Elsa stood at the top of the Arcelormittal Orbit in London's East End, watching as Sukie and Anna were fitted into safety helmets and harnesses.

"Oh, Elsa, you've wanted to do an abseil for years. What better day to do it than on your fortieth birthday?" Sukie held her arms out as the instructor checked she was firmly strapped in.

"Sukie McClaren! It has been a very long time since I said I wanted to do something like this. I was in my teens for goodness' sake. We want to do a lot of things then but that doesn't mean they're right for us!"

"It's Sukie Wallace now but I'll let you off because it's your birthday. C'mon, you know you'll love it. It's perfectly safe."

"Tell you what, Elsa, I'm all kitted up and ready to go," said Anna. "Why don't you watch me on the monitor to see how easy it is?"

She walked over to the edge and holding the ropes as the instructor had shown her, leant back, braced her heels against the edge of the steel platform and then slowly disappeared from sight.

Elsa felt a cold shiver go up her spine as she watched her on the monitor. There was no way she could do this.

She looked away towards Sukie. "Look Sukie, you go on and I'll walk back down to meet you. I can't do this."

"Won't, you mean!" Sukie replied harshly.

"I'm sorry?"

"It's not a case of 'can't' – it's a case of 'won't'!"

"Now you listen to me—"

"No, Elsa, YOU listen to me because you need to hear what I'm about to say. One of your biggest teenage dreams was to learn abseiling. Whenever we saw it in films, you always lit up and said one day you would do that. And do you know why you never did? I'll tell you. Harry! You never did it because of Harry. He was scared of heights and wouldn't allow you to try it. To keep him happy you stopped dreaming about it."

"That's not true!"

"Yes, it is, Elsa. It gives me no pleasure to say that Harry had the ability to be a selfish little git at times but I'm afraid it's the truth. He was my friend too, and I loved him dearly, but that doesn't mean I was blind to his faults."

"Harry wasn't selfish, how dare you!"

"Oh no... You asked me recently about your taste in music – well, that changed because Harry didn't like rock music and preferred bands like Simply Red and Coldplay. You went along with it because it made him happy. Or how about *you* tell me how many football matches and rugby tournaments you stood watching in the freezing cold because Harry wanted you beside him even though you hate football, you hate rugby and you *really* hate being cold. Now tell me how many ballets or musicals you saw at the theatre – because you like them, right? Oh yes, that would be none. Why? Because Harry couldn't stand them, and he wasn't prepared to make any effort to go even though he always expected you to make the effort for him. The problem, Elsa, was that you were so busy making sure Harry was happy you didn't stop to check if *you* were happy. Well, Harry's gone now, and you need to waken up to the fact it's not only your turn to be happy but it's your bloody right to be!"

Elsa looked at Sukie in disbelief, unable to take in what she'd just said.

"Right, I'm going down! I hope you'll give this a go, but if you're too chicken to be your own person, well... The stairs are over there!"

Sukie made her way to the edge, leaned back and, a few seconds later, she was gone, leaving Elsa staring at the spot where she'd been, her mouth still open with shock.

After a few seconds had passed, she lifted her jaw off the floor and ran through what Sukie had said. She knew she wouldn't have said such things without good cause – Sukie and Harry had been such close friends – but now the words had been spoken aloud, Elsa began to realise she'd made a good point. The Indian takeaways they'd always ordered because Harry wasn't keen on Chinese, even though Elsa preferred it to Indian food. The sport she'd had to endure on the television because he moaned if she put on the soaps or the period dramas that she liked but he didn't. The more she thought about it, the more she saw the truth in Sukie's words.

"So, love, what are you doing? Are you going to give this a try or not? You need to decide because there's another party on their way up."

Elsa looked at the instructor and a steely determination crept over her face.

"I'm going to do it! Sort me out please."

A few minutes later, she was perched on the edge of the platform, leaning out, ready to descend. She managed the difficult manoeuvre of getting off the platform to the ledge underneath and began to slowly work her way down the rope.

She'd barely gone a few metres when a gust of wind swivelled her round and she looked down. The sight of the ground so far below turned her legs to jelly. All of a sudden, she couldn't remember what to do. Her mind went blank, tears began to swim in her eyes and she couldn't see, so she squeezed them closed as the panic quickly crawled through her. Unable to move her hands, she tightened her grip on the rope. Her breaths came out in short, sharp bursts as her chest tightened and she froze, dangling all alone, two hundred and fifty feet in the air.

The Middle Men

Harry was in shock after listening to Sukie's words. He was standing at the back of the Orbital, as far away from the edge as possible. Even now, he had no head for heights. Beside him, William and Death were snorting with laughter.

"Ooh, check out the not-so-golden-boy now," said Death, chortling with glee. "That's what happens when you eavesdrop, you never hear anything good!"

"Harry, just ignore him. None of us are perfect."

"Thanks William. It's just... I thought our marriage was."

He looked over at Elsa as she began to don the safety harness. He couldn't believe she was even contemplating such a thing. She wouldn't have been doing this if he'd still been alive! Oh no, he'd have made sure of that—

He pulled himself up short when he realised what he was thinking. Shit! Sukie had been right. In that instant, the scales were ripped from his eyes. Harry saw all the occasions where he'd done his own thing, when he'd pleased himself and had expected Elsa to just fall in with his plans. And, being the sweet-natured person she was, she had done so without complaint because she only ever wanted people to be happy, even if it was detrimental to her own happiness.

Shame flooded through him as it dawned on him how selfish he'd been and how he hadn't been quite the great husband he'd always believed he was.

He looked at William. "That's why Elsa fell apart so badly after I died! I always put my own selfish wants and desires before hers and squashed her spirit. She didn't know how to revive it once she was alone."

William nodded. "Self-realisation can be a bit of a bitch, son."

Death prodded Harry with his scythe. "You never said you were scared of heights. You kept that quiet. So, me doing this won't bother you… much!" He flew off the end of the platform and disappeared over the edge. A second later his head re-appeared.

"Now you see me…!" He dropped back down again and all they heard was his voice calling up, "Now you don't!"

He bobbed up and down a few times, chanting his little mantra.

"Now you see me."

"Now you don't."

"Now you see me."

"Now you don't."

Harry shuddered as he watched him messing around. Just then, he saw Elsa make her way to the end of the platform. He looked up at the monitor as she took her first tentative steps over the edge and felt a small flicker of pride at the determined look on her face. She was so brave – much braver than him in the end. He watched as she slowly began to descend down the rope, his pride growing with each centimetre that passed through her hands.

That's my girl, he thought. You can do this.

Suddenly, she stopped. He saw her swaying in the wind, his pride shattering around him when he realised what had happened.

"Noooo!" he said aloud, "not now, not after you've made it this far. Come on, Elsa," he whispered, "you can do this. C'mon…"

When a few seconds had passed and she hadn't moved, Harry knew there was only one thing he could do. One little thing that might just begin to make up for his selfish acts of the past.

Not giving himself time to dwell on his decision, he ran towards the open edge of the platform and jumped off.

Death stopped bobbing and went to stand beside William who'd run forward when Harry had jumped. They both peered over the edge.

"Well, bugger me," said William, "I sure as heck didn't expect him to do that!"

Chapter Twenty-One

Elsa sat in the Jacuzzi, listening to Sukie talking about her house guest Danny, and filling Jean in on the details behind his stay. She looked at her mum and smiled, thinking of how difficult it must have been for her to keep secret the plans being made to celebrate this special day. Jean's forte in life was baking, not keeping secrets. She tuned out of the conversation – Sukie had already told her everything earlier in the day – and thought back to her abseil. It had been the strangest thing, but she was sure she'd heard Harry's voice coaxing her out of her frozen, petrified state.

She'd been holding onto the rope for dear life, unable to go up and too scared to go down when the wind had dropped, and everything went very still around her. Her hands began to slowly unclench – each finger had relaxed its hold as though invisible hands were gently easing them off the rope. There had been a tickle against her ear and she'd heard Harry's voice saying, "I've got you, Elsa, everything's going to be okay. You can do this. You're so brave. Remember your promise – living life for the two of of us…"

When those words had entered her head, she'd come back to life, the numbness which had overtaken her slipped away and the determination flooded back into her veins.

She'd opened her eyes, looked up at the sky above and had yelled, "For the two of us!" at the top of her voice as she began her descent once more.

Anna and Sukie had begun to chant her name as she'd slid down the last few meters. The elation she'd felt when her feet had touched the ground was like nothing she'd experienced before. She'd felt so alive! The blood had pounded in her head and her heart had pounded in her chest. She'd thrown back her head and let out a huge roar of joy as she'd realised *this* was what living felt like.

"Do you want some, Elsa?"

She snapped back into the moment to see Sukie holding up the bottle of champagne. With a grin, she picked up her glass and held it across for a refill.

White-knuckle, blood-pumping sport in the morning, she thought, followed by a luxury spa and treatments in the afternoon – now that is what you call a great birthday.

Sandra Harrison stared at the white stick in front of her, shock and dismay running through her in waves. She felt as though she was going to be sick. Except she'd already been doing that for the last ten days and it was this which had prompted her to visit the local chemist. She'd ended up visiting the chemist three times because she couldn't believe the results she was getting. In the end, she had to concur that six sticks could not be wrong.

She was pregnant!

A cold sweat broke out over her as the implications of

this began to sink in. She knew in her heart the father was Robbie. She'd been with him considerably more often than she'd been with Danny over the last five months. She could count the number of times she'd slept with Danny, since New Year, on one hand. The odds on it being his were very, very low. The problem was... how did she break the news to Robbie? He'd never given any indication their relationship was anything more than a bit of fun. He certainly didn't strike her as being the type who wanted to be serious and steady, he was always far more happy-go-lucky and just pleased himself. She was always last in his thoughts when it came to him having a good time.

If she was being totally honest with herself, however, Sandra didn't even know if she wanted to be stuck with Robbie long-term. From the little personal information she'd gleaned from him, she'd figured out he worked for a building company and was happy making just enough money to keep him in beer and chips from one week to the next. He never talked about the future, discussed his plans or even if he had any plans. He lived in the here-and-now and tomorrow could take care of itself. Danny, on the other hand, still had some prospects. She could now kiss goodbye to meeting some rich lawyer from Danny's workplace but Danny himself wasn't the worst option she could have. Okay, she might not love him, but she cared enough for him to make it work. He'd have to marry her though – she didn't plan to live in sin with a baby in tow. Knowing Danny as she did, however, she knew he'd do the right thing by her.

But... she pulled herself up short. She had to talk to Robbie first. It was the right thing to do, even if it wasn't what she really wanted to do. Although, what she really wanted to do, was crawl into bed, pull the covers up over her head and wish for the whole sorry mess to go away.

She dropped her head into her hands and sighed loudly. There was no point in wishing for something that was never going to happen.

A fleeting thought of getting rid of the baby crossed her mind but that's all it was – a fleeting thought. Her father would go through the roof when he found out she was up the duff but that would be nothing compared to what he would do if he were to find out she'd had an abortion. He was fairly relaxed on most things but that was one issue he had strong views on and he would never be able to condone his own daughter having one. Sandra knew she could never do that anyway. Her father aside, she simply couldn't bring herself to kill an innocent child. Instinctively, her hands crossed her belly, as though she was already trying to protect the life growing within it.

Letting out another sigh, she picked up the pregnancy sticks lying on the floor and carefully put them back in one of the paper bags along with all the packaging. She would stash them somewhere in her bedroom until she could dispose of them carefully. She wasn't about to risk putting them in the bathroom bin for someone in the family to find. She'd seen enough soap operas to know how that all worked out! No, she would tell her family when she was ready and when she'd spoken to Robbie and Danny. Once she knew how it was all going to pan out, then she would spill the beans. Until then, her lips were sealed.

She opened the bathroom door and peeped out, checking the coast was clear as she hurried into her bedroom and hid the package at the back of her wardrobe. She sat on her bed, picked up her phone and began writing a text to Robbie, telling him she had to see him.

Chapter Twenty-Eight

June

A few days later, Sandra was sitting at a table in the large window of a café in Covent Garden. Outside the street performers were doing their thing – juggling with balls and riding their silly, over-tall unicycles. She didn't see them though as she was too busy watching Robbie sitting opposite. She'd just broken the news. He'd practically downed his pint of lager in one and was desperately trying to catch the waiter's eye so he could order another.

"Are you sure? I mean REALLY sure?"

"Well, if you mean 'Am I sure I'm pregnant' then I can assure you I definitely am. I saw the doctor and she confirmed it. She thinks I'm about nine or ten weeks."

"What about that other bloke you've been seeing? Donny or something...? How do you know it's not his?"

"I'm not saying it isn't Danny's, however, given that I've only slept with him about five times since New Year, and you and I have managed that in one night – more than once might I add – then I'd say the odds are lying firmly stacked in your favour." Sandra took a sip of her mocha coffee in an attempt to try and quell the unease in the pit of her stomach. She didn't really know what she was expecting from this meeting – after all, unless Robbie turned round and declared himself the son of some Irish millionaire, and he was just slumming it to see how the other half lived – then there was no way she'd be walking down the aisle on his arm. No siree! She wasn't about to let the small matter of a baby get in the way of having the lifestyle she desired, and you didn't get that married to a brickie! Nope! Robbie wasn't a white-collar worker so she wasn't interested.

Robbie successfully managed to obtain a second pint of lager and stared into it for several minutes before replying, "I'm struggling to take this in, Sandra, I was always so careful. I just can't comprehend how you can be pregnant."

"Accidents happen, Robbie. It's not a position I've chosen to be in, believe me!"

"Well… I can't do this. I don't know what you want from me but, whatever it is I can't give it to you. I really don't know what to say."

For all her bravado, and strong words to herself, Sandra still felt her insides lurch at his words.

When she said nothing, he carried on. "I've never wanted children and never will."

"How do you know that… hmmm?" she couldn't help but ask.

Robbie looked across the table, his green eyes looking brighter than usual as the sunlight caught his face through the café window.

"I know because my own childhood was so difficult. My mum left us when I was eight and I had to help bring up my younger brothers and sisters. I was pretty much a parent before I was ten. When I was nineteen, and just about to move to England, Michelle, my girlfriend at the time, fell pregnant. She lost it two weeks before we were due to get married. I realised I felt more relieved than sad at this and that's how I knew I wasn't parent material. That's never changed. I've worked really hard and now have a good career. A wife and kids just doesn't feature in my plans."

"A career? You call being a bricklayer a career? You're just a labourer!" Sandra's words were venomous. Who was he to reject her?

"A labourer who's also a regional manager, darlin'!"

"Regional manager...?" she squeaked, her eyes as large as saucers.

"Yes, regional manager. I began as a brickie and general labourer, but I studied and worked my way up. I still do the occasional manual role though – just to keep my hand in and to create a good relationship on the sites." He named the company he worked for and they were big because even Sandra had heard of them.

She looked down at her now empty coffee cup, unable to believe what he'd just told her. He was a regional manager for a large construction company! How the hell had she missed that? *Because he didn't tell you, that's why!* said a small voice inside her head. She needed a few minutes to deal with this. She gave Robbie a smile and stood up. "I really need to go to the loo. I'll only be a few minutes."

She entered the Ladies toilets and stood for a moment to catch her breath before walking over to the sink. She washed her hands and checked her reflection in the mirror. She knew that she still looked good and tried to think of the best way to play this as she held her hands under the dryer. With this new information, Robbie had suddenly become, by far, the better marriage prospect. She knew she'd have to tread carefully though if she was to stand any chance of reeling him in. She also couldn't contain the feeling of relief which arose from knowing she didn't have to rely on Danny after all. She could finally kiss him goodbye and move onto creating the perfect life with Robbie. Despite all he'd said, she knew she could win him round. She'd always been good at winding people around her little finger, why should he be any different? It might take a little longer, but she could play the long game if she had to. The end result would be worth it.

She smoothed down her hair, touched up her lipstick, and then turned on her heel to go back out to the café. She saw Robbie scroll through his phone as she walked towards the table. No doubt checking his very responsible management emails, she thought. It was only when she sat down she realised he was scrolling through *her* phone.

"Oi! What do you think you're doing? That's my phone." She grabbed it out of his hands and thumbed through to see if he'd called anyone or sent a text. "What have you done?"

Robbie leant across the table and said quietly, "I've deleted my phone number and all of our text messages."

Sandra looked at him in dismay. "You've done what? Why?"

"Because it's the best thing to do, Sandra. We're never going to be the next Wills and Kate, it's not some big romantic love affair. All we had was some fun, some laughs and quite a lot of sex. But that was it, nothing more. You say this baby is mine, but I have my doubts. After what happened with Michelle, I've always been extremely careful to ensure it didn't ever happen again. You might have only slept with your other guy a handful of times but we all know that it only takes one slip-up for a baby to be created."

Sandra glared at him as he stood and pushed in his chair. Her eyes filling with tears, she saw all her newly-formed plans shattering in front of her. "But you don't have to finish it, Robbie. I haven't made any demands or asked you for anything. We could just carry on as before."

Robbie looked down at her, unmoved by the tears she was trying to hold back. "Sandra, I've met many girls like you over the years – the ones who still believe that the only thing they have to do is 'hook a good man' and they'll be set for life. Well, this isn't the eighteenth century and I'm not going to be that man. It's over. It's time for us both to move on." He bent down, kissed her softly on the top of her head and gave her shoulder a gentle squeeze before turning and walking out of the café.

Sandra sat and watched him through the window, seeing him walk away until he was swallowed up by the crowd. When she could see him no more, she looked down at the table, Robbie's empty pint glass still sitting across from her. For the first time in her life, she hadn't gotten what she wanted and she didn't know how to react to that. She sat at the table for quite some time as she slowly came to terms with how it felt.

After a while, she picked up her phone and slowly began to type out a text. Taking a deep breath, she hit the 'send' button. Thank goodness she still had her fall-back option.

Danny read the text message twice before exclaiming in disgust and throwing the phone back down on the table. Sukie looked at him and raised an eyebrow. He was normally rather mild-mannered so seeing his response was quite a surprise.

"Trouble at mill?" she enquired in a mock Northern accent.

"Girlfriend. Or, should I say, soon to be ex-girlfriend."

"I see."

She waited a few minutes to see if Danny would expand on his comment, but he didn't.

They were sitting in the garden and the sun was beating down. The twins were playing in their paddling pool and Pete was down in his basement studio going through his tour details with Kara. The only sounds were the twins babbling and splashing in the pool and the birds chirruping overhead in the trees. Sukie's much adored cats, Tony and Adam, had also wandered outside and, after chasing a few bumble bees and butterflies, were now lying sleeping in the shade of a nearby bush.

"How long have you been together?" she asked eventually. Danny had made no mention of a girlfriend and, in the four weeks he'd been here, his only visitor had been Guy. The initial two-week stay had been extended when the doctor had said Danny's arm needed to remain immobile for another four weeks. The damage had been extensive and, having checked how it was healing, he felt it would be more beneficial to rest the arm as long as was possible. After that, he wanted Danny to use it sparingly for a further two weeks, only doing gentle exercises on it while the tendons and muscles regained some strength. Sukie and Pete had had no hesitation in telling their guest he was welcome to stay as long as was needed. He was quiet, tidy, polite and excellent company to be in. He and Pete had enjoyed more than one night shouting at the television as the football season had drawn to a close and their respective teams were either winning or losing. Sukie had delighted in seeing Pete enjoying his company, he had so few friends. She hoped he and Danny would continue to be friends once he went back to London and resumed his normal day-to-day life.

Danny hesitated before answering Sukie's question. "We've been together for about three years. It was good for the first eighteen months or so but since then it's kind of limped along. I really should have put an end to it last year but... Well... I'm not very good at letting people down. I'm always loath to say or do things that might hurt or upset them, even when I know they need to be done. I think I'd hoped that she would do the deed instead, but she hasn't."

Sukie nodded to show she understood. "What's her name?"

"Sandra."

"Why hasn't she been to visit you? You've been here over a month."

He gazed at the twins splashing water over each other as he replied. "I've barely seen her since New Year. I let her down badly on New Year's Eve and I don't think she's really forgiven me."

For a second time, Sukie was surprised. Danny didn't seem to be someone who was unreliable. In fact, she would've put money on him being the very opposite.

"Why? What happened?"

Danny explained about him being ill and sleeping right through the celebrations. When he'd finished, Sukie immediately exclaimed, "But that wasn't your fault! You were ill. Very ill, from the sound of things. How could you be expected to attend a party when you could hardly speak and were aching from head to toe?"

She could see that Danny was trying to be diplomatic as he joked that Sandra was a woman who liked everything done her way. She called the shots and expected everyone else to do her bidding.

"You said 'soon to be ex-girlfriend'. When did you

decide you were going to grab the bull by the horns and finish it?"

"It's been growing for a while if I'm being honest. When I began painting again, earlier this year, the fact I didn't want to share the news with her was a big indicator. Guy found out by accident, but I was okay with him knowing, I knew he'd be in my corner. But Sandra... Well, she wouldn't be supportive, she'd laugh and tell me I was wasting my time." He paused for a moment. "I phoned her when I was in hospital, telling her what had happened – you know, the accident and me being stuck up here in Oxfordshire. She showed no interest in me whatsoever. Didn't ask how I was, where I was staying or even how I would manage with my arm being out of action. All she cared about was that she'd need to find someone else to go with her to a show we had tickets for. She didn't even wish me well when she hung up. This..." he nodded at the phone on the table, "is the first I've heard from her in over four weeks."

Sukie was shocked at how callous his girlfriend appeared to be. She didn't want to think badly of someone she'd never met but it was difficult to think nicely of the woman.

"Did she say why she was calling?"

Danny shook his head. "No, she simply said she hadn't heard from me in a while and she needed to see me, there's something she wants to discuss."

"Maybe she's come to the same conclusion as yourself, that there is nowhere further for your relationship to go, and she also wants to break it off."

"Maybe..." Danny pursed his lips. "I have to say, though, hearing from her has certainly brought me down. I now realise, even more, this has to end. Another few weeks or so and she'll be history. I can't wait."

Chapter Twenty-Nine

It was Friday morning and Danny was walking past the dining room door, on his way to the garden, when he heard Sukie exclaim loudly in a frustrated tone. Changing direction, he walked through the doorway to find her sitting with her head in her hands and swathes of papers and materials in front of her on the table.

"Everything okay, Sukie? Only, if you sigh any harder, those papers are going to end up all over the place."

Sukie looked up. "Oh, hi, Danny, how're you doing today?"

"Better than you I reckon. Anything I can help with?"

"Unless you're any good at interior design and can magic me up something which is understated, that my mother would like, and can turn a vast barn into a cosy reception room, I very much doubt it. Mum is allowing me to organise her wedding reception on the clear understanding that it's kept simple." She let out another big sigh.

Danny pulled out a chair and sat down. "Tell me

everything," he said.

"We've converted one of the old barns into a function suite, but I just can't see how to turn it into a cosy, intimate venue. I've been struggling to figure out how to decorate it. The high, pitched roof has been retained and, if the decoration is *too* minimal, it'll make the room feel cold and cavernous. We've installed a wooden balcony around the higher level, with a few secluded alcoves so guests can have some respite from the partying below, but even that won't help to break up the vastness of the room. I'm at my wits' end and running out of time. Beth is my mum and I want to be the one to make her day go smoothly. I don't get many opportunities to do something special for her.

Danny, seeing the strain on her face, said, "I'm rather rubbish at the interior design stuff myself, but I know a man who's a demon at it."

"Thanks, Danny but I really don't want to hand over to some unknown person for whom this is just another job. I'm doing it myself because I want it to be personal. Well... I'm trying to do it myself, I should say."

"The person I have in mind is someone you've already met, and I know he would love nothing more than to help you with this."

Sukie looked up in confusion. "I don't follow... Someone I've already met?"

He smiled. "Yes, someone you've already met. Guy! He's an interior designer and, at the risk of sounding biased, a damn good one too. I just know he would love to lend a hand. Plus, he also knows Beth so he's not someone impersonal, is he?"

"Guy's an interior designer? I didn't know that. Do you think he would help? And I mean HELP – I don't want him muscling in and taking over."

Danny took his phone out of his pocket. "There's only

one way to find out. Why don't you go and make coffee while I give him a call?"

Danny called Guy as Sukie left the room. When she returned ten minutes later, the table had been tidied, and he was putting all the paperwork into a neat pile in the middle. He looked up when she walked in. "Guy was over the moon when I said his help was needed. He's already on his way and should be here in about two hours – give or take, depending on traffic. I've given him the lowdown – understated, classy, very big room! He said he'll have some ideas for you by the time he gets here."

"What sort of stuff has he done before?"

He opened Sukie's laptop. "It would be easier to show you."

A few minutes later, Sukie was looking at a plethora of photographs from jobs Guy had done. There seemed to be everything from homes, to offices, to parties and even a few holiday resorts and hotels.

"Wow! Is there anything he doesn't do?"

Danny grinned. "I don't think he's done any boats or ships yet, but I believe he has some in his sights."

"But so much…" She pointed at the images on the screen, "and so varied. I always thought they specialised in one area."

"Most probably do but Guy gets bored easily. Variety is definitely the spice in his life!"

"Well, I hope he's happy to help me out, I certainly need it." Sukie took a large drink of her coffee as she looked again at Guy's work on the computer screen.

Three hours later, she was standing with Guy in the barn. He'd arrived with all the tools of his trade and had already drawn a floorplan of the barn which detailed all the doors, windows, kitchen and lavatories. He'd also taken measurements which he'd scribbled in his notebook.

"Right, I think I may have some suggestions for you."

"I'm all ears!"

"Well, I had a few ideas as I was driving up and I am delighted to see you've kept the old, wooden, horizontal rafters," he began, pointing above them, "because, to minimise the cavernous feeling you're most worried about, I'd suggest draping swathes of fairy lights, from side to side, across the beams. This would immediately lower the ceiling by creating a new one but, because of the lights, would ensure it didn't feel claustrophobic. We could also weave garlands of Beth's favourite flowers, or whatever she is having in her bouquet, through the balcony railings. What flowers is she having, do you know?"

"She's keeping that simple too – scarlet and cream roses, as far as I know."

Guy gave a little yelp of joy. "Oh, that is PERFECT!"

Sukie glanced at him in amusement. She loved that he seemed to have so many ideas, but she would love it if he could share them with her as quickly as he was thinking of them.

"C'mon, Guy, what are you thinking? Spill the beans!"

"Dark red table covers with cream roses as the centrepiece. You see, using pale colours will make the room look bigger but if we use dark colours instead, this will pull the space down and create a far more, cosy, atmosphere. I can also place dark red swags over the doors and windows."

Sukie closed her eyes and brought up a vision of Guy's ideas. She could already see it in her mind's eye and she liked what she was seeing. Oh yes, that could really work. She opened her eyes and gave him a massive hug.

"That sounds fantastic. I can already see it. She'll love it. Thank you. Thank you. Thank you!" Sukie squeezed him so hard he could barely breathe.

"Hey, I don't mind! I'm just delighted to be able to help *you* after the way you've cared for my best friend so well and welcomed him into your home with open arms."

They were strolling back to the manor house, when Sukie asked Guy about Danny's girlfriend. She was curious to hear his opinion on the type of woman she was. She wasn't, however, prepared for the vitriolic response he spat out at the mention of Sandra's name.

"Urgh! Please don't ruin a lovely afternoon by mentioning that flea-ridden, obnoxious harpy in my presence. The sooner Danny kicks *that* rancid baggage into touch the better. The woman – and I do the rest of womankind a disservice by referring to her as one – is incapable of loving anyone but herself. Selfish and self-centred doesn't even begin to do justice as a description of her. She's more common than a sewer rat but she thinks she's one step down from royalty!"

While he drew breath, Sukie replied, "So, you don't like her much, then?"

"I'd rather have dinner with Dennis Nilsen than spend a single moment of time with that social-climbing excuse of a cart-horse. I swear, pond scum has more appeal than Sandra Harrison!"

Sukie couldn't help grinning at his words. "How did they get together?" she asked.

"They met in a pub at some works night out and I wasn't there to save him. She got her hooks into him and he's too nice to dump her. Do you know, she actually told me at New Year she was only staying with Danny in order to meet the wealthy lawyers he works with?"

"You saw her at New Year?" Sukie remembered Danny's tale about being ill.

"Geez, no way! Seeing her at New Year would be the equivalent of seven years bad luck!" Guy wasted no time in telling Sukie everything. "She was really pissed off Danny had stood her up. She called me about five times that night, slagging him off and calling him all the names under the sun. Each call was more drunken than the last. I eventually turned my phone off but found a further two messages the next day. In one of them she calls Danny a total loser and says she's only staying with him so she can meet someone better, like one of the wealthy lawyers he works with. Surprisingly enough, I kind of forgot to delete that one. I still have it, should the day ever come when I need it."

"Wow! She really does sound a piece of work." Sukie was unable to hide her shock at what she was hearing. "Thankfully Danny appears to have seen sense and intends to break it off when he returns to London."

"Yeah, and not a minute too soon if you ask me! I just hope he doesn't change his mind. If she pulls the old waterworks routine, there's a good chance he'll fall for it and cave in." Guy shook his head dismally at the thought.

"Well, here's hoping he doesn't. He's far too nice to be stuck with someone like that."

They'd arrived back at the house and Sukie was glad Danny hadn't invited Sandra to visit while he was here, she really didn't fancy the idea of someone that cold and calculating being a part of their social life. Pete was finally beginning to open up to meeting new people again and someone like Sandra Harrison could cause major upsets. Sukie shuddered as she removed her outdoor shoes. No, the sooner Danny broke it off the better. She knew Beth was inviting him to the wedding and Sukie would not be a happy bunny if he turned up with this unpleasant woman on his arm.

Chapter Thirty

Elsa let out an almighty groan when her alarm went off at seven thirty the next morning. She'd had about three hours sleep, if that, and now she had to go to work. She could hear Anna snoring like a drain in the spare room across the hallway.

What had started out as a quick, Friday night drink in the pub after work had turned into a night on the town, complete with dancing. They'd met two blokes and Anna had immediately taken a shine to one of them. Gordon had shoulder-length shaggy blonde hair, was about six foot six, built like a brick outhouse and had a voice like thunder. He ticked all her boxes and she wasn't about to let him go. By the end of the night, she was calling him 'her mountain' and it was clear the attraction was mutual. Mike, his considerably quieter friend, had spent the evening chatting with Elsa, telling her about his forthcoming nuptials and how laidback his fiancée was. He was a lovely bloke and, at the end of the night, she'd kissed his cheek and wished him lots of happiness for the future.

She pushed back the quilt and sat up, immediately wishing she'd done it a bit slower as her head was thumping. She stood up, and staggering through to the lounge, opened the patio door to allow Puddle a trot around the garden. While he was out there, she made her way into the kitchen and put the kettle on for a strong cup of coffee. She had a quiet rummage in a drawer and found some ibuprofen tablets which she swallowed down with a large glass of water, hoping they would soon set to work. Also remembering vitamin C helped hangovers, she found her 'healthy stash' and took three of the extra strong tablets.

Behind her, she heard Puddle come back inside, so she opened the cupboard and took out his breakfast. She opened the tin and almost threw up when the smell invaded her nostrils. Urgh! Dog food was gross at the best of times but, when you had a hangover coupled with almost no sleep, it was the most evil stench known to man. Quickly scooping some into his bowl, she placed it on the floor, as far away as possible.

Elsa poured the hot water into her mug, and taking a sip of the coffee, felt the hit of caffeine run through her. She picked up her mug and took it with her into the bathroom where she stripped off her nightshirt, turned on the shower and stepped into the ice-cold blast of water. She had cold showers every day as they invigorated her and got her going in the morning, but she figured this one was going to have its work cut out for it today!

In less than an hour, she was ready to leave. She checked the patio door was closed and locked and tried not to feel too envious of Anna whose snores followed her out the front door. She locked it, dragged her feet up the stairs to ground level and walked gingerly to the showroom. On the first Saturday of every month, Jeff opened the showroom from 9 a.m. until 1 p.m. He said it was for the benefit of those who have to work all through the week. Yesterday, Elsa had told him he could have a long lie-in today, saying she would open up as he'd always done it previously. He'd mentioned he'd never been able to persuade his previous assistants to work on Saturdays. Elsa was now beginning to rue her offer, wishing she too had been unpersuaded to help out.

She didn't regret going out, it had been a long time since she'd partied after work but, oh boy, was she paying for it now. Thankfully, the ibuprofen and vitamin C had kicked in and her headache had receded somewhat, but she was shattered. She'd never been good on little sleep and that hadn't changed with age. She was grateful it was only half a day she was working.

The short walk to the showroom did little to revive her so, once she'd let herself in and disarmed the alarm, she headed straight to the coffee machine, poured in some water and switched it on while checking the pods in the basket. She was pleased to see they had a good supply of espresso – she was going to need several of those if she had any hope of still being awake at lunchtime.

Two hours later, Elsa had cracked open the third packaging crate from yesterday's late delivery. It was the last thing she felt like doing but she knew that, if she were to sit at her desk, she would almost certainly fall asleep.

She hurried through to the front showroom when she heard the pressure buzzer sound from the alarm underneath the outside foot mat. As she walked in, a man wearing a dinner suit, a dress shirt which was open at the collar, and an undone bow tie, semi-stumbled through the front door. He looked quite rakish and reminded her of the actors in that upper-class 1920's television drama she liked to watch.

When he straightened himself up, he looked at Elsa while letting out a small whistle. "Well, hello there, gorgeous. Aren't you a sight for sore eyes?" He staggered towards her. He was clearly drunk and she wasn't quite sure how she was going to handle this. Dealing with some drunken twit was the last thing she needed today.

"Excuse me, sir, but I think it would be best if you were to leave and return another day when you are better suited to view the paintings." There! That was both professional and capable. She could do this.

"I don't think so, darlin'. Today is a good day and the only thing I want to view is you!"

She quickly moved so that her desk was between them and drew herself up to her full height. "That is not going to be possible, so I suggest you leave right now. Please go!" She pointed towards the front door.

"Ooooh…! I see old Jeffy boy has got himself a little tiger. Where is the dodgy, old geezer anyway? Downstairs? I'll just go and see him." With a sharp turn on his heel, he made his way towards the office where the door to Jeff's basement flat was situated. Without thinking, Elsa grabbed the crowbar she'd been using to open the delivery crates from her desk and ran after the intruder. For someone so drunk, he'd moved with some speed and was already at the bottom of the stairs, standing outside the door to Jeff's flat.

Elsa came up behind him and raised the crowbar above her head.

"Sir, if you do not leave this MINUTE, I will have no choice but to hit you with this crowbar before I call for the police. Please don't make me do this, because I will." She didn't expect for one second she'd have to go through with the threat; she was just hoping it would be enough to scare him off.

The man turned round, looked at Elsa with her raised weapon, and laughter bubbled from his mouth before he fell back against the wall and slid down to the floor. He was still chuckling when he slipped over onto his side and passed out on Jeff's 'Welcome' doormat.

Jeff was sitting at his kitchen table, enjoying his leisurely morning. Once he'd finished this coffee, he would wander up the stairs to see how Elsa was getting on. There was a bell in the office which linked to the flat, so she could always call him if he was needed. He stared at the crossword puzzle in front of him. It was almost complete. Only two more clues to crack and it would be finished.

He was staring out the window into the garden, trying to break the cryptic clue, when he was startled by a commotion outside the door of his flat. Upon hearing Elsa's raised voice, he threw down his pen and ran to the door. He opened it just in time to see the body of a man slump onto the doormat and Elsa standing there wielding a crowbar.

Elsa screamed. "Jeff, I didn't hit him! I swear! He just collapsed. Honest!"

She was trying to explain when the comatose body in front of them suddenly farted loudly, turned over and began snoring.

Jeff let out a sigh. "Elsa, meet my brother, Charlie!"

Chapter Thirty-One

Jeff thrust the cup of hot, strong coffee under his brother's nose. With Elsa's help he'd managed to drag him onto the sofa and he'd been crashed out on it all afternoon. Jeff's anger had been simmering all that time and had now reached boiling point.

"Right you, time to waken up. C'mon, shift yourself!" He gave Charlie a sharp prod.

Charlie, groaning, tried to turn away but, in doing so, slipped off the sofa and landed on the floor at his brother's feet. Jeff couldn't resist giving him a sharp kick in the ribs before helping him to sit upright. He placed the mug on the coffee table and ordered Charlie to drink it.

Charlie took a sip and grimaced. "You could have put some sugar in it."

"You don't deserve sugar or anything nice. Maybe the awful taste will help you to sober up."

"What time is it?"

"After five." Jeff's tone was sharp, making Charlie wince.

"I don't suppose you've got any painkillers have you?

And can you talk a bit quieter please?"

"Yes, I do have painkillers but you're not worthy of any and no, I will not be quiet. In fact, right now, you're very lucky I'm not giving you the hairdryer treatment because it's certainly warranted."

"If I say sorry now, will you pass on the lecture?" Charlie's tone left no doubt that it wasn't the first time Jeff had given him grief over his drinking.

"No, I damn well won't! Charlie, you nearly lost me the best assistant I've ever had since starting this business. Poor Elsa was in such a state of shock, I had to send her home early. She was shaking like a leaf."

"Elsa?" He took a sip of his coffee and pulled at face at the bitter, unsweetened taste.

"Yes, Elsa! The new assistant I told you and Mum about last week." Jeff sighed. Their dad had died suddenly of a heart attack nearly eighteen months ago and Charlie hadn't dealt with it very well. The two of them had been very close, and it had been Charlie who'd joined him in his architect business. They'd been in a meeting together when their dad had, out of the blue, gripped his chest, made a strangling noise and fallen from his chair. By the time the paramedics had arrived, he was dead. Three months after that Charlie had begun drinking and partying to an excessive level. Somehow, he always managed to get himself to work on time, and still produce brilliant designs, but in the hours between leaving the office and going back in the next day, he was becoming a mess.

"Is she blonde and kinda cute?" he asked.

"Yes, she is, and you'll keep away from her. A scoundrel like you is the last thing she needs to meet." At thirty-seven, Charlie was showing no signs of settling down and always had a different woman in tow whenever Jeff met him for a drink.

"Okay, I get it. No touchy-touchy! I'll send her some flowers on Monday to say sorry. Will that suit you?"

Jeff snorted his approval before standing up and walking into the kitchen. He came back with the takeaway menu for the local curry house and waved it at Charlie.

"So, are you stopping the night? Fancy a Balti?"

Charlie looked up at his brother. It had been a while since they'd hung out over some naan bread and a lamb bhuna. "Oh, go on then. Just make sure you add several bottles of Cobra to the order," he said, and burst out laughing when Jeff rolled his eyes as he picked up the phone.

It was Monday morning and Elsa was sitting at her desk sorting out paperwork when she heard the pressure alarm buzz. She looked up to see an arm waving about, struggling to find the door handle. The owner of the arm was buried behind a massive bouquet of flowers. She hurried over to open the door and let the bearer in.

"Thank you. I thought I was about to drop these," a disembodied voice came through the blossoms. "They're a bit on the heavy side."

"I'm not surprised. That bouquet is massive. Here, put it on the desk." Elsa helped to carry it over. As she put the flowers down carefully, a woman's head popped over the top of them. She took a signature unit from her pocket, looked at the details and said, "They're for Elsa Clairmont."

"That's me!" Elsa exclaimed in surprise. Who on earth was sending her flowers? When she'd scribbled her name on the unit, the woman thanked her and left, closing the door behind her.

She looked through the foliage till she found a small card nestling among the leaves. Pulling it out, she opened it up and read it before snorting in derision. She threw the card onto her desk, went into the office and soon came back with a plastic bucket. She began dismantling the beautiful arrangement, placing the bulk of the flowers in the bucket. She then took a piece of paper out from the printer tray and wrote upon it, after which she stuck a bit of sticky tape along the top. Both the flower-filled bucket and the note were carried outside where the flowers were placed on the pavement and the note was stuck on the cast iron railings above them. Elsa walked back inside and returned a few seconds later with a jug of water which was poured into the bucket. She stepped back to admire her handiwork then headed back inside the showroom and closed the door firmly behind her.

Charlie Rowland was sitting on a bench in the square watching in disbelief. He'd positioned himself so he could see the expression of delight on Elsa's face when she saw what he'd sent her. He was less than impressed to find most of the bouquet on the pavement barely ten minutes later. He stood up, walked over to the flowers and read the note stuck above them:

Free to good home.
Please help yourself.
(Please leave the bucket!)
Thank you.

What the hell? Not stopping to think on the wisdom of his actions, Charlie stormed up the steps and into the showroom. He was greeted by the sight of Elsa arranging some daisies, roses, and gypsophila in a vase on her desk.

"I sent you those flowers! To say sorry!" he blustered.

"Yes, I know! I *can* read!" Elsa held up the small card.

"So why have you thrown them away?"

"I haven't 'thrown them away' I'm passing them onto to someone who will appreciate them more than I do."

"But they're lilies. There are loads of them." He'd spent a good thirty minutes with the florist, putting the bouquet together and couldn't believe Elsa was giving most of it away. "Why would you do that?"

"Simple. I can't stand lilies!"

"How can you not like lilies? *Everyone* likes lilies!" Or so the woman in the florist had told him.

"I can't stand the smell, it gives me a headache," replied Elsa.

"And the irises?" he asked.

"Nah, don't like them either."

"Tulips?"

"Meh! Not fussed either way really."

"Well, I'm glad to see you liked the daisies and the roses."

"Yes, they're lovely. Thank you." Elsa gave him a smile as she finished tidying the vase which now contained the remaining third of the bouquet.

"I really am sorry about the other day and for scaring you like that."

"It's okay. I think the lack of sleep was probably the biggest factor in my over-reaction."

"I see. Well, I really am sorry."

Elsa looked at Charlie. "Yes, I know. You've already said. Apology accepted. Now, can I help you with anything else because, if not, I've got paperwork to catch up with?"

Charlie realised he'd just been dismissed, and mumbling a goodbye, walked out of the door. A minute later he was back at the bench he'd been sitting on only a few minutes previously, trying to get his head around what had just happened.

He'd been dismissed!

He was never dismissed!

Women didn't do that to him!

He looked up at the window of the showroom where he could see Elsa sitting at her desk, head down, totally immersed in her work. It was quite clear she had already forgotten about him.

Two days later, Charlie was back on the bench in the square, waiting for his brother to go out so he could speak to Elsa alone. He hadn't been able to get over her response to his gift and her total lack of interest in him. It was the latter which rankled more deeply. He'd been sitting for an hour, when he saw Jeff walking out the door. He quickly raised his newspaper, hiding behind it, just in case Jeff should look over and spot him. He really wouldn't be happy if he thought Charlie was trying to make a move on Elsa after he'd been warned off.

He waited a few more minutes to make sure Jeff didn't return and, when he figured it was safe, he crossed the road and entered the showroom.

Elsa came out of the office when she heard the buzzer. "Oh, it's you again!" she said.

Charlie tried to play it cool by replying, "Actually, I've come to see my brother. Is he around?"

"No, you've just missed him. He'll be back in a couple of hours."

"I'll wait for him."

"If you feel you must."

"Is it okay if I wander through to look at the latest works Jeff has acquired?" he asked.

"Feel free," Elsa replied. "Give me a shout if you want information on any of the pieces."

With a small smile, Charlie walked through to the

216

back room, leaving Elsa to get on with her paperwork.

Elsa stood by her desk, unable to believe she'd just been quite rude to Jeff's brother. This was so unlike her, but he'd totally rubbed her up the wrong way on Monday. How dare he expect her to be GRATEFUL for the bouquet of flowers when he'd been the one in the wrong! Talk about an arrogant so-and-so!

That aside, however, he was her boss's brother, so she needed to rein it in and be more polite.

She put on her more professional voice and went through to ask, "May I get you a tea or coffee while you wait?"

Charlie hit her with a super-dazzling smile. "No, thank you. I'm fine."

"Okay. If you change your mind, please just ask." She returned to the showroom and, as she turned, she saw Charlie's smile slip and waver. I bet he's not used to being in the company of a woman who doesn't fawn over him, she thought. She stood in the doorway and pretended to straighten one of the paintings, all the while watching Charlie from the corner of her eye. His hair was the same colour as Jeff's – a sort of sandy brown – and she'd noticed they shared the same blue eyes. That, however, was where the similarity ended. While Jeff had a certain ruggedness about him – it had taken Elsa a few days to move past his striking resemblance to the Hollywood star, Clint Eastwood – Charlie was definitely more in the Brad Pitt or Ryan Reynolds mould. Slim built with smoother features. He was a few inches shorter than Jeff but, overall, he was a good-looking man. And he knew it! She could tell from the way he moved.

Fifteen minutes later, she heard Charlie calling her. Once she'd locked the front door and turned the sign, she went to find him. He was standing in front of a rare Picasso that Jeff had recently agreed to sell privately for its owner. When she arrived next to him, Charlie asked "Is this really a Picasso? I've never seen this one before."

"Yup, it's the real deal! It is called Portrait of Angel Fernandez de Soto. It's a very rare piece indeed."

"What can you tell me about it? It's captivating."

Elsa glanced at Charlie to see if he was trying to be funny, but he appeared genuinely interested and couldn't take his eyes off the portrait.

"Well," she started, "it was painted during Picasso's blue Period in 1903. The subject is a fellow painter and friend of Picasso's. The piece is also known as 'The Absinthe Drinker' as it is believed the glass in front of him contains absinthe. Picasso often referred to Fernandez de Soto as 'an amusing wastrel' although they must have been good friends because Picasso painted him several times. Sadly, he was killed in the Spanish Civil War."

"Wow! I'm impressed. How come you know all that?" he asked.

"That's the good thing about studying Art History at university," she replied, "they teach you this stuff." She gave him a quick smile and walked back down the stairs.

Charlie was more than a little shocked by Elsa's revelation. Jeff's previous assistants had been flaky little trust-fund girls who were just waiting to find either a rich husband or for their trust funds to mature. None of them had ever actually had any kind of art knowledge. It seemed Elsa had more going for her than he'd originally given her credit for. He acknowledged to himself that, because of her blonde hair and stunning looks, he'd automatically pegged her as some kind of bimbo. He, unusually, felt ashamed of himself for stereo-typing her this way. As he turned and walked back down to the ground floor, he decided this was as good a moment as any to ask her out for dinner. The more he spoke to her, the more she was intriguing him.

He found her standing by her desk in the showroom.

"Um, Elsa... I was wondering if you might like to go out for dinner one evening..."

"Now why would I want to go out to dinner with you?" she asked with a smile.

"So I can say sorry properly for upsetting you on Saturday."

"I thought the flowers were you saying sorry?" She fiddled with some brochures on a table in the open hallway."

"You gave most of them away so, as an apology goes, it was a bit useless."

She looked up at him. "They say it's the thought that counts. Your apology was accepted. There's no need to do anything further."

Charlie tried not to harrumph in frustration. He'd asked her a straightforward question, was a straightforward answer too much to hope for?

He pulled back his shoulders, cleared his throat and asked again. "So, would you like to go out to dinner one evening? We could go to Langan's Brasserie, you might be lucky enough to see some celebrities."

Elsa stopped fiddling and stared at him.

"I beg your pardon?" she asked, her tone barely above freezing. "Is that what you think of me? That I'm some simple-minded bimbo whose head can be turned by the sight of someone famous? Do I really come across as being *that* shallow?"

Charlie gulped as he realised he'd put his foot in it again. What was it with this woman that he always seemed to be the one who came off looking like an idiot?

"Err, no, of course you don't. It's just that Langan's is… err… Well, lots of famous people go there and there's always a… err… good chance of seeing someone…" he tailed off as he took in the hard expression on her face.

"So, to try and impress me, you think taking me to a place where I might see a famous person or two will do the job? You don't think taking me somewhere that actually has good food, good wine and good service is more important. Well, now that we both know you think so little of me, I suggest you leave before I *do* end up hitting you with the crowbar!"

Charlie sighed. "They also do good food and good wine…"

"Too late! Get out!" Elsa pointed at the door.

He looked at her for a few seconds before turning on his heel and leaving.

When she was sure he'd left the square, Elsa let out the giggles she'd been struggling to keep a rein on. Trying to impress her with celebrity spotting… Seriously? Okay, maybe once upon a time she'd have fallen for that sort of line but, when your best mate is married to the world's number one rock star, you soon get over being starry-eyed for people in the headlines. Even more so when you learn they are just ordinary people trying to do a job to support themselves and their families like everyone else. Celebrities? Pah, they're nothing special!

Mind you, she thought, it was still nice to be asked out. This was the first time she'd been asked out on a date since she was a teenager. She'd kissed a couple of boys at school before Harry had declared both his jealousy and his intention to marry her. She hadn't been on a date with anyone since. When Charlie had asked her, she'd played for time because she wasn't really sure what she should do next and had been on the verge of accepting when he'd chucked in the 'see some celebrities' comment. He'd *almost* redeemed himself until he'd come out with that one! If only he'd kept quiet…

Still giggling, Elsa picked up some invoices from her desk and walked into the office to file them away.

Chapter Thirty-Two

Charlie spent the remainder of Wednesday and all of Thursday trying to come up with something that would melt the lovely Elsa. He honestly couldn't remember the last time he'd had so much trouble trying to convince a woman to go out with him. He didn't think it had ever happened. Women had always been easy pickings for him, so finding one he needed to work for was a whole new experience altogether. Charlie wasn't sure if he liked it or not.

On Thursday evening, upon leaving the office, he walked into Mount Street Gardens en route to the tube station. When he saw Elsa there, throwing a ball for a Golden Labrador, he came to an abrupt stop. Once again, she had surprised him. Everything about her was so tidy, neat and precise, that a big lump of a dog was the last thing he'd have expected her to have as a pet – a small Yorkie or a poodle maybe, but not something quite so boisterous.

He and Jeff had had a Labrador when they were kids. Charlie remembered it being playful and funny. He'd loved that dog. What was it called again...? Oh yes, Brandy! Gosh, he hadn't thought about Brandy for years but seeing Elsa playing brought it all back. Not wanting to alert her to his presence, he walked back out of the small park and took the longer route through the streets instead. As he strolled, a plan began to form in his mind.

The following day, he walked into the showroom for the third time that week. Hopefully, it was going to be third time lucky.

He saw Elsa roll her eyes as he walked in and this made him even more determined that today he was going to win! Walking over to stand in front of the desk, he smiled and said, "Do you trust me?"

Startled by the question, Elsa replied, "Well... I can't say! I don't really know you."

Charlie replied, "Ok, do you trust that I wouldn't do anything unpleasant to you or behave inappropriately towards you?"

She thought for a moment. "Well... you *are* Jeff's brother, so I suppose, to some extent, that makes you sort of trustworthy, so, no, I don't think you'd do anything to me that was inappropriate."

"Good!" He gave her a smile and, leaning over her desk, pulled a sticky note from her small pad, picked up a pen and said, "I'll pick you up at 6 a.m. tomorrow morning. Address please..."

Elsa recoiled in her chair. "I beg your pardon? You'll do *what*...?"

"You heard me. I need your address, so I may pick you up tomorrow morning. We're going out for the day, but we need an early start. Oh, and you can bring the pooch."

"Have you been spying on me? How do you know I have a dog?" Elsa bristled when she heard this.

"Keep your blouse on, Elsa, I haven't been spying. You were playing with it in the gardens last night. I saw you when I was heading to the tube station after work."

"Oh!" The simple explanation deflated her indignation.

"So that finds me asking again – do you trust me? If so, give me your address so I may pick you and the pooch up tomorrow morning for a day out."

Elsa decided she may as well just give in – after all, it was becoming clear Charlie was not going away and, the longer she put him off, the more he would persist. She grabbed the pen from him and quickly scribbled down her address and mobile number, thrusting it back at him while saying, "There! The sooner I get this over with, the sooner you'll sod off and leave me alone!"

Charlie ignored her words as he smiled at the small piece of paper in his hand. He placed it carefully inside his wallet and turned to leave. Looking back when he reached the door, he said, "Remember, be ready for 6 a.m. and be sure to wear boots or shoes suitable for walking."

Elsa opened her mouth to ask a question, but he was already gone, the door slowly closing in his wake.

At 6 a.m. on the dot the next morning, Elsa heard a quiet knock on her front door. She opened it and saw Charlie standing there in jeans, denim shirt, a light-weight jumper and trainers. She looked back at his feet. "Are they going to be up to whatever crazy mission you are taking me on?"

He grinned. "Nope! That's why I have my sturdy walking boots in the car. I suggest you might want to do the same. Those will definitely not get you very far." He glanced down at Elsa's fluffy slippers as he spoke.

"Just changing them now," Elsa dug her walking boots

out from the back of the cupboard, gingerly placing her hand in each one. It was such a long time since she'd worn them, she wouldn't be surprised if a whole family of spiders had taken up residence inside. However, luck was on her side – all she found was an old pair of walking socks which she pushed back in. She'd need them later, she thought, as she pulled on a pair of shoes and put the boots in a carrier bag.

She straightened up, picked out a jacket then collected a bag of bits she had put together for Puddle and called him over from where Charlie was giving him a load of fuss.

"Sit!" Puddle did as he was told and she put his harness on him.

"Charlie, you may as well come over and be properly introduced."

Once he was beside her she said, "Puddle, meet Charlie, Charlie, meet Puddle. Now shake hands." At her words, Puddle raised his right paw. Charlie leant down, with a smile, and shook it gently.

"Hello, Puddle, you beautiful boy, I am very pleased to meet you."

He let go and, standing up, looked at Elsa with a raised eyebrow. "Puddle?"

"Yes, he likes water. More than he should and more than is healthy! For either of us!"

"I'll let you explain that one on the journey, but we'd better get a move on if we want to make good time." He picked up the bags at her feet and walked out to the car, leaving her to lock up and follow behind.

At the top of the stairs, Charlie opened the back door of his Lexus for Puddle to get in. Elsa was, although she wouldn't admit it, more than a bit impressed that he'd placed a blanket over the leather seats to make it more comfortable for the dog. She was further impressed when she spotted a dog bowl and a large bottle of water in the foot-well as he was closing the door. Without hesitation, Charlie turned and opened the passenger door for her, closing it gently once she was settled inside.

He was settling himself into the driver's seat and putting on his seat belt when he caught Elsa's eye. "What?" he asked at her smirking expression.

"You opened my door for me," she smiled.

Charlie rolled his eyes. "I'm not a complete Neanderthal. My mother did manage to drum some manners into me. Surprising as that may seem! Now, if you're ready, let's get going."

Four and a half hours later, the car pulled into the little village of Coniston in the Lake District. Charlie had driven a tad faster than was legal, but he'd been a considerate driver and Elsa had felt completely safe at all times.

They parked up and Charlie opened the boot of the car, handed Elsa her walking boots and said, "Time to change into these."

Once they were both kitted up in walking boots, and with light-weight jackets tied around their waists, Charlie shrugged a rather full-looking rucksack onto his back and closed the boot. Locking the car, he carefully stored the keys on a hook within one of the many pockets on the rucksack. He caught Elsa watching him. "You can't be too careful. Unless you want to risk being stuck here with me overnight…"

"No, you're good. Let's go!"

Charlie handed her a pair of hill-climbing sticks and said, "So, no complaints about the fact we're about to walk up a steep hill?"

"Nope!"

"Have I finally gotten something right?"

"Maybe!" Elsa smiled enigmatically, turning away to clip Puddle's leash on.

For a while they walked in companionable silence and, when they were on the path away from the road, she let Puddle roam freely. She had one of his waistline leads in her pocket if he began to wander off.

Elsa was thinking about the drive from London. They'd chatted for a time as she told Charlie about Puddle's penchant for water and the lake incident at New Year, explaining that was why he sometimes wasn't good for her health. Charlie had shared some of Brandy's antics that he could remember from his childhood, such as when he'd knocked over a tin of paint, panicked and had run all over the house trying to get it off his paws, leaving bright green paw-prints in his wake.

After a while, they'd both fallen silent, content to listen and laugh along to the comedian DJ on the radio.

"Are you okay?" Charlie's voice broke into her thoughts.

"Oh, yes, I'm fine. Thank you. Just saving my breath for the climb."

"I've got bottles of water in the sack and a small bowl for Puddle, so just let me know if you need anything."

"Thank you, I will. It sounds as though you've thought of everything. Thank you for being so considerate towards Puddle, I appreciate that." She was genuinely delighted with the effort he'd made for the trip and how much thought he'd given towards her dog's comfort. Elsa always felt that people who were considerate and thoughtful towards animals were usually pretty decent human beings.

Charlie replied with a smile, "No problem."

It took them two hours to reach the summit and Elsa stood catching her breath. It was windier up here, so she pulled her jacket off her waist and put it on. Charlie had walked off to one side and was unpacking the rucksack. She saw him pour some water out for Puddle who was quick to lap it up. This made her smile. Charlie had been very interactive with Puddle on the walk up and had called him to heel several times when he wandered too far from the track. She'd asked why he was keeping Puddle close by, expecting him to say he was just enjoying having her dog around. What he'd actually told her was that there used to be mines and quarry works on the hill and there were quite a few old shafts around. He'd smiled when he said, "I don't think it would impress you at all if your dog suddenly disappeared twenty feet down into the earth, would it?" When they'd gotten to the part of the track which was closest to the old quarry works, Charlie had suggested putting Puddle on his leash until they'd passed by.

She turned around to take in the view of Coniston Water which lay ahead of her. As she raised her face to the sun, she pulled the hairband from her ponytail and relished the feel of the wind blowing through her hair. She'd been letting it grow and it now sat just past her shoulders. She pushed her sunglasses up onto her head to keep her hair off her face and walked over to where Charlie had laid out a rug. Sitting down beside him, she noted he'd clipped Puddle's long leash onto his belt. She looked at him quizzically.

"It's so we can relax while we eat our lunch. He can wander about if he wants but can't go too far."

At the mention of lunch, Elsa's stomach let out a grumble. She'd only had a quick coffee before leaving this morning and they'd shared some chocolate on the journey up but that wasn't enough to sustain her after their long walk. Charlie snickered when he heard the rumbling and promptly put his hand in the rucksack. He pulled out a plastic container and passed it over to her, saying, "Cheese sandwiches." He put his hand in again, pulled out a second container, "Chicken sandwiches." He repeated this action twice more, producing plain salad sandwiches on gluten free bread and some cheese and ham ciabatta.

Elsa looked at the array of tubs in front of her. He'd also brought some smaller containers with mayonnaise and salad cream in them. He shrugged when she looked at him in amusement and said, "I didn't know if you were vegetarian, vegan, gluten free, couldn't eat dairy... Everyone seems to have some sort of dietary requirement these days so I was trying to cover all the bases."

Elsa laughed. "You had my phone number, why didn't you just call and ask?"

"I didn't want to risk giving the surprise away."

"Thank you, I really appreciate all the effort you've gone to. I'm assuming you did this and didn't just order in from some deli place..."

"Nope, all created with my own fair hands. Something you will notice immediately when you open these up and realise that finesse in cooking is not one of my better attributes. Give me a pen and paper and I will draw you a perfect building, but put a wooden spoon in my hand and I'll present you with the perfect disaster."

Elsa laughed while picking up the nearest container. Opening it and taking out a sandwich, she found herself holding two pieces of thick, unevenly cut, crusty bread door-steps with what could only be described as a *slab* of cheese, sitting between them. With her stomach letting out a second loud grumble, she realised a good hefty sandwich like this was exactly what she wanted. She smiled at Charlie and said, "This is absolutely perfect. Thank you," before sinking her teeth in and taking a bite.

Admiring the views in front of her as she ate, Elsa

found that she was quite touched by the efforts Charlie had made. He'd been attentive to Puddle's needs all day – from the blanket in the car, to stopping off at services on the drive up so he could have a drink and a wee, and now giving him some specially purchased dog biscuits and a bowl of water. Then there was the level of thought he'd put into the selection of sandwiches on offer. In that respect he needn't have worried – she could eat anything – but he'd been considerate enough to take on board that maybe she couldn't. She watched him from the corner of her eye and saw him sneak a piece of chicken to Puddle, who was very happy lying next to him. She felt herself softening towards him. Maybe he wasn't such a bad old thing after all.

Chapter Thirty-Three

They hadn't long finished eating when Charlie surprised Elsa further by producing a thermos of coffee and two massive slices of Victoria sponge cake, which they ate in silence, taking in the view and enjoying the quiet. A few other walkers had come up to the summit, and they'd nodded greetings each time, but they were sitting far enough over to the side to be out of the way of passing traffic. Finally, she asked, "So, have you done a lot of hill walking?"

Charlie didn't answer immediately. When he did respond he said, "This is the first time I've done it in almost five years. I used to walk with my dad. He loved getting away from the city and coming up here to stretch his legs out properly. That's what he used to say to me – 'Let's go and stretch our legs out properly this weekend, son. Let's go for a good, healthy walk away from the fumes and the city smells'. This climb was his favourite. There were a few others, the Peak District is a close second, but this was his favourite. We did this one the most."

Elsa immediately picked up the word 'was'. Quietly she asked "Was?" even though she knew what the answer would be.

"He died last year."

"I see." She didn't offer any form of platitudes because she knew from her own experience they gave absolutely no comfort to the recipient. She waited, giving Charlie the time to deal with the emotions which were most probably churning him up inside.

Eventually, he carried on. "I feel really bad because we hadn't walked together for some time. He asked me to go on several occasions and I kept putting him off. It was more important for me to go out with my mates and 'have fun'," Charlie used his fingers to create the quotes around these last two words which he'd spoken with great disdain, "than to spend time with him. After a while he stopped asking." He looked down at his hands, swallowing hard to control the tears he was close to shedding. Elsa stayed quiet, her instinct telling her it was probably the first time he'd spoken about this to anyone. She knew, better than most, the importance of talking about your grief and she didn't want to interrupt.

Charlie finally spoke again. "He died of a heart attack, Elsa. He was sitting right next to me, in the boardroom in our office. I couldn't do anything. I tried to resuscitate him, but to no avail. The doctors said he'd died immediately. The attack was so severe there was nothing I, nor anyone else, could have done. I knew then that I was to blame."

"Why were you to blame? You couldn't have prevented it." Elsa laid her hand gently on his arm.

Charlie looked away, unable to face her when he said, "Because I'd stopped him from stretching his legs. He didn't like to walk without me, he said. He preferred having me by his side. As he got older, that made sense.

If he'd fallen while on his own…" His voice trailed off.

They sat in silence again until Elsa asked, "Is this the first time you've spoken of this?" Charlie nodded.

"Why now? Why today? Why me?"

"I don't know. I was trying to think of how I could show you I'm not the complete asshole you think I am. When I saw you with Puddle, I thought if I came up with something that included him, you might think better of me. Then I remembered this walk, and suddenly I had to come here." Pausing, he looked at Elsa, "I think that, even if you had said no, I would still have come here on my own. Once the idea was in my head, it wouldn't go away. The urge to be here today was so strong."

"Maybe your dad was giving you a message. Maybe he was trying to get you here, so you could say goodbye and begin to move on. Maybe it's time to let go of the guilt."

"Do you think so? Maybe it's just me trying to appease the guilt myself."

Elsa thought back to the conversation she'd had with Harry on New Year's Eve, remembering his words when he told her she was clinging to his memory so tightly that *he* couldn't move on, that he was stuck in some kind of no-man's land. She'd had to let him go for both their sakes. She looked at Charlie. While she couldn't tell him of her experience, she could still give him the benefit of it. "Do you think your dad would want to see you the way you are now? From Jeff's response last week, I'm guessing that wasn't the first incident of you falling down drunk on his doorstep?"

Charlie reddened with embarrassment. "No, it wasn't. Since Dad's death I've felt totally out of control. I'm fine in the office, and my work is as good as it's ever been but, once I finish for the day and I'm on my own, I can't control the emotions inside me. The guilt, the loss, the pain of him not being here anymore… It all becomes too much so I drink and party to help me forget."

Elsa nodded. She understood that only too well. She may not have gotten drunk and partied all night but her obsession with health foods and working out down the gym until she almost dropped from exhaustion added up to the same thing – trying to maintain some form of control over something that could not be controlled. Death, in the end, always had the upper hand.

"Charlie, I think you were meant to come here to say goodbye. I believe those we love watch over us and it must hurt them to see us not living our lives to the fullest. They don't want us to be racked with guilt and remorse. They want us to carry on living. It is absolutely natural to feel guilty in the first few months – almost every human being does. We feel bad that we're still alive and the person we love is not but, eventually, the guilt needs to stop and we need to ensure it doesn't consume our lives. Life is for living. I'd bet anything that, if you could talk to your dad right now, he'd be horrified to know how you felt and that you were still carrying this pain inside. He was your dad; all he ever wanted was for you to be happy. He'd be really hurt if he knew you were in this pain because of him. No, you can't change that you didn't go on those walks, and yes, it will be a regret you'll have for the rest of your life, but it mustn't dictate the rest of your life. Instead, work on becoming the kind of man your father would have been very proud of. That's the best way you can remember him."

Charlie turned to look at her, tears blurring his eyes. "I just wish I could say sorry to him. Just once," he whispered.

"Then say it, Charlie. Say it here, say it now. If this was his favourite place, then he's probably here right now. Say it to the wind, he'll hear you. Let the wind carry your words to him."

She stood up and held out her hand. "Pass me Puddle's leash."

He looked at her in confusion.

"This is your private moment, Charlie. This is between you and your dad. You don't need an audience. I'll just be over there," she pointed towards the cairn on the other side of the summit. "Call me or come over whenever you're ready."

Elsa left Charlie sitting alone, mulling over how he felt. He hadn't opened up to anyone before – not to his mum and not to his brother. He'd carried these thoughts inside him all this time. He already felt lighter for having spoken them aloud. He glanced at Elsa as she played with Puddle and wondered why he'd sensed she would understand. What was it about her that had made him feel he could talk about this and that she wouldn't laugh or say he was daft? There was something he couldn't put a finger on... He turned back to look over the water and the hills beyond and thought about what she'd said. 'Let the wind carry your words to him'.

He stood up and pushed his fingers through his hair before taking a deep breath and whispering aloud, "I'm sorry, Dad. I'm so sorry I didn't give you more of my time. I'm so sorry I was too engrossed in my own life. And I'm sorry for being so selfish. I hope you can hear me, Dad. I love you."

He closed his eyes, feeling the wind blow around him. He felt it ruffle his hair, just like his dad used to do when he was a kid. As he stood in silence, he felt a presence next to him. Elsa had come back to stand beside him. He was grateful to her for that. It helped. A few minutes passed and then, in his ear, he heard his father's voice. *I hear you, Charlie. You have nothing to be sorry for. I love you, son. I will always love you...*

Charlie's eyes sprung open. What the hell...? He looked around and saw Elsa over by the cairn. She hadn't moved from there. He turned. There was no one else nearby. He was on his own. And yet...! He had definitely felt someone by his side. He was sure of it. Just as he was sure it was his father's voice he'd heard in his ear. The air had been cold, but he hadn't imagined it. He looked down at the lake below and slowly felt the guilt begin to ease away. For the first time since his dad's death, he felt almost peaceful.

After a few minutes, he walked over to Elsa and Puddle. "If you're ready, we should begin to make our way back down."

Elsa looked at Charlie and could already see a change in him – his face was more relaxed and his shoulders had dropped. Not asking any questions, she helped him to pack the remnants of their picnic back into the rucksack.

The journey down the hillside, and back to London, was made in silence. Charlie changed the radio station to one that played classical music. It was very soothing and the atmosphere in the car was peaceful.

When they arrived back at her flat, Charlie helped to carry her stuff to her door. She opened it and pushed Puddle inside. Not saying a word, Charlie gave her a gentle hug and a kiss on the forehead before turning and walking back up the stairs. Elsa waited for the car to pull away before she closed the door.

The Middle Men

Harry and William watched Death as he swooped around the summit of the hill, his black robes floating in the wind behind him.

"Woohoo, look at me! I'm Batman!"

"Batman? Pfft! The Joker more like!" William was still nursing a bit of a grudge over Danny's accident. He couldn't yet see how it was supposed to have helped.

"Oh, leave him alone, he's having some fun. Give him a break," said Harry.

After a few minutes, Death came to lie beside them on the grass. Pointing at the few fluffy clouds in the sky he said, "Rabbit! Duck! Flower! Airplane!"

Harry started laughing. "That *is* an airplane!"

"I know that," replied Death, "but William here is SO old, I wasn't sure if they'd been invented before he died."

"Cheeky bugger!" William couldn't help but smirk. All these years as mates and Death still gave out to him.

"Aye, aye! What's this?" Death sat up.

Harry and William also sat up, to see what Death was looking at. They saw two figures nearby – an older man standing alongside a younger one. They looked like father and son. They watched for a few moments after which the younger man walked away, leaving the older man standing on his own. Some time had passed by when he turned around and began walking towards them.

"Alright there, Arthur?" asked Death.

"I am now, thank you."

"Is that you moving on?"

With a smile, Arthur Rowland replied, "Yes, I believe so. I'm ready to go now."

Death shook Arthur's hand. "Good luck, mate. Look after yourself."

"Thank you. You too."

Arthur nodded at William and Harry before walking away. Within a few steps he began to fade until, barely a moment later, he was gone.

Harry and William looked at each other in surprise. It wasn't often they saw someone moving on right in front of them, most of the beings usually went off somewhere private.

"Well he wasn't for hanging around, was he?" said Harry.

William and Harry looked over at Death who was now floating horizontally in mid-air, his robes once again billowing behind him. His left arm was stretched out in front of him, his hand curled up in a fist and he was yelling "SUPERMAN" at the top of his voice.

William glanced at Harry and said drily, "Can't say I blame him, do you?"

Harry shrugged and was about to respond when he saw how far Charlie and Elsa had walked down the hill. He called out, "C'mon, guys, it looks like we're out of here," and they began following the trio back to the car.

Chapter Thirty-Four

"Hey, you guys, wonderful to see you. Come in, come in!" Sukie held the door open for Guy and his husband to enter.

"Sukie, this is my husband Nigel. Nigel, this is Sukie Wallace."

"Hi, it's lovely to meet you and, if you don't mind me saying, you are bloody gorgeous! Guy didn't tell me his other half was a model. Move over Will Smith!"

Nigel laughed, the deep, hearty sound filling the hallway nearly as well as he did. At six foot three inches in his socks, and with a physique suitable for any rugby player, he was certainly an eye-catching man.

"Mrs Wallace, you are far too kind."

Sukie felt herself melting at the sound of his rich Jamaican tones. "Nigel, your voice is wonderful. I could listen to it all day. And please, call me Sukie."

Guy moved over to stand by Sukie and said, "Sukie Wallace, are you making a move on my man?"

With a grin, she replied, "Guy, I've seen you eyeing up *my* man when you thought I wasn't looking, I'm simply returning the favour!"

They all burst out laughing.

"So, you *have* been eyeing up Pete Wallace on your visits…" Nigel gave Guy a stern look.

Still laughing, Guy looked at Sukie. "Well, clearly YOU can't be trusted with a secret!"

She threw her hands up in front of her saying, "Guilty as charged!" before turning towards the stairs. "Come, let me show you to your room where you can refresh at your leisure. We're outside in the garden, so join us there when you're ready."

Danny was going home the next day and they'd decided to hold a small leaving party for him. Sukie was really going to miss him. Pete was now very busy preparing for his forthcoming tour – his first since he'd been shot – and having Danny around had been both company and a distraction for her, keeping her mind away from the constant worry which now plagued her.

Walking out into the garden, she announced Guy and Nigel's arrival, saying they'd be down shortly. Kara and Gareth had arrived last night and were staying for most of the week to work with Pete on the tour details.

She went over to the twins and moved the parasols to ensure they were in the shade. Since Danny's arrival they'd both taken to drawing and it was quite comical at times to walk into a room and find the three of them sitting together, drawing to their heart's content. She really hoped they kept it up when Danny left, it was great for keeping them quiet.

Sukie got up to make introductions when she saw Guy and Nigel coming towards them, but Pete got there first so she moved over to sit down next to Kara instead and topped up both of their wine glasses before asking,

"How are things looking for the tour, Kara?"

"Very good, Sukes, very good indeed. Having fewer dates than before is a bonus and Pete's happier now we've split it into two smaller tours, so he does half of the gigs this year, time out for Christmas and New Year and then the other half in February and March."

"What about the security? Has that been tightly vetted? Are we sure there won't be a repeat incident?" Even as she was asking the question, Sukie knew it was a stupid one. Pete being shot the first time, during a performance in Italy, had been a highly unusual occurrence meaning the chance of it happening again was almost impossible. That didn't stop her worrying about it though. Lightning striking twice happens far more often than people realise.

Kara placed her hand on Sukie's arm to reassure her. "It'll all be okay. Security guards in the UK don't carry guns and it will be incredibly difficult for someone to get one into the auditorium. All the venues are equipped with bag and body scanners so everyone, and every bag, will be x-rayed upon entry. I understand your concerns, Sukie but, honestly, he's going to be fine."

Suddenly, they heard Pete's voice exclaim, "Oh, that's a great idea. Let's do it!"

"Let's do what?" Sukie asked.

"Visit that pretty little pub in the village. The one we always say we want to visit whenever we pass by," Pete replied. "Nigel was asking what it's like inside and I had to confess we hadn't yet been in."

"If I had a pub like that on my doorstep, I'd never be out of it," said Nigel.

"We've been saying for a while we'd like to go in, but it's never been the right occasion. And I'm always worried about Pete being mobbed. I don't think his disguises would last for long under close scrutiny."

Sukie's uncertainty was clear in her voice.

"But there are quite a few of us today, Sukie, I think it's safe to say there is safety in numbers. We always said we wanted our lives here to be as normal as possible but, the longer we stay holed up in the house, the more of a novelty we become to the locals. If we want to be treated as normal by the villagers, then we need to act it. And that means going to the pub on the odd occasion."

Sukie knew that now the idea was lodged in his mind, Pete really wanted to go. "What about the twins?" she asked.

"I'll look after them."

Sukie turned to her mum. "Don't you want to come with us?"

"No, darling, I'll be fine. Jordie and I have been in a few times already. It's very nice. You'll like it."

"You've been to the pub and not told us?"

Beth grinned at her daughter. "Yes, Sukie, Jordie and I do have our own lives, you know. We don't have to tell you everything. And, being a LOT lower profile than Pete or yourself, nobody bothers with us apart from when they need to serve us. So off you go, have some fun, I'll stay here with the twins. Look, they're almost asleep anyway so they'll be no trouble."

The rest of the party were already gathering their bits and pieces together so, with a shrug of her shoulders, Sukie realised she might as well join them.

Within a few minutes, everyone was walking along the pathway that came out at the side of the church. Upon their arrival in the village, there was a quick discussion over which pub to visit – 'The Inn on the Green' which overlooked the village or 'The Cat and Cow' down past the car park where Danny had parked up that fateful day. The decision was unanimous – 'The Inn on the Green'.

The pretty hanging baskets, thatched roof and olde-worlde, bay windows were far too appealing to ignore.

The woman behind the bar looked up from the lemons she was slicing when the party of seven walked in the door. It was a quiet Saturday afternoon and Pete surmised the local cricket team must be playing away as there weren't many customers.

The bartender was washing her hands as Pete nervously approached the bar.

"Good afternoon, Mr Wallace, welcome to The Inn on the Green. What can I get you?"

"Um.... er... Good afternoon. May I have two lager-tops, one dark ale and four glasses of dry white wine please?" Pete was slightly taken aback at her forthright greeting. He was used to people trying to play it cool and pretending not to know who he was. The bartender's straightforward, no-frills approach was very refreshing and he felt his nerves easing away.

"No problem, Mr Wallace. Would those be pints?"

"Yes, and please, call me Pete."

"I'm Percy Meadows, the landlady." Percy stuck her hand across the bar. Pete shook it as she carried on, "It's lovely to see you in here, I hope you'll feel comfortable enough to become a regular. I can assure you that you'll never get any hassle here and, if anyone tries anything, they'll be out of that door faster than a jet-propelled fart!"

Pete laughed at her words and, as four glasses and a bottle of wine in an ice-bucket – "That's more practical than glasses" – were placed in front of him, he picked them up and carried them to the table. He was grinning as he collected the remaining drinks, paid the bill and sat back down. Sukie raised an eyebrow towards him, asking if everything was okay. He smiled and nodded back. Yes, everything was absolutely fine.

He took a long drink of his shandy before turning to

Danny to ask what his plans were for when he returned to London.

"Get back to work and catch up with that. I'll be lucky if I can see my desk on Monday. Give Prissy loads of fuss because I've missed her terribly, and then I'll begin sorting out the two paintings you've commissioned. They'll be my priority."

Pete exchanged a look with Sukie who smiled back at him.

He cleared his throat, and spoke a bit louder to get everyone's attention. "I have a small announcement to make. Or rather, I have some good news for Danny, but I know he'll be happy with me sharing it."

He turned towards Danny and asked, "Danny, have you heard of the art dealer Jeff Rowland?"

The look of awe on Danny's face answered the question. "Have I? Who hasn't? He's a legend in the art world. Anyone who gets to show in his gallery is practically guaranteed world-wide success."

Pete smiled at his reply. "Well, there's a chance that *you* might be his next success. I've spoken with him and he's agreed to see you. He wants you to provide him with a selection of your work. To give you time to prepare, he's asked if the first Saturday in August would be acceptable. That's just over a month from now. Can you do that?"

His face shining with excitement, Danny replied, "Oh, my goodness! Jeff Rowland has agreed to see ME?"

"He sure has. Are you okay with that?"

"Pete, I am MORE than okay with that and the timing is perfect. I'll be there! Thank you."

Hey, don't thank me, Danny. All I did was orchestrate an introduction. The rest, my friend, is up to you."

A short time later, Pete noticed Danny wasn't joining in the chatter. When he looked, he saw him staring into space, no doubt already thinking about what he could show to the most revered art dealer in the country.

Chapter Thirty-Five

July

Danny was standing at the bar in the pub in Covent Garden. It was Friday evening and the place was rammed tight with bodies. When he'd sent Sandra the text, asking for them to meet, he'd suggested one of the quieter, smaller pubs down a nearby side street but Sandra had replied she would meet him here.

He took another sip of his beer and noted he'd already drunk half of it – a sure sign he was nervous. He was officially breaking things off with Sandra tonight. They hadn't seen each other for over three months – he'd worked out he hadn't seen her since the last week in March – and had barely spoken to each other since then. It made perfect sense to end it all properly, so they could move on. Given that Sandra had only sent him one text, and hadn't bothered to call him the entire time he'd been living with Pete and Sukie, he guessed she wouldn't be too upset anyway.

Guy had already read him the riot act and had told him that, under no circumstances, was he to change his mind. If she began crying, he was to ignore her and stick to his guns. Danny had already said he didn't anticipate any objection from Sandra to which Guy had just grunted while muttering, "We'll see…"

He looked at his watch and saw that, as usual, Sandra was late. Seeing a couple get up from a nearby table, he quickly grabbed his pint and moved over to it. He hadn't fancied trying to break the news to her while standing at the bar.

From where he was now sitting, he could see the clock over the bar. Sandra was fifteen minutes late. Danny sighed. He just wanted her to hurry up and arrive. The sooner she got here, the sooner he could break the news and the sooner he could get out of the place. He'd never liked this pub – too many tourists and too much false atmosphere. He licked his lips nervously and took another sip of his beer, as he willed her to get a move on.

Sandra stood outside the pub watching Danny through the window. She'd planned this evening down to a 'T' and turning up twenty minutes late was the first part of her plan. Let Danny sweat for a bit, thinking she wasn't going to turn up and then, when she did, he'd be so grateful to see her he would forgive her tardiness. Once he'd bought her a drink – she didn't yet know how she was going to avoid his curiosity when she asked for something non-alcoholic – she'd indulge in a bit of small talk before dropping the bombshell. She already knew how the rest of the evening would pan out – Danny would be shocked, then surprised, then overjoyed with her news. He would immediately ask her to marry him and they'd go back to hers to break the news to her parents. They wouldn't get married until after the baby was born, however, as she wasn't walking down the aisle looking like a beached whale. Oh no! She had that all planned out too. But…, first things first! She was about to walk into the pub as a single woman for the last time. When she walked out, she'd be engaged. She ran her fingers through her hair and checked her lipstick on her reflection in the window before taking a deep breath and pulling the door open.

Danny glanced up and saw Sandra sashaying towards him. He tried not to smirk at how ridiculous she looked. Some women have the ability to walk in such a manner that it looks sleek and sexy, some do not. Sandra fell squarely into the latter category. When she caught him looking, she gave him what, she no doubt believed was, a sexy pout. Yet again, she was unable to carry the gesture off in the intended manner. She reached the table and Danny stood up to pull out the chair opposite for her to sit down. He asked what she wanted to drink and didn't bat an eyelid when she requested a soda water with lime. He shuffled his way through the crowd to the bar. While waiting to be served, he tried to quell his churning stomach as he thought of what he was about to do.

Once served, he made his way back, sat down, and passed Sandra her drink. He took a large swallow of his beer before looking at her, preparing to do the deed. Small talk first, he thought, I can't just come out and say it.

"How are you, Sandra? You're looking well," he said, noting how her eyes were sparkling and her skin was glowing. He wondered if she'd been on the sunbeds again.

"Thank you, Danny, I'm very well as it happens."

When it became clear she wasn't going to return the greeting or make an enquiry after his own health, Danny asked her how work was going and how her parents were keeping. Each time she gave him a short, sharp answer but still didn't ask anything in return. It wasn't long before they fell silent.

Danny eventually cleared his throat and said, "I've got something to tell you."

Sandra smiled. "Funny, I've got something to tell you too."

"Really? Well, in that case, after you." He knew she was about to break it off with him and breathed a sigh of relief. He wasn't going to be the bad guy after all. His relief however, was short-lived.

"Oh no, Danny, after you! After all, you said it first." Sandra smiled again.

Shit! Clearing his throat again, he drew in a breath and said, "I think it's time we split up, Sandra. This relationship is going nowhere, so the best thing for both of us would be to knock it on the head and go our separate ways."

Sandra didn't reply as she sat with a dreamy look on her face.

"Err… Sandra, did you hear what I said?"

"Oh, if you insist, yes, I'll marry you… WHAT? What did you just say?" Sandra sat bolt upright.

Danny looked at Sandra open-mouthed. Marry her? Was she off her trolley? Where on earth had she gotten that idea from? He felt sick at the very thought of being stuck with Sandra for the rest of his life. Now that he'd finally woken up to what a self-centred creature she was, he couldn't wait to be done with her and get on with his life. He'd finally seen what Guy had picked up on so quickly when they'd first gotten together. He took another drink of beer and quickly repeated what he'd said.

Sandra's mouth opened and closed a few times before a malicious little smirk took it over. "Who the *hell* do you think you are, Danny Delaney, breaking up with me? Don't you realise that you're the lucky one in this relationship? Well, *sweetie*, I don't think we will be splitting up, because you see… There's really no easy way to put this… I'm pregnant!"

Chapter Thirty-Six

Almost choking on his beer, Danny spluttered it across the table. He pulled a tissue from his pocket and tried to mop up some of the mess, using the time to take in what Sandra had just said.

"You're what? Are you sure?" he finally replied. "How did that happen? And when – I haven't seen you for over three months?"

Sandra sniggered as she witnessed Danny's shock. "Yes, I'm sure. The doctor reckons I'm about thirteen to fourteen weeks which works out exactly when we were last together."

"You've been to the doctor and had it confirmed?" He felt a cold sweat break out across his body. He'd hoped she'd said it for a joke, in retaliation to his news, but now that she was talking about doctors, he was beginning to realise Sandra was being completely serious.

"Yes, it's been confirmed. Here's the proof." She threw a picture in front of him. It was the photo from her scan the week before. The dates were clearly printed along the side. He couldn't argue with her on this one.

"Are you sure it's mine?" Danny couldn't get his head around this. He always took precautions. Even if the lady in question said not to worry, she was on the pill or similar, he still wouldn't take the risk. He'd been an accident. His mother had screamed it at him often enough over the years – telling him time and time again how he'd ruined her life. He didn't want to be responsible for some other child growing up in similar circumstances.

Sandra reared up as she replied indignantly, "What are you suggesting, Danny Delaney? Are you calling me a slut? How dare you! I haven't been with anyone else. This is your child and I expect you to stand by me and do the decent thing."

"I'm sorry," he said. "It's the shock, you know. We haven't seen each other for three months. This was the last thing I was expecting to hear."

Sandra pouted again before finally replying. "Yes, fair enough. I get that. I've had a few weeks to get my head around it all."

"So, what are you planning to do? Are you keeping it?" He really didn't know what classed as appropriate questions in these circumstances.

"Of course I'm keeping it, Danny! It's our baby, why would I want to get rid of it?"

He shrugged. "I don't know. We've never talked about children, I don't know if you want them or not."

"Well, I've never been against the idea."

"I see. Naturally I'll support you and I'll be there for you in whatever way I can. You just need to let me know. I'll sort out a bank account for maintenance purposes."

Sandra stared at him. "What do you mean 'you'll support me'? Huh? What do you mean 'you'll open a bank account for maintenance'? Eh?" Sandra narrowed her eyes and spoke harshly. "You'll fucking marry me, Danny Delaney. I'm not going to be a single mother, living in a council house with some snot-nosed brat hanging off my skirt! You're responsible for this, so you'll treat me right. You're going to propose and then we're going home to tell my parents the good news. For fuck's sake, I've got a bottle of champagne chilling in the fridge. Tesco's finest range too – none of that cheap stuff!"

Danny looked at Sandra and saw the meanness on her face. She didn't care about him, she didn't care about anybody. She just cared about herself. This was all about her.

"Sandra, I am not marrying you. You can get that idea out of your head right now."

"Oh yes you are! Once I tell my father what you've done, he'll make you marry me."

Danny couldn't prevent the snort of laughter which burst from his lips. He liked Joe Harrison. He was a nice man but totally under the thumb of his blowsy wife Anita. Anita and Sandra were two peas in a pod. If he wanted to see Sandra twenty years from now, he only had to look at her mother. It was not comfortable viewing. She treated Joe badly, talking to him as though he was dirt. She'd always felt she'd been short-changed with her lot in life and this same belief had been passed on to Sandra. If he had cause to be scared of anyone in that family, it was her mother, not her father.

Danny took another drink of his pint, feeling better for his outburst. It had broken the tension inside him although, looking at Sandra, he could see she was furious with him.

He leant forward and said, "Sandra, this is the twenty-first century. Your father cannot force me to marry you. Times have changed and, I can quite categorically tell you, I will not be marrying you. Now, I suggest you go home and we can meet again tomorrow to discuss this further. Do you want me to walk you to the station?"

"You're a bastard, Danny Delaney. How dare you do this to me! I'm ruined now. Well, we'll see. You'll marry me! Let me tell you that right now. I'll damn well make sure you do."

Danny sighed. "No, you won't, Sandra. Now, do you want me to walk you to the station?"

Sandra stood up as she answered him. "No, I damn well don't. You can stay here and rot!" With her words, she picked up her drink and threw it in Danny's face before turning around and storming out of the pub.

Chapter Thirty-Seven

Sukie gazed around the barn. Guy had worked wonders and it looked fantastic. The fairy lights twinkled above her head and around the door frames. The deep red table cloths looked fabulous and the cream centre pieces were beautiful. It was exactly what her mother had asked for – simple, classy, and elegant.

In the kitchen, she could hear the caterers setting up and the waiters were already putting the finishing touches to the tables. The polished glasses sparkled in the sunlight streaming through the windows. The weather forecast had predicted today was going to be a warm one and, not wanting the barn to get too stuffy, the double doors along the side were open wide. They led into a marquee which had been erected for dancing purposes later. Some air conditioning units were already blowing in there and the cool air was wafting through into the barn.

They had fifty guests in total, made up of friends and family, including Jordie's parents who had arrived last night. They were a lovely couple although his mum, Mags, was a spirited one. She'd told them a few stories last night which had had them all in fits of laughter. Beth had met her a few times and had warned Sukie what to expect. Sally, Jordie's sister-in-law, and Pete's housekeeper at the schloss, had flown in from Austria, having promised Pete that the lady from the village, who she'd entrusted the care of his beloved dogs to, was more than capable of looking after them for three days. Laura, Beth's best friend, was her matron of honour.

It promised to be a great day and everyone was looking forward to it.

Sukie left the barn satisfied everything was in place and under control. Time for her to go and get the twins dressed, and herself. She didn't think her mum would be too impressed if she turned up wearing the stained jogging pants she was currently sporting.

When she arrived back at the house, she found Guy walking up and down the hallway, his phone held tightly to his ear. She raised her eyebrows, silently asking him if everything was okay. He just shook his head and walked into the dining room, closing the door behind him. He and Nigel had arrived yesterday afternoon and Danny was driving up this morning. Sukie was looking forward to seeing him again. She'd missed his gentle, easy company. She knew she wasn't the only one. Pete and the twins had also been a bit lost without him. In the weeks he'd been here, he'd gone from being Poppy's saviour to becoming a member of the family. Sukie made a mental note to tell him this when she saw him later. She glanced at the time on the grandfather clock in the hallway and quickly ran up the stairs. She was walking Beth down the aisle and it would be very bad form if she stole the bride's thunder by turning up late herself.

Guy listened to Danny on the other end of the phone. He couldn't believe what he was hearing. Not for one second did he believe Danny was the father of Sandra's baby. He knew that he was careful about taking precautions and the reasons why. He wondered if the conniving bitch had stuck a pin in the condom when Danny was out of the room. He wouldn't put such a thing past her and said as much.

"Guy, even if she did, there's not much I can do about it now. If that kid has my DNA then I'll be expected to pay for it, regardless of how it came to be conceived."

"I hope you'll be demanding a DNA test as soon she's pushed it out."

"Well, that might be a bit soon, but I'll certainly want one."

"Pity they can't do them in the womb, it would save a whole heap of heartache in the long run." Guy couldn't help but be scathing in his remarks. He hadn't liked the stuck-up little madam from the minute he'd set eyes on her and he didn't trust her in the slightest. It all seemed a little too convenient for his liking. How many times over the last three years had she and Danny had sex but, oh so conveniently, the very last time was when she'd fallen pregnant. Guy reckoned she'd begun to realise that Danny was waking up to her manipulative nature so she'd found a way of keeping him by her side. Guy still had the voicemail message she'd left him at New Year and, when he got back to London, he was going to make sure Danny heard it. In the meantime, until that DNA test was done and it was proven to be Danny's child, he was never going to be convinced that it was.

"So, what's happening now?" he asked.

"I don't know." Danny sighed at the other end of the phone. "It's really thrown me, obviously, and I still haven't come to terms with it yet. She's agreed to meet this afternoon to discuss it further.

"What's to discuss, Danny? Until you know for a fact

the baby is yours, you don't need to have anything to do with her."

"Guy, I'm the product of a woman who was badly let down by the man who fathered me. It turned her into a bitter and twisted alcoholic druggie which, in turn, made my childhood an absolute misery. There's no way I could inflict that on another child. It wouldn't be fair. And, if it *is* my child, then I want to know I did right by it from the start. Not when I had too!"

Guy couldn't say anything to that. They'd discussed Danny's upbringing many times and he'd shared some of the horrors his mother had put him through. Danny always excused her by saying it was the nature of the disease. Alcoholics hurt those they are closest to. Guy refused to buy that however. He thought it was a disgrace that the one person who was supposed to look after you, nurture you and keep the bad people away had turned out to *be* the bad person in Danny's young life. He'd only met Danny's mother once – when Danny had received a phone call from the hospital, saying his mother had been taken in with a suspected overdose. They'd been out together at the time so they'd both gone to the hospital. Now that he thought about it, he could see a lot of Danny's mother in Sandra Harrison – petulant, whining, moaning about her lot in life, and thinking she deserved better but hadn't cared enough to try and be something better. She just thought it was delivered to you on a silver platter.

"So, if you're seeing her this afternoon, does that mean you're not coming up for the wedding?" Guy already knew the answer. The fact the wedding was due to begin in ninety minutes and Danny was still in south London told him he wasn't coming.

"I can't, Guy. I've barely slept a wink all night and I feel like an extra from The Walking Dead. I wouldn't trust myself behind the wheel of the car right now. Besides, I need to talk to Sandra and get some things sorted out. Now that the shock is wearing off, I need to put some plans in place. Until I'm told otherwise, I need to consider that the baby is mine."

Guy sighed. Danny's decency could sometimes be his undoing, but he understood where his friend was coming from. The best he could do was to be there for him and support him through this. Giving him a hard time wasn't doing that.

"What do I tell Sukie and Pete? They've been really looking forward to seeing you."

"Tell them the truth. Tell them what's happened. I want them to know the real reason for my not being there. I don't want to make any petty excuses that might make them feel I've let them down. Sukie'll understand. Tell her I'll call her through the week."

"No worries, mate, I'll do that for you."

"Thanks, Guy, I appreciate it."

"Danny, before you go, I just want you to know that I'm here for you. Whatever I can do to help, you just let me know, okay? You're not alone in this. I'll do whatever you need."

"Be nice to Sandra?"

"Don't push your luck! I have limits!"

The two of them burst out laughing and then said their goodbyes.

Guy ended the call, and putting the phone back in his pocket, let out a stream of expletives that would have made a coalminer blush. It looked as though Danny had been caught out by the oldest trick in the book and there wasn't a damn thing he could do about it.

He gave the pouffe in front of the fireplace a hard kick before going to find Sukie to break the bad news.

Sukie was standing at the back of the barn beside the photographer. The day was going well and her mum and Jordie were now officially married. Beth looked absolutely radiant and Jordie looked as though he had won every lottery on the planet. He hadn't stopped smiling all day. It warmed Sukie right through to see them both so happy. After all these years on her own, it was wonderful to know Beth would have someone so loving and caring by her side in her later years.

She took a look around the room and realised there was nothing left for her to do. The speeches had been made, the toast had been raised and, in a few moments, the barn doors would open, leading the way into the marquee for the dancing to commence. She could finally kick back and relax.

She tried to catch Guy's eye – she wanted to know more on why Danny hadn't made it. She knew he'd been really looking forward to it and she'd hoped to introduce him to Elsa, thinking he may have liked to know someone from the gallery before he had to take his work in for Jeff. At the thought of her best friend, Sukie scanned the room until she found her sitting talking to Kara. She narrowed her eyes as she peered at Elsa. There was something different about her, but she couldn't put her finger on exactly what it was. She was considerably more relaxed, and Sukie could see more of the girl her friend had been when she'd been in her twenties – confident, outgoing and funny. Looking at her now, and seeing these positive changes, it dawned on Sukie just how hard it must have been for Elsa. She realised she had become used to the heavy sadness her friend had been shrouded in. There was no doubt the move to London and her new job with Jeff had done wonders for her. Sukie caught sight of Guy moving behind Elsa and managed to get his attention. She discretely gestured to the balcony area above them. Guy nodded he would meet her up there.

She'd only been waiting five minutes when he appeared at the doorway to one of the alcoves. It looked like a little fairy-tale den with the small dormer window, low ceiling and fairy lights strung across it. He was carrying an ice-bucket and two wine glasses which he placed on the table in between the two soft, deep sofas. Sukie was reclining across one of them, her shoes off and her feet on the little windowsill, trying to catch a breeze through the open window. Guy poured her a glass of prosecco and handed it over.

"Oh, thank you, Guy. I know I've had a few of these today but this is the one I'm really going to enjoy. I'm now officially finished in my role as wedding co-ordinator. Cheers!"

She took a long drink of the wine, before lying back on the sofa cushions. "Okay, spill the beans. Why's Danny not here today?"

Not mincing his words, Guy repeated everything Danny had told him. Sukie sat up as he relayed the phone call from that morning.

"No! She can't be… Seriously…?" She looked at him in disbelief.

"Yes, seriously!" Guy's flat tone said it all.

"Oh no! How is Danny? That must have been one hell of a shock. Especially as he was supposed to be finishing the relationship last night! He called me before he left work to say he was dreading seeing Sandra but he was absolutely sticking to his intention to go through with it. I wished him good luck!" She looked at Guy in dismay.

Guy gave a wry grin. "I don't think you jinxed him, love!"

"Did he say how Sandra was coping? It must be quite a shock for her too."

"Knowing how low my opinion is of her, Danny

didn't go into too much detail on that. I'll find out more when I see him next week and I'll keep you updated."

"Yes, you must."

Sukie picked up her glass, and draining the rest of her wine, she held it out for Guy to refill. She felt heart-sore for Danny. Just as he was beginning to sort out where he wanted to go with his life, life had come right back and kicked him in the nuts! Some folks just never seemed to get the breaks.

Chapter Thirty-Eight

Two weeks later, Danny was standing in his attic looking through his artwork, trying to decide which pieces to put in his portfolio for Jeff Rowland. He knew a cross-section of everything he had was best but due to the time he'd been in Oxfordshire, most of what he had was drawings. So far, he'd managed to get two oil paintings done and a third was now drying in the corner. He'd also had an idea for a quartet of smaller pieces and would be starting them tomorrow. Hopefully he'd complete them by the middle of the week if he worked into the night. He was staring at some water colours, trying to decide if any were good enough, when he heard a knock on his front door. Sighing, he went to answer it. He already knew it was Guy and he really wished he'd use the spare key he'd been given. It would be so much easier, especially now that he was painting again and was often deep in concentration when Guy came round – which was proving to be rather a lot since Sandra had dropped her bombshell. If he didn't know better, he'd have said Guy was checking up on him, making sure he wasn't getting too cosy with her again.

He opened the door and Guy walked in. "Hey, Dan, look what came out this week. I figured we could watch this over pizza and a few tinnies – what d'ya reckon? Up for it?" Guy held up the DVD of a film they'd both been keen to see. In his other hand he had a see-through carrier bag with several cans of lager and beer in it.

"Hmmm... I don't fancy pizza. But I could certainly do a Chinese."

"I'm not fussed as long as it's food. I'm starving."

Danny laughed at Guy's comment – he was always starving. He'd never known anyone eat the way he did. And he never put on any weight either. Guy told him it was his daily 'step routine' to blame for that – up the stepladder, down the stepladder, up the stepladder, down the stepladder. And that would be just one curtain he'd be hanging. When you factored in the other nine... Who said being an interior designer was an easy job?

"Here, let me put these in the fridge to chill and you can help me to decide which paintings to take to Jeff Rowland before we order food. You'll be more impartial – I'm struggling a bit."

"Okay, no worries."

Danny went into the kitchen while Guy made his way up the attic stairs.

He joined him up there a few minutes later and saw Guy had already pulled out a number of pictures and was lining them up in the light coming through the skylights.

"Definitely these two, without a doubt," he said, pointing at two pictures he'd put side by side.

"Are you sure you're not being biased with those choices, my friend?" Danny grinned as he looked at the two pictures of Prissy lying sprawled out on her back, catching a sunbeam that was streaming through a window. The first picture was a standard portrait and he'd managed to capture the essence of his haughty little madam perfectly. The second was a copy of the first but he'd decided to have a play about and had tried a cubist style – it had worked surprisingly well and Guy had adored it from the first moment he'd laid eyes on it. Danny had promised him he could have it after he'd been to visit Jeff.

Slowly, Guy picked out six more pieces and lined them up together. He stood back to look at them all side by side. Eventually he turned to Danny and said, "Yup! I'd say those are the ones to take in. You've got a good mix of subjects and I think they show your versatility."

Going over to stand beside him, Danny nodded his agreement. The eight paintings in front of them were the same ones he'd felt he should take to Jeff Rowland, but he'd wanted to see which ones Guy would choose. Happy they were in agreement, he moved them carefully to one side, ready to be wrapped for transportation in a couple of weeks.

He turned back to Guy and saw him standing in front of his second easel, looking at the other painting he was working on. It was the first of the two paintings commissioned by Pete and Sukie. This was the one of Jordie holding Drew up in the air. He planned to add it to those he was taking to Jeff, if it was finished in time.

Without preamble, Guy said, "This is exceptional. Truly, it's by far the best of everything you've done. The way you've caught the light here and the shadows there, I almost feel as though I'm back in Sukie's garden, watching Jordie swinging Drew around. It really is stunning."

"Thanks, Guy. I feel that one's a bit more special too, but I put it down to actually knowing the subjects. I can't wait for Pete and Sukie to see it. I hope they like it."

"Like it? Mate, they are going to LOVE it! Take my word for it."

"Cheers! Well, now that's done, let's go and sort out that takeaway before you fade away to nothing eh?"

Ninety minutes later, having demolished a hefty plate of noodles, chicken, and prawn crackers, Guy asked Danny if he'd seen or heard from Sandra recently.

"Sort of! I get a couple of texts every other day. She's usually whining over something. Her last one said she's going to have to stop working because it's too tiring to stand all day."

"I thought she always had that problem. She gets tired just thinking about work!" Guy's dry tone said it all and Danny couldn't disagree with him. It was no secret that Sandra was lazy. In the three years he'd known her, he'd lost count of how many jobs she'd been through. She seemed to move on every two or three months. She'd tell Danny she was bored, or the other members of staff were horrible to her but, eventually, he began to suspect she was being fired and the 'horrible' people were probably her bosses telling her to pull her weight.

Danny smiled. "She followed it up with telling me I would have to support her and give her a weekly allowance."

Guy spat out the mouthful of lager he'd just taken. He grabbed some kitchen towel from the coffee table in front of him and dabbed at his top while looking at his friend in horror. "Please tell me you didn't agree to that?"

Danny laughed at the sight of Guy looking so horrified. "No, I didn't but I did turn it back on her though. I said I wasn't giving her money, but she was welcome to come and live here, in the spare room, if that helped in any way."

"How does that turn it back on her?"

"She doesn't give her parents any money, but she doesn't know I'm aware of that. She was trying to make out that it was unfair for them to have to pay for her. So I said she could come here and live rent free and I'd be happy to buy in extra food."

"Please tell me she didn't say yes…" The thought of her getting her feet under Danny's table was too much for Guy to bear thinking about.

"Of course she didn't! She'd have to do housework and actually look after herself here, especially with me being at work all day. If she stays at home, she's got mummy dearest to run around after her and be her little slave. This way, however, she can't say I haven't offered to help. And, it was all on messenger, so I have a copy if she ever tries to pull a fast one on me."

Guy looked at Danny with something akin to admiration. "Nice one, mate!"

He picked up two fresh cans, popped them open and poured them into their glasses. He lifted his up, tilted it in Danny's direction and said, "So, here's to you finally growing a pair! Long may they last!"

Danny smiled, nodding at Guy as he took a drink. He had to admit he did feel just a little bit proud of himself for standing up to Sandra. It had given him a little bit of a buzz inside that he rather liked the feel of.

Chapter Thirty-Nine

Elsa picked the tray up off the worktop and carried it through to the lounge, placing it on the coffee table. She carefully lifted the teacup and saucer and put them on the table, doing the same with the matching teapot, milk jug and sugar bowl. She also had a small plate with two Jaffa Cakes on it. She returned the tray to the kitchen before sitting down on the sofa. She poured herself some tea and added the milk. She didn't take sugar, but Harry always had, and the bowl was there for that reason.

She took a sip from the pretty china cup, sat back on the sofa, crossed her legs and pulled the large book by her side onto her lap. She gently stroked the soft white, leather embossed, cover before carefully opening it.

Tucked inside the cover was a pressed white rose from her wedding bouquet. Harry had pulled it out and presented it to her as part of his wedding speech when he'd declared the flower in his hand represented his heart and he was giving it to Elsa to look after and cherish until death did them part. She brought the flower to her lips, remembering how Harry had kissed it before he'd given it to her.

She put it to the side and turned the thick heavy page which announced that this was the wedding album of Harry and Elsa Clairmont. Her hand came to rest on the thin piece of tissue paper which protected the photographs and she could make out the hazy picture underneath of them both kissing as a flurry of confetti and rose petals flew around them.

She stopped to take another sip of her tea and check that Puddle wasn't up to mischief in the garden, giving herself a moment to steady her insides before moving the tissue aside. She looked at the photograph in front of her. Eleven years ago today it had been taken and they had both looked as carefree and happy as any other young couple on their wedding day.

Her breath caught in her throat. She hadn't looked at the album for seven years. Harry had died just a few weeks short of their fifth wedding anniversary. Prior to that, they'd had a little ritual whereby, on each anniversary, they would stay at home together, make themselves a 'proper' pot of tea using the dinner service they'd been given as a wedding present and go through the album, remembering their special day, after which they would watch their wedding DVD.

After Harry had died, Elsa had buried the two items away at the bottom of the wardrobe in the spare bedroom where she would never see them and, when she'd moved into Sukie's flat, she had repeated the act, covering them up and rushing out of the room as quickly as possible. Even seeing the box the album was stored in had been too much for her. She couldn't bear the thought of looking at it without Harry by her side and it had been easier to put it somewhere where she never saw it at all.

Now, however, it was time for her to face this final demon. She'd come so far this year, but she still had this last hurdle to get over. Today was their wedding anniversary and it felt like the right time to do it. Somehow, it seemed symbolic. Once she'd done this, she would be entirely free to move on. She had closed so many doors already this year. After this, her old life would finally be over. There would be no more ghosts to carry forward. She'd have finally laid them all to rest.

She picked up a Jaffa Cake, nibbling around the edges as she turned the pages, seeing Harry gazing out at her time and again. So far, she was managing not to cry, which was a surprise. She had the box of tissues nearby, ready to soak up the deluge. When she turned to the next page, she began giggling. For there, on the crisp, creamy page was a big chocolatey smudge. She remembered it so well. It had been their second anniversary, and they'd both been snuggled up on the sofa, eating their Jaffa Cakes when Harry had dropped a bit of chocolate on the page. He'd flicked it off and, in doing so, had left a long chocolate smear in its wake. Elsa had been furious. She'd always been so careful with the album – when they'd first gotten it back from the photographer, and everyone had been clamouring to see it, she'd always ensured that all hands were spotless and she was the only one allowed to turn the pages. She'd breathed a big sigh of relief when it had finally done the rounds of friends and family and could be stored back in its box. So, when Harry had been the one to mark it... Well, the sparks had flown!

Now, however, she was so glad it had happened. She lightly touched her finger to the smudge and smiled – another special memory that she hadn't appreciated at the time. One thing was for sure, losing Harry and the journey she'd been on since had made her realise how much we all take those we love for granted and how many ordinary days are actually very special because of the small things that go on to become treasured memories.

Slowly, she made her way to the end of the album, stopping only when she got to the last photograph. This had been their favourite. The photographer had finally ceased snapping away, and was packing away her outdoor equipment, when the two of them had sneaked away to enjoy a solitary moment behind some bushes, where they'd tried to absorb the events of the day. They'd been looking into each other's eyes, whispering 'my husband' and 'my wife' and giggling at the sound of it. They hadn't been aware of anyone, least of all the photographer, coming to usher them inside for the indoor shots. When she'd found them, and noticed a beautiful rose arbour above them, she had quietly raised her camera and taken a shot. As she'd expected, the natural, un-posed photograph had turned out to be the best of the lot. There had been several copies made of that one.

Elsa looked at it now and smiled again. Quietly whispering "my husband" she put the tip of her finger to her lips, kissed it and then placed it on Harry's face. She sat in the fading dusk for a while longer, lost in her thoughts and memories.

Eventually, when darkness had all but fallen and she could no longer see clearly, she closed the album, set it to one side and stood up to switch the lamps on. She called Puddle in from the garden and closed the patio doors before turning and walking to the sofa. She carefully placed the album back in its box, carried it through to the bedroom and, moving some jumpers, placed it on the top shelf of the wardrobe.

She no longer felt the need to bury it away. She had gotten through the day, and the evening, without shedding any tears. It had been close but she'd made it. She was closing the wardrobe door when she caught sight of her reflection in the mirror. She looked at herself, seeing the physical changes this year had brought. She was no longer skinny and gaunt, she'd filled out nicely and the haunted look that had been in her eyes for so long had gone. She felt like she'd been through hell since Harry had died but she'd survived it.

She had finally let him go.

She was no longer moving on.

She had moved on.

Chapter Forty

August

Danny carefully carried his paintings and sketches down from the flat and laid them gently in the back of his car. He had a selection of sheets, blankets and towels between the larger pieces that wouldn't fit into his portfolio case. He was trying not to feel nervous but failing dismally. His insides were churning worse than stormy seas and the one piece of toast he'd eaten for breakfast hadn't stayed in his stomach for very long. He still felt like he could throw up again even though his insides were empty.

Guy had come round to see him off and wish him luck but, seeing the state Danny was in, he'd nipped back home and returned with some herbal concoction to calm him down.

"I'm not taking it, Guy," he said, "but I appreciate the gesture."

Guy stood on the other side of the car and putting his

hand in his pocket, he pulled out Danny's car keys. "Well, you're not going anywhere until you do!" He waved them in the air.

Danny let out a gasp! "Give me those *right now*!"

"No! Not until you take some of that mixture." He nodded at the bottle he'd thrust in Danny's hand.

"Guy, I do not need to take this. Just give me the keys will you…"

"Dan, I am not letting you get in this car until you do something to calm those nerves. Look at you, you're shaking. You are *not* getting behind the wheel of this vehicle in that state. It's for your own good."

Danny tried to ignore his trembling hand as he looked at his watch. He didn't have time for games. He was due at the Jeff Rowland Gallery in just over an hour and he still had to fight through Saturday morning traffic to get there. "Guy, I'm going to be late. Give me the keys."

"Then drink the damn stuff and you can get going. But, until then, forget it!" Folding his arms in front of him, Guy stood his ground.

Danny uttered a few choice swear words, undid the bottle in his hand and squeezed several drops into his mouth. He shuddered as the bitter liquid hit his tongue and went down his throat.

"There, I've taken it. Can I go now?"

"Sure you can, here you are!" Guy chucked the keys over.

Danny caught them and was moving towards the car when he stopped and turned to Guy. "Do you think I'll be good enough, Guy? Do you think he'll like my work?" he asked in a small voice, his fear making it shake.

Guy walked over and placed his hands on his friend's shoulders. "Danny, what will be, will be! Personally, I think you have a lot to offer and your talent is tremendous. The Royal Academy thought so too, just keep that in mind when you speak with him. You're going to be just fine. Now go…" He pushed Danny towards the car.

As he pulled away, Danny looked in the mirror and saw Guy give him two big thumbs-up. He couldn't help but smile.

Fifty minutes later, he was in Berkeley Square and driving round to the gallery. As luck would have it, there was a space right outside. He parked up, got out and locked the car behind him. He may as well introduce himself first before hauling everything out.

He walked up the steps at the front and could see a tall man inside. The man turned and moved towards him when he stepped through the open door. Danny's first thought was, *What the hell is Clint Eastwood doing in here?* However, as the man walked closer and the sunlight from the window fell on his face, Danny saw that it wasn't Clint Eastwood but, by golly, he was a darned close second to the bloke!

"Good morning, may I help you?" The man's rich, soft, tones soothed Danny's nerves a little more. Guy's herbal stuff had helped but there was a limit to its effectiveness. He still felt jittery.

"Hi… Err… Good morning. I've got an appointment with Jeff Rowland."

"That would be me then, and I'm guessing you must be Danny Delaney as I have no other appointments today."

"Urm… Err… yes, that's me."

Jeff smiled at the man in front of him. "Have you brought me some of your work to look at?"

"Oh… Yes, yes. It's still in the car. I didn't want to drag it in straight away."

"Well, let's get it in now and we can put it out of the

way while we have a chat."

Together, the two of them walked out to the car and began to unload it. Once all the pieces and the portfolio case were inside the showroom, Danny locked the car again and followed Jeff back inside.

"If you could help me to carry these through here please…" Jeff picked up one of the oils, taking it through to one of the viewing rooms at the back. Danny did the same and followed him. Soon all of his work was lined up around the room but then, much to his surprise, Jeff shooed him out, switched off the light and closed the door. Seeing Danny's face, he smiled. "Let me show you around the showroom. Then, we can make some coffee and sit up on the roof terrace while I talk you through how this works."

"Here we go, have a seat over there." Jeff pointed Danny towards the small table and chairs in the corner. "Would you like a tea or a coffee? I'll go and bring some up."

When Jeff had gone back down the stairs, Danny gathered his thoughts. He loved the gallery and had been very impressed with the quality of the works Jeff had in stock. Some of the Old Masters he had hanging were very rare and almost never seen by the public. He felt hugely honoured to have been allowed to view them. If nothing else came of this trip, at least he would have that to take away with him. As he waited for Jeff to return, he took in the view around him. There was something quite special about London rooftops. Ever since he'd watched the chimney sweep scene from the film Mary Poppins, he'd thought there was something magical about seeing all the chimney pots from this angle. He could see a few other roof-top terraces on nearby buildings, but they were not currently occupied. It was very peaceful, and Danny felt the tension begin to ease from his body. He was here now, his work was downstairs in Jeff's viewing room and there wasn't much more he could do.

"Here we go!"

Danny turned to see Jeff walking towards him, a tray of beverages in his hands. He got up and helped him lay it out on the table. Once he was seated across from him, Jeff began explaining how he worked.

"You might be wondering why we're sitting up here and not downstairs looking through your work."

Danny nodded that he was.

"Well, firstly, I find it is easier to be more objective when the artist is not standing looking over my shoulder. Secondly, I like to take my time going through the pieces offered and noting how they make me feel. This part of the process is very important as art should make our emotions awaken. If an artist cannot make me 'feel' his work then I cannot display him in the gallery because I can't promote something I don't believe in. Thirdly, art is like music. Sometimes you'll buy an album and not really like it the first time you listen to it. But then, the second time round, it's not so bad. By the third or fourth listen, you've gotten used to it and you really like it. It has grown on you. Art is like that for me. So, I could look at your work in front of you, say I don't like it but then find myself thinking of a specific piece over the next few weeks and realise I did like it after all."

Danny smiled. "Yes, I can understand that."

Jeff carried on. "It can, however, work the other way too. Something I absolutely love the first time I see it, can wane very quickly. There are no guarantees. And that is why we're sitting up here enjoying the lovely weather."

"Thank you for explaining, I really didn't know what to expect."

"That, Danny, is only the beginning. If I decide I like

your work, I will put three or four of your pieces on display in the gallery. If those few pieces generate interest, and sell, then we will discuss putting on a full-scale exhibition and launching you into the world of art. All sales will be split fifty-fifty."

Danny's excitement was rising as Jeff spoke – an exhibition of his work? At the Rowland Gallery? That would be amazing.

Jeff's next words, however, brought it right back down to earth. "On the other hand, if, after four weeks – and it will be no more than four weeks – your work and I are not enjoying each other's company, I will get in touch, ask you to come and collect your items and thank you for taking the time to show them to me. I may, depending on what you have presented to me, suggest other galleries to approach if I think you might be a better fit for them."

Danny took this all in. Of course there was every chance Jeff wouldn't like his work, art was, after all, very personal. He just had to hope that Jeff thought he had talent and was prepared to work with him.

Jeff stopped to take a drink of his coffee. "So, now you know my process, why don't you tell me about you. Maybe you could start with when you first began painting and take it from there…"

For the next hour, Danny filled Jeff in on his early days at school, to being offered the scholarship at the Royal Academy and why he'd turned it down.

"I picked up a brush again, for the first time in twenty years, just a few months ago."

"May I ask what brought that on?"

Danny knew he couldn't tell Jeff what had happened at New Year. He'd tried to tell Guy once but no matter how hard he tried, he hadn't been able to do it! Deciding to temper the truth, he replied, "I began feeling very restless and had an overwhelming urge to do 'something'.

I didn't know, however, what that 'something' was. And then one night, I felt this urge, or pull, to dig out my art stuff and begin drawing again. I tried to put it off but, in the end, I couldn't resist. Eventually, I went up to my loft where my art materials had been stashed and well... here I am."

This time it was Jeff who nodded in agreement. "I've heard other artists say pretty much the same thing – there comes a point when the urge and desire to hold a brush or a pencil becomes too much and you have to succumb. I must say, I'm looking forward to viewing your work. Now, I'd like to make a note of all your contact details."

Danny realised their meeting was now over. He stood and followed Jeff down to the office where he pulled out the diary and Danny gave him the information he required. Jeff said, "Elsa will put this onto the system on Monday and she'll send you an email confirming the pieces we are reviewing. You should have met her today but the manager for the Knightsbridge gallery is ill, so Elsa is covering for her."

"That's unfortunate! I was looking forward to meeting her. Sukie spoke a lot about her when I was staying with her and Pete."

"Ah, not to worry, you'll meet her the next time you visit."

They shook hands and Danny said goodbye.
When he got into his car, it was nearly five full minutes before his hand stopped trembling enough for him to put the key in the ignition.

Chapter Forty-One

Elsa stood beside Jeff in the viewing room, looking at Danny's paintings laid out in front of them. It was Monday afternoon. Neither of them had spoken for about ten minutes. Jeff eventually broke the silence. "Well?"

She tilted her head to the side and took another minute before answering. "I like them!"

"What do you like exactly?"

"Lots of things! I like the way he uses the paint. You can see how the alternating between soft strokes and heavy strokes gives his work depth and definition. The use of colour to express and convey emotion is superb and his portrayal of light is excellent. These all draw you into the painting, yet the subject matter is simple and uncomplicated. I *love* this set – it's fabulous." She pointed at the four small paintings in front of her on the table. Titled 'My Generation', they showed four couples standing beside, or leaning against, some railings with Blackpool Pier behind them but each couple was wearing different clothing which depicted the nineteen forties fifties, sixties and seventies. Elsa had been drawn to them as soon as she saw them.

"What do you think? You haven't said anything yet." She looked at Jeff. He'd been very quiet so far.

"I'm not sure, to be honest. They're not setting me on fire, but I don't dislike them either. I'm not denying the talent – that is very evident – but I feel as though something is missing, although I can't say what."

"Well I think they're great. Even the watercolours look good and I'm not usually a fan."

Jeff grunted his response and looked back at the paintings. Nope! He simply wasn't feeling them.

"Tell you what, why don't we hang some out there," Elsa pointed to the hallway at the foot of the stairs, "and see how we feel after looking at them for a few days? We've got space at the moment. That large shipment isn't due in for another ten days."

"Yes, okay. That sounds like a plan for now. I'll leave you to decide what to hang and where," said Jeff and he walked out of the room.

She stood looking at the paintings again. They had a number of spare frames and mounts in the storeroom which they could put some of these in. They wouldn't look as good as if they'd been professionally framed but they would suffice for the purpose of viewing Danny's work. The more she looked at them, the more she wanted to keep looking. She really hoped Jeff would come to see them as she did.

A few hours later, Elsa stood back to scrutinise her handiwork. She was pleased with what she'd achieved. The centrepiece was the oil painting of Jordie and Drew. It really took your breath away. On one side she'd put together the sketches and watercolours Danny had done of his nineteen fifties couple. He'd drawn several of the young man with his leather jacket and quiff, holding the hand, embracing, kissing or laughing with his faceless, blonde pony-tailed girlfriend. The views behind them included the Blackpool Tower, Big Ben in London, Brighton Pier and, of course, the picture that had set off a whole chain of events – the row of thatched shops in Lower Ditchley. In the middle of the sketches and watercolours she had placed the four small 'My Generation' oils. Elsa had named this side of the display 'The Rock 'n' Roll Lovestyle Collection'.

To the right of Jordie's portrait, she'd put up Danny's drawings of Drew and Poppy playing in the garden, along with some of Beth and Sukie. He hadn't included any of Pete – Elsa surmised he hadn't felt comfortable either sketching him or, more likely, hadn't felt it appropriate to include any at this time. She put the three oil paintings of a white cat – his? she wondered – beside the portraits. In one picture, the cat was curled up, sleeping peacefully on a green cushion. The definition of the long fur was, to Elsa's eye, quite exquisite. She suspected each brush stroke had been laden with love. On either side of this, she had placed the other two pictures showing the cat lying in a sunbeam. One had been painted in a cubist style which she really liked and it made her smile each time it caught her eye.

She stepped forward from her musings to slightly straighten the cat painting and realised that, as she'd been hanging his paintings, she could feel herself being drawn to Danny Delaney. She felt as though she was getting to know him through his work and now she really wanted to meet him. From what she had been told by Sukie, and looking at the art in front of her, he seemed to be a kind and caring man. She was looking forward to when they did finally meet up. Just then, her mobile phone began to ring through in the front showroom and, giving Danny's work one last, lingering, glance, she spun on her heel and hurried through to take the call. It was probably Anna confirming what time they were meeting tonight.

That evening, Elsa and Anna were sitting at what was becoming 'their table' in the corner. They were in a pub in Shepherd Market which was now their favourite place to meet up. The pub dated back to the 1800's and Elsa loved its Olde Worlde charm with its dark wood and little snuggy nooks. She'd ventured upstairs a few times but the tight staircase with its uneven steps was not so easy to manoeuvre when coming back down after a few glasses of wine. If Gordon was with them, as he was tonight, then they were a definite no-no. His height and the low ceiling were not a match made in heaven. Gordon and Anna, on the other hand, most definitely were. Gordon had taken Anna's phone number that first night and had earned himself massive brownie points when he'd text her an hour after saying goodbye to see if they had both gotten home safely. Since then, the relationship had slowly blossomed and Anna had confided in Elsa that she had high hopes for this one.

"So how are things going with you guys?" Elsa asked. Gordon and Charlie were at the bar getting in the drinks. In one of those little funny quirks of fate, it had transpired Gordon and Charlie knew each other. Gordon was a surveyor with a large commercial surveying firm and he'd worked with Charlie on a number of his projects. This had gone a long way towards turning the little twosome of Anna and Elsa into a regular foursome.

Anna looked over at Gordon chatting to Charlie before answering. "Really good, Elsa, really good! I'm taking it slowly though. I don't want to rush things like I've done before. I *want* to dive in head first, but I'm forcing myself not to. I reckon that's where I've been going wrong, too much too soon. So I'm holding myself back a bit and I'm finding it's making everything more enjoyable and special. Does that make sense?"

"Of course it does. You're allowing yourself to enjoy the anticipation aspect of the relationship. And that is just as special. Plus, you're giving it space and time to grow. The most beautiful flowers don't grow in a day, Anna. You have to nurture them and give them time in order for something worth having to develop."

"Yeah, that's a good way of putting it. And, so far, it still feels as though it could be something beautiful."

"I hope it is, Anna. You deserve it." Elsa smiled at her friend while giving her arm a gentle rub. Over the last three months, they'd become very good friends. Elsa was delighted, and grateful, to have met her. She'd certainly made a big difference to her new life in London.

"So, what about you and Charlie? Any further progress there?"

"Not in the way you mean, Anna," she replied, laughing at Anna's comical eyebrow twitching and lewd expression. "We haven't even snogged so just behave yourself!"

"What? Not even a little peck on the cheek?"

"Well, yes, we do that when we meet up and when we say goodbye. But it hasn't gone beyond that."

"Do you want it to?"

Elsa thought for a moment before replying. "I'm not sure, if I'm being honest. I really enjoy his company and he makes me laugh. He's calmed down since we went up to the Lake District and doesn't appear to be drinking so much now, which is good. As for us, I'm not going to push it. I'll just let it develop at its own pace."

"That's fair enough. Although, I hope it does blossom into something more, then we could have a double wedding!"

At this comment, they both burst out laughing.

Charlie and Gordon heard the laughter floating across the pub, and looked over to see the ladies bent double over the table. Smiling at their happiness, they turned back towards the bar, still waiting to be served. They all loved this pub but it was always so busy, that was its only drawback.

"So, any further progress on Operation Elsa?" Gordon asked.

"Not so as you'd notice. She's not giving me any signals to show she's interested in taking this to the next level."

"Hmmm... Do you think she's still got one on her after how you met?"

Charlie and Gordon's business friendship had moved into being a personal one further to the time they were now spending in each other's company. Charlie hadn't had a good friend for some time. His best mate Artie had gone out to work in Dubai over two years ago and he'd left quite a large hole behind him. With the loss of his dad on top of that, Charlie had felt very detached and he knew his recent wild behaviour had been a poor attempt to fill the void left by losing the two people he'd cared most about. Gordon's presence, along with becoming a part of this foursome, had given him stability again. He didn't miss the shallow party life at all. He'd confided some of this to Gordon and also that he had feelings for Elsa, but he was scared of doing the wrong thing and scaring her off or pushing her away.

"Mate, as far as first impressions go, it certainly wasn't the best."

"Nor was the second or third from what you've told me!" Gordon had laughed when Charlie had first told him and he laughed again now.

"No, that's for sure. I've certainly got some ground to make up."

"I would say so. Oh, two lagers please and a bottle of Pinot Grigio with two glasses. Thank you." The barman walked off to get their order and Gordon turned to look at Charlie. "Well, my friend, I think you may need to push it to the next level soon because, if you stay just friends for too long, it'll be harder to move past that. I know you want her to *be* your friend but, you don't want her to *just* be your friend. If you want your relationship with Elsa to be more than friendship, you need to make it happen. I'm just saying…"

"Yeah, I know. You're absolutely right. I think I'm just a bit scared of losing the friendship we have. I really need it. And you guys too. All of this has made such a difference for me."

Gordon picked up their drinks and, pushing through the crush, yelled over his shoulder "Yeah, well, a feint heart never won a fair maiden. Man up!"

Charlie followed in his wake, thinking over what Gordon had said. He was right. It was time to gently push this relationship up a notch. He wasn't sure how he was going to do that exactly, but he hoped something would come to mind, and come to mind soon.

Charlie decided, as he walked Elsa home at the end of the evening, that he was going to give her a 'proper' kiss goodnight. He didn't know how it would turn out, but he was prepared to have a shot. What was the worst that could happen? She slapped him around the face? Or, far more likely – now that he knew her better – she'd give him a karate chop on the neck or a kick in his particulars! She might be little, but she knew how to defend herself.

When they arrived at her gate, he turned to face her, his heart beating furiously in his chest.

"So, do you still want to meet up tomorrow?" he asked.

"Sure, I'd love to. What do you want to do?"

"Well, the weather report says it's going to be another warm day, so I wondered if you fancied a picnic down at Richmond Park. You mentioned tonight you haven't been there yet?"

"Oh, that sounds fabulous! Puddle will enjoy getting a good run out." She clapped her hands together and continued, "I'll do the sandwiches this time. Technically, it's my turn."

"Are you sure? It was my idea." He smiled at her enthusiasm.

"Of course I'm sure," she replied, smiling up at him.

"Okay, I'll pick you both up about eleven?"

"Perfect. We'll see you then."

"Great. Well… err… I'll… err… get off..." He swallowed hard and thought *here goes*. Leaning down, he found himself looking into Elsa's big blue eyes before his own eyes caught sight of her slightly parted lips and he hesitated. He glanced back up into her eyes. Was that a twinkle he saw there? Was she reading his mind?

Oh, get on with it! a little voice said in his head.

So he did. Instead of the usual peck on her cheek, he placed his lips gently on hers.

He felt her start with surprise and pull slightly away but then she leant into him. Carefully putting his arms around her, he gently pulled her closer. His kiss was soft and tender although, now that she was in his arms, he wanted to hold her as tightly as possible. He felt lightheaded and a galaxy of stars exploded behind his closed eyes. He couldn't recall any other kiss making him feel this way. This was a first.

A moment later, he felt her pulling away. With great reluctance, he opened his eyes and released her. He couldn't decipher the look on her face, but she was smiling – that had to be good, right?

She stepped back through her gate, closing it behind her. "Tomorrow, at eleven," she said. "Goodnight." She walked down the stairs, opened her front door and closed it gently as he watched from above.

Charlie waited until the outside light was switched off before he walked away, feelings of joy coursing through his body. Having a quick look round to ensure there was no one about, he punched the air above him. "YES!" he yelled at the sky.

He couldn't wait until tomorrow.

Elsa closed her front door, switched off the outside light and leant against it. She touched her lips with her fingers – she could still feel the soft pressure of Charlie's lips against them. He'd been so gentle, almost as though he'd been afraid of scaring her. She'd liked that. It was so long since she'd kissed a man, she wouldn't have been comfortable with a big full-blown snog. This had been just right.

It still felt strange though – only being used to Harry's kisses, she was surprised by how different this had been. It had been nice. There hadn't been any fireworks or a thunderbolt rushing through her body, but it had been nice. Very nice actually! While walking down the hallway, she realised she would be quite happy to kiss Charlie again. She smiled at the thought as she walked into the kitchen to see what she'd need to sort out for their picnic tomorrow.

Chapter Forty-Two

Jeff was walking down the stairs when, reaching the bottom and turning towards the office, his eye was suddenly caught by one of Danny's paintings. They were still hanging on the wall and had been for two weeks – Elsa hadn't yet moved them and had been working around them. Jeff suspected she was doing this on purpose while she waited for him to come to a decision. What was grabbing his attention now, however, was the painting of Jordie and Drew. The angle he was standing at had the sunlight picking up the expression on Jordie's face. It was a face that was full of tender love. The child being held above him was not only laughing but was also looking down both adoringly and trustingly, knowing the man who held him would never let him fall. He felt his breath catch in his throat and he coughed suddenly while swallowing down hard. The painting was making him feel very nostalgic. He had a memory of his own father holding him in a similar manner when he was a child, and he recalled that he'd had that same trust in him.

Jeff stepped back to look once again at the paintings

and sketches on the wall. Finally, he saw what Elsa had seen straight away. She'd framed the pictures to their best advantage and they now looked what they were – exceptional. He liked all of the work and Elsa had grouped it very cleverly. He found himself being pulled towards the scenes with the young fifties lovers. He could now feel the emotion being invoked – the young couple wanting to be alone but unable to give in to the intense emotions running through them as it was still very much taboo to do so back then.

He came to a decision and walked through to find Elsa in the showroom.

"Elsa, please could you do me a favour. Send Danny Delaney an email asking which of the pieces he would be happy to sell. I'm going to give him a trial run."

"Oh, brilliant! That's great news, Jeff. What made you change your mind?"

"I haven't 'changed my mind' young lady. I simply hadn't made my mind up yet. That's why I don't make instant decisions. You never know when something that seemed ugly before, can suddenly turn into an object of beauty."

"Well, you'll be delighted to know I've already asked Danny the question and the only two we can't sell is Jordie & Drew and the cubist version of the cat in the sunbeam. We've got free rein on the others."

"Good. Then I'll leave it to you to do some rearranging. Put a few pieces in here and we'll see what kind of interest they get."

"Right on it, guvn'r!" Giving him a mock salute, Elsa made her way through to the back to decide which items she was going to relocate.

Jeff came back out of the office two hours later and found the showroom had been changed in its entirety.

Elsa had moved her desk over to one of the corners and had put up a couple of floating walls. On these, she'd placed all of Danny's work.

He turned to her saying, "This all looks fantastic, but I only meant for you to bring out one or two items, three at the most. You've got the whole lot here, including the Jordie which is not for sale. You need to put some away. Elsa…! I'm talking to you."

"Shhhh!" was her reply. "Look, watch this man…" She pointed discretely towards the window. "That's the third time he's stood there looking at that painting."

"What painting?" Jeff was sure he'd placed a Renoir in the window that morning.

"I've put one of the cat oil paintings there."

"You've done *what*?" Jeff was horrified. He never placed trial artists in the window. Dear goodness, what would his competitors think? "Get it out of there right now, Elsa!"

"I will! Once that chap comes in to buy it."

"Look, he's not going to…" Jeff halted as the man began walking up the steps to the door.

"Look busy!" Elsa hissed as she suddenly picked up the phone and began talking to the dial tone. Jeff promptly turned and picked up some paperwork sitting on the desk. When the gentleman came through the door, Elsa smiled, raised a finger and mouthed she would be with him in a few minutes. Putting her hand over the mouthpiece, she whispered, "Please, have a look around. I won't be long."

While she continued her pretend conversation, Elsa looked the man over. Her trained eye noted his designer clothing. His shoes were handmade and the suit was Savile Row. As he came to stand by her, looking at Danny's Rock 'n' Roll collection, he scratched his face. Her eagle eye spotted the Bulgari watch on his wrist. Elsa liked to wear a bit of designer herself and was quick to recognise it on other people.

When she'd finished her 'call', she approached the gentleman.

"Is there anything I can help you with, sir?" she enquired politely.

"Err... the cat painting in the window..."

"Ah, that would be 'Priscilla on her Pillow'."

"It's beautiful. I'm thinking it would be the perfect present for my mother's birthday. She has a white cat, which is almost identical, and I just know she would love it."

"If I may say, sir, that would be an excellent choice. Who wouldn't love it? It really is a stunning piece of work."

"It is very eye-catching. I think I must have walked past your window about three times to look at it. And I'm more of a dog person!"

"Would you like me to put it up in the viewing room for you, sir, where you can look at it while sitting with a cool drink in your hand? Or a hot one if you prefer?"

"Yes please."

As Elsa walked towards the window, the gentleman asked, "How much is it?"

"Twenty-five thousand pounds, sir," she replied, not breaking her stride and picking it off the easel. She ignored Jeff's sudden coughing fit as she carried it to one of the viewing rooms, while asking the gentleman to follow her.

When she had sat the client down with a glass of iced tea, Elsa popped back to the office, allowing him to consider the painting further with some discretion. Jeff looked up when she walked in, saying, "Twenty-five grand? Seriously?"

"Oh, yes, and it was very nearly thirty!"

"He's never going to pay that for an unknown artist."

"He was never going to pay anything less. Have you seen his clothes? For this man, money very much equals quality. If I'd made the price too cheap, he'd have walked away."

"Very well, I shall trust your judgement on this one."

"Thank you, Jeff. You won't be disappointed."

An hour later, the customer, Mr Weir, left the showroom, his black Amex card lighter to the tune of one hundred and fifteen thousand pounds. When Elsa had informed him that Danny Delaney was an upcoming artist and that, in a year's time, he'd be adding one, if not two, zeros to the current retail price, he'd insisted on adding a few more pieces to his initial purchase. Elsa had given him a 'discount' on the condition that he'd be agreeable to lending his pictures back to the showroom for the Danny Delaney exhibition being planned for later in the year. She also explained he'd be a V.I.P. guest due to now owning some of Danny's early works. Mr Weir was more than happy to agree.

Once he'd given Elsa all his details and left, Jeff came out of the office shaking his head. "I cannot believe you did that! And Danny is not going to believe it either!"

"I think he's not going to believe he's about to be offered an exhibition in the Jeff Rowland Gallery…"

"Yes, about that…! Exactly who is in charge around here? I believe I'm supposed to be the one calling those shots!"

"Oh, Jeff, are you really going to look a gift horse in the mouth? This is just the start. Danny Delaney is going to be B-I-G! You mark my words!"

Jeff looked at Elsa. She was proving to be a great asset to his business and he couldn't deny that she had great selling instincts. Her eye for quality was also impeccable.

If she thought Danny should be exhibited, then he wasn't going to disagree.

"Ok! Fine! Let's get the diary and see what we can do."

Elsa smiled as she turned towards the office. She already knew Danny's rising star was about to become stratospheric.

Chapter Forty-Three

September

Danny was sitting in the hospital with Sandra beside him. They were waiting for her to have her twenty-week scan. Except it was her 'over twenty-two, nearly twenty-three weeks' scan as she'd forgotten her original appointment two weeks ago and she'd had to reschedule.

They both sat in silence, lost in their own thoughts. Danny was still dumbfounded from the contents of the letter he'd received from Jeff Rowland.

A thick creamy envelope had been lying on the mat behind the door when he'd arrived home from work last night. He'd nearly passed out when, upon opening it, a cheque for over seventy thousand pounds had fluttered out. He'd quickly scanned the contents of the letter and had managed to take in that the gallery had sold a large portion of the work he'd left with them and, as a result, they would like to offer him an exclusive rights contract and arrange holding a launch exhibition.

He'd read the letter four times, trying to digest its contents. This was followed by taking himself off to the kitchen where he'd poured himself, with a very shaky hand, a stiff whiskey! Finally, he'd called Guy. He needed to share this great news with his best friend.

The letter had asked him to either call or email to arrange a suitably convenient time for him to come in and discuss the matter further. It was too late to phone, so he'd composed an email – with the 'help' of Guy whose excitement had been no help at all – and sent it off for Jeff to receive this morning. He'd advised them he was out of the office today but would be happy to drop by at any other time in his lunch break, or after work – whichever was most convenient. A reply had come through at ten thirty this morning, asking him to come by during his lunch tomorrow.

He was so excited, he could barely sit still, causing Sandra to tut a few times as he sat beside her. She knew nothing of this development and Danny had no intention of telling her. If she were to find out he'd just earned such a vast sum of money, he'd never see the back of her and she'd be trying to spend it before the cheque had even cleared.

He stood up. "Do you want a coffee?" he asked. Maybe moving about would curb the restlessness in his limbs.

"No thanks," was Sandra's scathing reply. "I've already had to drink about a ton of water as it is, do you really think I need, or want, to drink anymore?"

"Well, I need one. I'll be back in a few minutes."

"What about the scan? I don't want to go in by myself." Sandra's tone quickly changed to a whine.

Danny tried not to sigh. "Look, I'm just going to be around that corner. If you get called in before I'm back you only have to shout. I'll hear you. Anyway, we're early so I doubt you'll be called yet."

While walking to the vending machine, he thought about how he didn't want to be here. When Sandra had first mentioned the twenty-week scan, and told him this was when they'd be able to see what sex the baby was, he hadn't said very much. Seeing the baby moving on the monitor would make it all seem very real and he wasn't sure if he was ready for that. He'd called Sukie a few nights earlier for her thoughts on the matter. She'd been very sweet and had asked him how he felt, where he wanted this to go and how he felt about becoming a father. She'd explained to him that, if he was sure he wanted to be a proper father to the baby – as in, actually involved with it, having custody as it got older, etcetera – then he would benefit from attending the scan because this would be his first real contact with it. She'd explained that it was a hugely sentimental moment for the mother too and he had to be prepared for Sandra being emotional. Sukie had also advised him that a woman's hormones become very erratic during pregnancy and he needed to cut Sandra some slack. She'd suggested that Sandra may have forgotten her original scan appointment due to having pregnancy scatterbrain. While he'd concurred this was possible, Guy had been less forgiving and had just accused her of being an irresponsible piece of trash! He was already trying to talk Danny into applying for full custody, feeling the child would be far better off with him. Danny had quickly dispelled him of that notion!

He arrived back at his seat just as Sandra's name was called. He took a quick drink of his coffee – burning his mouth in the process – then placed the cup in a nearby waste bin and followed her into the scanning room. He waited as she got herself into position on the table where she pulled up her loose-fitting sundress and pushed down the very large pants she was wearing. The sight of those began to bring home to Danny the reality of the situation. The only underwear Sandra normally wore were those tiny, skimpy thongs which looked less like underwear and more like something for flossing your teeth.

"Ok, Sandra, are you feeling relaxed and comfortable?"

Sandra said she was. The sonographer tucked some paper towelling above and below her tight, round belly and squeezed some gel over it, apologising for it being cold. The instant she began scanning, the shape of the baby popped up on the screen, accompanied by the sound of a strong heartbeat. Sandra grabbed Danny's hand while squealing, "Look, Danny, look! It's our baby. See its tiny hands moving – it's waving to us."

"Do you want to know if it's a boy or a girl?"

Sandra turned to Danny. "Well, do you?"

He shrugged. "I'm not bothered. You can if you want to."

She took a moment to think before replying. "No thank you, let's go for the surprise."

"No problem. Oh look, baby is urinating. Can you see it?"

Leaning across Sandra to get a closer look at the squirming, piddling, waving, shape on the screen, Danny was able to make out the head, the hands and its feet. He was gobsmacked! For the first time since Sandra had broken the news, he felt a stirring inside him. This little being was his baby. He'd made this and he knew then, that he would do everything in his power to protect it.

Sandra took in the wonderment on Danny's face as he looked at the baby and almost did a fist-pump of joy. He didn't know she hadn't forgotten her appointment at all but, because he'd been rather non-committal about attending when she'd first broached the subject, she'd wanted some extra time to work on him, to make sure he came with her.

Sandra was far more cunning than most people gave her credit for. She knew that, once Danny saw the baby on the scan, he'd be right on board with giving her more support and it would help her no end in persuading him to marry her. No matter what he might think, she still had every intention of walking down the aisle next summer and she'd use every trick in the book to make it happen.

As she looked at him now, she could tell from his expression he was already smitten. He was finally in her power and she'd be able to make him do whatever she wanted. If he refused, she'd just deny him access to the baby. She had no qualms about blackmailing him into marrying her, if that was what it took.

Her plan had worked!

Chapter Forty-Four

The following day, Danny made his way through town to see Jeff. As luck would have it, he had a meeting near Piccadilly Circus later this afternoon, so he could stay longer than he'd previously expected. He was also looking forward to finally meeting Elsa.

He arrived at the showroom and Jeff hurried forward to greet him. Shaking Danny's hand vigorously, he locked the door behind him and put the 'Closed for Lunch' sign in the window.

"Danny, it's great to see you again. Do come through. We got in some sandwich platters for lunch – would you like to sit up on the terrace again?"

"Thank you, Jeff. Yes please, that would be lovely. It's great to see you again too."

He took a quick look around him as they climbed the stairs and wondered where Elsa was. He really wanted to meet Sukie's best friend.

Jeff walked over to the small fridge in the corner of the conservatory and began taking out trays of sandwiches and finger food, the latter of which consisted of sausage rolls, onion bhajis, chicken skewers and mini quiches. He placed them on top of the fridge and looked over to Danny asking, "What would you like to drink? I've got bottled lager, white wine, orange juice or water."

"I'll have some water, thank you."

"You sure you don't want a beer?" Jeff held up a bottle for Danny to see.

"No thank you, I'd better not. I have a meeting this afternoon, best if I attend with a clear head," he replied with a smile.

Jeff put the beer back in the fridge and brought out two bottles of water. "That's what I like to see," he said, "an artist who goes easy on the alcohol. I've had problems in the past with artists who were rather fond of a tipple and I now tried to avoid them if I can. They're more trouble than they're worth." He carried the bottles out to the table on the terrace but, when he turned to go back for the sandwiches, he found Danny standing behind him with a platter in each hand. He placed them on the table next to the water, invited Danny to sit and, removing the wrapping from the platters, he passed over one of the plates Elsa had laid out earlier. "Please, help yourself," he said.

Danny looked around him. "Is Elsa not joining us?"

Jeff took a quick glance at his wristwatch. "Yes, she should be. I expected her to be back by now. She dropped a carton of milk just before you arrived and her suit took the brunt of it. She was going home to change and then via the supermarket on her way back to pick up some more."

"Maybe she got held up," Danny said. "It's lunchtime so the supermarket might be busier than normal."

"Hmmm… Possibly. Anyway, tuck in, before everything begins to wilt in the heat."

Danny chatted as he loaded up his plate. "I do like it

up here. It's so peaceful. Even though it's all hustle and bustle down below, you can barely hear it. It's lovely."

Just then, the sound of a siren wailing loudly pierced the air. Both men looked at each other and burst out laughing.

"You were saying?" laughed Jeff.

"Nothing! Just ignore me!" Danny sniggered before biting into his sandwich.

For ten minutes neither of them spoke, eating their lunch together in an easy silence. When they'd had their fill, they sat back and Danny waited for Jeff to begin. He was, after all, here at his invitation.

"Were you pleased with the payment you received for your work?"

"Oh yes! Very pleased! That was far more than I could ever have expected."

"You've got Elsa to thank for that. Credit where it's due – she saw something in your work which, I confess, I initially didn't. She hung it all with great care and, in doing so I eventually saw what she saw. I strongly suspect that, had she not done so, we wouldn't be sitting here now."

"Then I'm looking forward to meeting her even more."

Jeff looked at his watch again. "I really don't know where she can be." With a small shrug, he carried on. "To cut a long story short, once I finally saw your potential, I asked Elsa to hang a few pieces in the showroom – just to see what kind of reception they would get. I think I explained that to you previously."

Danny nodded, agreeing he had.

"Anyway, Elsa decided you were having a mini-exhibition because she put just about everything you'd submitted out there. We had interest very quickly and, within a few hours, we'd sold a number of your pieces.

Well… I'm saying 'we' – it was all Elsa. She talked you up big time. I thought the first buyer may have been a fluke but, the next day we had three more and the day after another two. By the end of the week, all we had left were a few sketches of your cat and the two oil paintings we weren't permitted to sell, although we could have sold them both six times over."

Danny couldn't help the happiness brewing inside him. People liked his work that much? It's one thing when friends say they like your creations, it's quite another when people are prepared to pay serious money for them.

"I really don't know what to say, Jeff. If it helps, I'm as surprised as you are."

"Well, we need to discuss where we go from here. I would like my gallery to represent you and I'd be honoured if you would allow me to launch you with an exhibition."

Danny looked at Jeff, trying to take on board what he was hearing. Even though he'd been expecting it – the letter he'd received had said as much – it was still quite something to hear it from the horse's mouth.

"Going on from there, you would be exclusive to my gallery for three years. You may not produce work for anyone else, and everything you create must come through me. I will take the responsibility of framing your pieces. I have an arrangement with an excellent framer who will display your work to its full potential. My PR company will also run all your publicity and arrange any interviews. Everything you do in the public eye must go through them. You, to clarify, pick up the cost of your own materials. I once had an artist who thought I supplied all that, so I now make it clear that I don't. For every item of yours I sell, you will receive fifty percent. If that appears unreasonable, I advise you that most galleries take between sixty and seventy percent. How does that all sound to you?"

Danny took a drink of his water in an attempt to clear his throat. He was quite choked up from hearing Jeff's offer and needed a moment to recover. He really never thought this could happen to him. Finally, he was able to speak.

"I think that all sounds more than reasonable, Jeff, and nothing would give me more pleasure than to work with you."

"Excellent. Then all I have to say is welcome aboard!" With these words, he stood up and stuck his hand over the table for Danny to shake on the deal.

Danny stood too, surprised he'd managed it as his knees were trembling so much, and shook Jeff's hand.

They'd both sat back down, and Jeff went through a few more details.

"Looking at the calendar and seeing what other galleries have planned for the next few months, I'd like to make your entrance into the art world a bit of an extravaganza. Something quite spectacular! So, I've decided to launch you on New Year's Eve. We'll throw a huge party here in the showroom and I'll only be inviting the most elite clients on my books. I plan to make it quite amazing!"

Danny blanched when Jeff mentioned the date of the exhibition. With all that had been going on lately, he'd forgotten he was living – quite literally – on borrowed time. He sneaked a glance at his left wrist, and seeing two little brown freckles still sitting there, he surmised he may be here for New Year's Eve, but there were no guarantees on what New Year's Day was going to bring.

"—I will also require quite a lot of artwork from you. A minimum of forty pieces, nearer to sixty would be ideal."

Jeff paused when he noticed how pale Danny had become. With a small laugh, he said, "There's no need to look so scared. The pieces don't need to be large, Danny, I'm not asking for the ceiling of the Sistine Chapel, although about twenty sizeable ones are required. The rest can be small to medium in size. The more variety we offer, the more pockets we can fit. I'd suggest you concentrate on your Rock 'n' Roll Lovestyle collection as it was very popular, very popular indeed."

"My '*what*' collection?" Danny looked confused.

"Oh, sorry. That's what Elsa named your pictures of the young fifties couple. It does work rather well, if you ask me. I'd also suggest more paintings of the cat. It was very popular."

Danny bristled slightly at hearing his precious Prissy being called 'it'. "The cat is called Priscilla, as it happens."

"How perfect! That collection will be called 'Pictures of Priscilla' – oh, this is fabulous!"

Danny blinked as Jeff actually clapped his hands. It had to be said, his enthusiasm was infectious and Danny was already beginning to sense ideas forming. It was one heck of a workload but he'd manage it. He still had holidays to take – he was sure he could do it.

Jeff was still talking and Danny pushed his thoughts to one side to listen. "I would also suggest a few other miscellaneous pieces," he continued, "one-offs that are not part of either collection. These can be anything that tickles your fancy and, because they'll be unique, we can sell them at a higher price as their worth will grow over the years. Think you can manage all that?"

"Oh yes, Jeff, I most certainly can. I'm already looking forward to it. I'll begin this evening."

"Do take some time to think over everything I have

said, Danny. Three years is a big commitment, so you must be sure that it suits you and will work for you. Elsa will type out the contract and you'll receive two copies. You must sign one, have it witnessed and return it to me. The other you keep for yourself. If you feel unsure, please speak with a solicitor who will go through it with you."

"Thank you, Jeff. I don't think I'll be changing my mind, but I do promise to think everything over before signing. Now, I'm afraid I need to leave. I still have a day job to contend with."

"Not for much longer, Danny. Come the New Year, I think you'll be waving the day job goodbye."

While walking down the stairs, Danny expressed his regret at not meeting Elsa. It was clear he owed this new career development to her.

"Yes, I'm sorry you weren't able to meet her today. I really don't know what could have happened to her. Not to worry, there will be plenty more occasions."

"Please pass on my thanks to her. Her belief in my work has changed my life, what more can I say?"

"I'll be sure to let her know."

At the front door, the two men shook hands once again and said their goodbyes.

Danny stood on the edge of the pavement and checked the road for traffic – after what had happened in Lower Ditchley, he was a lot more cautious. He crossed over and cut through the square as he hurried to get to his meeting. He was now a REAL, fully-fledged, artist with a gallery behind him. He felt as though he was floating on air and it was taking a great deal of self-control not to hop, skip and jump with joy. He just had to content himself with silently squealing inside instead.

Elsa flew round the corner, with a carrier bag clutched to her chest, just as Danny walked through the gates of the square. She ran up the steps and rushed through the showroom door. Jeff came out of the office to find her standing, panting heavily.

"Where on earth have you been? You were gone for ages."

"Is he still here? Is Danny still here?" she gasped in between breaths.

"No, you've literally just missed him. He only left a couple of minutes ago."

"Oh bugger!" She walked into the office and sank into a chair, feeling the disappointment sweep through her.

"What took you so long?" Jeff put the carton of milk in the fridge.

"I was in the queue at the supermarket when the woman in front of me suddenly fainted. She hit her head on the counter as she went down and was knocked out cold. We called for an ambulance and then, as we waited, she began to come round. She was really dazed and confused and I didn't feel I could leave her until I knew she was being properly looked after, so I stayed until the paramedics arrived. I didn't have my phone with me," she pointed to it lying on the desk, plugged into the charger, "to call you and let you know what had happened."

"Well, don't worry about it. There'll be plenty of opportunities for you both to meet as Danny has agreed to work with us. You need to get to work on typing up his contract as I'd like it to go out in tonight's post if possible. Once we get it back, we can begin organising his launch."

"Have you decided on a date for that yet?"

"Yes, we're doing it on New Year's Eve. It's going to be AWESOME!"

Jeff walked back through to the showroom, leaving Elsa sitting alone in the office. The words 'New Year's Eve' were spinning around her head. She had successfully put that date to the back of her mind but now it came rushing right up to the front, elbowing everything else away from its path. Would she still be here for New Year's Day, she wondered?

She looked down at her wrist where the two freckles were still... "Oh!" she exclaimed. "When did that happen?"

"You what?" called Jeff.

"Nothing, just talking to myself," she called back.

"They have places for folks who do that you know!"

Elsa ignored Jeff's comment as she stared at the solitary freckle now sitting alone on her wrist.

When had the second one disappeared?

And, more to the point, *which* task had she unknowingly completed?

The Middle Men

"Oh… Aye, aye, aye like dis vereee much. Oh Aye, aye, aye like dis vereee much! Cheeky cheeky boom…! Cheeky cheeky boom!"

Death had the worst singing voice Harry had ever heard. It was so bad, he made Elsa sound like a classically trained soprano.

"Will you please shut up! It's not funny!" William and Harry were sitting on a bench in the middle of Berkeley Square wondering how the big 'meet up' they'd planned between Danny and Elsa had gone so terribly wrong. William was not taking it well at all.

"Oh dere now, my li'l chickadee, what be da matter wit you?"

"You know what's wrong," growled William "And what the hell are you doing wearing that stupid outfit?"

"Oh dere now, honey-chile', is you saying you don' like me Carmen Miranda danc-eeing?"

"I don't know what's worse – the bloody awful singing or that terrible Caribbean accent. Why are you dressed like that anyway? You look stupid!" Harry was in agreement with William – this was not the time for Death to be messing about. Things between Elsa and Danny were not working out as they'd hoped, and it was proving to be very frustrating. That was two attempts which had now fallen through – the first had been Beth's wedding and now today.

Furthermore, the longer they were apart, the greater the chance of Elsa becoming more involved with Charlie and it gave that scheming wench Sandra more time to worm her way back into Danny's affections.

"Oh, come now, boys, you have plenteee of time steeell. Eet's only early September, you know. You've heard de expression 'De path of true love never runs smooth'. Geeve eet time. Now cheer up. Eet's a hot, hot, hot summer's day. Eet's jist like being een da Caribbean. So come along and sing wit me... Ooohhh... Aye, aye, aye like dis verrree much. Oh aye, aye, aye, like dis verree much..."

Watching Death shimmy off up the path, William said, "I suppose he's got a point. Well, two actually. It is only early September and true love never comes easy."

"Yeah, I suppose. Although I'll feel better once we've got them paired up."

"I know, lad, but then, Rome wasn't built in a day."

"Oh, don't you start with the clichés William. That muppet over there is bad enough!"

"Shall we go and drown our sorrows over a few blagers?"

"Yeah, that sounds good." One of the good things in the Middle Realm was that someone had come up with an infusion of beer and lager – it had all the earthy flavour of a beer, but with the light texture of a lager. Harry was very partial to it.

"C'mon then."

Harry stood up and looked over at Death who

appeared to be doing some kind of twerking motion against a tree. "Are we taking him with us?"

"Do you want to sit next to him dressed like that?" asked William.

"Err... No!"

"Exactly! You've just answered both questions."

When they saw Death make his way to the furthest corner of the garden, William and Harry legged it out of the nearest gate, the thought of having to sit beside Carmen Miranda in the pub making their feet move more swiftly.

Chapter Forty-Five

Elsa carefully lifted the quilt and slipped quietly out of bed. She picked up her dressing gown and tiptoed from the bedroom, taking care not to waken Charlie who was still sleeping.

She padded down the hallway to the kitchen where she switched on the kettle to make herself a coffee. She carried it into the lounge and opened the patio door to let Puddle out into the garden. She left the door ajar, sat down on the chair and curled her feet up beneath her, watching her dog bounce around the garden as she sipped her drink.

Charlie had stayed over for the first time last night but they hadn't progressed beyond cuddling and kissing. She'd sensed he was beginning to feel a little frustrated at how slowly their relationship was developing and she knew the time had come for her to tell him about Harry. Thus far she'd managed to avert his questions about her past – she didn't want to see the look of pity that always came into people's eyes when they knew she was a widow. She was sick of it defining her and the person she was. Or rather, the person she had been. There was no doubt that, this year, she had found closure and had put it behind her.

There was also another reason for telling him. Today was the September music festival in Hyde Park and Pete was the headline act. She had guest passes for the four of them – Anna and Gordon had jumped at the invite to join her and Charlie – and she'd finally be introducing Charlie to Sukie. She couldn't risk anyone saying something and causing an upset, so it was better for her to tell him her story herself.

With this in mind, she'd asked him round for dinner, fed him a homemade pork and apple casserole and then, sitting him down on the sofa with a large glass of wine, proceeded to tell him about her life before she moved to London.

When she'd finished, he'd looked at her for a few minutes before saying, "Life's a right bitch at times, isn't it? I feel a right selfish twat now, going on about my dad when you'd had to contend with all that."

Her response had simply been, "Everyone has their right to grieve in their own way and in their own time. I'd come to terms with my loss, you hadn't. I needed to listen to you more than you needed to listen to me. I know how many people let me spill my heart out to them over the years. It was my turn to pass that gift on to you. I just need you to understand why I can't rush our relationship – everything is very different and it's taking me a while to adapt. I'm simply asking you to be patient with me."

Charlie had patted the sofa next to him and said, "Come here."

She'd moved over to sit next to him and he'd put his arms around her, pulling her close and tenderly kissing the top of her head. "There's no rush, Elsa, we'll go as slowly as you are comfortable with. Now I know why, I'll worry a lot less that you don't care for me."

She'd been quick to assure him she definitely cared for him and that was why she didn't want to risk jeopardising the relationship by moving too quickly.

Satisfied with her answer, Charlie had changed the subject, refilled their glasses and they'd put on a Bruce Willis DVD which they'd watched curled up together on the sofa. By the time it had finished, she'd fallen asleep on his shoulder. Charlie had stayed completely still, loath to disturb her slumber. She'd eventually woken up in the early hours of the morning and he'd been about to call for a taxi when she'd taken his hand and asked him to stay. They'd spooned until she'd fallen back to sleep. She'd woken this morning to find them both still curled up together.

Elsa snapped out of her reverie when she felt Charlie's hand on her shoulder and his light kiss on her head.

"Hey, how're you doing this morning? Are you okay?" His voice was gentle.

She looked up and smiled. "Do you know, I *am* okay, thank you. I was a little out of sorts when I first got up, but now, I'm good."

"No guilty feelings or anything like that?"

"No. In fact, I think I'm feeling guilty at the fact I don't feel guilty, weird as that may sound."

"No, I get you."

She stretched her legs out in front of her and made to stand up. "Let me get you a coffee."

"No, it's fine. You stay there and relax a bit longer. I'm going to go home to freshen up. I'll be back in a few hours. What time are Anna and Gordon arriving?"

"Twelve o'clock."

"I'll be back by then. See you later." Charlie bent down and placed a soft, lingering kiss on her lips. With a gentle stroke of her hair, he turned and left, closing the

the front door quietly behind him.

Charlie took the slightly longer route to the tube station, to ensure he didn't bump into his brother, and thought over what Elsa had told him. It had taken a lot of restraint on his part not to ask a million and one questions about her husband. He'd concluded that the less he knew, the less he'd feel he was competing against him. He was astute enough to know he'd never win against a ghost.

As he walked through the quiet streets, the thought which had hit him last night, while she'd slept on his shoulder, came back to visit him. He'd wondered at the time if it was the effect of the wine and her close proximity which had triggered it but here, in the cold light of day, he knew it for a fact.

He was falling in love with Elsa.

Chapter Forty-Six

The four friends were in high spirits as they traipsed along Piccadilly in the direction of Hyde Park. Anna was bouncing like a jelly bean as she hadn't attended a big gig like this for quite a few years and she was really looking forward to. When Elsa revealed they actually had 'Access All Areas' passes she barely managed to contain herself. Gordon was grinning happily at her enthusiasm despite already being told that she'd be up on his shoulders for a better view. There were, Anna said, some advantages to dating a mountain! They were walking up Park Lane towards the entrance to the park, following the crowd to the gates of the fenced-in festival area, when Anna groaned loudly as she saw the queues in front of them.

"Aw gee, it's going to take forever to get through there," she said dismally.

"Then it's a good thing we're not going in that way. Come on, follow me!" Elsa had memorised Kara's letter which had accompanied the passes so knew there were two areas for fast-tracking the VIP guests. Their special passes would see them through with minimum hassle.

They were approaching the fast track gate and Elsa brought out the passes, complete with lanyards attached. "Here you are, pop these over your heads and hold onto them tightly – just in case someone with light fingers takes a fancy to them."

While they waited in the considerably smaller queue, Elsa wondered how Sukie was feeling today. She'd been on the phone two nights ago, telling Elsa her fears. This was Pete's first gig since being shot and, while he appeared to be rather relaxed about it, Sukie was turning into a nervous wreck. Elsa had tried her best to convince her there would be extra security measures in place and she was certain Kara would have ensured that every handbag and rucksack was thoroughly searched.

Once they were through the gates, complete with body scanners, she sent Sukie a text to ask how she was feeling and to let her know they'd arrived and had been fully frisked upon entry. If they were being so particular with the VIP guests, then she was in no doubt that all the gates were being as thorough.

Five minutes later her phone beeped with Sukie's reply. She said she was doing okay so far, all things considered, and advised they wouldn't be on site for another few hours but she'd text when they got there. She finished by wishing them a fun time and looked forward to meeting up later.

Elsa put the phone securely away in her bag and, turning to the others, said, "Right, let's go and find a bar! I'm in the mood for cider! And after that, I want to find a good spot where we can enjoy the music."

"Here it is! Here's the gate we need." Danny looked behind at Nigel and Guy. They'd arrived on the wrong side of Hyde Park and walking round most of the perimeter to get to the fast track entrance had left Guy very unamused. Danny was trying not to smirk as he glanced down at the reason for Guy's bad humour. Or should that be two reasons... In the hope of seeing Pete again, Guy had dressed more smartly than he normally would when going to a gig. This meant the brand new shoes he was wearing were pinching his feet and making him grumpy.

Danny had never been to a big music festival before and was a little apprehensive. He wasn't too fond of large crowds like this but, when Pete and Sukie had invited Guy, Nigel and himself along, he couldn't bring himself to say no. Besides, he wanted to see Pete perform and there was no way Guy was going to refuse the opportunity to parade around an event like this while sporting a VIP pass.

Soon they were safely through the gate and Guy was rubbing the plastic on his pass, making it shine in the sunlight, his earlier sulk slipping away as he preened and fiddled with the lanyard. Danny, spying a bar, offered to go and buy some drinks.

"There's probably a free bar backstage, we could go and use that." Guy was champing at the bit to use his pass in its rightful capacity.

"There probably is but, as Sukie and Pete aren't going to be here until after five o'clock, I don't think it would be right to go backstage just yet. So what do you want to drink Guy?"

Guy gave a small flounce which made both Nigel and Danny laugh. "Oh, get me a white wine. And make sure it's something decent, dah-ling! I'm not spending the day drinking rat's piss."

With a chuckle, Danny headed to the bar. It was hilarious when Guy acted up on his sexuality. He didn't do it often but, every now and again, he'd become rather camp and play it up. The first time he'd witnessed it,

Danny had asked why he did it. Guy's answer had simply been, "Because I can, dah-ling, because I can!"

To pass the time as he stood waiting to be served, Danny watched the crowds still pouring in through the gates. He surmised that, in another few hours, it would be murder trying to get a drink although he guessed there would be plenty of facilities around to cope with the numbers. He turned back to face the bar and tried to see what wine was on offer but the tall, solid man in front of him blocked his view. He hoped he didn't end up standing behind him later. He was the size of a mountain and he wouldn't be able to see a thing. Just then, the mountain spoke to the man on his left, "Here Charlie, you take these drinks to the girls. I'll settle up here and bring ours."

Blimey, thought Danny, he even has the voice to match his stature – loud, deep and rumbling. A moment later, when he began to move away from the bar, the mountain caught Danny's eye. He said, "There you go, mate, squeeze in quick while I hold this lot back for you."

Danny flashed him a grateful smile as he eased into the space. "Thank you."

"You're welcome. Have a great day," the mountain replied before he disappeared off into the crowd.

"Now this is more like it! *This* is civilised. Not like the rabble out there!" Guy raised the wine glass that was actually made of glass, and not the plastic offering he'd been disgusted to receive earlier.

He was back-stage in the VIP tent with Danny and Nigel, trying very hard to keep his cool among all the celebrity guests walking around. He was convinced he'd seen both Robbie Williams and Gary Barlow earlier. He'd also overheard a conversation which suggested that Sir Elton John was expected to drop by too. He'd almost danced on the spot when he heard that. Elton John? Now he WAS a legend!

He picked up the drinks from the bar and made his way back towards Danny, Nigel, and Sukie who had since joined them. When he looked closely, Guy could see the tension on her face. She needs to relax, he thought. He understood the reason for her concerns but felt she had to be less anxious, if only for Pete's sake. He was sure Pete was nervous enough about going on the stage later, without having to cope with Sukie's fear too. But, there again, how would he feel if Nigel had been shot and was now preparing to go back into the very same environment where it had happened? Would he be cool, calm and collected? No, of course he wouldn't! He would be a hysterical wreck. With this thought in mind, he decided to cut Sukie some slack.

He went to stand beside her, gently placed his hand under her elbow and led her to a nearby chair. "Sit down, poppet, let me rub those shoulders for you before you end up wearing them as earrings."

"Oh, Guy, I can't help it. What if—"

"Hush right there, Sukie. Shhhh!" he whispered in her ear. "Nothing is going to happen. It was a one off and the security today has been even tighter than usual. Look at all the gigs he did before Verona, where nothing happened. Pete's going to be fine. Have some faith."

He felt her shoulders begin to lower under his touch. Guy hoped she would try to enjoy Pete's performance later. This was his big come-back gig – it had to be better than any other gig before it.

As Guy massaged Sukie, Danny and Nigel walked over to them. They'd been chatting with Gareth but he was now heading off to run the checks on the lighting rigs. Pete was due on stage in just over an hour.

"Is Elsa here today?" While they had communicated over a number of emails, Danny still hadn't met her, and he really wanted to thank her for all she'd done to bring Jeff round to signing him on.

"Yeah, she's around somewhere. I thought she'd be in here by now. I've sent her a text but there's been no reply."

"Maybe she's simply enjoying some of the bands. It's a good line-up today."

"I hope she is. Elsa's had it rough in recent years and she deserves to be able to finally let her hair down."

"Oh! I'm sorry to hear that, may I ask why?"

Sukie smiled at him. "Sorry, Danny, not my story to tell."

"Not a problem, I get it." Danny appreciated the loyalty to her friend. "Anyway, I think we're going to head back out front. I know Guy wants to see Pete in all his stage-presence glory, so we're loving you and leaving you. Thank you so much again for the tickets and tell Pete I'll see him very soon."

He bent down to give Sukie a hug and a kiss on the cheek. Guy and Nigel did the same with Guy whispering reassurances in her ear as he said goodbye.

Amidst another flurry of kisses, they walked out of the tent to go and find a good spot to watch Pete's performance.

Sukie felt her phone vibrate in her pocket and, pulling it out, found a message from Elsa saying they were on their way backstage. She quickly text back telling her she'd meet her outside the tent. Elsa came through the gates just as she stepped out into the sunshine. Sukie ran over and they both embraced tightly.

Sukie hadn't seen Elsa since her mum's wedding and, while she had begun to look better then, she now looked absolutely wonderful. She was still growing her hair and today it had dried in its natural soft curls. She'd put on more weight; her skin was glowing and her eyes were sparkling. The short, severe geometric bob, bony skinniness, and the lifeless eyes with dark circles underneath were all gone. Elsa had finally morphed back into the happy, carefree woman she had once been and Sukie was ecstatic.

"Oh, Elsa, it's wonderful to see you and my… Look at you, you look fantastic. London is clearly agreeing with you." Sukie grabbed her and hugged her again.

Elsa squeezed back just as hard. "Thank you, Sukie, I feel great too. Here, let me introduce you to some friends."

Anna hugged Sukie, delighted to see her again. "Sorry we're late coming backstage," she said, "but the Acid Kows are one of my favourite bands and I just had to watch them perform."

"No problem," Sukie replied. "If you hang around here, they'll turn up in a bit. I'll make sure you're introduced." Anna's squeal made her smile.

She then shook hands with Gordon and Charlie. Jeff mentioned his brother occasionally and she liked that she could now put a face to the name. He didn't look much like Jeff, but he had a friendly face. Sukie also clocked the way his arm snaked around Elsa's waist and how her friend seemed happy with that.

With the introductions over, Sukie told them to go and get some drinks from the bar and food from the buffet. She turned to Elsa and said, "Come and see Pete, he's hiding away in his dressing room."

Elsa told Anna and the boys that she'd be back shortly and followed Sukie outside. Once she was sure they were alone and out of earshot, Elsa put her hand on Sukie's arm and brought her gently to a halt.

"How are you doing, babes?" She could feel Sukie trembling slightly beneath her hand.

Sukie's eyes filled with tears. "Oh, Elsa, I'm trying so hard to keep it together but, the truth is, I'm terrified. I keep telling myself everything will be okay, it's not going to happen again but it's not helping."

The tears began to flow down her face. Elsa put her arms around her friend as she sobbed on her shoulder, gently rubbing her back and letting her cry herself out all the while thinking back to the many occasions when Sukie had held her in such a similar way.

Finally, the sobs began to subside and Elsa pulled some tissues from her bag. She handed them to Sukie who wiped her eyes and then blew her nose with an almighty snort. Elsa looked at her in surprise before bursting out laughing. A few seconds passed and then Sukie joined in. Eventually Elsa asked her, "Do you feel better for that?"

"What? The crying or the snorty nose blow?"

"Both!"

Sukie gulped back a hiccup and gave her a watery smile. "Strangely, yes I do. Thank you."

"Hey, no need to thank me," replied Elsa, still gently stroking Sukie's arm in, what she hoped was, a calming manner.

"I don't know what's wrong with me Elsa. Normally I wouldn't let anything like this faze me and I KNOW he's going to be okay, but I just can't seem to help myself."

"Sukie, don't be so hard on yourself. Things are very different for you now – you're a wife and a mother. You have other people to consider in your life, so your values have changed. The fear you're feeling is not just about you, it's about your children too. You become more risk aware once you're a parent. That's all it is. You're not turning into some hysterical, swooning woman from the nineteenth century."

"Oh, Elsa, you put it so well – that's exactly how I've been feeling and I couldn't fathom out why I was being this soppy. Thank you." Sukie gave Elsa a tight hug. "I feel somewhat relieved to have a reason which sort of explains this anxiety."

"You'll be fine by tonight, once the gig is over. It's his first one since... well... you know..., it makes perfect sense for you to be concerned. You'd be a pretty crap wife if you weren't."

"Pete would probably say that I was anyway."

"No, he wouldn't, and you know it. Besides, if he did, he'd say it once, but I don't think he'd say it a second time," Elsa grinned.

"Damn right he wouldn't! He'd be in hospital having his jaw rewired!"

With a laugh, Sukie took her arm and they began walking again.

They arrived in front of the tour bus, with the vast caravan behind it, and Sukie led the way inside, flashing her pass at the security guards at the door. "Any problems, guys?" she asked.

"No, Mrs Wallace, everything has been quiet," said the first guard.

"Thank you."

Sukie knocked on the door before walking in. Elsa followed behind. Pete was lying on a large sofa which took up half of the room. Elsa gawped as she took in the opulence of the motorhome. Well, if it could be called that. A hotel on wheels would be a better description. She'd seen something similar on the television last week when Charlie had been watching the Formula One racing.

Pete stood and walked over to Elsa, giving her a hug.

"Hey, how *you* doin'? Looking good, honey!" She

laughed at Pete's silly New York accent. "Can I get you a drink?"

"I'll have a cider please, Pete, thank you. I was drinking that earlier so better I stick with it. I'm a bit long in the tooth to be getting drunk at music festivals."

Pete walked over to the bar area in the corner as Sukie turned to Elsa. "So, tell me more about Charlie! I saw his arm wandering around your waist earlier and you didn't seem too bothered by it…" Sukie raised a questioning eyebrow.

Elsa blushed and was happy for the bottle of cider Pete handed her. She took a slow drink, giving herself time for the colour in her cheeks to recede.

Finally, she lowered the bottle, and replied simply, "It's early days, we'll see how it pans out. For now, I'm just enjoying his company."

"I'm glad, Elsa. If you're happy, then we're happy." Pete nodded in agreement with his wife.

Just then, there was a knock on the door and Kara walked in. "They're prepping the stage for you now Pete, ten minutes till you're on."

"Oh, crap, is that the time?" Elsa put her hand to her mouth as she exclaimed. "The others! They'll be waiting for me, so we can go back out front to find a good spot to watch the show."

"Why don't you all watch it with Sukie at the front of the stage? You know, in front of the crowd-barrier?" Pete looked at his wife. "Your presence will probably help her to relax and maybe even enjoy it."

"Oh wow, Pete! That would be amazing." Elsa's eyes lit up at the prospect. Pete might be her best friend's husband but that hadn't stopped Elsa being his number one fan.

With a smile he picked up his jacket and as he put it on, he said with a cheeky wink, "You can even come up and dance on the stage with me!"

Elsa let out a squeal of delight. Sukie, on the other hand, simply rolled her eyes and, speaking in a mock stern voice, said, "The only 'dancing' going down tonight, Pete Wallace, will be the mass riot towards the stage if you don't move yourself and get over there now! Go on, beat it! Elsa and I will make our own way across."

Pete came to stand in front of Sukie and, placing his finger under her chin, he gently raised her face up until she was looking into his bright green eyes. "I'll be fine, my love, I promise you. Italy was a one-off. Please try to relax and enjoy the show." Pulling her into his arms, he held her tightly before kissing her gently on the lips. Then, with a smile at them both, he left the room.

Elsa noticed Sukie's smile waver as she watched the door closing behind him, so she sprang into action. She downed the remains of her cider, turned to Sukie and, holding out her hand, said, "Well, come on then. Let's go! Anna is going to be absolutely STOKED when she finds out we'll be right at the front."

Sukie smiled at her words. Never mind Anna, Elsa was almost bouncing herself at the prospect of seeing the gig so close up. She took the proffered hand and the two women left the room in high spirits. Sukie could feel herself beginning to unwind a little. Elsa was right – everything *was* going to be just fine.

Chapter Forty-Seven

October

Danny was painting in the loft when he heard banging on his front door. He groaned at the interruption – he needed to get on with these pieces for Jeff. He put down the brush and walked downstairs. He was approaching the door when he heard giggling on the other side. Oh great, he thought. It was Sandra and Kylie!

A few days after the hospital visit last month, Sandra had started to behave as though they were still a couple. She'd sent him texts on a daily basis and turned up at the flat twice in one week. Danny had let it pass on the first two occasions but, on her third visit, he'd finally said something. Sandra had turned on the water-works and had worked herself up into a right state. Finally, thinking only of the baby, he had reluctantly agreed they could try again. She now visited every other day or evening with Kylie by her side as she did the driving. Sandra hadn't managed to pass her test despite five attempts. She never stayed the night – "Sex might hurt the baby," she said – although she was being more affectionate towards him. As he watched her bump grow, he was finding it more difficult to stay detached although something deep inside was preventing him from fully committing to her. Something... and Guy!

When Danny had told Guy they were trying again, for the sake of the baby, he'd gone ballistic. They'd never had a full-blown row in all their years as friends but they did that day. Danny had tried to explain how torn up he felt inside, that he didn't want to be with Sandra but he couldn't live with the guilt of not giving the baby the best chance possible. He'd told Guy straight that he couldn't bear for any child to have the upbringing he'd had. Guy, in turn, had called Sandra all the names he could think of, telling Danny she was using him. This had resulted in Danny totally losing his temper and Guy walking out of the flat, slamming the door hard behind him. Their friendship had been very cool since and it was Nigel who was holding them together right now.

Danny held back the sigh on his lips when he opened the door. There would be no more painting done until they left. Sandra knew he was painting now – she'd caught him covered in paint too many times – but he hadn't told her about Jeff, the gallery or the launch at the end of the year. If she knew about those, she would immediately don the airs and graces of entitlement and begin to act like the Queen of Sheba. Danny was under no illusion there. The smallest whiff of 'celebrity' or anything similar would turn her into a screaming diva. She watched all the reality shows on the television and had even applied to a few of them. God forbid she was ever successful. There would be no living with her then!

Suddenly remembering he had no milk in the fridge, he called out that he was popping to the shops. While he shrugged on his jacket, yells for chocolate and crisps came at him from the lounge.

The flat was eerily quiet when he returned home twenty minutes later. He dropped the carrier bag on the kitchen worktop and, walking into the lounge, found Sandra and Kylie sitting in silence, their faces stony and disapproving.

"What's wrong? Is the television broken?"

Sandra, pursing her lips, replied in a cold and icy tone, "We were just wondering when you were going to tell me about *this*!"

'This' was a piece of cream embossed cardboard in her hand which Danny recognised immediately. It was an invitation from Pete to attend Sukie's birthday party at the end of the month. It had been stuck under a magnet on the fridge door. He wondered if Sandra had been snooping around (he knew she did as he'd caught her once) or if she'd gone into the kitchen for genuine reasons. Either way, she'd found it and now he was going to struggle to get out of taking her with him.

"It only arrived yesterday. This is the first time I've seen you since then."

"So, what exactly is it?"

"I think you know what it is, Sandra, your reading's not that bad!" Danny responded shortly. He wasn't going to pander to her dramatics.

"Well, the first question is, exactly *when* were you planning to invite me? And the second is when did you become so pally with Pete Wallace that he's inviting you to his wife's birthday do? Hmmm?"

"To answer your second question, I became friends with Pete when I had that accident back in April. You know… the one you never bothered to ask me about. If you *had* actually cared enough to pay me any attention, I would have told you I was staying as Pete and Sukie's

329

guest while I recovered."

Sandra looked at him through narrowed eyes, then asked, "So why did Pete Wallace take you in?"

"His mother-in-law was there when the accident happened. She stayed by my bedside in the hospital because she didn't want me to wake up from my operation alone." Danny hoped his abridged version of events sounded convincing. "It was just one of those crazy things in life that happen unexpectedly."

"So, were you planning to invite me? I am your girlfriend, after all."

Danny hesitated. He had actually planned to use the event as an opportunity to mend the rift with Guy. He'd already agreed with Nigel that the three of them would travel there and back together. Guy didn't know this and would only find out when he got in the car. That wouldn't happen if Sandra was in tow. The sight of her would be the proverbial red rag to a bull! Danny couldn't help but feel he was stuck between a rock and a hard place. He knew he'd have to take Sandra along. She'd only blackmail him with 'baby visiting rights' if he didn't.

He let out a deep sigh. "Of course I was going to invite you. Like I said, the invite only arrived yesterday."

"Get in!" After giving Kylie a high-five, Sandra leaned over to the coffee table, grabbed Danny's laptop, switched it on – without even asking – and brought up the internet. "Hey, Kylie, scooch over here and help me look for a dress. It'll need to be something awesome if I'm going to meet Pete Wallace."

"Err... I think you'll find the invite states 'smart casual' on it. You don't need to go too overboard." He suddenly had visions of Sandra arriving in some gold lamé creation that would be completely inappropriate.

Sandra treated Danny to a withering expression. "Danny, you're a bloke. You know nothing of these things. Now, why don't you make yourself useful and make us a cup of tea. We're dying of thirst here."

Knowing he was wasting his breath, he turned away and walked into the kitchen. He picked up his phone and sent a text to Nigel to let him know their plans had been scuppered.

Chapter Forty-Eight

"Please, Charlie, have another slice of cake." Jean Benton leaned over the table and offered the plate of sliced fruit cake to the nice looking young man sitting across from her.

"Thank you, Mrs Benton but I really couldn't manage another slice. I've had two already, although it is very delicious."

Elsa's mum blushed at the compliment. "I'll pack you some up to take away with you. And my name is Jean."

Elsa and her dad grinned at each other. Her mother was all a-fluster because Elsa had decided to kill two birds with one stone by taking Charlie to meet her parents before going on to Sukie's birthday party. When she'd called to let them know, Jean had actually let out a scream and dropped the phone. She'd listened to the commotion in the background, waiting patiently for her father to come on the line as her mother had been so excited she'd been unable to talk. David Benton had finally gotten the details from Elsa which he'd relayed to his wife when she'd calmed down.

They both understood why Jean had gone on a mad baking spree and why the already immaculate house had been scrubbed from top to bottom. Elsa bringing a man home to meet her parents was a pretty big deal and, in Jean's eyes, it didn't get any better than this. Her daughter had begun to live her life again – something both Jean and David had almost given up hope on.

"Why don't I refill the teapot? This one has gone cold."

"Here, let me help you, Mum." Elsa picked up some of the empty plates from the table and carried them through to the kitchen. Her mum was filling the kettle as she walked in.

"Well, Mum, what do you think? Is he passing muster?"

"Is he? Oh, Elsa, he's lovely, such perfect manners and a total gentleman. He's quite easy on the eye too!"

"Mum!"

"What? I might be old, darling but I'm not blind. I can still appreciate a handsome face you know!"

The two women chuckled. "Oh, Mum, you're incorrigible!"

"I know! It's great, isn't it?!"

Elsa couldn't help laughing while her mother busied herself with rinsing out the teapot although, looking at her, she suddenly saw how much Jean had aged. The laughter died in her throat as she realised the effect Harry's death, and her own subsequent grief-stricken behaviour, had had upon her mum. She hadn't once given any consideration to how worried Jean had been or how it had felt for her – being unable to reach or console her daughter who was suffering in the depths of her pain.

She walked over and, gently taking the teapot from her mother's hands, placed it on the worktop before taking her in her arms and hugging her tightly. "Oh, Mum, I am so sorry for what I put you through. I was so wrapped up in my own pain and sadness that I didn't give any thought as to how worried you must have been. You were always close by, but I couldn't let you in. I couldn't let anyone in."

"Hush now. There's no need to apologise. Yes, it was difficult, knowing there was absolutely nothing I could do to ease your torment, but I always hoped one day you would find your way back. And here you are! You've come through the darkness and you're walking in the light again. I can see you're happy. You're glowing with life, just like you did when you were young. You're living again, what more could any mother want for her child?"

Elsa tried to stem the tears her mother's soft words had induced, but to no avail. It seemed that saying sorry and thank you to those she cherished the most, for having hurt them so badly, always resulted in her sobbing on their shoulders – first with Sukie and now with her mum. She said as much to Jean, who stepped back and looked into her daughter's eyes. "My darling girl, the tears you're crying are wiping the darkness from your heart. They're washing away your pain and freeing you from your sadness. Every tear you shed is a little more weight off your shoulders. These are good tears, healthy tears. Don't be ashamed of them."

She gave her mum a watery smile and straightened her shoulders. "There! Feeling lighter already!"

Jean grinned at her daughter. "That's my girl! Now go and sort your face out, you look like a bad drawing of Alice Cooper!"

Through in the lounge, Charlie and Elsa's dad had been bonding the way men do. Firstly they'd discussed football, the teams doing well in the first two months of the season and who they thought would be relegated seven months later at the end of it. From this, they moved on to talking about Charlie's work and what buildings they felt were architectural masterpieces and those they considered to be an abomination to the eyes. The Scottish Government building in Edinburgh fell strongly into the latter category for both men.

"My father and I always agreed that the lines of a building should flow. Sharp edges and corners are disagreeable and make for disagreeable people inside them," said Charlie.

"I like the sound of your dad, he talks sense."

"Yes, he did." Charlie was unable to hide the sadness in his words and David quickly picked up on it. Elsa's suffering over the years had taught him the signs.

"No longer with us, son?" he asked.

"Err… No." Charlie cleared his throat. "Heart attack, twenty months ago. Still gets me at times."

"Yeah, it does that. Always catches you unawares does grief." David nodded as he spoke.

"Anyway, sir, I have something I would like to discuss with you please." Charlie changed the subject quickly. He didn't want to be dwelling on his dad.

David looked at him with interest. "Oh, sounds intriguing."

With a small cough, Charlie cleared his throat. "I'd really like to surprise Elsa by taking her away for a few days. I was thinking of a nice city break – maybe Bruges or Amsterdam or perhaps even Barcelona, but I don't know where is safe."

"Safe?"

"Somewhere she hasn't previously visited with Harry."

"Ahh…! Of course!" David nodded his understanding.

"I want her to make fresh memories with me, not be

remembering old memories of another time."

"I'll let you in on a little secret. Elsa has always wanted to visit the top of the Eiffel Tower at night. I don't know why exactly. I think perhaps she saw it in some movie or another when she was a kid, but I do know it's been one of those 'bucket list' type things ever since. She never visited France with Harry, so you should be 'safe' to go there. I know she would love that."

"Oh wow! David, thank you. That's exactly the sort of thing I had in mind – somewhere totally new and fresh."

"No problem, it's a pleasure to help."

"Please don't say anything to her. I want it to be a total surprise."

"Don't worry, Charlie, your secret is safe with me."

"What's safe with you, David Benton?" asked Jean, walking back into the lounge.

"Oh, nothing dear, just a bit of boy banter. Here, let me move that mat for you…"

David winked at Charlie as he stood up. Charlie smiled back. He was already forming a plan in his head and couldn't wait to return home to begin sorting out Elsa's surprise.

Chapter Forty-Nine

Danny looked at Sandra's outfit in dismay. Was she for real? What on earth had she been thinking?

Sandra twirled in front of him. The red-sequinned, floor-length dress, with the halter-neck top, deep waistline cleavage and slashed-up-to-the-thigh split would not have suited her short, curvy body at the best of times. Her being seven months pregnant meant it looked bloody awful.

"Sandra, I *told* you the dress code was 'Smart Casual'. I made that very clear to you."

"And I told *you* that men know nothing of these things. I bet all the women will be dressed up to the nines when we go downstairs."

"And I bet you they won't! Sukie and Pete don't do 'flashy', they prefer everything to be simple and relaxed."

"Hmph! We'll see!" Sandra threw her head back, as she returned to the bathroom.

They were in the same bedroom Danny had occupied earlier in May. When they'd arrived, Sukie had said, "You're in your old room again tonight. I always think of it as your room these days. Whenever Pete and I discuss household things, I always find myself saying 'Danny's room'." She'd smiled at him as they'd walked up the stairs.

Danny had smiled himself at her words and had been about to respond but, before he could speak, Sandra had snorted, pushed past Sukie and stormed into the room, citing an urgent need to use the toilet after the drive up from London. Danny had tried not to look embarrassed at her lack of manners, giving a small grin at Sukie's surprised expression. "Pregnancy hormones?" he'd suggested. Sukie's response had been very non-committal, but he could tell Sandra had not made a good first impression.

He got dressed in his own outfit of charcoal chinos and chambray shirt but couldn't help worrying over how Sandra would behave tonight. She'd been in a strange sort of mood on the drive up from London and, Danny knew from past experience, these were the occasions he'd found her to be the most unpredictable.

He kneeled down to pull on his shoes and tied the laces, while calling out, "Are you ready yet? It's time we went downstairs to join everyone." A glance at his watch, told him it was just after eight p.m. Sukie had said most of the guests would be arriving around eight. He wouldn't put it past Sandra to try to engineer a 'fashionably late' entrance in order to gain some attention.

"Nearly," called the disembodied voice from the bathroom. "A few more minutes…"

"No, Sandra, no more minutes. Now! I am not going to be the last to arrive so get a move on. You were ready when you came out to show me your ridiculous outfit so move it, or I'll go down without you."

Sandra walked out of the bathroom with a fierce scowl on her face. "I'm getting really sick of you bossing me

338

about, Danny Delaney!"

"And I'm getting really sick of you always aiming to be the centre of attention, Sandra Harrison, so I'd say we're evens!"

She picked up her small clutch bag and threw him a filthy look before flouncing out the bedroom door. Danny closed it gently behind him, unable to prevent the soft sigh that escaped his lips. Tonight was going to be a l-o-n-g night.

Sandra stood in the corner of the room, watching the other guests move around. It hadn't taken long for her to realise she should have listened to Danny. Everyone else was indeed wearing casual attire and, beside them, she looked like a stuffed Christmas turkey in red baking foil. She was sure there had been a few sniggers too when they'd walked into the room. She cradled the glass of orange juice in her hands and tried not to look too self-conscious. Thankfully, she'd managed to sneak some wine into her OJ when Danny had been distracted by a couple he'd introduced as Kara and Gareth. Catching sight of Kara's up-and-down look at her outfit, Sandra had barely even bothered to be polite and simply muttered a brief hello before taking a long drink from her glass.

Now she was alone and Danny, having gone off on the pretext of getting more drinks, was nowhere to be seen.

"Hello, dear, I'm Beth, Sukie's mum. How do you do?"

Sandra found a small, slim, silver-haired lady standing next to her. Her hand was out, waiting to be shaken, and a large genuine smile was on her lips.

She felt the warmth in the woman's greeting and responded more graciously than she had to Kara.

"Hi, Beth, I'm Sandra."

"Ahh, Danny's girlfriend! How great to meet you.

How are you getting on? And, I must say, I LOVE your dress, it's quite stunning!"

"Oh… thank you. I love it too, but I think it might be a bit OTT for this evening."

"Yes, well… I would have to agree with you on that one. I did try to talk Sukie into making this a black-tie event, but she was having none of it. She's not very keen on the old dressing up malarkey."

Sandra had no reply to that so took another sip of her wine and orange juice. She hadn't had any alcohol since May, when she'd found out she was pregnant, but tonight she wanted a bit of Dutch courage to cope with being surrounded by all the showbiz people she was anticipating meeting. The result was she could now feel the alcohol zipping its way through her veins, and her nerve endings felt like they were popping. She saw a waiter coming her way, and turning her back on Beth, grabbed another glass of wine and one of orange juice from his tray. Quickly, she poured the wine into the juice and took a slug before turning back to Beth. With a friendly smile she said, "So, it's quite something that Danny and Pete know each other – what with Pete being famous the whole world over and Danny barely knowing his next door neighbour."

"Well, under the circumstances, they couldn't be anything but friends. If you can't be friends with the man who saves your daughter's life, then who can you be friends with?"

"Saved his daughter's life? I don't know anything about that?"

Beth shook her head. "Now why doesn't that surprise me? That Danny is far too modest for his own good." Beth took a sip of her own drink before proceeding to fill Sandra in on the events back in April. When she'd finished, a very shocked Sandra said, "But none of this was in the newspapers or on the television."

Beth replied, with a pat on Sandra's arm, "No, dear, it wasn't. Pete was adamant his daughter wasn't going to be splashed across the newspapers, so he ensured it was kept very hush-hush! He didn't want the paparazzi sniffing around, bothering either his family or the villagers."

"Hmm, interesting… And how is his daughter now? Was she badly injured?"

"No, thankfully. She hurt her wrist and had the joy of wearing a cast on it for a few weeks but she's right as rain now. We all owe Danny a great debt of gratitude. We will always be eternally grateful to him."

Sandra murmured her agreement then excused herself to find a toilet. One of the few upsides to being pregnant was that she had a readymade excuse for getting herself out of situations she no longer wanted to be in. Her mind was spinning from what she'd just heard and, as she walked along the corridor to the bathroom, she was already thinking of ways to use the information to her advantage.

Chapter Fifty

Sukie was standing talking with Danny, Guy and Nigel out in the conservatory. Guy and Danny had agreed on a truce as neither of them wanted to create a bad atmosphere on Sukie's special night. As they chatted and laughed, Sukie could see Guy's recent cold front towards Danny gradually warming up. They'd been on non-speaking terms for several weeks now and she knew Danny was hoping being here tonight would help their relationship to heal. Guy was his closest friend and he'd told her a few times that he really missed him being around.

Danny looked at Sukie and asked, "So, will I finally meet the elusive Elsa tonight? I can't believe our paths still haven't crossed."

With a peek at her watch, she replied, "Yes, she should be here shortly. She was having dinner with her parents before coming over."

"Why didn't she arrange to do that tomorrow?" asked Guy. "Isn't it more normal to have Sunday dinner with the folks?"

"I believe she said something about getting – and I quote here – 'absolutely shit-faced and wanting a nice long lie in on Sunday morning followed by a great big fry-up brunch before heading back home'." Sukie smiled as she recalled Elsa's words on the phone. With every day that passed, she was becoming more and more like the girl she used to be.

She suddenly realised, as she was speaking, that she hadn't seen Pete for a little while. This was most unusual for he normally stayed close by on the rare occasions they attended parties. She asked the lads, "Have you seen Pete recently?"

"I saw him heading towards the library about ten or fifteen minutes ago," replied Nigel.

"Oh? The library is out of bounds tonight, I wonder why he went there. Excuse me, chaps, I think I need to go and find my husband." Sukie smiled as she moved away.

She was making her way along the small side hallway towards the library when she noticed, as she drew closer, that the door was ajar, and she could hear voices from inside. She'd just placed her hand on the door handle when the rough clacking sound of an East London accent came floating through the opening.

"Pete, I'm asking you, why do you want to be hanging about with an old bird like Sukie when you can have a younger, firmer model like me, eh? Put your hands on these babies, don't they feel well good?"

"Stop that! Please, will you move away?"

"Oh, stop playing hard to get, Pete, you know you want me. I ain't got bits saggin', baggin' or draggin' like that dried-up old cow you're with now. She's ancient, man. Once I push out this brat inside me, you an' me could have a real good time together. C'mon, have a squeeze of these big tight titties!"

"Look, I'm telling you to get off me! Now! Will you

please move?!"

Sukie pushed the door open quietly and took in the sight of Pete sitting in the winged Queen Anne chair by the fireplace and a fat, pregnant Sandra straddling him, her red-sequinned dress hitched up to her waist. She was pulling at Pete's hands, trying to put them on her vast heaving breasts inside the deep-cut cleavage of the dress. Sukie saw the horrified look on Pete's face and noticed he was trying to resist but his movements were being hampered by the high arms on the chair.

"What the HELL do you think you are doing with my husband, you fat slut?"

Sandra looked over. "Oh, piss off. He's with a real woman now. He wants to be with me."

Sukie stormed over, looked down at Danny's girlfriend and then, leaning down, grabbed her blonde hair just above the neckline at the back and pulled her from her husband's lap.

"Ow! Ow! Ow! Let go of me, you bitch. That hurts…"

"How *dare* you come into my home and accost my husband. How *dare* you abuse our hospitality this way! Guy's right about you, you really are a nasty, tacky little tart!"

"Oh, please, if your husband didn't want me, he'd have soon pushed me off his lap. Have you asked yourself why he didn't?"

Pete had risen from the chair the instant Sukie had pulled Sandra off him. He snarled, "I'll tell you why – because you're heavily pregnant and I couldn't risk pushing you off and possibly hurting the baby if you'd fallen. Believe me, if you *hadn't* been pregnant, you wouldn't have gotten anywhere near me! And you *still* haven't told me why you were in here." Pete turned to Sukie. "I saw the door was open and the light on as I was heading to the kitchen. I came to see why and found her in here. She told me she felt a bit faint and, when I went over to assist her, she pushed me onto the chair. It all happened just moments before you arrived."

"I did feel faint!" Sandra answered mutinously.

"Yeah, of course you did!" Sukie's tone left no doubt that she didn't believe a word Sandra was saying. "Anyway, move it, you saggy-arsed heifer. You're coming with me!" Sukie tightened her hold on the fistful of Sandra's hair in her hand.

"Ow! Will you let go!?"

"Not until you are out of my house, you repulsive strumpet! Pete, please could you change your shirt. I don't want to smell the odious cheap perfume this tawdry tramp is wearing on you all night!"

She marched Sandra along the hallway and over towards Danny, who was still standing where she'd left him a few minutes earlier. "Danny," she said, "I'm so sorry but you have to leave. You need to get this woman out of my house before I punch her lights out! She is five seconds away from having her teeth so far down her throat she'll need to put her fingers up her fat arse to bite her nails!"

Danny's face fell when he saw the fury on Sukie's, and the way she was holding Sandra by the scruff of her neck told him that Sandra had managed to ruin yet another night out. "What's happened?" he sighed. "What have you done now?"

Sandra glared at him but said nothing. He looked at Sukie who said, "Let's just say I have found her behaviour unacceptable and I want her gone. Now! Please take her away, Danny." She released her hold on Sandra and pushed her towards Danny who took her firmly by the arm.

"Of course, Sukie, I am so sorry."

"It's not your fault Danny but please, do yourself a

favour. Get rid of her! She's not good enough for you."

"I've been telling him that for three years Sukie, maybe now he'll listen!" Guy couldn't refrain from adding his tuppence-worth to the conversation.

"Oh, shut yer face, ya queer little poof!"

Guy laughed at the insult. He leant forward and made a point of looking Sandra up and down before replying, "Honey, the Americans have a phrase for the likes of you and it's 'trailer trash'. And that is *exactly* what you are – vile, intolerable trash!"

She opened her mouth to respond but Danny glared at her. "DON'T even think about replying. Just button it. You've clearly done enough damage for one night."

With those words, he gave Sukie another look of apology as he pulled Sandra upstairs to get changed and packed.

"Here we are, just on the left." Elsa directed Charlie to where he needed to turn to enter the gates of the Ditchley Manor estate.

"Blimey, it must be a rubbish party!" said Charlie.

"Why?"

"Someone's leaving already!" He nodded at the headlights coming down the drive towards them. He pulled into a passing place and waited for the oncoming car to go by. At that moment, Elsa's mobile began to ring. She bent down to her handbag lying at her feet and the sweep of the headlights from the other car helped her to locate the phone hiding deep inside. She was already speaking as she sat back up.

"Hey, Sukie!"

"Hi, Elsa, I was just wondering when you would be arriving."

Elsa frowned. It sounded as though Sukie was crying. "I'm practically there, babes," she said. "We're just coming up the driveway now. We had to stop to let another car pass by, but I'll be with you in a minute or two. By the time you to get to the front door, we'll be there. What's wrong?"

She elbowed Charlie, mouthing at him to drive faster. A few seconds later they drove around a bend and the manor house came into view. Elsa could see Sukie standing on the steps waiting for her.

Charlie had barely stopped the car when Elsa jumped out, running over to her friend as fast as her high heels would allow. "What's wrong? Why are you upset? What's happened?"

"Upset? Upset? I'm not upset. I'm absolutely bloody furious!"

Elsa pulled back in surprise. "Oh!"

She looked at Charlie who shrugged lightly. She gestured for him to follow them as she led Sukie back inside.

"What's been going on, Sukes?"

"Danny's fat, ugly, pregnant bitch of a girlfriend tried it on with Pete!"

"She did what?" Elsa felt a lurch in her stomach at Sukie's words. Danny had a girlfriend and she was pregnant? She didn't know Danny had a girlfriend, never mind a pregnant one. But then, why would she, she'd never even met the bloke. It didn't make sense – why should she be affected by this news? Trying to ignore the unexplained sensation of jealousy, Elsa put her arm around Sukie's waist.

"You wanna tell me all about it? Let's go and get a drink and you can fill me in on your evening thus far. Sounds like I've missed all the fun already."

Sukie laughed. "Oh, Elsa, you have no idea…"

While they walked through to the conservatory, she filled Elsa and Charlie in on what had occurred. When she'd finished, she turned to Elsa saying, "I only have one more thing to say on the matter and then the subject is closed."

"What's that?"

"I hope that fucking baby comes out sideways! That'll teach the bitch a lesson!"

Elsa and Charlie were still laughing when Sukie took them over to meet Guy and Nigel and, for the rest of the night, they put every effort into getting 'absolutely shit-faced'.

The Middle Men

William and Harry, sitting on the bonnet of Danny's car, held their heads in their hands in despair. They couldn't believe what had just happened. They had been *so close* to getting Danny and Elsa together but then Sandra had stepped right in and ruined it.

"How could that have happened? HOW did that just happen?" Harry raised his head and howled into the wind.

William swivelled round to look at Death who was car surfing on the roof of Danny's Ford.

"I'm feeling me good vibrations, I'm feeling me excitations, boom di bop, boom di bop…"

"Did you have anything to do with this? Is this all your doing?"

Death stopped singing and leaned down. "What did you say? I can't hear you, the wind is rushing about up here."

William shouted at the top of his voice, "DID YOU HAVE ANYTHING TO DO WITH THIS GOING WRONG?"

With a large sigh, Death sat down and slid down the

incline of the windscreen to sit beside his friends. "Guys, with my hand on my heart, or where it would be if I had one, I did not – and have not – interfered with any of your plans. The only thing I am guilty of is engineering Danny's accident. Everything else since has been a simple case of life taking its own course."

"Then why does it keep going wrong?" Harry asked.

Death put his arm around the shoulders of his young friend. "Because The Universe has bigger plans than we will ever know about and what we want is not always what we get."

"Can't you do something?"

"As much I wish I could, William, I'm afraid I too have limits. Interfering with The Universe is way above my pay grade. Those guys up there are like the uber-ultimate in computer programming nerd-geeks. They're still pissed with me because Danny and Elsa got to go back. Apparently, that caused quite a ruckus."

"Oh, I'm sorry," said Harry, "We didn't think you'd get into trouble over that."

"Hey, don't sweat it, lad. It's good fun messing with them as long as I only do it every other century. It wouldn't do to make a habit of it."

"Harry, I've been thinking—"

"Careful there, William, you know that plays havoc with your angina…"

"Oh, fuck off, Death! As I was saying, Harry, I was thinking… What exactly did you do to help Elsa? You know, in the early days?"

"Very little, William. When I saw the news broadcaster filming in Berkeley Square, I noticed it was the channel Elsa usually watched. All I did was move the angle of the camera a little so the brass plate for Jeff's gallery stayed in shot. After that, I just had to hope she'd see it and it would prompt a reaction. Which fortunately, it did."

"I think you're forgetting something there, Harry. Tell William everything."

Harry rolled his eyes. "Okay... I might have also engineered a situation where 'things went bump in the night' to get the previous occupant out of Pete's Mayfair flat, freeing it up for Elsa to move into. But that really was all. Everything else she's sorted for herself. Why do you ask?"

"Hmmm! I was hoping there was something I could have used to try and sort Danny out as he seems to have ground to a halt. I can't see any way forward from here." Harry and Death glanced over their shoulders to look at Danny sitting behind the wheel. At this moment in time, they agreed with William – they couldn't see how Danny was ever going to complete his last two tasks either.

Chapter Fifty-One

November

Danny was in his loft, looking at the paintings propped up against the wall. He couldn't believe he'd managed to produce so many since September. He'd used all of his holiday allowance, he'd worked every night after work or, when Sandra had foisted her company upon him, after she had gone home. Fortunately, that hadn't been a problem of late as he hadn't seen her in the two weeks since Sukie's party and he wasn't missing her in the slightest either. He was, on the other hand, missing watching the bump grow. Since seeing the baby on the scan, he'd softened to the idea of being a father. It was just a pity his choice of mother hadn't been better.

Danny counted the paintings – forty-four. Jeff had said between forty and sixty. He still had six weeks before the launch, but Elsa had emailed him to say they needed to have the bulk of the pieces on site by the first of December to allow time for them to be framed. Now that he'd checked what he had, he was about to reply advising that, if it was practical, she could have them sooner and he'd get the remainder to her by the first of the month.

He was wandering back downstairs when he heard the front door being unlocked. Guy had finally taken to using his spare key whenever he visited in order not to disturb Danny if he was painting.

"Hiya, Guy, how're you doing tonight?"

Danny closed the door and followed him into the kitchen. He could smell the curry wafting from the bags in Guy's hands. "Are you feeding me again?"

"Well, if I don't, you won't eat. Or you won't eat anything of substance. Toast is NOT substance!" He countered Danny's argument before he'd even opened his mouth. He'd heard it all before.

"Guy, I don't want to sound ungrateful, mate but you need to stop coming round here all the time and feeding me. Nigel is going to get very pissed off with barely seeing you. I don't want you risking your marriage over me. I'll be absolutely fine."

"You're not risking anything. Nigel and I have spoken about this and he has no problem with me coming round. It's actually worked out well because his band has a big gig coming up next month and they're doing extra rehearsals for it. He's out himself most nights. Besides, this is only a temporary thing. Once we're into December, the pressure will be off, and you can relax before the big night."

Danny was trying not to think of his launch night but, given its date, it was proving to be difficult. He glanced at his wrist. The two freckles were still sitting there, mocking him, letting him know he was a failure and that he couldn't even complete his tasks! He let out a sigh. He didn't know what more he could do. He'd thought returning to his painting had been a life change, but it was clear his freckles didn't agree. He only had six weeks left and he knew there was nothing for him beyond that.

"I'm just sending a quick email to the gallery and then I'll be with you," he said to Guy.

"No worries, we should be ready to eat in five minutes," Guy smiled back as he walked out of the kitchen.

They hadn't long finished eating, and were clearing away the leftovers, when Danny's mobile rang. Picking it up, he saw 'Unknown Caller' on the ID screen.

"Hello?"

"Good evening, am I speaking to Mr Daniel Delaney?"

"Er… yes, you are. Who is this?"

"Hello, Mr Delaney, I am Ward Sister Collins at St Thomas's Hospital."

Danny nearly dropped the phone. St Thomas's Hospital…? Sandra… The baby… Something had happened…

In his panic, he missed what the woman was saying and had to ask her to repeat it.

"I said, your mother has been admitted onto my ward and you are listed as her next of kin. She fell down some stairs and is in a pretty bad way. She's asking for you."

"Oh! I see. Give me a moment till I get a pen and paper…" He scribbled down the details, thanked the nurse and hung up, breathing a sigh of relief as he did so.

Guy read the information Danny had written down, looked at him and asked, "What gives?"

"My mother's in hospital again. Apparently, she fell down some stairs. She's asking for me."

"Are you going? I'm just thinking of the last time you saw her and how nasty she was to you…"

Danny looked at him. "I don't want to, but I suppose I

should. She is my mother after all."

"She's your mother through birth, Danny, but not in any other way. I'm not going to say 'Don't go' but I think you're mad if you do."

Danny let out a sigh. Deep down he didn't want to see her, he knew she wouldn't have changed but he also couldn't help think that this would be the last time he'd see her. In six weeks, it was game over for him. Finally, he replied, "I'll go tomorrow after work."

Guy shrugged. Family ties were the one thing that could never be explained. "Do you want me to come with you?"

Danny smiled. "No, I'll be fine. But thank you for offering, I really appreciate it."

"Well, let me know if you change your mind. It won't be a problem."

"Thanks, Guy, you really are the best mate a bloke could have. I'm so lucky you're mine."

"Yeah, I know. On both counts!"

Danny burst out laughing at Guy's total lack of modesty and felt some of the tension slip away. He wasn't looking forward to seeing his mother again but that was tomorrow's problem. Tonight, he was simply going to have a rare evening of relaxation with his best friend.

Chapter Fifty-Two

Danny stood outside the hospital and looked up at the giant edifice in front of him. When he was last here, he'd seen his unborn child for the first time. Now he was here to see the woman who had brought him into the world.

He'd struggled all day, unable to concentrate at work, and as finishing time had drawn closer, the churning had begun in his stomach. Standing here now, he really felt as though he could throw up. The sandwich he'd eaten at lunchtime really was threatening to make a reappearance. He took a bottle of water from his bag and had a long drink – anything to delay the moment when he had to face his mother again.

He wondered, as he replaced the bottle in his rucksack, if other adults felt the same way towards their parents. Surely it wasn't natural to feel such resentment towards the woman. Guy had said he wasn't alone in this. Many people had had difficult upbringings and they'd found cutting all ties with their family was the only way they could move on. Danny wished he could do this but the sense of guilt he'd feel would be more than he could cope with. He'd been burdened with a strong sense of duty and always doing what was right. He wasn't strong enough to walk away. He knew that and so, unfortunately, did his mum.

He pulled himself up straighter and with a heavy sigh, he walked into the building. The sterile smell that permeated these facilities immediately assaulted his nostrils as the automatic doors swooshed closed behind him. He stood for a moment to get his bearings and looked for the direction boards to find the ward his mother was on. He checked the paper in his hand and soon found it on the signs with colour-coded arrows by its side.

He stood in the lift with three other people, and felt the churning in his stomach accelerate at the same speed as the lift ascended up through the floors. Each time it stopped, Danny was tempted to get out and find another lift heading back down to the ground floor. When it finally stopped on the floor he needed, his feet felt like they were encased in lead boots and every step was heavier than the last. He only just got out of the metal box before the doors closed behind him. He stood looking at the signs in front of him, all the while trying to regulate his breathing which was becoming more and more laboured. He'd never had a panic attack before – was that about to change?

The signage said he needed to turn left. He walked along slowly until he came to the doors leading into the ward. He pressed the bell and smiled his thanks to the young nurse who let him in.

"Good evening, I'm here to see Edith Delaney."

"Ah yes, she's here but, before I take you to her, Ward Sister Collins would like a word with you." The nurse showed him into an office and closed the door behind him.

A few minutes later a woman came in. Her air of authority was wrapped around her like a cloak. She moved behind the desk, leaned across and put out her hand. "Good evening, Mr Delaney, I'm Ward Sister Collins. We spoke on the phone last night."

Danny stood to shake her hand and then sat back down when she did likewise.

"Mr Delaney, your mum fell down the concrete stairs in the block of flats where she lives. We think she may have fallen down the full flight, judging by her injuries, but she herself cannot actually remember."

"Was she drunk?" Danny knew this would be the crux as to how the conversation progressed.

"Her blood alcohol level was extremely high when she was admitted. It has been necessary to delay the operation she requires until this has reduced. She's currently on pain relief although, due to the alcohol, she can't have a strong dose, so she is still in some pain."

Danny nodded, not in the least surprised by this news. He'd have been more surprised if the Sister had said his mother *had* been sober. He didn't know the last time she'd gotten through the day without a drink. He doubted she did either!

"So what operation does she require?"

"She needs a hip replacement. Her bones are very brittle and it appears her left hip and leg took the brunt of the impact when she fell. Both are broken. Once we are able to operate, she will require quite a bit of respite care – especially for the first six to eight weeks. Will she able to come and live with you during that time?"

Danny nearly fell off the chair with shock. Of all the worst possible tortures he could think of, this would surpass the lot. He couldn't think of anything he'd hate more.

"Err… My flat is a top floor flat and the only access is

up stairs. There's no lift."

Sister Collins pursed her lips at this information. "What about your mum's home? Can you move in there?"

"She lives on the fourth floor and the lift spends more time being out of order than it does being operational."

"I see. Well, in that case, we'll need to try and get her into residential care while she heals. I'll speak with Social Services and see what we can do."

"Thank you, Sister, I appreciate your help with this."

"Right, then I'll take you to your mother. Please come with me."

Danny stood and followed the Ward Sister down the ward. He could hear his mother's strident tones as she complained to someone about how much pain she was in. She let out a screech when she saw him coming towards her.

"Oh my, look at what the cat has finally dragged in! Took your fucking time to come, didn't you? Are you too high and mighty these days, now that you work in *'The City'*?" She spat out the last two words as though they were a nasty taste in her mouth.

"I had to go to work, Mother. I came as soon as I could after that."

"Yeah, course you did."

"So, how are you feeling? The sister told me about your leg and hip."

"I'd feel a lot fucking better if they gave me some decent painkillers."

"You know they can't because of the alcohol in your blood. I'm sure they explained that to you."

"Yeah, yeah, a likely story! They just like to treat us old people like shit, so they do!"

Danny looked at his mum. She was only fifty-nine yet looked more like seventy-nine. Her ravaged body was testament to the long years of smoking, drugs and alcohol abuse. The bitterness which had kept her company all her life hadn't helped either and the lines around her mouth were deep and plentiful.

"So, have you had any more promotions at work?"

"No, I'm still a supervisor which means I'm not earning any more money." Danny knew exactly where this line of questioning was going.

"Why does that not surprise me? You always were a fucking useless waste of space. Geez, the worst thing that ever happened to me was giving birth to you. You ruined my life."

Danny sighed. It hadn't taken long for her usual rant to begin.

"Yes, so you keep telling me, Mum. I think we can safely say that, after forty years, I've got the message on that one!"

Edith Delaney glared at Danny as her hand clenched on the bed-covers.

"Don't you back-chat me, you little guttersnipe. When I think of all the things I gave up for you, with no thanks in return. It wasn't easy for me to put food on the table and clothes on the backs of two kids all on my own. I could have been something if it hadn't been for you. My life was going somewhere until you came along. And you're nothing special either. Just look at you for fuck's sake – as ugly as Frankenstein, soft as putty and no fucking back-bone. It's a miracle you've managed to hold down a job this long – they must be desperate to keep on a shitty, hopeless fucker like you." Her clenched fist hit the bed with every vitriolic word that fell out of her mouth.

Danny felt himself begin to tremble. Her rant had sent his mind racing back to his childhood and he could feel the blows raining down on his back as the memories of the beatings he'd received washed over him. His mother saw his fear and used it to add more emphasis to her abusive tirade.

"Oh, not saying anything now, are you? No, I thought not. You're pathetic. You're nothing, you've always been nothing and you will always be nothing! You're a walking abortion, that's what you are. I should have drowned you at birth and done us all a fucking favour!"

Danny couldn't take any more. He knew it had been a mistake to come here. He sprung up from his chair and rushed down the ward. His chest was tight, and he was struggling to breathe. His ears filled with the sound of her cackling laughter which had followed on his heels. He arrived at the doors, grabbed the door handle with his left hand... And stopped!

His eyes fell upon the two freckles still sitting on his wrist. As he stood looking at them, all the years he had suffered at the hands and mouth of that woman boiled up inside him. The slaps, the kicks and the battering's came hurtling back to him, the times she'd stubbed her cigarettes out on his arms. He remembered the days when his stomach had ached from hunger because she'd spent the little money they had on cheap vodka, and the embarrassment of the kids at school calling him Prozzie Boy because they knew she would sleep with anyone who'd buy her a drink. The final straw, however, was the knowledge that she had purposely stopped him taking up his art scholarship. She'd ruined her life and, not content with that, she'd also tried to ruin his.

In that moment, he began to feel a sensation of calm spreading through him. His mother was still cackling in her bed, but it was no longer having an effect on him. The churning in his stomach had stopped and he felt almost peaceful.

He spun on his heel and, with his head high and

shoulders back, he strode back along the ward until he reached his mother's bed.

"Ooh, look at the silly little boy pretending he's a man. Come back to find the balls you've never had…"

Danny walked up and leaned over his mother. "Be quiet," he hissed at her. "Just be quiet! I am sick and tired of being blamed for your failures—"

"Well you were—"

"I told you to be quiet!"

Edith closed her mouth, although her eyes opened wide, when she heard the authoritative tone in his voice. "You've had forty years of spilling your nasty words upon me, well now it's my turn to speak. You have got a cheek to call yourself a mother. You never once mothered me. All you have EVER done is abuse me – both verbally and physically. I was a CHILD and yet you used me as a punchbag, taking out all your frustrations at YOUR failings on me. I didn't ask to be born but you made sure I suffered because you couldn't keep your fanny in your pants! But, do you know what the absolute worst thing was that you did to me? Going OUT OF YOUR WAY to stop me going to art school! I KNOW you tried to bribe my teacher. I KNOW you intentionally did everything you could to ensure I didn't take that chance. Yeah, I know about it! That's surprised you, hasn't it?"

Edith's mouth had dropped open when she heard those words.

"Well, you listen to me and you listen good because this is the first and last time I will say this. You were, and still are, nothing but a selfish, evil, old bitch! YOU fucked up your life – not me and not Patrick. You! But you could never accept you were anything less than perfect. It was always someone else's fault. Well let me tell you now that it was NO ONE else's fault. You had opportunities to make a better life for us, but you had such a high opinion of yourself that none of them, in your eyes, were ever good enough. Well guess what? I am *not* the failure you've always made me out to be. I have a good job, I have a nice home and I have good friends. Those alone prove I am not a failure. But, just to add a little cherry to the top of the icing on the cake, I am now a professional artist! People have paid good money for my work. *Very* good money! Furthermore, I am having a large exhibition with a very up-market Mayfair gallery at the end of the year. And, do you know what the best bit of all this is? Let me tell you! You will *never* see a penny of my success. I could have looked after you, got you the best of care and ensured you never had anything to worry about for the rest of your life. You, however, have shown me once again, but for the last time, that you do not love me, you have never loved me and you will never love me. Well, Mother dearest, that works both ways. From this moment forward, you are dead to me. I have never loved you and I never will. Everything I did for you was from a sense of duty, but why should I have a sense of duty towards you when you never had one towards me?"

Danny straightened up. He could practically see the anger and resentment flowing from every pore on his mother's body.

"Right, *Mother*, I suggest you take a good hard look at me now for this is the last time you will ever see me. Goodbye! And good luck... For you're going to need it!"

He bent down, picked his rucksack off the floor and walked back towards the door of the ward. As he passed the office, he saw the Ward Sister sitting at her desk. He quickly turned, knocked on the door and walked in.

"Sister, I'm just letting you know that, from this moment on, I am no longer the next of kin for Edith Delaney. Please could you remove my contact details from her file."

"Oh, but… Well, who can we contact? Is there anyone else?"

"Yes, you can put in my brother Patrick."

The Ward Sister pulled up the file on her computer and removed Danny's name and phone number. She typed Patrick's name into the Next of Kin box.

"Phone number?"

"I don't know it. You'll need to look it up on the internet. HM Prison Wormwood Scrubs. It shouldn't be too hard to find. Goodbye."

Walking out of the office, out of the ward and out of his mother's life, Danny felt lighter than a feather. He was shocked by the weight of the resentment he'd been carrying all these years.

By the time he walked out the front doors of the hospital, he was shaking like a leaf! He managed to make his way to a nearby bench before his legs gave out under him. He got the bottle of water from his bag and took a long drink. He really needed something stronger but, until he got home, this was the best thing on offer.

He was putting the bottle back in his bag when he caught sight of his wrist again. He still had two freckles, but one had faded. It was still there but not as dark as it had been and certainly not as dark as the one next to it.

Clearly, he still had something else in his life he needed to change but it would seem he was now on the right path.

Danny picked up his bag, threw it over his shoulder and, with a newfound lightness in his step, began whistling as he walked towards the tube station.

Chapter Fifty-Three

Elsa looked up upon hearing the pressure buzzer and was surprised to see Charlie walk in.

"Oh, hello? What are you doing here?" She walked over and gave him a brief kiss on the cheek. "Is everything okay? You look a touch worried?"

Charlie smiled and put a gentle hand on the small of her back. "I'm absolutely fine. I've come to see Jeff – is he around?"

"Yes, he's in the office."

"Then I shall go and dig him out. Are we still okay for dinner later?"

"Absolutely! I'm looking forward to it."

"And are you still okay with me staying over at yours tonight?"

Charlie smiled when Elsa blushed at his words. Even though he'd now 'stayed over' on numerous occasions, he never took it for granted and always checked she was okay with it. Elsa grinned at him. "Yes, of course it is. You know how much Puddle likes you being there."

He rolled his eyes. "Do you like me being there?"

"You wouldn't get to stay if I didn't. Now stop fishing for compliments and go find your brother!"

Charlie popped a light kiss on her nose before walking towards the office. He was not looking forward to the next thirty minutes.

"Hey, bro, how're you doing?"

Jeff looked up from the auction catalogue he was going through. "Charlie! Long time, no see! How are you?" He jumped up from his chair and went over to give his brother a hug. Although they'd chatted on the phone and by email, they hadn't actually seen each other since Charlie's drunken escapade in June.

"Really great, thanks Jeff. I was wondering... do you have time for a coffee downstairs? I need to run something by you."

"Sure. I'll just let Elsa know. You head on down and put the kettle on."

A few minutes later, the two brothers were sitting at the kitchen table exchanging their news. Jeff was filling Charlie in on his latest new talent – Danny Delaney. Charlie was biting his tongue not to say anything as Elsa had already told him everything.

"Err... Jeff, can I stop you there. I need to get this off my chest."

Jeff looked at him and narrowed his eyes. "Get *what* off your chest?"

"Erm... Do you remember back in June, when I had my little... erm... incident on your doorstep, and you told me to stay away from Elsa...?"

"Y-e-s..."

"Well, I kind of didn't and we've been dating pretty much since then!"

"You WHAT? I specifically told you to keep away from her. She's happy here and I don't want you messing her about. I don't want to lose her, she's the best assistant

I've ever had!"

"Jeff, I promise you that messing her about is the *last* thing on my mind – you can trust me on that!"

"How can I? You've never dated the same woman for more than three months. You've been through more girlfriends than I've had cups of coffee!"

"Well, as I've now been seeing Elsa for about five months, I think that should tell you something."

"Hmmm… That is a first I suppose."

"Jeff, you can trust me, I really do like her. A lot!"

"How much is 'a lot'?"

Charlie swallowed hard. He was about to tell his brother his biggest secret. "I love her. I'm in love with her. And have been for nearly three months. Well, it might be more, but I've known for nearly three months."

Jeff gawped at him. "Wow!" he said eventually. "Does Elsa know?"

"Oh gosh, no! And please don't tell her either. I don't think she's ready to hear it yet and I don't want to scare her off."

"Bloody hell, Charlie! You really ARE in love with her! I've never known you to worry about a woman's feelings before." He took a sip of coffee before continuing, "But why has Elsa never mentioned this to me?"

Charlie squirmed in his chair. "Because I kind of asked her not to… I told her that you wouldn't be happy with me."

"So, you got my assistant to lie to me? Well, that's rich!"

"Knowing Elsa, I'm sure she didn't actually lie. Have you ever asked her if she was seeing anyone?"

"Well, no. That's her personal business."

"Exactly! And has she ever alluded to seeing anyone?"

"Not that I can recall…"

"So, she hasn't lied to you!"

"Hmph!" Jeff took a longer drink of his coffee. He looked at Charlie. "Well, she's clearly a good influence on you. You don't smell of booze and you look healthier."

"I feel great! Better than I've felt in a very long time."

"So, why are you telling me this now? I'm guessing there's a purpose behind it all."

Charlie's face lit up and he leaned across the table in excitement. "I'm taking her to Paris at the weekend and I want to clear it with you for her to have two days holiday on the Monday and Tuesday afterwards. I've booked it for three nights, you see. But, it's a surprise so I can't ask her to do it."

"And do you think she'll like Paris?"

"Her father told me it's somewhere she's always wanted to visit but has never been to yet."

"You've met her father?" Jeff nearly choked on his coffee.

"And her mother!" Charlie grinned at the shock on his older brother's face. Oh, how he wished he'd thought to film this.

Jeff just shook his head.

"I also have a second little favour to ask you…"

"What?"

"Would you mind looking after Puddle while we're away? I can't very well arrange to put him into kennels and I don't think Elsa would agree to that anyway."

Jeff sighed. "Sure, no problem! Drop him round before you go."

"Aw thanks, bro! You're the best!"

"Hmmm! I think I need another coffee!"

Charlie stood up to oblige, delighted his plans were all coming together so well.

Chapter Fifty-Four

"Oh, my goodness! I can't believe it! This is amazing!" Elsa wriggled on her seat, taking in how roomy and spacious it was. She was sitting with Charlie on the Eurostar, in Premier Business Class no less, waiting for the train to leave Waterloo Station.

Charlie had surprised her with the news last night when she'd mentioned they hadn't made any plans for the weekend. After squealing at him that she didn't have anything ready for a weekend away, and then planting a big kiss on his mouth, she had rushed into the bedroom to sort herself out. She still wasn't exactly sure what she'd packed, and she just hoped it was appropriate for walking around Paris.

Elsa couldn't believe Charlie had put so much effort into keeping this a surprise. When she'd mentioned Puddle, he'd immediately informed her that Jeff was looking after him. She then brought up that he'd booked three nights away, but she hadn't booked any holiday time from work. He reassured her it had also been cleared with Jeff.

Now they were sitting in the best carriage on the train, waiting for their adventure to begin. She pulled out the small tourist guide to Paris, which she'd bought in the station just before boarding the train, to decide where and what she wanted to visit. It felt a bit weird with it all being last minute because normally she was a planner and she'd have had each day's itinerary all worked out. She turned the pages and read up on the Moulin Rouge – "We have GOT to go there!" – Montmartre – "for all the artists and the Sacre Coeur" – The Latin Quarter, Notre Dame and, without question, the Louvre. She would just die if she didn't get to see the Mona Lisa. She worked her way through the guide, exclaiming over almost everything it suggested. How was she ever going to manage it all in just three days?

Charlie smiled as he listened to her excitement but noticed that she hadn't yet mentioned the one place that was so special – the Eiffel Tower. He hoped she didn't bring it up because he wanted to try and keep it as another surprise. If she did mention it, however, he was prepared to tell a little white lie and say he'd booked tickets for Monday morning. The truth was he'd booked them for Sunday night. The lift would take them straight to the top and he didn't think Elsa would mind too much if she didn't have to climb the stairs, not after the amount of walking he was anticipating they'd be doing over the next two and a half days.

Upon their arrival at the Gare du Nord in Paris, they were met by a driver standing at the end of the platform who took their luggage, showed them to their car and whisked them through the city – well, as fast as it is possible to 'whisk' in the heavy Paris traffic – to their hotel on George V Avenue. Eventually, they pulled up outside the Four Seasons Hotel and Elsa's jaw pretty much hit the floor. She looked at Charlie in disbelief! "We're staying HERE?"

"Oh yes!" he answered gleefully. He'd really gone to town on this trip and he wanted Elsa to enjoy every single minute of it. From what he'd been able to work out – from conversations with her parents, and with Elsa herself – she hadn't been on holiday for about eight years. He wanted to be sure everything about this trip was as special as it could possibly be.

Elsa looked around the reception area of the hotel in awe. It was now decorated for Christmas and looked stunning. Two large gold Christmas trees stood on plinths, and green pine garlands, with brilliant white fairy lights woven through them, adorned every doorway and archway. The highly polished marble on the floors and walls reflected the twinkling lights and multiplied them around the room.

She realised with a jolt how close it was to Christmas. She'd been so busy in the gallery, with various exhibitions and getting Danny's launch organised, that time had stopped being counted in months and was now measured by days and weeks. It had become 'so many weeks till the launch' or 'X amount of days for the framers' or 'the invites can be collected in a few hours'. Seeing the festive décor also brought it home again that she still had one freckle on her wrist and less than six weeks to do something about it.

She pushed the thought to the back of her mind as Charlie approached her with their room key in his hand. Elsa had left him to sort out the arrangements in fluent French, realising her very poor, quite embarrassing, school-girl fumbling of the language was not required. He smiled at her and said, "Come on, then, let's see what broom-cupboard we've been put in."

He put his hand gently on the small of her back and guided her towards the elevators. Elsa bit back the retort that she was quite capable of walking there unaided. She knew Charlie was simply being thoughtful, but she did sometimes find his old-fashioned manners a bit irritating. She wasn't a china ornament and she was noticing he was beginning to treat her as though she was. She'd give it a bit more time and, if it got any worse, she would have to say something. What was it Sukie would say? Oh yes! Set your boundaries and stick to them. Well, it looked as though some boundary-setting was going to be required fairly soon.

They exited the lift on their floor and Charlie pointed Elsa towards the bedroom door. Except... It wasn't a bedroom! According to the small plaque at the side, above the doorbell, it was The Penthouse Suite! She turned to him in wide-eyed surprise.

"The Penthouse Suite? Seriously?"

"Oh yes, seriously!" He grinned with at her with joy. The women he'd dated in the past would have expected nothing less. The fact Elsa had not expected this made him love her just a little bit more.

He put the key-card in the reader, opened the door and stood aside to let her enter. He'd counted to five when he heard her gasp of delight and walked over to her side to enjoy her awe-struck silence as she gazed around the stunning room in front of her. The floor to ceiling windows let in the bright autumn sunlight which reflected off the golden décor on the walls around the room, making them appear as though they were gleaming. The large corner sofa and the cream and gold armchairs screamed at you to lounge upon them. Walking through, Elsa stopped dead when she came to the bathroom. The floor and walls were encased in polished, shining beige marble and the bathtub was the size of a small swimming pool.

Charlie followed her as she carried on exploring and muttered something about needing a stepladder to get into the vast king-size bed. She was about to walk into the dining area when he rushed over.

"Stop! I have a special surprise for you, but you need to close your eyes."

"Oh, what?"

"You heard. Close your eyes."

Elsa closed her eyes. Charlie's heart did a little flip at how trusting she was. He really hoped his surprise was a good one.

Elsa waited with her eyes closed and, after a couple of seconds, she felt Charlie take her hands.

"Right, I need you to step up twice... That's it... Its' okay, I won't let you bump into anything. Just let me guide you. Easy... To the right a little... Okay, stop for a moment."

She waited patiently, hearing Charlie fumbling about. Suddenly, there was a cool blast of air on her face and the noise of the Paris traffic roared towards her. Charlie took her hands again and led her outside. So, The Penthouse had a roof terrace, did it? She felt Charlie placing her hands on cold metal before he whispered in her ear, "Okay, you can open your eyes now."

Elsa slowly did so and found herself speechless. The sight that filled her eyes was just too much. Her mouth opened and closed but no sound came out for, in front of her, was a spectacular, uninterrupted view of *the* iconic Parisian landmark. It was so close, she almost felt as though she could touch it.

Eventually she managed to squeak, "The Eiffel Tower. It's the Eiffel Tower."

Charlie slipped his arm around her waist and pulled her close to him. "Yes, my darling Elsa, it's the Eiffel Tower. And that…" he turned her slightly and pointed, "is the Sacre Coeur, the steeple right in front of you is the American Cathedral and that, in the distance, is the rooftop of the Palais Garnier, also known as the Paris Opera House."

"Noooo! As in 'Phantom of the Opera' fame?"

"Yup, the very one. And… there really is a lake underneath it."

"Oh, get away with you. You're just messing with me now." Elsa flicked his arm lightly with her hand.

"No, I'm not, as you will see for yourself tomorrow morning on our guided tour."

"Oh, my goodness! How exciting!" Elsa clasped her hands together with happiness. Her earlier irritation with Charlie had completely vanished. How could she be annoyed with someone who clearly cared enough to work out exactly which kind of tourist attractions she'd most like to see?

"Where else are we going? What else are we seeing?" Her excitement was now bubbling over.

"That would be telling." Charlie smiled. "For now, though, how about we change into some walking shoes and take a stroll through the Parisian streets and soak up the uniquely wonderful Parisian atmosphere?"

Elsa could scarcely believe what a fabulous afternoon she was having. From the hotel, they'd turned right and had wandered down Avenue Georges V towards the Seine. They should have turned left when they reached the junction at the end, with the intention of heading towards Notre Dame Cathedral, but Elsa had spied a small sign with the words 'Musée d'Art Moderne' upon it. She didn't need her poor French to work out what that was. Barely giving Charlie a chance to object, she'd grabbed his arm and dragged him along behind her. She knew about this place. It was home to Matisse, Chagall and Picasso to name but a few. There was no way she was missing out on this.

Once Elsa was satisfied she'd seen nearly everything in the art museum, they retraced their steps and strolled through the Jardin d'Erivan towards the Place de la Concorde, taking in the hustle and bustle around them – the constant sound of car horns blaring and tourists talking in myriad tongues as they passed by. There was a quick stop to admire the hieroglyphics on the obelisk, and as night began to fall around them, they walked up the tree-lined Champs-Elysees towards the Arc de Triomphe. By the time they reached the famous monument, it looked utterly stunning, all lit up against the darkening sky.

"Do you want to climb up to the viewing area?" Charlie asked her.

"What? You can go up there?"

"Oh yes. It's a bit of a climb – about two hundred and eighty steps or so, but I've been informed it's worth the effort. Are you up for it?"

Elsa gave him a steely look. "Damn right I am!"

"Follow me, there's an underpass on the other side which takes us to the entrance." Charlie took her hand and they walked round, crossing several roads until they reached it. Twenty-five minutes – and one very energetic climb – later, they stood on the roof and watched the motorised frenzy down below. Elsa made a mental note to never drive in Paris – so many cars, coming from all directions? No thank you, she would pass on that one. The car headlights and taillights all blended together and the effect made her think of a huge Catherine Wheel firework, with its many sparkly tails spinning out from where she stood at the centre. The Eiffel Tower was majestic as it dominated the skyline in all its lit-up glory. The beacon on the top sliced the night sky as it alerted everyone to its presence. Elsa walked around the edge of the structure twice, absorbing the essence that was Paris. She still couldn't believe she was here. For a brief moment, she felt a tinge of sadness for it had been a city both she and Harry had planned to visit together. Gazing over at the Eiffel Tower, she whispered into the wind, "I made it, Harry. I wish we could have done this together. I hope you can see me, wherever you are." She closed her eyes for a moment before taking a deep breath and forcing a smile on her face. "I'm living my life for both of us, my darling, just as I promised!"

A moment later, Charlie came over and put his arms around her waist. "Impressive huh?"

"Fantastic," she replied. "Thank you so much for bringing me here. It's wonderful."

"Are you hungry yet? I have a table booked in one of the hotel restaurants for later this evening. Shall we wander back, and you can relax for a little while. It's been a long day."

"That sounds good to me."

They made their way down to ground level and out onto the tourist filled avenues. From the monument, it was a quick walk back to the hotel.

Elsa wasted no time, when they reached their room, in having a soothing soak in the mini pool in the bathroom. She was exhausted but happy and could feel herself relaxing after the brilliant but busy day. The water began to cool and she contemplated topping it up but thought better of it. She needed to move herself and get ready for dinner. She pulled the plug out to let the water drain away, raised herself out of the bath and dried off, adoring the feel of the ultra-thick, soft, fluffy towels. This really was the epitome of luxury. She moisturised her face and applied her make-up, then went back into the bedroom to get dressed. Thank goodness she'd had the foresight to pack a little black dress and some heels. She didn't think it would have been very well received if she'd arrived at the restaurant in her jeans and walking boots.

She was just putting the finishing touches to her hair when Charlie walked in from the lounge area. He'd also changed and was wearing a smart, charcoal grey suit. The colour really suited him and further enhanced his handsome features. He looked very dashing and she happily took his arm to walk down to the restaurant.

Chapter Fifty-Five

The following morning Elsa was up bright and early. Charlie had suggested having breakfast in the suite but she'd rejected the idea as she wanted to visit the breakfast buffet. The photographs in the hotel brochure had made her mouth water and she wanted to see it for herself.

After showering in the *massive* shower cubicle, Elsa quickly passed the hairdryer over her hair, pulled it up into a ponytail and turned to Charlie expectantly. "Hurry up, slowcoach. Not only am I starving hungry, but we have got LOADS to see today. I want to see EVERYTHING!" Elsa threw her arms out wide, tilted her head back and spun around, laughing as she did so.

Charlie smiled at her obvious happiness. He'd been worried she might find the trip a bit too much, too soon, but it appeared as though he had nothing to be concerned about.

"Two minutes till I get my shoes on and then we're good."

Elsa was not disappointed when they walked into the

breakfast restaurant a short time later. The buffet opened up in front of her and she gave a small shiver of delight. There were tables laid out with cold meats, cheeses, breads and cakes. The cold meats consisted of several different flavours of salami, hams, thin-cut pork and beef. The cheese selection looked like a rainbow with all the various options including a brilliant red Gouda cheese ball, a very tempting green, sage-flavoured cheddar and a piece of brie that simply oozed from its dusty white skin. The smell of the freshly baked breads assaulted her nostrils, vying with the rich, deep coffee aroma which circled the room. As if all this wasn't enough, the cake table was laden with the most delicious looking pastries and cakes she had ever seen. The pain au chocolat, croissants, cinnamon rolls, brilliant yellow, buttery brioche, and her all-time favourite, pain aux raisin, just about sent her cross-eyed with joy. Quickly grabbing a plate, she loaded it up with little bits of just about everything. She wanted to try the lot!

Charlie chuckled at her enthusiasm. "We have another two breakfasts after this one, babes, you have plenty of time to taste most of the selections."

"Ha! That is where you have it all wrong! Today I taste everything so that the next two days I can fill up on what I really like the most. There is method in my apparent madness." She smiled at the waiter as he approached to fill their cups with coffee.

"Well, it is going to be a busy day, so I suggest you take on plenty of fuel to keep you going," Charlie answered, tipping his coffee cup at her before taking a large mouthful and savouring it for a moment. "Ahhhhh!" he said. "You really can't beat a good cup of real Parisian coffee."

The day passed in a blur as Charlie swept Elsa from

one place to another. They had strolled to the Palais Garnier to give their breakfast some time to settle. Elsa had been thrilled to learn the real story behind The Phantom of the Opera. Seeing the lake – well, she'd hardly seen a lake, more like some odd-coloured water through a square concrete hole in the floor – had been very special and the opulent splendour of the auditorium had been breath-taking. The next stop was the Picasso museum which had just been a brisk walk away through the streets. The building alone was breath-taking – from the sage-green woodwork on the multi-paned windows to the cobbled courtyard where they briefly queued to get in and the marble hallways and walkways inside. And all this was before the pleasure of seeing the unique works of the man himself.

From there, they'd jumped onto one of the many open-topped buses and let it carry them up to Montmartre where they'd admired the brilliant whiteness of the Sacre Couer. Charlie then surprised Elsa again by walking her a short distance from the soaring edifice to the nearby Espace Dali. The climb up the stairs had been a little steep, although not as bad as the Arc De Triomphe the evening before. She'd eyed up the funicular which ran alongside them but, remembering the vast breakfast she'd consumed, decided taking the stairs would be good for her. It had amused her somewhat that the rather unassuming building, with its white shuttered windows, held one of the most amazing collections of modern-day paintings and sculptures. She couldn't help but feel humbled by the effort Charlie had put into organising this trip, ensuring all the things she'd most wanted to see were on the agenda.

She 'oohd' and 'ahhd' her way around most of the Dali exhibits, Charlie trailing patiently behind her, after which they'd taken a quick trot through some side streets so she could photograph Vincent van Gogh's house and the Moulin Rouge. They'd then caught another tour bus which dropped them off quite near to the hotel.

Charlie closed the door to the suite behind him as Elsa flopped onto the large corner sofa, pulled off her walking boots and collapsed backwards, pulling her feet up beside her.

"Oh, my goodness," she exclaimed. "Today has been wonderful but oh boy, am I shattered now. Please tell me we're having room service tonight."

Charlie looked at his watch. "I'm afraid not, my pretty one. You have ninety minutes to freshen up, change into something less casual – but not as dressy as last night – before we go back out again."

Elsa could not hold back the groan. "Oh, Charlie... Seriously?"

"Yes, seriously! Although it won't be as frantic as today, I promise. It'll be far more relaxed."

She dragged herself upright. "Well, in that case, I have time for another soak in the pond before we go out. I'm going to need it to help revive me."

Charlie hadn't lied that his plans for the evening were more relaxed. A taxi drove them to the pick-up point for the Baton Mouches where they enjoyed an hour on the Seine, taking in the sight of Paris from the water. They'd managed to commandeer the seats in the prow of the boat which gave them the very best views of Paris in her night attire. Once back on dry land, they walked over the Pont de l'Alma, into a warren of small streets which brought them to a petite, typically French, café-restaurant which was very cosy inside with small round tables bearing red-checked tablecloths and old wine bottles topped with candles and rivulets of melted wax down the sides. The smell of garlic hung heavy in the air and there was even a musician in the corner, playing softly on an accordion. It was as French as it was possible to be, and Charlie could see Elsa loved it. He persuaded her to try some frogs legs – she didn't really get the chicken thing, but they did taste nice when dipped in the thick garlic butter. The main course of chicken breast in a mushroom sauce on a bed of rice had her almost groaning with pleasure. The chicken was so succulent it barely needed to be touched and it fell apart. The mushroom sauce was so subtle and the rice perfect. The accompanying Chardonnay was chilled to perfection.

Elsa placed her cutlery on the empty plate and leaned back, exclaiming this trip had been totally focused on nothing but food and art.

"Well, Elsa, you're in Paris. The city is famous for both of those. I'd say you're embracing the culture to its fullest."

"I suppose so, although my stomach is also stretching these trousers to *their* fullest."

Charlie smiled. Since they'd met, Elsa had put on weight and it really suited her. She'd lost the waif-like appearance she'd been carrying in the early days of their friendship and looked far more robust and healthy now. The longer hairstyle set off her lovely high cheekbones and her skin glowed.

His eye caught sight of the clock on the wall and he motioned to the waiter to bring their bill. "Time for us to be moving on," he said.

The waiter arrived at the table with the bill and, once he'd settled up, he led Elsa out the door and back into the night air of the city. They were surrounded by restaurants and the smell of garlic, onions and meat was almost cloying.

"Come, this way…" Charlie put his arm through Elsa's and walked beside her.

"Where are we going now?" she asked.

"I thought you might like to see the tower all lit up and with fewer tourists around. It'll be heaving when we return tomorrow."

"Oh, that would be nice. Lead the way, Monsieur."

They crossed the main road and walked along Avenue Joseph Bouvard, the shining tower on their right-hand side. They then cut through the gardens, strolling along the leafy, lamppost-lined paths until they came to the paved area upon which stood one of the most famous landmarks in the world – The Eiffel Tower.

Elsa cranked her head back as far as it would go, trying to see all the way to the top.

"I'll bet Paris looks amazing from up there," she said.

Charlie took her hand. "There's only one way to find out. Come on…"

"Wha—? Are we going up there now?"

"We sure are," replied Charlie, as he led her towards the entrance.

Elsa couldn't believe this was happening. She'd wanted to see Paris at night, from the top of the Eiffel Tower, since she'd been about seven and now it was about to happen. She began to tell Charlie this when they entered the lift, but stopped when she saw the expression on his face.

"You already knew this, didn't you? How did you know?"

"Your dad told me."

"Oh!" She didn't get a chance to say anything further as they had to change to a second lift which would take them to top.

When the lift halted and they walked outside to the viewing platform, Elsa felt her breath catch in her throat. The vision of Paris beneath her, all lit up, was beyond

383

anything she had ever expected. She walked round slowly, taking it all in. Charlie walked beside her, smiling with joy at her happy expression. The platform wasn't as busy as it would be in normal daylight hours, so they were able to walk with ease.

The strong breeze had pulled at a few tendrils of her up-do and these kept whipping across her face. Elsa absent-mindedly swept them away, oblivious to Charlie's loved-filled expression as he watched her.

Finally, having circled round twice, Elsa came to a stop on the south facing side, looking down on the beautifully lit up Champs de Mars.

"Would you like some champagne?" Charlie asked.

"Champagne? Up here?"

"Oh yes, champagne up here. This is Paris after all. Look…" Charlie inclined his head to the small booth just a few feet away.

Elsa giggled. The thought of sipping champagne at the top of the Eiffel Tower tickled her. It was something she'd never thought likely. "Oh, go on," she replied, "why not? We only live once."

Charlie returned with their drinks and found Elsa was deep in thought as she stood gazing across the landscape.

"Penny for your thoughts?" he said lightly, handing over the plastic cone filled with the golden fizzing liquid.

Elsa started at the sound of his voice. Taking the proffered drink, she smiled. "I don't think they'd be worth that. You'd be asking for change."

"Try me," he said.

"I was just wondering if people who live in beautiful cities such as Paris or Rome really appreciate the splendour around them or do they just accept it as a normal part of their life. I've lived in Oxford almost all of my life and barely see its beauty. The tourists are considered a nuisance most of the time. You live in

London – how often do you stop to properly look at what stunning architecture it has?"

"Erm… Quite often as it happens. You know… With it being a part of my job!"

Elsa burst out laughing. "Doh! Spot the blonde!" she quipped.

"I do know what you mean though." Charlie smiled. "We're so busy living our day-to-day lives that we rarely take time to absorb the history or elegance of our surroundings."

A strong gust of wind blew across them and the loose curls flew across Elsa's face again. Charlie stepped up closer to her and gently moved her hair away. He put his free arm around her and pulled her into an embrace. Looking into her shining, blue eyes, he said, "Thank you for coming away with me. This has been a wonderful weekend."

"Oh, Charlie, I should be thanking you. Thank you for bringing me here, for putting so much thought into it all and for being *so* patient as I've forced you to look at a tonne of artwork. And this, tonight, is the icing on the cake. You've done so much for me, you really have. Thank you."

Charlie leaned in and placed a warm kiss on her lips. Elsa felt herself melt. He really cared for her. He had more than proved it this weekend.

Their kiss deepened and then Charlie slowly moved his lips along her jawline, towards her ear. He whispered, "I love you."

Elsa froze at his words and pulled back to look at him. His shocked expression told her he hadn't planned to say those special words to her and now he was worried he'd gone too far. She felt a little flutter in her stomach. With a smile, she stepped back into his arms and whispered, "I love you too."

The Middle Men

"Daaaa dadadada dada, dadadadadaaaada, Dadadadadadaaaadadadada…"

Harry put his head in his hands. "I'm not looking, William. I refuse to look!"

William patted his shoulder. "That's probably a good move, lad. I can tell you now, it's not pretty!"

William looked up at Death as he jiggled about on top of the Eiffel Tower beacon. He was dancing his own obscure version of the can-can while dressed in the full flouncy skirt regalia, including a black bouffant wig and some peacock feathers. His scythe twirled around in his hand like some cheerleader fronting the Thanksgiving Day parade.

"She told him she loves him… She told him she loves him…!" Death chortled with glee as he imparted this detail to the two men standing below.

"She loves him yeah, yeah, yeah…" he crooned, morphing into a Beatles outfit, complete with the mop-top haircut.

Harry made to stand up. "I'll bloody kill him…"

William stayed him with his hand and sat him back down again. "Don't rise to it, Harry. You know what he's like. He's just winding you up because HE'S AN ASSHOLE!" He shouted the last three words to ensure Death could hear him above the tuneless racket he was making.

"I heard that!" Death said, suddenly appearing at William's side.

"Good! You were meant to!"

"I didn't expect them to still be together," Harry moaned. "With his reputation, he should have been long gone by now."

"Don't worry, Harry, there's still time. It's over a month until New Year's Eve. A lot can happen in a month." William tried to keep his young friend's spirits up. It wasn't easy however as he too was beginning to worry their grand plan wasn't going to work.

"Or not happen…" Death snickered.

"OH, SHUT UP!"

Death grinned at the unified response his words had received. He gave a shrug, bounced back up to the top of the tower and, donning his flouncy skirt once again, performed another couple of jigs and twirls. This was so much fun he thought and pondered on why he hadn't done it before now.

Chapter Fifty-Six

Danny laughed as he watched Guy trying to throw darts at the playing cards on the wall at the back of the stall. He was desperately trying to win one of the over-sized, stuffed, Minion toys which were hanging around the exterior. Nigel had told him the darts were blunted, and the flights were useless, but Guy was determined to give it his all. It was the 'giving it his all' that had Danny laughing. Guy's efforts were making him red in the face and he was beginning to lose his temper. Still smiling, Danny turned away to look out at the lit-up spectacle in front of him.

On a last-minute whim, he'd had a sudden notion to visit the Winter Wonderland in Hyde Park. Now that he'd submitted all the paintings required by Jeff, he was having some time out to recharge himself. The problem was that, having pushed himself so hard since August – painting almost every night – he was finding it difficult to switch off and relax. He'd caught up with some of the lads from his football team and had made his apologies for his lack of appearances in the last three months. Once he'd explained why, however, they'd been very supportive and had even asked if they'd be able to attend his launch. This had been a surprise as Danny had expected them to take the piss. It had transpired a couple of them were rather partial to some nice artwork and the rest of the evening had been spent discussing various new and old artists and making comparisons between them.

Today, however, he'd been bored. It was just over two weeks until Christmas and the television channels had been showing back-to-back Christmas movies. He needed to get into a Christmas frame of mind, but they weren't the answer. That was when he'd called Guy and Nigel to see if they fancied a trip to the yearly winter extravaganza. When they'd said yes, he'd gone online and had been able to book some last-minute tickets for the various attractions. What a stroke of luck that had been because he knew from past experience that the second to last Saturday before Christmas usually sold out quickly.

"I give up!" Danny turned back at Guy's loud exclamation and saw him throw his hands up in disgust. He stomped away towards a nearby stall that was selling mulled wine. Nigel's big shoulders shook as he tried to contain his laughter. Danny smiled at him and together they followed Guy over to the drinks stand.

Once they were holding the little plastic cups and warming up their cold hands, Guy said to Danny, "We were thinking of maybe having a goose for Christmas dinner this year, Dan, how do you feel about that? I know we always do turkey, but I saw Nigella cooking one up the other night on the television and it looked fabulous. I'm really keen to give it a go."

Danny shuffled his feet awkwardly. This was going to be fun... Not!

"Errrm... I'm afraid I won't be joining you for Christmas Dinner this year."

"Why not? You always come to ours for Christmas. We've done Christmas together for years!"

"Yeah, I know, but Sandra—"

"I might have known that fat old strumpet would be involved!"

"Guy, it's not like that. She came round the other night – it was as much of a shock to me, opening the door and finding her there, let me tell you – and she was hugely apologetic about her behaviour at Pete and Sukie's."

"Took her long enough to get her arse in gear, didn't it! She should have been apologising from the minute it happened, not six bloody weeks later!"

"Yeah, I know. I was quick to point that out to her. She said she'd been too embarrassed to face me—"

"Embarrassed? That one? She can't even spell the damn word! She's got more front than bloody Brighton. She's never been embarrassed in her life!"

"Are you going to keep interrupting me or can I finish?" Danny glared at Guy.

"Okay... I'll keep it shut for now! I know you're only keeping her sweet because of the baby." Guy made a show of biting his lip.

"Anyway, her family want me to join them for Christmas dinner."

"Why? You weren't invited the last two years. What's changed this time?" Nigel asked the question before Guy could let rip again.

"The baby's what's changed. Both sets of her grandparents will be there, and her parents want it to look as though we're together. It's only for one day. I'm not very happy about it myself but, for the sake of the baby, I

390

need to at least try to make an effort."

"The sooner that baby arrives, the better!" Guy muttered. "I want that DNA test done as soon as possible. Then we can all move on with our lives."

Danny couldn't disagree with him on that.

Just then, someone jostled him from behind. He looked round to see a very tall bloke grab onto one of the solid, fixed, drinking tables which were dotted around the area.

"Sorry about that, mate," he said to Danny. "Slipped on some ice and lost my balance. Did I make you spill anything? Can I get you another?"

Danny noticed a petite, dark, curly-haired woman and another man laughing beside him. "No, you didn't spill anything. I'm fine thanks."

"Okay, if you're sure."

Danny grinned as he replied. "I'm quite sure. Honestly. But thank you again for checking. Merry Christmas!"

"You too, mate!"

Danny turned back to Guy and Nigel and wondered why the man had seemed familiar as they walked away.

"Hi, Mum, how are you?" Elsa answered her ringing phone and motioned to the others to carry on and she would catch them up. They were walking towards one of the bar areas to get some warming drinks, so she knew where to find them. "Hang on a minute, Mum, let me find a quiet spot."

She saw a space between two stalls, next to a hedge, and slipped into it. Immediately the noise level dropped. "That's better, I can hear you now. We're in Hyde Park at the Winter Wonderland and it is rammed!" She listened to her mother's reply.

"Yes, I am with 'that lovely man' as you so sweetly

put it. Yes, Charlie." She rolled her eyes. Her mum had really taken to Charlie and she kept making a point of telling Elsa how lucky she was to have met him, especially after he'd taken her to Paris.

"What's he doing for Christmas dinner? Spending it with Jeff and his mum I expect, I haven't actually asked him."

She listened as mother spoke some more. "Yes, it is only the three of them..." Her mum carried on talking. "You what? Are you sure?" Elsa sighed. "Okay, I'll ask them. Yes, I will do it as soon as I can and let you know. Now, I have to go, I'll speak with you next week when I have an answer for you. Love you, and love to Dad. Bye!"

Elsa ended the call and put the phone securely back in her handbag. Pulling her hat back down over her ears and putting her gloves on again, she made her way to the bar where Anna, Gordon and Charlie were waiting for her. Charlie handed her a cup of mulled wine.

"Elsa, you've just missed Gordon doing his Bambi impression!" Anna was still laughing.

"Yeah, he slipped on a bit of ice and nearly sent some poor bloke flying." Charlie filled her in on the details.

"Oh, gosh! Are you okay, Gordon? Is the other bloke okay?"

"I'm fine and so was the chap I bumped into. Thank you for asking though, it's more than some people have done!" He glared at Anna and Charlie as he spoke, setting them off into fits of giggles again. He looked back at her, saying, "The next time we come out, Elsa, what say we leave the children at home! They're just too embarrassing and don't know how to behave in public." Anna pulled a silly face at his words. "I rest my case!"

Elsa laughed and took a drink of her mulled wine, loving the warm feeling flowing through her. She was feeling very happy today. This was the first time she'd visited the Winter Wonderland and the atmosphere was certainly festive. There were pretty little wooden stalls, selling their Christmas wares, fun-fair rides with people screaming on them, and a plethora of hot food huts sending their aromas wafting into the air. It all added to the Christmas ambience and it certainly imbued the spirit of the season into the visitors flowing through the gates.

"How's your Mum? Is everything alright at home?" Charlie asked while Gordon and Anna playfully bickered over Gordon's Torvill and Dean moment.

"Oh yes, everything's fine. She sends her love. She's also asked if you, Jeff and your mum would like to come up to Oxford and join us for Christmas dinner."

"Oh!" Charlie straightened up in surprise. "I hadn't really thought about it but I think that would be nice, Elsa. Last year wasn't a great one as you can imagine, being the first one without Dad. If it's only the three of us again this year, I suspect it will be just as bad and I'll most likely spend most of it in a drunken stupor. Let me talk with Jeff and Mum and see what they say."

"Cool. Let me know as soon as you can and I'll pass it back to my mum so she can get everything organised."

"I will. And thank you." Charlie popped a kiss on Elsa's very pink nose. "Now, shall we see who can scream the loudest on The Hangover?"

She took one look at the high tower which dropped people from a great height at high speed. "I think that will definitely be me!" she said as they finished their drinks and made their way towards it. Charlie put his arm around her shoulders and held her close to his side. "Don't worry, my little friend, I'll protect you."

Elsa looked up and laughed at his words before pulling his head down to give him a kiss. Yup! She was definitely happy. Very happy indeed!

Chapter Fifty-Seven

Christmas Day

Danny stood on the doorstep of Sandra's house, waiting for his knock to be answered. He held a bag of gifts at his side. The door opened and Sandra's sister, Alison, stepped aside to let him in.

"Hi, Danny, come in, come in. How lovely to see you. Merry Christmas," she said, closing the door behind him.

"Hi, Alison, Merry Christmas. It's nice to see you too." He put the bag of gifts on the floor as she took his coat. He'd always gotten on well with Alison on the few occasions they'd met. Her work as a doctor meant she was often on duty whenever Danny had called by to pick Sandra up.

"Thanks, Danny. Come on through. I should warn you the whole family is here. Aunts, uncles, and cousins too. It's a bit crazy."

She opened the door to the lounge and a thunderous roar of noise hit him. He walked in and his eyes immediately fell upon a large table running from the lounge, through the dining room and out into the conservatory. He did a double take at the vastness of it.

"Errr, Alison, just how many people are here today?"

"About twenty-five if you count the kids," she replied.

"I see. So just a small get-together then."

Alison laughed. "Come on, let me sort you out with a drink. I think we're sitting down to eat soon. And, knowing my sister, she'll be dying to see what you've bought her for Christmas. I hope it sparkles a lot or we'll never hear the end of it!" She smirked as she spoke.

Alison walked into the kitchen with Danny following behind.

"Mum!" she shouted over the top of the hubbub, "Where's Sandra? Danny's here."

Anita Harrison looked round and smiled. "Hi, Danny, how are you? Has Alison got you a drink yet? I think Sandra's upstairs, but she'll be down in a few minutes."

"What can I get you, Danny?" Alison gestured towards a large table that was groaning under the weight of the alcohol on top of it.

"Can I have a soft drink please – a Coke or something, I'm driving."

"Sure, coming up. Will you be okay to have some wine with dinner?"

"I think one glass will be alright." Danny smiled.

Just then Anita and one of her sisters started yelling at everyone to begin sitting at the table for they were nearly ready to serve dinner.

"Here, Danny, you sit there with Sandra beside you." She pointed towards the top of the table in the lounge, near to the door. "Sandra can't go more than half an hour without needing the loo – it makes sense to put her up there. The size of her these days, there's no chance of her being able to squeeze by if she sits further down."

He'd just sat down when Sandra walked in. She was now huge, and Danny thought she looked like she could pop any minute. Today was her due date but they'd been assured it was not unusual for first babies to take their time in coming out. She had roughly ten days grace before the doctors would begin to consider alternative options.

Danny stood up and held out the seat next to him for her to sit on. Rubbing her belly, she sat down and flashed him a glimmer of a smile.

"How are you feeling?" he asked as she wriggled on the chair, trying to get comfortable.

"Bloody massive, if you must know. I'm sick of it now. I just want it out. My back is in agony, I'm shattered because I can't get comfortable to sleep and I've forgotten what my feet look like. I've had enough."

"Oh!" Danny didn't really have an answer and was grateful when a bowl of prawn cocktail was placed in front him.

For the rest of the meal, all five courses of it, Danny didn't get much opportunity to speak with Sandra. One of her aunts had been placed to his left and she was quite a chatterbox. She pretty much claimed his attention for most of the afternoon.

They were onto the coffee, cheese and biscuits, port and sherry part of the meal when Sandra's loud voice suddenly broke into his conversation with the chatty aunt.

"Danny, how much longer do I need to wait to get my Christmas present?"

Everyone stopped talking and turned to face them. Danny blushed under the weight of all the eyes upon him.

"Ermm, you can have it now, Sandra, I have them here under my chair."

He bent down, pulled out the gift bag and handed out the few presents he had brought. There was a footballer autobiography for her father, a set of old, leather-bound medical books for Alison, and perfume for both Sandra and her mum. He handed them out, feeling sure they would all be appreciated.

Joe and Alison were quick to open theirs and both thanked him for the lovely, thoughtful gifts. Alison was especially pleased with hers.

He turned to Sandra and was surprised to see a mutinous expression on her face.

"What's wrong? Don't you like it? Have I bought the wrong one?"

"Perfume? You've given me perfume? Where's my engagement ring? I thought you were going to propose? You made me think you were going to ask me to marry you!" Sandra's eyes filled with tears as her voice rose, growing louder and louder with each word.

"I... What...? How...?" Danny stuttered as Sandra turned into a wailing, watery mess in front of him.

"Danny, what's going on here? Have you changed your mind? Are you no longer planning to marry my daughter?" Joe's low, firm tone broke through the noise Sandra was making. Danny looked at him, sitting directly across the table. "Joe, I never... That is... I'm not planning... Erm... It was never agreed..."

"Young man! If you've gotten my daughter pregnant, and a baby is coming into this world, then the decent and correct thing for you to do is to marry her. It is totally immoral for you to lead her on with an expectation of a wedding simply so you can have your way with her. I will not have that!"

"But I never..." Danny tried to explain the situation but found himself floundering as everyone glared at him, disappointment and disgust written across their faces.

"You made me think we were going to be married. That's why I kept the baby..." Sandra sobbed loudly beside him. "I thought today would be the day you were going to propose."

Danny opened his mouth to protest again when the penny dropped. Sandra had orchestrated this! She had purposely allowed her family to believe he would be proposing today. He'd bet that was why so many of them were in attendance – they all wanted to be present for the special moment.

He looked closely at Sandra and saw the gleam in her eye as she knew her manipulative little plan was rolling along as she'd hoped.

Danny sighed to himself. He had two options here – he could either create a scene by denying everything, which would most likely result in lots of shouting, crying and a ruined day for several people, or he could just go along with it for now, propose to Sandra and then break it off later when they were alone. Coming to a quick decision, Danny took the paper hat off his head, placed his napkin on the table and, pushing his chair back out of the way, knelt down on one knee, picked up Sandra's hand and said, "Sandra Anita Harrison, will you do me the honour of becoming my wife?"

Chapter Fifty-Eight

Elsa pulled the duvet up to her chin and turned to snuggle into Charlie's back. She wasn't quite ready to get up yet. Everyone had been late to bed last night, or this morning, to be precise. When they'd returned from the midnight service at the local church, they'd consumed warm mince pies and champagne while exchanging stories of Christmases past. It had been almost two in the morning by the time goodnights were being said. She closed her eyes and drifted off back to sleep.

She woke a second time, a few hours later, wrapped up in Charlie's arms and he was softly kissing her ear.

"Stop that," she wriggled, "it's tickly!"

"Then turn around and give me a proper kiss."

"No, because we both know where that will lead, and we need to get up. Save it for later." She turned around, gave him a kiss on the nose and, throwing the quilt back, got out of bed. She went over to the window and peeped through the curtains to see if they'd been lucky enough to get a white Christmas this year. Nope! No snow although there was plenty of frost, so it was white but not in the manner they had hoped for.

"Right, lazy bones, if you're planning to stay there a while longer, I am commandeering the bathroom." She tickled Charlie's toes as she passed the bottom of the bed. He pulled his legs up under the duvet while she laughingly gathered up her things.

"See you shortly," she quipped, walking out the bedroom door. Her parents had put her and Charlie in the granny flat annexe over the garage. She'd been surprised by this, but her mum had explained that it simply made it easier to arrange everyone.

Elsa stepped into the shower and began shampooing her hair as she thought about Charlie. She liked him and he was great fun to be with. She did love him, she hadn't lied when she'd said it to him in Paris, but it was not the all-consuming kind of love she'd had for Harry. And she was fine with that. Right now, she didn't want that kind of commitment, she was happy just having a bit of fun. Although, catching sight of the freckle still on her wrist, there may not be many days of fun left. She had come to realise that Charlie was not the 'true love' she'd been tasked to find. She was, strangely, okay with knowing that, having failed to meet all three conditions, her life would change considerably seven days from now. This last year had shown her she was a person in her own right, not the half person she'd always been when Harry had been alive. She'd been by Harry's side since they were teenagers and everyone had always seen them as two halves, only whole when they were together. All decisions and choices had been together. Therefore, having to make many decisions for herself this year, Elsa had found herself feeling quite liberated. She felt she'd become her own woman and, although sad it had taken so long for her to face up to being alone, she could honestly say that, whatever occurred on New Year's Eve, she was ready for it.

She wasn't going to be maudlin today, even though it would be the last Christmas she'd spend with her parents. No! She was going to enjoy and relish every single moment of it and remember their smiles and laughter. She was going to savour every memory made today so that she could look back on it with happiness wherever she ended up next.

She rinsed herself off, turned off the shower, stepped out and briskly dried herself. It was time to go and make this a day worth remembering.

"Why have elephants got big ears?" asked Charlie.

"We don't know, why have elephants got big ears?" chorused everyone sitting around the table.

"Because Noddy won't pay the ransom!"

A collective groan went up as Charlie regaled them all with his collection of Christmas cracker jokes. They were so bad, he made the ones they'd told earlier before lunch seem almost award winning.

Seeing Charlie opening his mouth, with the intention of subjecting them to more pain, David Benton stood up and said, "Why don't we move back into the lounge and sort out Christmas presents?"

Elsa followed her dad's lead. "That sounds like a great idea. Would anyone like some tea or coffee?"

It seemed everyone did, so Elsa and her mother cleared the remaining plates from the table and took them through to the kitchen. Elsa piled them neatly on the worktop, ready to go into the dishwasher when the current load was finished.

"Are you having a nice day, dear?" Jean asked her daughter as she placed cups and saucers on a tray.

"I'm having a really lovely day, thank you. And thank you for inviting Charlie, Jeff and Brenda – they really have made the day even more fun."

"They certainly have. I can't believe some of the stories Brenda was sharing about Hollywood."

"Indeed! Talk about hair-raising! I think it was the first time Jeff and Charlie had heard them too, judging by their expressions," laughed Elsa.

Jeff and Charlie's mum, Brenda, had once been a very famous Hollywood star and she'd kept them well entertained over the last two days with tales of her filming experiences – some of which had left her two sons quite embarrassed!

Elsa carried the tray through and, placing it on the coffee table, she helped to sort everyone out with their drinks before taking up a spot on the floor near to the Christmas tree. "I'll be Santa, shall I?" she asked, as she began to pull out presents and distribute them accordingly. Soon the room was filled with sounds of joy and appreciation as everyone opened their gifts and enjoyed their surprises. Elsa was delighted with the bottle of perfume and gorgeous red jumper which Charlie had thoughtfully given her. He had been equally delighted with the bottle of aftershave and new leather briefcase she'd given him.

"Right, I think that's us folks. There's nothing else under there." Elsa peered under the tree to ensure she hadn't missed any stray gifts which might have gotten pushed towards the back.

"Shall we put on a Christmas movie?" she asked.

"Ermm…" Charlie coughed and cleared his throat.

Everyone looked at him.

"There is one present still to be given but I wanted to make it a bit more special. I hope you don't mind."

He stood up and walked over to Elsa. He put his hand out for hers and pulled her up into a standing position. Charlie then took a small box from his pocket, went down on one knee and opened it. He looked up at her and said, "Elsa Clairmont, please would you do me the greatest possible honour and be my wife. Will you marry me?"

Elsa stared at the diamond ring twinkling in front of her but all she could hear was a rushing, whooshing sound in her head. Her blood ran cold and her shock was evident across her face. As the momentary loss of sound cleared, she became aware of her mother, Brenda and her father all exclaiming with joy that this was indeed a wonderful surprise and what a beautiful couple they would make. Jeff seemed to be the only one not joining in the premature celebrations. After all, she hadn't said yes yet. She caught his eye and he gave a very small shrug, indicating this was as much of a surprise for him as it was for her. When she saw the glow of happiness on the faces of her mum and dad, she knew saying no would put a downer on the day and she couldn't bring herself to do that to them. Not with it being their last one together.

She looked down at Charlie, still on one knee in front of her, still holding up the ring in its box, the excitement on his face beginning to slip and embarrassment slowly taking its place. Elsa knew this wasn't the time or place for disappointment, so she quickly came to a decision. She forced a bright smile onto her face, and beaming down at Charlie, she replied "Yes, Charlie Rowland, I will marry you."

Chapter Fifty-Nine

<u>*30th December*</u>

"I WANT MY ENGAGEMENT RING TODAY! I am not going into that hospital until I have a ring on my finger!" Sandra was yelling down the phone at Danny.

"But, Sandra, you're heavily pregnant and could go into labour at any time. You don't want to be traipsing around the West End, getting bumped and jostled by the crowds in your condition, it would be crazy." Danny was not only trying to make her see sense but also trying to buy some time. He did *not* want to put a ring on Sandra's finger, no matter how short a time it may be for. He looked at the two freckles still sitting on his wrist. He'd failed his tasks big time, but he wanted to be sure that when the time came, he could face Death with a reasonably clear-ish conscience.

"I won't be 'traipsing around the West End' as you put it, since I already know which jewellers we're going to." She went on to name one of the more expensive shops on

Bond Street.

Danny blanched. "Sandra, I can't afford to buy a ring from there."

"Yeah you can. You can use some of that seventy-grand cheque that you got!"

"How do you know about that?" His voice was cold and hard as the anger coursed through him.

"I saw it on your bank statement."

"And what were you doing looking at my personal paperwork? That is private. You have no right to be snooping through my things."

"I'm going to be your wife, I have every right!"

Danny bit back his retort. She wasn't worth the hassle. "I'll meet you at the tube station at one thirty," he said and hung up. Normally he'd have walked round to Sandra's house, but he was damned if he was going to carry on being nice to her now. He only had another thirty-eight hours and this farce would be over. After that phone call, he could hardly wait!

An hour after meeting her, Danny rang the doorbell of the Bond Street establishment which Sandra had set her heart upon. The smiling assistant unlocked the door and stepped back to let them in.

"Good afternoon, sir, madam. How may we help you today?"

Before Danny had a chance to reply, Sandra took over. "I'm here for an engagement ring so show me what you've got."

She missed the look of distaste which crossed the young man's face, but Danny didn't. He sympathised with him. Sandra had been both rude and arrogant. "We'd be most grateful for your assistance please." Danny hoped his smile and more pleasing tone would soothe any rumpled feathers.

The sales assistant returned his smile. "Certainly, sir. Please come this way. Would madam be more comfortable sitting down?"

"Well DURRR... What do you think? Of course I would!"

Danny made a mental note to check the chair for any sharp objects before Sandra sat on it. She was not making the trip any better for him with her imperious attitude.

Once they were both sitting comfortably, the assistant began bringing over a selection of rings. Sandra couldn't decide if she wanted a solitaire or a cluster, an emerald cut, a princess cut or a round. Two hours later, she was still dithering and Danny had just finished his third cup of coffee.

"May I get you another coffee, Mr Delaney?"

"No thank you, I think three cups is more than enough. If a glass of water isn't too much trouble though..."

"No problem at all, Mr Delaney, no problem at all."

It suddenly occurred to Danny, when the young man returned with the drink, that the assistant had called him by his name. But he hadn't given him his name...

"Excuse me, but how do you know my name? I'm quite sure I haven't mentioned it. Have we met before?"

The young man blushed and swallowed hard, not knowing quite what to say. Danny looked round and saw the other assistants in the shop huddled together over a computer tablet. They were looking at him and then looking back at it.

He stood up and walked over. "May I?" he asked and picked it up without waiting for their consent.

When he saw what they were looking at, the colour drained from his face.

'UNSUNG HERO SAVES SINGER'S BABY' screamed off the screen at him. Underneath was a photograph of him alongside a picture of Poppy sitting on

Pete's knee. He recognised the photograph – it usually sat on a cabinet in Sukie and Pete's library.

He turned to look at Sandra as it all came together in his head. Sandra hadn't been looking for a quiet place to sit down on the night of Sukie's party, she had been snooping! Somehow she'd found out the events around how he'd become friends with the Wallace's and had decided, even then, to cause trouble.

He took the tablet over to where Sandra was still sitting trying on rings, oblivious to the tension which had suddenly sprung up around her. Danny slammed his hand hard on the table, making everyone jump.

"You bitch! You evil, twisted, nasty, money-grabbing, fucking bitch! How dare you! How dare you take this story to the papers! How dare you intrude on the lives of my friends like that! You are beyond contempt. If you think I could marry a manipulative cow like you, then you have got another think coming!"

He looked to the assistant who was hovering close by. "Put all of these rings away please, there is no longer a need for them. I wouldn't marry this disgraceful piece of humanity if she was the last woman on earth."

He leant down and stuck his face up close to Sandra's. "You and I are finished! Over! Done! Have you got that? And, furthermore, this child will be having a DNA test. Once I have proof that it is mine, I will be suing you for custody. After this stunt, I really don't fancy your chances of keeping it. Now I suggest you get up and get out because these very nice people don't need a scumbag like you littering their shop!" In his anger, Danny had forgotten how little time he had left.

He strode over to the door.

Sandra stood up. "Danny, I'm sorry. I just wanted to make some extra money for us, for our baby, for our future."

"I don't want to hear it, Sandra. There is no coming back from this one." He turned the door handle, but it wouldn't open.

An assistant ran over. "Sorry, sir, I need to enter the combination. It's for security reasons, you know…"

Danny stood back to give him some space. He heard Sandra crying noisily behind him. Well, he was done with her and her crocodile tears. As soon as the assistant opened the door, he stepped out just as she let out a scream.

"DANNY…"

He hesitated before turning, ready to give her one last parting shot.

Except… he didn't get a chance to say anything.

Sandra was bending over clutching her stomach and a large puddle was forming around her feet.

Her waters had broken.

The baby was coming.

Chapter Sixty

Elsa stood back and looked at the display in front of her. She tilted her head from side to side, before deciding she was now finally happy with it. She slowly looked around, surrounded as she was, on all sides, by Danny's work.

She was standing up on the top level of the gallery. She still loved it up here where the large windows and skylights at the front of the building made it a light, airy space, even at night, when the backdrop of the night sky would be perfect for some of Danny's pieces.

She heard footsteps on the stairs behind her and walked over just as Jeff reached the top. "So, what do you think?"

Jeff looked around him and walked through to the large exhibition room. He took his time to scrutinise every piece of art which was hanging up. He inspected the frames for fingerprints, he checked the labels at the side to ensure they were with the right painting, he double-checked again that they also displayed the right price. Once he had done all of this, he walked back to where Elsa was nervously twisting her hands. He looked down and gave her the largest of smiles. "Elsa, it is perfect!"

"I can't believe the photographer let us down with Danny's headshots. We won't be using him again! If only I'd had a copy of the photograph, I could have found someone else."

"Elsa, it wasn't his fault he had a technology failure. Besides, I think it makes Danny a little more mysterious if no one knows what he looks like. After all, it hasn't done Banksy any harm, has it?" Jeff smiled. "Look, you have done a magnificent job. Well done! I am so *very* proud of you! I have to say it, Elsa, the best thing that ever happened to this gallery was you walking through that door in March. Thank you for everything you've done."

Elsa beamed in delight at these words of praise. They both knew it had been an incredible act of faith on Jeff's part when he'd agreed to her request to set the exhibit pieces up herself. She'd really enjoyed the challenge although she felt it was more a labour of love. In some strange way, she felt responsible for Danny and wanted to do the best she could for him while she was still here to do so. In less than thirty-six hours, it was all going to change and she didn't know what came next. Would all that had happened this year simply cease to be, or would it stay the same but without the memory of her in it? It had already dawned on her that she hadn't thought to ask Harry what came next if she failed the tasks.

She stepped back and bumped her leg against the plastic box containing the glasses the caterers had dropped off earlier. She leant down to rub the tender area and let out an exclamation.

"Oh, for goodness' sake! Not again!"

She looked at the back of her leg where a large hole

had appeared in her stocking. This was the third time in as many days that her new ring had caught and ruined her nylons. She was getting heartily sick of it. She pulled the ring off her finger. It was a beautiful ring; there was no doubt about that. It was a brilliant, round cut, solitaire set in white gold with two smaller diamonds on each shoulder. It was simple, elegant and looked perfect on her finger. In truth, it was not far off what she herself would have chosen if she'd been included in the decision.

The problem was she wasn't ready for this and certainly not with Charlie. She did love him, there was no argument there. She cared for him deeply and she most certainly didn't want to hurt him in any way, but she knew, deep down, he was not a true love. She didn't love him in the way upon which a marriage should be based. Although, given what the next thirty-six hours was bringing, it was a moot point anyway.

She went to slip the ring back on but then hesitated... No! She wouldn't put it back on again. She'd had it on and off her finger so many times over the last five days but now she knew she couldn't put it back on again. She slipped it carefully into the little pocket on her waistcoat, looked around one last time then put out the lights and made her way downstairs.

Jeff had just finished putting up the rope fencing which would keep the visitors away from the main gallery and guide them towards the stairs. Not that it would have made any difference if the rope fence was there or not as all their other works of art were safely stored away in the viewing rooms which were securely locked.

"So, that's us. Are you ready for tomorrow night?"

Elsa looked at Jeff. He didn't realise just how loaded his question was.

"Yes," she replied simply. "I'm ready."

"Okay. Then get yourself home, have a lovely relaxed

evening and I'll see you back here tomorrow night at six o'clock."

"Goodnight, Jeff."

Elsa walked home quickly. It was a cold night and the weather forecasters had already said the chances of snow were very high. The wind was blowing in from the east which meant some Siberian snow could be coming their way.

The first thing she did, when she got indoors, was put Charlie's ring back in the presentation box. She would return it to him tomorrow. She may not know what tomorrow night was going to bring her way, but she wanted to face it with a clear conscience.

She heard the ping of her phone and, when she picked it up, she saw a text from Danny telling her Sandra had gone into labour (she assumed Sandra was his girlfriend) and he was currently with her at the hospital. He didn't know how long it would be but he couldn't see it being a problem for the following night. He just wanted to keep her in the loop.

Elsa smiled as she read his news. How appropriate, she thought. One in, one out!

She changed into her jeans, called Puddle and put on her jacket for a brisk walk around the square. Her plans for the night included a long soak in the tub, a bottle of champagne and a Chinese takeaway. She wanted her last night to be one of pure self-indulgence. She might really go to town and put on her BBC DVD of Pride and Prejudice. Five hours of Colin Firth was an acceptable last request for any woman.

Chapter Sixty-One

New Year's Eve

Danny tried not to grimace too much when Sandra squeezed his hand again. She had now been in labour for twenty-four hours and was no nearer to delivering the baby. The midwife had just been in and had advised them she was only four centimetres. There was still some way to go yet before they hit the requisite ten centimetres, but the doctors were becoming concerned that there was a risk of infection to the baby and were now talking about delivering via a caesarean section.

Sandra, however, had gone off-the-scale crazy when she'd heard this. She didn't want a great big scar on her stomach. She'd never be able to wear a bikini again and she'd said as much.

Her mum and dad were waiting outside, and they'd been taking it in turns to sit with her. Danny stepped out and motioned to Anita that she might want to take over. She was probably better placed to talk some sense into

Sandra.

Danny had just sat down beside Joe when he noticed a very familiar looking nurse walking down the corridor. It was Ward Sister Collins – the same sister who'd been caring for his mother. Before he could turn away, she saw him and walked over to stand in front of him. "Mr Delaney, how interesting to see you again!"

"Ward Sister Collins, nice to see you. What are you doing down here in Obstetrics?"

"This is actually my ward. I was doing holiday cover when we last met."

"I see." Danny shuffled his feet, not quite sure what he could say next.

"Would you like an update on your mother's health and whereabouts?"

"No, thank you, I think I made my feelings on that matter quite clear the last time we spoke."

"Yes, you did, but I'd hoped you may have had a change of heart since then."

"Nope! It is still one of the best decisions I have ever made." Danny gave her a smile. "Now, if you'll excuse me…" He walked off towards the toilets. He didn't actually need to go but he had to get away from that woman before Joe felt the need to ask any awkward questions.

Once inside, he checked his phone. Damn! It was five o'clock. He should be at home by now, getting ready for the exhibition, but there was no way he could leave. He quickly fired off a text to Elsa, apologising for the problem and saying he would still be there but he might be late. He also sent one to Guy, telling him the same thing. He was making use of the facilities when Guy's reply pinged on his phone. Danny smiled when he read it. As expected, it was full of vitriol towards Sandra, but he did finish off by saying he hoped the baby was okay and wasn't unduly stressed. You could tell Guy had a penchant for television hospital dramas.

Three and a half hours later they were told Sandra was finally ready to begin delivering the baby. Danny was given some scrubs to wear and made to 'scrub up' before he was allowed in with her. When the doctor asked if he wanted to 'watch at the business end' he quickly declined. There were some things he simply didn't need to see. He chose to stay at the top of the bed and did his best to speak words of encouragement which he hoped Sandra was finding soothing. Although, given the language she was hurling at him, he strongly suspected she was not.

Just then, the midwife spoke. "The head is out. Not long now and your baby will be in your arms, Sandra."

Danny glanced at the doctor and saw a look pass between him and the midwife. "Is everything okay? Is the baby okay?" he asked.

The midwife smiled at him. "Yes, Danny, baby is absolutely fine."

"Here it comes, one last push, Sandra, come on, you can do this..." The doctor called words of encouragement as the baby finally slipped out.

"Congratulations, you have a baby girl."

"Oh, Danny, do you hear that, we have a daughter." Sandra looked up at him with a tired smile on her face.

Danny swallowed down the lump in his throat. "Yes, so it would seem."

"Can I hold her?" Sandra tried to sit up.

"In a few minutes, Sandra. The midwife needs to weigh her and give her a check-over first. In the meantime, you need to do a bit more work to push out the placenta and then we can get you all tidied up. Danny, do you want to pop out and relay the good news while we finish up here?"

Glad of the opportunity to get a bit of fresh air, and a moment to gather his thoughts, Danny left the room and went to find Sandra's parents to tell them the news.

The doctor came out a short time later to tell him he could now go back in. Joe and Anita stood, as though to follow him, but the doctor stopped them. "I think we should give Danny and Sandra a few minutes on their own with the baby first. This is a big moment for them."

Danny walked through the door where the midwife was standing holding a little swaddled bundle in her arms. "Here, Danny, would you like to take baby over to Sandra?"

He took the baby in his arms and looked down at her. Her little face was all scrunched up and she was curling and uncurling her tiny little fingers. She really was rather cute.

He walked over to the bed and carefully placed the baby in Sandra's arms. "Well, Sandra," he said, standing back, "I don't think we need to bother with the DNA test, do you? Goodbye!" With those words, he turned on his heel, walked out of the room, out of the hospital and out of her life.

Sandra looked down at the baby in her arms. Somewhere, in the deepest recesses of her brain, a faint memory stirred. Her forehead pulled down into a frown as she tried to grasp a hold of it. Something stirred again. Then it stirred a bit faster before finally arriving at the front of her mind with all the speed of a bullet train.

The memory took her back to the last Saturday night in March. The night Robbie had cancelled their trip to the cinema and she'd gone out with Kylie instead. They'd gone on a bit of a pub crawl before deciding to go clubbing. Unsurprisingly, she'd been quite drunk by the time they got there and she'd begun chatting up a bloke she'd bumped into at the bar. One thing had led to another and the night ended with them both having a hot and sweaty tryst in the alleyway behind the nightclub. He wouldn't tell her his name, so she'd called him Idris because, to her gin-soaked eyes, he'd been the double of Idris Elba...

Sandra gently stroked the face of the little coffee-coloured bundle lying in her arms and wondered how the *hell* she was going to explain her way out of this one.

Chapter Sixty-Two

Elsa looked at the text that had just arrived on her phone. Danny was on his way home to shower and change. He hoped to be at the gallery for just after eleven o'clock. She checked her watch. It was nine-thirty.

She went to find Jeff and relayed the news to him.

"That's good. I really didn't want him to miss this. It's all going so well."

"I think we can call that an understatement, Jeff," she replied as she grinned up at him. Almost every painting had a red sticky dot on the card next to it. She had been running around like a crazy thing taking people's details and logging them on her clipboard against the piece they were purchasing. The interest and enthusiasm for Danny's work had exceeded all expectations. People had immediately fallen in love with it.

"Did he say if it was a boy or a girl?"

"Sorry?" Jeff's voice broke into her thoughts.

"Danny. Did he say if the baby was a boy or a girl?"

"Oh no, no he didn't! How strange…"

"Not to worry, he's got a lot going on right now. We'll

find out the details when he arrives."

Elsa smiled. She really hoped she got to meet him before she had to leave. After all of this, it would very bad luck to miss him.

"And what about my brother? Any sign of him yet?"

She felt a tremble in her stomach. Charlie had gotten stuck at the office, trying to sort out an unexpected problem which had come up with one of his foreign clients. He'd promised to get there as quickly as he could.

Elsa wished now that she'd told Charlie sooner that she was breaking off the engagement. His delay meant she wasn't enjoying the evening as much as she should be. She simply wanted to get it done so she could make the most of the last few hours she had left. She spied Sukie and Pete and walked over to them.

"Hey, you guys, I'm so glad you could make it. After yesterday, I didn't know if you would come along."

Returning her hugs, Pete and Sukie smiled. "Now why would we let a small matter of Danny's lying bitch of a girlfriend stop us from being here tonight? We know she was behind it. Pete found her in the library and that's where the photograph of Pete and Poppy used to live. We didn't need Sherlock Holmes to work it out. We've passed the information over to our solicitor and he's going to look into the legal ramifications of the matter. Let's just say that I don't fancy being in her shoes over the next few months."

"She had the baby tonight. I don't know what she had but Danny should be here in an hour or so, he can give us the news then."

"Oh good, I can't wait to see him. I want to let him know we hold no hard feelings against him, but he needs to do something about her or we'll have a problem. I don't appreciate some jumped up little scrubber causing trouble for my family." Sukie's expression left Elsa in no doubt that she wasn't about to let this go.

"Out of interest, Elsa, I don't suppose you know how long she was in labour for, do you?"

"I think it was about twenty-six, twenty-seven hours…"

The smile on Sukie's face rather belied her words when she replied, "Oh, dear, how unfortunate."

Danny looked at his watch as he ran up the stairs at Green Park tube station. Ten past eleven. He'd have just enough time to thank Jeff for all he'd done, thank Elsa for all she had done and then make his peace with Pete and Sukie – if they'd turned up – before Big Ben started chiming.

He arrived at the gallery just as another man was giving his name to the security guards on the door.

"Oh, Charlie Rowland. Are you related to Jeff by any chance?"

Danny looked quizzically at the man in front of him as he gave his own name to the doorman. He felt he'd seen him before somewhere…

"Yes, I'm his brother. And, Danny Delaney, would you happen to be the artist this is all in honour of?" Charlie smiled.

Danny laughed. "I'm afraid so, that would be me."

"Well done and congratulations. Elsa has put a LOT of time and effort into this, I really hope it's a great night for you."

They both walked through the salon, towards the stairs. "You know Elsa, do you?"

"Yes," Charlie replied over his shoulder, "I'm her fiancé."

"Oh! Erm… Congratulations." Danny couldn't explain

420

why the pit of his stomach suddenly felt as though someone had just pulled out the plug and all of his innards were being sucked down a great big, black hole.

He heard the noise of people talking and laughing and it grew considerably louder as they climbed the stairs.

Danny couldn't believe his eyes when he reached the top floor. All around him people were standing talking and, from what he could make out from a nearby conversation, they all seemed to be singing his praises.

"Catch you later, Danny, I'm off to find Elsa. Well done, it looks like you're a massive hit." Charlie gave his arm a squeeze and he headed into the crowd to find his fiancée.

Danny looked around and eventually found Jeff standing over by the wall. He walked across to him.

"Hey, Danny! You've made it, well done. And congratulations on becoming a father! Was it a boy or a girl?" Jeff pulled him into a big hug before giving his hand a hearty shake.

"Oh… It was a girl but I'm not the father."

Jeff stepped back and looked him. "How do you know that?"

Danny smiled. "Well, let's just say I am one hundred percent Caucasian, Sandra is one hundred percent Caucasian, the baby is not!"

"Oh!" Jeff's shocked expression said it all.

"Indeed! But it made it easier for me to make the final break. It was long overdue." Danny knew this to be more than true as, while having his shower earlier, he'd discovered he was down to only one freckle on his wrist. The one which had begun to fade after he'd broken all ties with his mother had now completely disappeared.

"Well, from what Sukie and Pete were saying, it sounds like that was a good move on your part."

"Are they here? I was hoping they would come so I

could explain and apologise."

"I don't think you have anything to worry about, Danny, they both know that you had no involvement."

"Thanks, Jeff."

"You're welcome. Oh, and as you're passing by, you might want to note how many of your paintings have red dots on them. That means they're sold!" Jeff winked before turning to talk to the man who'd just arrived at his side.

While making his way through the crowd, trying to locate Sukie and Pete, Danny couldn't believe how many of his paintings had been purchased. He was gobsmacked that people had taken to his work in such a big way. He finally saw Pete standing in the far corner and he made his way over.

He gave them both a big hug before saying, "Pete, Sukie, I am *SO* sorry about the paper thing. I really had no idea she was planning to do that. I'm really embarrassed. Have you had much trouble as a result?"

Sukie was quick to reassure him that he had nothing to be concerned about and they didn't blame him in any way. As they chatted, Danny's eyes kept sweeping the room. He didn't know what Elsa looked like, but he had a feeling he would know her when he saw her.

"Is Elsa here tonight?" he butted in as Sukie was explaining it had been Beth who'd furnished Sandra with the details of the accident in April.

"She's around somewhere..."

"Please excuse me. I don't mean to be rude, but I need to find her. It's almost midnight and I feel it's only right to thank her for what she's done for me in *this* year, rather than next..."

"Of course, mate. Off you go, we'll see you next year." Pete chuckled at his little joke while Sukie rolled her eyes.

422

"Lame! So lame! *Beyond* lame..." she muttered while smiling into his eyes.

Danny pushed through the crowds once more, his eyes searching for Elsa but she was nowhere to be found. People were moving around him and he kept coming up against people he'd passed just a few minutes earlier.

It was ten minutes to twelve when he gave up looking. He really hoped she knew how deeply grateful he was for everything she had done for him. He owed her for so much but, most of all, for making him believe in himself. Something he'd never managed in all his forty years. He cherished the knowledge that he would leave this world a far better man than the one who'd been returned to it one year ago tonight.

Danny was so lost in his thoughts that it was a surprise when he found he'd wandered into the corner behind the catering screens. He tried the handle of the door which led up to the roof-terrace, expecting it to be locked, and was surprised to find it open. He quickly glanced over his shoulder, and making sure no one was watching, slipped up the stairs, closing the door behind him. He had no idea how this thing was going to pan out, but he didn't really want an audience when it did.

Chapter Sixty-Three

"Charlie, I'm so sorry. I should never have said yes when you proposed last week but I didn't want to embarrass you in front of everyone. This felt like the lesser of the two evils."

Elsa was hidden away in the office with Charlie. It was the only place which guaranteed complete privacy tonight. This was too sensitive a moment to risk anyone interrupting them.

"You led me on, Elsa. You said you loved me. I thought you meant it."

"Oh, Charlie, I did mean it. I do love you but not in the way I should love someone who I intend to marry. I wish it was, because you are a wonderful, caring man. You gave me so much this year, more than I can ever express. You helped me to move on and I will *always* be grateful to you for that." Elsa was trying not to cry. She felt so bad right now, but she had to be strong because it was Charlie's heart she was breaking, and she had no right to shed tears.

She looked at the clock above his head. It was ten

minutes to midnight.

She had to leave.

She took Charlie's hand and pressed the small box gently into it. "I have to go now, Charlie, you can stay in here for as long as you need to. I'm really sorry."

She backed out of the office and closed the door behind her before running up the stairs. When she arrived at the top, she stood for a moment and took one last look around her.

Jeff was standing talking to one of the clients, both of them clearly discussing the painting in front of them. She rose up on her tiptoes and was just able to see Sukie and Pete, both of them laughing while gazing at each other with love-filled eyes. Next to them, also laughing, were Guy and Nigel. She'd only met them a couple of times, but they'd been very warm and kind to her. She hoped they continued to live a love-filled life together.

She looked about once more. She didn't know what Danny looked like, but she'd always felt she would recognise him when she did finally meet him. However, it looked as though it wasn't meant to be. Her watch told her she only had six minutes until midnight. She sighed as she looked at the last freckle on her wrist.

She'd tried.

She'd tried so damn hard.

She turned away and slipped unseen behind the catering screen. She opened the door for the roof-terrace and crept through it. She'd known it would be unlocked as she had made sure of that earlier, before all the guests had arrived. A sharp pull made sure the door was closed firmly behind her and she walked up the stairs, through the conservatory and out onto the terrace. The moon was shining brightly, and the snow had finally begun to fall. It was already lying on the ground, creating the soft muffled effect the atmosphere took on when snow was falling.

It was then she noticed a set of footprints laid out in front of her. She looked up to see a figure leaning against the railings.

She marched over and said in her most official tone of voice, "Excuse me, but the roof-terrace is off limits to clients tonight. If I could ask you to return the party downstai—"

The figure turned around and, in the moonlight, she recognised the face of the man she had met three hundred and sixty-five nights ago.

"Oh my—"

"— it's you!"

"You were in my dream..." they said together.

"Except it wasn't a dream, was it? In the end..." Danny looked down at the woman in front of him – the woman whose face had been so elusive, hidden away deep in his mind and who he hadn't been able to paint, no matter how hard he'd tried.

"No, it wasn't," replied Elsa quietly. "I'm Elsa, by the way."

"I'm Danny."

Elsa smiled up at him. "I think I knew that. Somehow..."

"Did you get three tasks to complete?" he asked.

"Yes. I managed two, bombed on the third."

"Yeah, me too!" Danny looked up at the moon. "What do you think happens now?"

"I really don't know but I'm ready for it. I've done the best I could and if that's not good enough, then tough!"

He smiled at her feisty words. He wished he'd met her sooner, he figured they would have been good friends. He pulled his gaze away from the moon to look at her. "At the risk of sounding like a bit of a wuss but... would you object to us holding hands? I don't know where we're going to end up, but I'd feel a bit better if I thought there was a chance of arriving there beside someone I already kind of know."

Elsa smiled at him. "I think that sounds like a perfectly good plan."

Below them, they heard the sound of loud voices beginning the countdown to the end of the year.

Ten…

Nine…

Eight…

Elsa slipped her right hand into Danny's left hand.

Seven…

When their remaining freckles touched, they both felt a strong tingling sensation surge through them.

Six…

They looked at each other in wide-eyed surprise.

Five…

"Did you—"

Four…

"—feel that?"

Three…

Elsa felt small electric tingles coursing through her

body. She looked into Danny's soft brown eyes, saw again his beautiful, kind face and felt her heart perform little summersaults. Her stomach began quivering as a feeling of excitement and incredible joy rushed through her.

Two...

Danny gazed at Elsa, losing himself in her deep, sapphire eyes. His body felt so light, almost like it was floating and it was only Elsa's hand in his that was stopping him from flying off into the night sky. He could feel his heart beating furiously inside his chest and his breath came out in little short gasps.

One...

HAPPY NEW YEAR!

Danny turned and carefully brushed snowflakes off Elsa's face.

"Happy New Year, Elsa," he whispered.

"Happy New Year, Danny," she replied.

As Big Ben's chimes floated towards them on the wind, Danny leaned down and placed his lips on Elsa's. He kissed her gently, pulling her slowly into his embrace. He could feel her heart beating against his chest and when she wrapped her arms around him and held him tightly against her, his kiss deepened as he felt himself becoming lost within her.

Elsa felt every part of her being melt when Danny began to kiss her. She gladly stepped into his embrace, wanting to be as close to him as possible. She held onto him tightly, already knowing she would never let him go.

She felt his heart beating against her chest – one beat…
two beats… By the third, their hearts were beating as one.

So lost were they in their embrace, they didn't hear the
party-goers singing Auld Lang Syne.

They didn't hear the people running in the street
shouting Happy New Year to each other.

And they didn't hear the last chime of Big Ben hanging in
the air.

The Middle Men

Three figures stood in the shadows, watching the young couple who were so wrapped up in their embrace, they were oblivious to everything.

"Well, you two, it looks like you have somehow managed to pull this off. I hope you're both pleased with yourselves!"

Death already knew the answer to his question as Harry and William had been high-fiving each other for the last few minutes. This time it was Death's turn to roll his eyes.

"When you two have quite finished, can we please be serious for a moment?"

Harry and William turned towards him, trying to keep their faces straight.

Death thought they looked like two naughty schoolboys who had been caught getting up to mischief but didn't care. He sighed to himself. He was really going to miss these guys. They had been good friends over the years despite all the bickering that passed between them. But, he consoled himself, there would be new friends. It was the way it had always been and the way it would always be. Friends came and friends went. Such was the circle of his existence.

He cleared his throat.

"You both know what this means. You're released from the incumbents who held you here in this realm. You're both free to move on."

"But we don't have to, do we? We can choose to stay here if we want to, can't we?" William asked.

"Yes, you can choose to stay, but I feel it would be better for you both to take the next step in your journey."

William looked at Harry. "How do you feel, Harry? Are you ready to go?"

Harry looked at the couple still embracing behind him. "Yes, William, I'm ready to move on. Death is right. I need to go now. As much as it pains me to see Elsa in another man's arms, I know it's now my turn to let her go. I have to leave her to live her new life."

Death looked at Harry. "Good luck, Harry. Knowing you has been a pleasure."

"Thank you, Death, being your friend has been a wonderful experience. You're a good guy. William, I hope we meet again, wherever we end up. You've been a really great friend too. Goodbye."

With a smile and a small wave, Harry slowly faded away until he was gone.

"What about you, old man? Are you going or staying?"

William sighed. Harry was right. He'd been here long enough. It was time to move on.

"I'm leaving too."

"I'm going to miss you, you mardy-faced, whining old git. We've had some good times together."

"We sure have," William replied with a smile. "I can't believe I'm saying this but I'm going to miss you too.

Look after yourself, make sure you find new friends and don't ever stop being an asshole!"

Death laughed while watching William slowly fade away until he too was gone.

Now standing alone, he looked at Danny and Elsa as they continued to kiss. Fireworks were exploding above their heads and, with their bodies silhouetted against the night sky, it looked exactly like the happy ever after of a Hollywood movie.

Time to go, he thought, but, as he also slowly faded away, he had a huge grin on his face for there was one secret which he'd never shared with Harry or William.

Death truly was a sucker for a happy ending.

The End.

ABOUT THE AUTHOR

Kiltie Jackson grew up in Scotland, moved to London before finally settling down somewhere in the middle.

She now lives in Staffordshire with five cats and one grumpy husband.

Her debut novel 'A Rock 'n' Roll Lovestyle' was released in September 2017. 'An Artisan Lovestyle' is the second book in 'The Lovestyle Series'.

If you would like to read more about Kiltie, you can find her on the following:

Website: www.kiltiejackson.com

Facebook: www.facebook.com/kiltiejackson

Twitter: www.twitter.com/KiltieJackson